Praise fo...

Ni...

"Laura Renken is a master ... l-
ing combination of spark a... ...ness and
satisfied. A true Platinum read."   —*Bridges Romance Magazine*

"Renken's voice is fresh and exciting. Her characters are three-
dimensional and unique—no carbon copies here—making for a read
you won't put down. If you're looking for a swashbuckling adventure with a feisty heroine you can empathize with and a hero you
won't forget, pick up *Night Shadow*. Newcomer Laura Renken is
definitely an author to watch."   —*Scribes World Reviews*

My Lord Pirate
A Golden Heart finalist for Best Long Historical Romance

"Positively sublime . . . the plot is tight, the action mesmerizing, the
characters a blast to witness. Brava!"   —*Romantic Times*

"The best book I've read all year . . . Ms. Renken weaves a story like
no other. Her heroic characters come to life and invite you on an adventure that's so breathtaking it leaves you aching for more. Passion
and piracy, loyalty and love, *My Lord Pirate* delivers it all with powerful panache. This one's so much more than just a 'must-read.' "
—*Bridges Romance Magazine*

"Waves of thrills as unpredictable as the battles and storms on the
high seas make *My Lord Pirate* a spectacular story. It's sensual, tan-
talizing, and luscious."   —*Rendezvous*

"Ms. Renken's characters come to life and jump off the pages. She's
put a new twist or two into the classic pirate story that readers will
be sure to enjoy. Don't miss the chance to read her new book."
—*Old Book Barn Gazette*

Don't miss these other Seduction Romances . . .

HEART OF A WARRIOR by Betty Davidson
HERO FOR HIRE by Sheridon Smythe
A HUSBAND BY LAW by Cynthia Sterling
MY LORD PIRATE by Laura Renken

Night Shadow

Laura Renken

JOVE BOOKS, NEW YORK

This is a work of fiction. Names, characters, places, and incidents are either the product of the author's imagination or are used fictitiously, and any resemblance to actual persons, living or dead, business establishments, events, or locales is entirely coincidental.

NIGHT SHADOW

A Jove Book / published by arrangement with
the author

PRINTING HISTORY
Jove edition / September 2001

All rights reserved.
Copyright © 2001 by Laura Renken.
This book, or parts thereof, may not be reproduced in any form
without permission.
For information address: The Berkley Publishing Group,
a division of Penguin Putnam Inc.,
375 Hudson Street, New York, New York 10014.

Visit our website at
www.penguinputnam.com

ISBN: 0-515-13155-5

A JOVE BOOK®
Jove Books are published by The Berkley Publishing Group,
a division of Penguin Putnam Inc.,
375 Hudson Street, New York, New York 10014.
JOVE and the "J" design
are trademarks belonging to Penguin Putnam Inc.

PRINTED IN THE UNITED STATES OF AMERICA

10 9 8 7 6 5 4 3 2 1

With much love and affection,
I dedicate this book to my three wonderful children,
Brent, Ross, and Shari,
who by your very presence
have given me the wings to fly.

Chapter One

Caribbean
1691

A re we going to die, *señor?*" The youth's voice trembled over the ship's groans.

Sitting with his back against the dampened bulkhead,
Marcus Ryan Drake, condemned to the terror of the darkness, opened his eyes. His heart pounded against the wall
of his ribs. Mother Mary and Jesus, he hated storms. And
more than death itself, he feared drowning.

He hated the sea.

Somewhere a mast splintered and chains crashed to the
deck. Gnashing his teeth, Marcus cast his gaze aloft.
Screams pulsed through the ship's middle deck like a
dying heartbeat. On Marcus's right, a boy no older than ten
curled against him as if his body alone could shield the lad
from the terrors of the storm.

Marcus frowned. He was not anyone's savior and
wanted only to rid himself of the role. About as helpless as
kittens in a wolf's den, the old man on his left and the kid
had come on board in Hispaniola with him. The very
youngest and oldest of the condemned, and Marcus sat

uselessly chained to both. They'd rendered any escape attempt impossible.

"Are we, *señor*? Are we going to die?" the boy cried again.

With the helm hard over, Marcus could feel the vibration of the rigging against his back. The noise hummed through his body over the wind and the crash of waves. He gave the stately galleon another hour before she lost her crosstrees and mainmast. The idiots couldn't sail a flat tub in becalmed seas much less a four-hundred-ton Spanish galleon ensnared in the stranglehold of a storm.

"No, *amigo*." Marcus moved his arm over the boy's back and cursed the bastards who'd condemn a child to die. "It will take more than a storm to get us."

"I'm not afraid, *señor*. I'm not." The lad's voice sounded small. "*Mi madre*, she is in heaven."

At thirty, Marcus held a checkered belief in the Almighty throughout a life more aptly filled with misdeeds of piracy and mayhem than good for his fellow man. Jehovah's Paradise was not a place he'd likely glimpse. Even in passing.

Thunder shattered the skies. Drawing his legs as close to his chest for warmth as the chains on his ankles allowed, he draped his manacled wrists over his knees. The press of trapped, unwashed bodies nailed him to the worm-ridden deck of the hold and assaulted his senses. It was the stench of abandoned humanity, forsaken by compassion, and condemned to a merciless death.

A reckless grin burned his cracked lips. In a matter of weeks, his captors had reduced him, second son of English aristocracy, to an animal: a beast who would fight for the recompense of eating an occasional rat or anything else that crawled on more than two legs.

Marcus remembered little of the sea battle that had left him seriously wounded. Abandoned in Tortuga by those who thought him dead, he'd barely survived his wounds, only to face eventual betrayal by greedy townspeople who had traded his life to the Spanish for the price of a bottle of rum. Nor did Marcus know for sure what had happened to his betrothed, who had been with him on his brother's ship. The confidence that his brother, Talon, had escaped Tortuga with the *Dark Fury* gave Marcus the spark of hope he needed to survive this miserable darkness.

If Talon knew he was alive, he would find him. *Dark Fury* had not gained her ruthless reputation by perpetrating mere foreplay on her enemies. She made piecemeal out of vultures like this. As would he.

And in that vow, Marcus found strength.

Hell, he had little else in this world.

Except for the bandage that someone had wrapped around his wounded shoulder and ribs, a pair of leather breeches was all that was recognizable from the man he'd once been. A black beard matted his face. Filthy hair hung in dark, wet tangles over features once considered the bane of female virtue. One eyelid remained swollen after the last beating he'd received for smashing his chains across his guard's face. The bastard had tried to whip the old Spaniard chained to Marcus's left.

Marcus held no love for Spaniards, but he'd never condoned barbarous treatment of any man no matter his creed. Beside him in the darkness, the old man hadn't moved in hours. Marcus struggled with the man's chains and set him against the bulkhead out of the stinking bilge water. A gnarled hand trembled across Marcus's chest in search of the boy. The old man's raspy words were lost to the wind and waves, but the boy gripped his hand and seemed to find comfort. The profound attachment these two shared was not lost on Marcus, and he found his throat tight.

Torchlight suddenly filled the hold, illuminating the dank walls and pale faces; eyes blinking back with terrified confusion. Marcus shut his own against the pain that shot through his skull. Another wave smashed the ship. The man carrying the torch stumbled back against the bulkhead. His light flickered. Yanking down his filthy, blue woolen jacket over a swollen belly, he straightened his bulk and resumed his search among the cowering prisoners.

He stopped in front of Marcus. "You." A scuffed boot nudged his ankle. "*Venito.*"

Marcus merely blinked in feigned ignorance. He wasn't going anywhere with this gossoon.

"You are a *capitán, sí?*" he demanded in broken English.

Marcus was conscious of the eyes suddenly turned on him. He'd betrayed his identity to no one. "How do you know that?"

"When we bring you on board, they say you *muy* valiant against my people. You are English pirate?"

The galleon shuddered on a swell and dropped into the sea. A stout pillar was all that kept the guard from flailing backward into the other prisoners.

"We have passengers, *señor,*" the man flared in a burst of indignation that matched his arrogant goatee. "We are in need of help. Our *capitán* is washed into the sea, as is most of our crew. We will all die."

"*Ja*, I will sail widt you, captain," a Dutchman with bushy blond hair called out. Two Englishmen, a Frenchman, and a hairy Scotsman echoed the same words. Chains rattled as the call was taken up by still others down the line of bedraggled prisoners.

The boy's chained hands tightened around Marcus's forearm. The youth's wet black eyes watched him. Marcus didn't deserve such trust. Not from any of these souls who now looked to him as if he held the power in his hands to save them. He wanted to laugh in disgust.

The black boots clicked in an official summons. "The *señorita*, she will speak with you, now."

Marcus glared up into the guard's face.

"You will come with me, *señor.*"

At a motion of his gloved hand, two haggard men stepped into the sphere of light, their once immaculate blue and white uniforms dripping with water and seaweed. Epaulettes dangled from torn sleeves. Gold buttons were missing. These men were not guards, but the ship's officers. Only the ornate silver hilts of their sabers, attached to their waists with slings, gleamed.

One man unshackled his chains from the boy and the old man while the other dragged Marcus to unsteady feet. His legs ached as blood flowed back into his veins. Unfolded to his height, Marcus stood two inches over six feet. He had to duck to keep from hitting the thick ceiling beams. Every muscle burned.

Balancing against the drunken lurch of the ship, Marcus started walking. Behind him, the prisoners grew rowdy. Over the shriek of wind, chains clattered like sabers. Another wave hit the ship. Salt water seeped through the unsealed wood and washed over his naked feet as it forged aft. The Spanish officers crowded closer. Hampered by heavy leg irons, Marcus struggled up the short ladder to another hold. The scent of hay and manure clouded his senses. He heard the high-pitched whining of frightened horses.

Two lanthorns banged against stout, brass rings pinned to the wooden bulkhead. What stopped him was the tall, elegant, feminine figure pacing within the bright circle of light thrown onto the straw floor. Her coif had tumbled in disarray over her shoulders and down her slim back to reach past her hips. Only the silver comb drooping crookedly in her hair gave any hint to its once dignified state. Thunder rattled the hull. His guard urged him forward. With hands clasped to the hilt of their sabers, the two Spanish officers remained ready in the shadows.

The woman's dark head snapped up at his approach, and Marcus met the most glorious, sapphire eyes he'd ever seen. Her wet, black and silver embroidered skirts clung to long legs. She was taller than most men; her elegant height a contrast to the dainty flower of femininity he usually admired. Indeed, the top of her dark head measured to just beneath his nose.

Her gaze dropped down his grimy length. Gaping at his filthy toes, she then moved her eyes over his naked torso.

Her shapely mouth inched a fraction wider before she finally settled her full attention on his shaggy face. Thick black lashes framed her disbelief in a cerulean portrait of uncertainty. "You are the English sea *capitán*?"

A mocking smile showed he still possessed all his teeth. "To put it kindly, your highness."

"This is he?" she queried the guard in rapid Spanish. "We are to trust our lives to such as this?"

Panic underscored the lift of her chin. Her hands twisted. Knowing that she'd risked her life to cross the deck and face him, Marcus imagined she was a woman who faced demons on her own terms. That she was frightened now told him she believed their predicament to be serious.

"What have you done to him, Ramón?"

"*Señorita* . . . the man is insolent."

Looking around, Marcus settled his gaze over the woman's shoulder onto the fine, red stallions housed in padded stalls. "If I may be so bold as to inquire?" he asked. "Who the hell are you?"

Her beautiful gaze shifted. Clearly she was astonished to discover him capable of coherent speech. "This is my brother's ship." She clamped her hands to her side. "We have no *capitán*. Our quartermaster can barely keep us afloat."

Another wave burst over the ship. Seawater rained through the main hatch seals into the hold. Despair flashed in her eyes. The guard leaned his great bulk into the ship's movement and soared with the swell. Marcus had long since lost his sea legs, and stumbled ungracefully into the beautiful señorita. They both hit the stall door. Marcus caught himself, but not before his body made full contact with hers.

Beneath the layers of sodden silk, her skin was warm and provocative; her curves soft, a promising reminder that he'd not touched a woman since his captors pulled him from a watery grave in Tortuga. That was months ago. She smelled of rainwater; clean like a fresh-scrubbed babe doused in perfumed talcum. Her heady essence stayed him longer than the situation warranted.

"Get off me." She shoved against his chest.

Marcus allowed the guard to pull him backward. "*Señorita*," he stifled a grin.

Her chin hitched a second notch. "Will you help us?" she asked.

He braced his legs against the swell and regarded her coldly. "No."

"*¿Oyes el trueno?* Do you not hear the thunder? Do you choose to die?"

He held up his manacled wrists. Iron rattled on his ankles as he shifted his stance. "Maybe any man prefers death to this."

"Among our passengers there are children on board. I do not wish them to die in this horrible way. *Por favor*, I do not wish to drown."

Her vulnerability sobered him. "There is no pleasant way to die."

The girl held his stare unflinchingly. Terrified as she was of the storm, she checked her fear behind a show of bravado that would do any condemned man proud. The galleon pitched. Marcus rode the ship's movement.

She gripped the stall door for balance. A whisper of gold flashed just above the full bounty of her breasts. A cross.

"Unchain him, Ramón. *Por favor.*"

The burly guard glanced uncertainly at the other two ship's officers. Fumbling over his fist-size key ring, he dropped to his knees in front of Marcus.

"I don't own your papers, *señor*," the girl replied.

"But you know who does. The same man who owns us all."

"You'll have your freedom. If I have to buy it out of my own pocket, you'll have it. On my word."

"On your life, highness."

The brass key scraped against the metal bands on his ankles. Iron manacles clattered to the floor.

"And not just *my* freedom."

Her blue eyes widened tragically. "I cannot guarantee everyone's freedom. I can only try, *Capitán.* . . ."

"Drake," he filled in. "Marcus Drake." If he didn't think the girl could grow any paler, he was mistaken. "You know me?"

Her fists clenched. "Who doesn't know you or your rogue brother? I would be wealthy for the bounty on your head alone."

"Only if you are acquainted with the crooked bastard in Puerto Bello who offered it. His excellency, the *alcalde*, would most likely hang us both before parting with one doubloon of that bounty."

The guard looked anxiously from Marcus to his mistress before hastily resuming his task. Keys jangled as he moved to the bracelets on Marcus's wrists.

"You'll forgive my lack of manners," Marcus said. "I haven't the pleasure of your name."

Her sapphire gaze bent severely on his. "If I had known 'twas you, the most vile pirate on the main, I'd not have humbled myself with begging for my life."

A dark brow lifted in amusement. He disliked airs. "What would you have done instead, *Highness*?"

She didn't have a ready answer and was wise enough to tamp her mouth shut. Patiently awaiting his release, Marcus looked toward the stalls where the prized thoroughbreds paced nervously.

"Those are a fine pair of stallions."

Her face softened and she turned to gaze fondly at the pair. They continued to raise a fuss, and she reached her hand to caress first one, then the other. Divided in half by thick, center slats, the wooden barrier imprisoned the two.

"They are brothers. I have raised them from colts."

"You are fond of your horses?" He met her gaze steadily and her rare beauty struck him anew.

"Yes." Her eyes shimmered with unshed tears. "I would not see them harmed, sir."

"Yet, you treat men no better than vermin," he said with sarcasm. "Fascinating."

Her lips parted in mute response.

In moments the fetters on his wrists had dropped to the floor and he was free. Absently rubbing his chafed wrists, Marcus pulled his gaze from the woman's and turned to the guard. "Unchain every man who has ever sailed anything. They're needed topside. And bring the others out of that pit to the hold."

"We cannot do this, *señor.*"

"Do it, Ramón," the girl quietly bid. "And bring the others out here. Give them blankets if you can find any."

"But *señorita—*"

"Do it now, Ramón. What good are these men if they are dead?"

Ramón bowed in formal courtesy, and Marcus again wondered who this firebrand was to cower his stouthearted captors with such manly finesse.

"There is an old man and a boy chained in there. I want their irons removed. I want them fed. Give them whatever corn mash you feed your horses if you have to. They have not eaten for two days." He looked down at his scantily clad body. "And I need clothes," he added. "Even the Caribbean is unpleasant in this weather."

She nodded to one of the Spanish officers. "Is that all?"

The lanthorns banged against the bulkhead with a methodical *click, click*. Light fluttered with amber brilliance in her eyes. He took a step nearer to her and saw the pulse leap on her throat. His palms were damp with restlessness. Already his blood hummed through his veins. But it was the repulsion in those sapphire eyes that would follow him into the storm and bind him in a way chains never would again, as if he, Marcus Drake were not fit to scrape the horse dung off her royal slippers.

A leisurely grin marked his insolence in pirate splendor. "Rest assured, Highness, before this is over I'll have more than my freedom from you." Seeking further inspiration from her horrified expression and comely blush, he gallantly bowed over her hand. "Of course, I will bathe first."

She snatched her hand away and slid her palm down her sodden skirt. "You have your freedom. That is all you will ever get from me, Englishman. Now go before we end up spending eternity together at the bottom of the sea."

"Eternity will be spent with the woman I love. And that will never be you, *Highness*." Marcus executed a mocking salute before wheeling around. One of the two remaining Spanish officers followed on his heel. "Nor the sea," Marcus vowed, silently cursing his own tumult and the plight of anyone whose life depended on him.

Especially hers.

Chapter Two

*D**ios*, what have I done?"

Maria Liandra Espinosa y Ramírez, proud daughter of Spain, had never been reduced to begging. Nor had she been more afraid in her life. Grandmama had taught her to always stand tall.

Look them in the eye, Maria Liandra, and never let them forget who you are.

Her scathing gaze followed the odious sea *capitán* as a Spanish officer led him from the hold to the upper galley. Without chains, his powerful body moved with lithe grace that bespoke of countless years pirating the seas. Clearly, he was more sound in mind than his offensive appearance implied.

She shivered. Certainly she hadn't expected his voice to be so deep, or refined. Nor had she expected him to be so tall. Her height, though clumsy as Aunt Innes often complained, held advantages when dealing with men. But not with him. He *was* insolent, she decided, touching her sticky palm to her skirt. And dangerous.

He'd once been imprisoned in Puerto Bello, long before he took to pirating the seas. Her uncle, the *alcalde*, probably held his papers, which would explain his presence on this ship with the others. But it was her brother that had condemned him to die. Her brother that put the tall price on his head. Why would her uncle want him at all?

This English pirate might be a reputed thief, womanizer, and certainly a criminal, but he was no fool. If he discovered her identity, he would feed her to the sharks.

Yet, he was all that stood between this ship and the sea.

The ship's master, the second in command, came to stand beside her. She looked into the familiar face of her friend and smiled tremulously. Miguel had practically grown up with her. They shared the same adoration for her grandmama, who had founded the mission where Miguel had lived after his parents died. His four older sisters were nuns.

"How did the Englishman come to be on board, Miguel?"

"He was in Tortuga ailing from wounds he received during a fight there. Someone betrayed him to your Uncle Carlos for the bounty on his head. I do not know why the *alcalde* wants him. I only know that he will not let the Englishman go."

Liandra pressed fingers against her aching temples. She hated that her hands trembled.

"*Es peligroso*," Miguel concurred. "It is a very uncertain predicament. But I know your brother is only a few days behind us. He will not give up searching for you."

"I have endangered your life, Miguel. I am sorry."

"No one can fault you for this, *Doña* Maria."

But deep inside, her reasons for not delaying departure were less than admirable. This voyage was about more than bringing much-needed supplies to her beloved mission, where she'd spent much of her life with Grandmama. She'd wanted to be there for her mother's birthday. It was her way of showing her only parent that she existed, like a small child waving a hand and shouting, "Just once, look at me, Mama. I'm alive." A glance at her horses clenched her heart. She'd raised them to give to her mother, who had once possessed the finest horses in all of New Spain.

Somewhere in the ship, glass crashed and shattered.

"*Doña* Maria." Miguel offered his arm. "Ramón will be here soon with the other prisoners. I must take you back to the children. Your niece needs you. And Isabella will be no help to her in this storm."

"*Sí*, you are right."

Before she gained two paces, voices announced the arrival of the other captives. She watched in shock as Ramón led a file of barbarous, half-clothed, filthy men stumbling from the bowels of the ship. Many leered as they passed single-file out of the hold. Her fingers twisted in the loose folds of her skirts.

Criminals, all of them. The full scope of her iniquity began to take shape. This was her fault her people were in danger. She'd given the order to sail out of Hispaniola. She should have awaited her brother's escort to Puerto Bello. If she had, they would not be caught in the throes of this disastrous storm. She would not have consented to letting condemned prisoners freely roam the ship.

She would not have met the arrogant Englishman and made pledges that would send her to hell.

Surrendering to the pitch of the ship, Liandra gripped the stall and turned to face her horses. Her tongue felt thick. Her mouth dry.

But her word was her soul. Even if it was given before she knew his identity. Before she knew that he could never be freed.

A swell lifted the galleon. Above her on the deck, the English *capitán*'s voice suddenly filled the distance between the storm and her torment, which was truly no distance at all. He'd taken command.

Her gaze swung to the rafters. A vision of silver eyes and the promise of retribution became one.

"*Doña* Maria—"

Miguel snapped Liandra's attention aft. Ramón had taken most of the men on deck. The last of the prisoners drifted out of the hold. Still chained, a dozen confused men stood bunched in the shadows.

As she studied the pathetic, mismatched lot, an over-whelming disgust with herself took hold. The Englishman was right. Her horses received better care than these people did.

She moved forward. The ship pitched dangerously and Liandra would have toppled facedown had Miguel not caught her arm.

"I have to help them," she said.

"You have done everything you can. When Ramón returns, I will take you back to your room. Go sit down. Your brother will have my head if I allow harm to befall you."

An urchin caught her eyes. Her stomach lurched. She could not sit down. This was the youth the sea pirate expressly wanted freed. Wearing only rags, and barefooted like the others, he huddled with a gray-haired man. His teeth chattered and his thin body trembled with cold. At least he and the older man behind him were now unchained.

"We need blankets and supplies for these people."

Miguel sighed with masculine annoyance.

Her purpose renewed by the task at hand, Liandra's first thought was to go to the lower decks to check for food.

"*Doña* Maria!" He stepped in her path. "The decks are flooded."

"I gave my word, Miguel. I will help."

"I cannot allow it."

She gnashed her teeth. Those pompous words riled her temper beyond repair. A woman was supposed to act help-less. Such ignorance was surely the brainchild of men. Miguel knew better!

Liandra stepped around him to face the captives. But before she could speak a grizzled picaroon spat at her slippers. "We got us a real Spanish duchess, boys." A few brave snickers followed the example of the old tar. "Don't be thinking yer any better than us, ye Spanish tart. We can take care of our own without yer righteous charity."

Liandra felt herself pale. The man's wrinkled flesh molded to his ribs. With gnarled hands, he tightened the rope on his baggy canvas breeches and sat in the straw. Her hand on Miguel's arm stayed him from making an example of the prisoner.

"Do you understand now why it is better that you stay out of the way?" he quietly vented.

Standing alone, she watched Miguel herd the other prisoners single file against the wall. Something crashed to the deck. Water slithered through the cracks in the main deck hatch above and the lanthorn light flickered. Hugging her chest, Liandra turned and stumbled to the stall. She leaned against the door for balance. Even her horses wanted nothing to do with her. The storm had left the brothers battered. Finally, she sank to the ground. With her back against stall doors, she pulled her knees to her chest.

Miguel went through the room, stacked wall-to-wall with sacks of maize and food supplies for her horses. He tested the nets that held the barrels in place. Liandra stole a glance at the boy. Dark eyes returned her gaze, and made her breath catch. A tremulous smile greeted her study and sparked in her that lurking want of affection.

It was the most absurd of all her emotions, this childish yearn to feel needed. Yet, it drove her constantly to take risks that would appall her regal peers.

Liandra smiled back.

As if her mere gaze had harmed the child, the gray-haired man beside him pulled the boy away. Her gaze dropped to the tattered lace sleeve of her once elegant gown. She was shaking.

Somewhere tin pans banged against walls. The galley was up the steep stairs toward the prow. "Ramón should have returned by now," Miguel said as he took up his position beside her.

"They are all freezing down here."

"You have a good heart, *Doña* Maria. But they are all criminals. You are not responsible for putting them on this ship."

Tears suddenly gathered in her eyes. She turned

abruptly away. 'Twas unseemly to betray her emotions in front of others.

She thought of the Englishman outside in the storm. And wondered at the hidden nature of a pirate who'd place the welfare of a boy and an old man before his own. His tenderness for the two merited her full attention to caring for them as promised.

Dragging the wet hem of her dress, Liandra stood and rode the pitch of the ship with new determination. "Miguel, the officer's berth will have blankets."

She knew he would argue, and could not bear it. Without giving him a chance, she hurried to the ladder. The ship labored against the waves. Divided by narrow gangways, the ship lacked any coherent route from stern to bow. Liandra quickly became disoriented. Forced to stoop in the darkness, she struggled to remember the layout of a dozen other ships she'd sailed on with her brother. Puzzles, like letters, desperately confused her. She squeezed her eyes shut. Everything always felt backward.

Think, Liandra, think.

The officer's berth suddenly appeared in front of her when she opened her eyes. Light sputtered. Encased in brass, the lanthorn rattled against its brass keep. Hammocks littered the floor like decapitated bodies. Her hand clutched at her heart. Barrels slammed against the bulkhead. The place was a deathtrap. Bringing a fist to her lips to quell their trembling, she whirled back into the dark gangway.

Food, blankets, and other supplies were stored in the passenger hold at the stern of the ship. She'd put the supplies in there herself. But she couldn't get there from here.

Dios. She had to go out on deck.

When Liandra finally reached the galley, she threw open the door leading to the deck and breathed deeply. The roar of waves drowned out her pounding heartbeat. Rain hammered like shards of ice against the deck. The waves had swept the deck completely of extra provisions; hen coops, casks of sugar, and the launch. Stepping over the coaming that prevented water from running into the hold of the ship, she tented her hand over her eyes and looked aloft.

In the rigging, every man, captor and prisoner alike, worked feverishly side by side. She stared in awe. Within an hour of taking command, the Englishman had rallied the crew and stripped the spars of all but the forecourse weather shroud, the sheet pulled taut in the wind. They were now running before the storm. Already, the galleon rode easier on her bow.

At once, she noted her country's red and gold flag had been removed from its esteemed place of honor on the mainmast. Her eyes narrowed. The insolent sea pirate had proved very bold indeed.

Suddenly apprehensive of being discovered by the sea-roving outlaw, she stepped back beneath the forecastle deck. Above, the tall spindle masts and crosstrees stretched the length and width of the great galleon, an opalescent patch of dawn riddled the swirling mass of purple clouds.

A chill passed over her. Even as she watched, the precious seed of light began to shrink. Heart pounding, Liandra set her attention on the quarterdeck, more specifically the door that opened to the passengers' cabins. A lifeline had been strung from forecastle to quarterdeck.

She needed the supplies stored in the hold just below those cabins. But more than that, her niece, and the two boys she was taking to the mission in Puerto Bello were inside. Probably frightened. She would reassure them, then return to the hold. Despite their dislike of her, the prisoners still needed care.

She would not go back on her promise to the Englishman.

Gripping the line, Liandra took a deep breath. Silver bubbles slimed the deck. She slipped. Squeezing her eyes shut, she ran across the pitching deck and came up hard against the oaken door to the passengers' cabins. The portal was bolted solidly from the inside.

"Isabella!" She pounded. The air around her seemed to

grow heavier. Her ears crackled. "'Tis me. Open this door."

Liandra knocked again. This time with more force. "What are you doing? Open this door!"

Her hysterical cousin had probably barred the door when Liandra hadn't returned from the hold. Isabella possessed a bent for self-preservation that put her mother, Liandra's Aunt Innes, to shame. But this was going too far. "Isabella!"

Nothing. Liandra bent an ear to the oaken portal. Still nothing.

She began to be afraid.

A strange new sound whistled in the sulfurous air. The wind had started to shift, and slowly, she turned to look over her shoulder at the sky.

"Madre de Dios!"

Liandra crossed herself.

A vast tormented wall of clouds rolled toward them from the south. Lightning pulsed like a monstrous heartbeat throughout its tumbling mass, a savage display of power and beauty. Even as she watched, the tempest grew in fury until the wind howled through the naked rigging like a banshee. All around her, men started lashing themselves to the deck. She whirled and pounded her fists on the door. Her throat tightened. Frantic, she kicked and screamed.

"Let me in, Isabella. Open this door!"

The wind tore at her skirts, sucking at everything that wasn't bolted down. Her hair blowing horizontal in the wind, she whirled and flattened herself against the doorway. The pewter sky had melted into a churning mass, indistinguishable from the sea. Never in all her life had she faced such wrath. It speared her heart, seared her skin, and flowed like lightning in her veins. Her body shuddered.

The Englishman's voice came from somewhere across the deck. Over the roar of wind and waves, he remained in command. A human force to combat nature's fury.

Blinking the rain and tears from her eyes, she found

him, a defiant specter against the storm, high on the fore-castle deck. The wind seemed to bear him into the lower rigging as he shouted orders across the deck to the helm.

Her breath clogged her throat. He looked nothing like the abominable rogue she'd confronted in the hold. He wore the knee-high boots of her Spanish guard. A red ker-chief bound his wild hair. Sea spray molded the white shirt to hard-muscled flesh.

His courage in the face of the storm's wrath humbled her.

Suddenly, his gaze cut across the deck.

Her drumming heartbeat slammed to a stop. Liandra knew the instant he discovered her. The thunder became one with his expression. In that brittle moment, her fear of him rivaled that of the storm.

A wave crashed over the bow of the ship.

The shock of cold water slammed against Liandra. She grabbed the lifeline just as her feet were swept from be-neath her. Two men, caught in the savage pull, swirled past her. Choking beneath the deluge of salt water, Liandra held on to the lifeline, felt her palms slip, and squeezed with all her strength. The sea dragged at her skirts. Unrelenting. Punishing in force. Filling her mouth and nostrils. A crate hit her shoulder. Her desperate grip slipped. She cried, but no voice sounded from lungs that burned like the fires of hell. And then the ship righted itself. Seawater ebbed and flowed around her burning muscles, releasing her. Liandra fell to her knees, choking on bile.

All around her, the wind roared. Somewhere her frozen consciousness registered movement over her fingers as something tried to pry her hands from the line.

"No!"

Another wave smote the strangled word from her mouth. Desperately she tightened her grip on the lifeline. She would not let go. She would not die.

A man's voice penetrated the roar in her ears. She turned her head. A tangled mass of hair hung in her face. Salt burned her eyes. The Englishman was there, bending over her, trying to pry her fingers from their grasp on the line.

Sheer terror kept her hands locked on the rope. His fingers covered hers. "Let go!" he yelled over the shrieking hell.

She watched in horrified fascination as her fingers let loose their grip, and she gave her life over to the English pirate.

The Englishman lifted her to her feet. The surge had dragged away her slippers. Liandra flung her arms around his neck, felt the heat of the man beneath the icy wet cloth of his shirt, and clung to his terrible strength. The force of God's wrath could not tear her from him.

He gripped the line and staggered through the slanting rain. Before they reached the other side, the prow dropped into another trough. Only the strength of the Englishman's arm wrapped around her waist kept her from being swept overboard. His other arm looped the lifeline. His muscles strained with the weight of fighting the giant combers washing over the starboard rail. Somehow, he made it back beneath the forecastle deck.

One strong arm wrapped around her bottom, bracing her firmly against his thigh, and stopping long enough to shout orders to the helmsman, a brawny Dutchman who'd lashed himself to the wheel, he pulled open the galley door. The wind tried to snatch the portal from his grip. The sea heaved and slammed the door behind them. Together they tumbled into the shelter of the narrow gangway. They hit the wall. His breath came hot and hard over her icy cheek. Her lungs burned with the need for air. The sea had washed the stench from him.

And suddenly the darkness seemed less terrible with him near. His beard felt coarse against her tender skin. Even in her panicked state, she felt his muscled thigh between her legs as he held her flat against the wall. She felt the deep pounding of his heart against her breast. Her limited imagination of the male physique had not prepared her for the reality of his body. Untamed muscles coiled beneath her feverish touch. She'd never touched any man, certainly not in such an intimate manner.

"Don't collapse on me now, Highness."

She straightened with a jerk. Darkness prohibited contact with his eyes, but did not ease the awful throbbing between her legs. Her whole body vibrated like the masts. "I n-need no h-help to stand." She was breathing hard.

"Of course not." He braced one hand against the planked wall. The pitching deck kept him pinned to her body. "Regal pride does not allow you to be human. What the hell did you think you were doing out there, anyway?"

"She m-must have b-barred the door." Her voice cracked. "I-I w-wanted only to g-get blankets. I th-thought—"

"Don't think. You might get me killed, yet."

Humiliation burned her face. "My cousin, she is in there. And the ch-children. They n-need me."

"Looks like from where I stand they don't even like you."

Tears burned her eyes. "They are all f-frightened," she explained, but could find no worthy excuse for such cowardly behavior from her family member. Her desolation lay in the truth that Liandra's life had meant so little to Isabella.

"You are too kind, Highness."

"Liandra—" Her hands fisted in his wet shirt. Her skin remained warm where he cupped her bottom. "My name is Liandra."

"You can let go of me now, Highness." She felt his amusement. "Unless you wish me to comfort you."

She pushed his shirtfront. But shoving against him was akin to hitting a wall. That he should jest at a time like this was the greatest of insults. Did he not have one serious bone in his body?

"You, E-Englishman—your offensiveness is only superseded by your insolence."

"Highness." His hand tightened around her backside, pulling her intimately against him. Seawater dripped from his face to caress her lower lip. "I've gone to a lot of trouble saving you today. And now that I've experienced more of you," his harsh whisper nudged the small whirl in her ear, "I've decided I like the special conditions laid out between us."

Her tongue lapped at the beads of water on her bottom lip. "There were n-never special conditions."

"Ah, but there are now." The silken words promised much to her beleaguered imagination and did naught to abridge her deathlike grip on his shirt. His breath joined hers. "I would have more than my freedom."

"Are you . . . insane?"

"No. I'm an Englishman," he gloated. "A lowly Drake."

The smug boast was almost enough to rejuvenate her temper. Then the ship rose on the crest of a huge wave, and hysteria stabbed at her breast. *"Madre de Dios,"* she cried. "Let the ship be safe and I'll gladly sleep with the devil himself."

The force of her terror seemed to sober him. Perhaps he hadn't expected her to surrender. Or merely she'd robbed him of the pleasure of further torment. He was a Drake, after all, and probably enjoyed torturing animals and helpless women.

"Liandra," he wrapped his hands around her shaking ones, "I won't let you die."

The breakers hitting the ship told her differently.

"Let go of me, pirate." She untangled herself from his loathsome embrace before she sobbed like a babe against his shoulder.

He abruptly released her. "Don't go on deck again. I can't always be around to save you."

Liandra braced her hands, palms flat, against the wall behind her. "God should sweep you overboard, Englishman!"

The galley door opened and closed, but not before his laughter drifted back to her on the wind. Marcus Drake left his presence behind in the very air she breathed.

What was happening to her?

Her hand went to her throat seeking the comfortable reassurance of the necklace Grandmama had given her. She
cried out. 'Twas gone. The ship hurled her against the
bulkhead. She dropped to her knees. Finally, after futilely
searching the planking, Liandra stumbled back to the hold
only to helplessly confront yet another horror.

Her stallions kicked and reared in terror, slamming
against the stalls, jolting loose planking. The furious sea
had thrown them into a new bout of panic that would
surely kill them.

The boy and the old man stood before them. Maize was
scattered over the floor of the hold. Miguel carried two
coarse lap bags in one hand, his rapier in the other.

With a cry, she flew to her horses.

Miguel snatched her arm, swinging her around. "The
boy, he knows what he is doing!" he yelled over the crash
of waves.

Placing the bags over the stallions' heads, the dark-
haired urchin succeeded in capping their wild terror. The
boy turned to her with a smile so generous she felt the
breath catch in her throat. "They will be safe now,
señorita."

He cared.

So few cared about anything that was important to her.

Thunder crashed. She raked her gaze past Miguel, over
the prisoners. In the fading light, they watched her. Rats'
eyes, she thought in panic. *Dios*. She hated rats.

She started shaking uncontrollably. She couldn't speak.
Couldn't move her tongue to say even the smallest of
words of gratitude to this boy. She'd lost her necklace. Her
once beautiful hair lay in wet tangles around her face.
Water poured through the planking in icy rivers, and soon
they would all drown.

Fighting back tears, Liandra sank to her knees. Blood
oozed into the wrinkled creases of her palm. A cut marred
her skin just below her little finger, where the lifeline had
torn into her flesh.

A sob filled her lungs. In her mind, she saw those two

poor souls swept overboard. She was alive . . . and shouldn't be. The Englishman had saved her from being sucked into the same icy oblivion when her own selfish cousin had left her to die.

Indeed, who would have missed her had she vanished today?

She didn't belong to anyone. Her brother lived his ornate life everywhere but home. Gabriel loved his precious Spain more than he loved her. Her mother . . . her mother didn't even know her.

Only Grandmama had cradled her heart and kissed her tears.

"Señorita?" Someone tugged her soaked and tattered skirt.

Liandra lifted her head. The boy knelt beside her. In his hand was one of her pitiful horse blankets. Carefully, he laid it over her shoulders. Humbled by his kindness, Liandra, staunch survivor, buried her face in her bloody hands and cried.

Chapter Three

The salt-scented breeze drifted over Marcus. Awareness trickled through his fatigue. The deck rose and fell in seas still heavy with the passing storm. For three days, strong winds buffeted the ship. Spars and blocks slapped against the naked masts. Opening his eyes, he blinked past the aching brightness hammering his head. The rope binding him to the foremast dug into the muscled flesh around his ribs. He sat with knees drawn to chest, his forearm pillowed against his cheek. A puddle of sunshine warmed his back. His clothes were already stiff as sackcloth.

Drawing in a deep breath, Marcus lifted his gaze past tangled rigging and up to the blue dome of sky. Every muscle protested his slightest movement. Gritting his teeth, he drank in the precious sunlight. Breathed its cleansing essence. And mocked fate yet again.

His demons would have to wait another day to claim him.

All around him men stirred, but none seemed overly enthusiastic to return to their labors. They would be as weak as he.

Marcus turned to better assess the ship's damage in daylight. The galleon was a clumsy fifty-four-gun ship. The old girl had weathered the tempest, but not intact. The ship dragged half the mainmast in a tangle of shrouds and broken spars. Last night, when lighting filled the sky, for a space of hours night was light as day. He'd never witnessed anything like it. Just below the shattered crosstrees, a jagged black line scorched the thick length of mast. Charred rigging and chains lay in a scattered heap over the deck.

Working the tight knots on the rope around his waist, Marcus pulled his gaze to where the lifeline had cut into the bend of his elbow. He opened his fist to reveal a small golden cross on a tender, roped, filigree necklace.

Hers.

Sun glinted off the yellow gold. The necklace had caught the lace cuff of his shirt when he'd plucked Liandra out of the storm. Last night he must have pulled it from his pocket.

He latched it around his neck then yanked the rope free of the mast. His first thought was for the welfare of his crew. His second was to see to a particular *señorita* still in the hold.

"*Ja,*" a voice boomed. The blond Dutchman heaved his bulk up the stairs from the main deck. Shadows cast by the weather shroud blocked the glare of the sun. "You are not so dead."

Marcus had last seen the man lashed to the wheel. Daylight revealed a scar that ran the length of his cheek. A patch covered his right eye. Canvas breeches cut off at the knees and a leather jerkin protected little of his flesh.

"It is goodt day to breathe," the Dutchman said most cheerfully. "You have slept well, Captain?"

Marcus grinned. "Like a babe." Slowly he climbed to his feet and began coiling the stiff rope around his arm. His biceps pulled at the fancy fabric of his shirt. "We are in need of grog and food."

"The barrel strapped beside der mizzenmast is half-full after last night's downpour."

"That won't be enough water."

"Maybe there be supplies still in der lower decks."

Marcus tossed down the rope. "The galleon is riding too low in the water to hope she isn't flooded. Put men on the pumps."

The Dutchman's hazel eye moved shrewdly to the stern castle where the passenger cabins lay. "I have heardt that such places have food and water to ward off a siege. Our friend Ramón, he was very quick to hide when we come on deck. Maybe he goes inside to keep the silver. *Ja?* There are two others that go inside with him."

"Silver?" Dread chilled his veins.

"*Ja.* Some of us saw der silver come on board when we stopped in Havana."

Stepping to the rail, Marcus considered the enormity of the problem. Greed was difficult to control, but more manageable than hunger. Shadows from the ratlines and shrouds checkered the deck. The captain's pilot book and charts, the quadrant, and logbook would be in there. More than anything, they needed the provisions inside. And soon. The men could not continue without food.

His thoughts shifted to the hold. He rubbed his thumb over the smooth, golden cross against his collarbone. The woman, Liandra, waited with the boy. He would need her assistance. But the cowards bolted even her out. She'd known about the flooded lower decks that first day and tried to secure blankets and supplies for the prisoners. A task no one else saw fit to do. For all her haughty bearing, her grit in the face of the storm still astounded him.

He flexed his sore wrist. The little fool had almost gotten him killed. "The only other way into those cabins is through the stern galley windows," he said. "You can bet your life the first man through will be shot." He scanned the blue sky. The galleon was running free before a north-westerly breeze. "Send someone aloft. Find out if there is land nearby."

"You will set a course, Captain?"

He knew what the Dutchman really meant. The prisoners outnumbered the Spaniards. Dutch was asking Marcus to lead them against the Spanish.

Legs braced, Marcus rode the swell of the sea. The men were no longer casually idle, but watching him. His gaze traveled over the bearded faces, their cheeks and eyes hollowed by hunger and exhaustion.

A more scurvy lot he'd never faced. Nor better sailors.

For three miserable days they'd worked the sails at great peril and followed his orders. Every one of them. Including the Spanish crew.

Did the men know that his own mother had been Spanish aristocracy? Marcus had considered this unwelcome course of events when he'd demanded that the haughty *señorita* free these men. Marcus also knew they would take the ship whether he joined them as their captain or not.

The tense silence called up a reckless grin as he took his place among thieves and outcasts. The brethren code did not allow for weakness and he would show none.

"Aye," he said. "We go to Port Royal."

"We were hoping your loyalties lay wit'us. Captain."

He had no loyalties to anyone but himself. Business took him to the city of sin. It was a path he gambled would lead to his brother, Talon.

"Draw up articles. Make it clear that any man who harms the passengers or crew on this ship will not live to see freedom. If there is silver on board, everyone will get his share. I will kill the first man myself who does not heed my word."

The Dutchman's good eye assessed him. "*Ja.* I believe you wouldt."

Marcus started down the stairs. Suddenly realizing he didn't know anything about the Dutchman, he retracted his steps. Not many men forced him to tilt his chin to look them in the eye. The Dutchman topped him by a solid four inches.

"You handle the helm like you were born to the task. How is it a man with one eye can maneuver a ship?"

The big man actually appeared to blush. "Every bit of canvas has its own beautiful music. Like a fine woman in bed. *Ja?* No two are alike in soundt or touch." He chuckled at his own poetry. "*Mein* name is Groot. Groot van Dokkum," the Dutchman said.

Marcus grinned. "Groot. The name means big. It fits."

"You speak Nederlands?" His voice was not without admiration.

"Enough to know what your name means."

"My friends, they call me Dutch. It is honor to finally meet you, Marcus Drake."

"Oh?" Conscious of tension inside, he lifted a brow. "How so?"

"You are man with both Spanish and English enemies, *ja*? A man without a flag." The Dutchman rolled back on the heels of his hairy feet. "I was in Port Royal when His Excellency, the governor, tried to hang your brother last year. You sailed *Dark Fury* right down der governor's throat and blew his many fine ships to kindling. You are most famous. We were sorry to learn that you died in Tortuga before anyone could collect der bounty on your head."

"I'm relieved to say that my wounds were not fatal. So what brought someone of your stature to this end?"

"El Condor."

The name sobered Marcus. Anyone who sailed the Main knew Gabriel Espinosa, the famous El Condor.

"That Spanish son of a bitch, he sank our fine vessel. Thirty guns we hadt. Der rest is history, as you English say." He held up has bruised wrists where the shackles had torn his thick flesh. "I go now to work der cacao fields in Panama."

Marcus sat his hands on his hips and stared out across the turbulent sea. White caps marred the surface. Clouds rolled on the horizon. El Condor was an adversary worthy of his name.

Before there ever was a *Dark Fury* that combed the Spanish Main, Gabriel Espinosa had Talon and him condemned for piracy. Marcus still bore the scars of his captivity in Puerto Bello, and the irreconcilable hatred of the man Espinosa helped to mold: a man without name or country. Without morals. Without honor.

A survivor.

Releasing a breath, Marcus swung his weary gaze aloft. If he should meet El Condor, it would be on his own bloody terms—and not in this tub. More than anything, Marcus would not be taken back to Puerto Bello.

A shadow passed over the ship. A glance found the sunlight wrapped in clouds. "Hoist the staysails, Dutch. Get this ship up to speed." Marcus loped down the stairs to the main deck. "And Dutch?" He turned on his heel. "After you've set the sails, find and stow all weapons and powder on board this ship."

No man would argue the need to fight if that time came.

For Marcus, he would kill the man who chained him again.

"Captain?" The Dutchman stopped him again. "We'll needt that food and drink."

Marcus's stance reflected impatience as he followed the man's gaze. Glancing over the curve of his shoulder, he eyed the oaken door leading to the passenger's cabins. His hand closed around the delicate gold cross beneath his shirt. Heat radiated into his palm.

He grinned. "Leave that to me, Dutch."

Liandra came awake in slow degrees. Her nose itched. Her stomach ached. She had the ungodly sensation that she was twelve years old again, still hiding in the hay cart to escape her strict *dueña*. She'd been visiting Uncle Carlos and Aunt Innes in Puerto Bello. The fair was in town. Thousands of people had descended on the coastal village. In her dream, she smiled as she remembered the fireworks. She'd never witnessed anything so grand.

A crunch of straw alerted her. Water plopped onto her nose. Opening her eyes, she shoved her tangled hair out of her face, and her gaze stopped on a seemly pair of black boots. The boy, Alejandro, remained asleep beside her.

Her memory came roaring back with a groan.

The English pirate regarded her from his lofty height. Her heart quickened at the look of concern in his unguarded gaze. He knelt to better assess her tattered form. A once-white shirt marked by a ruffle at his neck contrasted with the deep tan on his neck and the red kerchief that bound his wild hair. Tucking a finger beneath her chin, he tilted her face to the light.

"Are you all right?" he asked.

His small courtesy slipped beneath her guard. *Dios.* A little kindness and she would melt. She struggled to her elbow. The storm might have bested her, but Marcus Drake would not. "Are we still alive then?"

"Aye, your highness." Silver eyes raked her face with what could only be considered amusement. "Your ship is saved, as I promised."

Blood rushed into her head. Her foolish words blared back at her. *Let the ship be safe,* she'd cried in her fit of terror, *and I'll gladly sleep with the devil himself.*

She should cut out her tongue for such idiocy. That he would dare hold her to her insane promise was an affront.

White teeth flashed behind his scruffy beard. "As much as I enjoy our . . . discussions, Highness, first things first," he continued as if conversing with prone women was a matter of course.

She sat up. The hold stank of unmucked stables and worse. "I will promise you nothing else."

"And I would not ask anymore from you." His eyes went over her with an intensity that belied his casual voice. "But it seems that one of your esteemed countrymen, Ramón I do believe is his name, has the key I need to unchain these men."

He swung his arm indicating the filthy prisoners shuffling up the ladder to the deck. Liandra blinked in relief. They had taunted her; she was glad to see them go. Beside her, the boy continued to sleep. But the grandfather now stirred.

"Ramón has locked himself in with the passengers," Marcus said.

Miguel hissed, startling her. "I should have known the coward had done something like that when he did not return," he said.

He stood near the stall. Liandra noted at once, he no longer retained his sword. And a vague sense of unease began to take root.

"Perhaps he was worried that pirates have overrun the ship," the Englishman offered. "And he is merely protecting your other passengers. Which means I won't keelhaul him when I finally get my hands on the bastard."

Liandra was suddenly frightened for Ramón's life. "You cannot blame him. Isabella probably panicked and ordered the door locked."

His eyes flashed. "What kind of man leaves a woman to fend for herself in the company of pirates? For any reason?"

With no more effort than it took to lift a babe, he pulled her off the ground. She gritted her teeth. Pain surfaced. Her legs were wobbly. She stumbled against the hard wall of his chest. And her gaze flew helplessly to his. "I"—she grappled behind her for the stall door—"I-I can stand on my own."

Easing his eyes over the swell of her breasts, made more visible by her torn sleeve, he set her upright. "So you've told me."

Furious heat blossomed on her cheeks. Sleep with the devil, indeed. He stood before her now, arrogantly poised, a mocking tribute to the total disgrace of her whole life should she allow him to lay one finger on her person. Isabella may find pleasure in such carnal ventures, but Liandra would surely die first.

The shroud on her horses had long since been removed. They whickered nervously over her head.

"We need to get into the rooms," he said. "Talk to your cousin. Before the crew riots and someone gets killed."

Glancing at the riffraff around her, she decided it was safer for the children—for her brother's daughter—that the portal stay locked. She crossed her arms. "I will not betray them. I've already done enough, don't you think?"

His laughter was light.

Her temper flared. "It will take a cannon to open that door."

"Indeed." He backed her flat against the stall. "Are you suggesting I blow up the door?"

He smelled oddly of heat and sunshine, a potent combination of male sensuality. He reached over her shoulder and petted her horses. Butterflies flapped in her belly.

"Even you can't be that cruel," she scoffed.

"Don't count on it, Liandra."

He then dismissed her and spoke to Miguel. "I'll send some of your men down. Have them retrieve any water barrels not yet under the sea and any food they can find."

Though his expression was not hopeful, Miguel nodded.

Liandra could do little more than blink stupidly. These men talked around her as if she were incapable of speech.

The pirate turned back to her. "You'll have to stay down here a little longer. The deck is no place for a woman or children at the moment."

"*Sí*," Miguel agreed. "I will stay with the *señorita* and the boy."

The boy suddenly stirred awake. "*Señor!*" He sat upright, rubbing his eyes. Straw clung to his black hair. "We are free, now?"

Looking from the boy's grandfather to his sleepy face, the Englishman knelt. "You are free, Alejandro," he quietly said. Then to her surprise pulled an oilcloth from beneath his shirt. Carefully unfolding the yellowed edges, he revealed a chunk of cheese. The lad's dirt-streaked face lit like sunlight.

"If it's too much, *amigo*, share it with the others," he bid. "It's all I could find."

"But what of you, *Señor Capitán*? You always give us your food."

"I have eaten. *Muy* full." He curled his right arm in a display of manly biceps. "See? I am strong."

Liandra marked the gentle exchange with astonishment. She knew the Englishman lied. Discovering this mere pittance of food had been lucky. They'd eaten maize and drank all that remained of the fresh water. The Englishman stood and, for a moment, her puzzled gaze caught his. His bearded face cracked into an insolent grin.

"Would you care to test the man as well?" he challenged.

"Why of all the—" she crossed her arms "—I would not."

"The weather bodes ill for us all. Stay below, Highness," he called over his shoulder as he followed the other prisoners out. "Under no circumstances come on deck. You'll soil your royal toes."

Her eyes narrowed. "Royal indeed! A man could be flogged for speaking to me with such disrespect."

He dared to laugh at her in front of the others. Any benevolence he'd sparked in her heart vanished. The man was a hairy boor.

"He is not so bad," Miguel said in the stinging silence that followed.

Wary of the old grandfather standing nearby, she grabbed Miguel's arm and led him to the stairway out of earshot. Her skirts swished in the straw. "The Englishman must not get through that door," she whispered. "Besides harming the children, have you considered what he will do if he finds the *capitán*'s logbook?"

His expression turned grave. She was the sister of El Condor. The very name doomed any member of his family who fell into enemy hands. And El Condor's daughter was on board.

"My brother is the *Almirante* of the New Spain treasure fleet. They could blackmail Gabriel."

"The logbook will be written in Latin, *Doña* Maria."

"But he could torture one of the crew to interpret the book." Her temples throbbed. It was her responsibility to protect them all. "He mustn't be allowed to hurt our people, Miguel. While you are checking for food, see that every grain of gunpowder is thrown overboard. If there is a fight between crews, 'twill be with fists. How many people can die with fists?"

He regarded her gravely. "Not as many as this storm has already killed. We at least owe those men their lives back."

Lowering her gaze, Liandra knew Miguel was correct. Noise in the hold announced the arrival of the Spanish crew. She straightened. None looked beaten, except maybe by fatigue. After Miguel took them to the lower decks, she looked from the boy to his grandfather and swallowed the bitter taste of shame. Miguel was correct. The prisoners had saved the ship. She would never forget the Englishman's courage in the face of that deadly storm.

Still, something deep inside warned that she'd unleashed a far greater peril. Marcus Drake was more dangerous to her than the storm.

Before ten minutes had passed, Liandra found herself at the portal leading to the deck. Hesitating only a moment, she threw open the door. This was still her brother's ship, and she would not be imprisoned in the hold. Nor would she be manipulated into doing the pirate's bidding.

Bright sunlight glinted against her skull. She squinted. Stepping outside, she walked directly into a wall of human flesh.

"*Ja,*" the wall chuckled. "He saidt you would follow."

Her head snapped up to confront the cyclopean gaze of a laughing Dutchman. A canvas patch, the color of the sails, covered his left eye. He looked over the knob of a nose that belonged more on the face of a pretty girl than this behemoth. Blond hair whipped in the wind.

"You are stubborn, just as der captain said." To her disbelief, the smelly oaf carried her back beneath the forecastle overhang. "Der captain says you stay below until he is ready to fetch you."

"I'll not be fetched by anyone. I demand—"

"He also says that you must not be afraidt," the hazel-eyed brute recited. Then placed a bulbous hand over his heart. "That no matter how hungry der crew gets, we will not eat your horses. Yet."

Liandra gasped in horror. "You can tell him . . ." She stopped.

What was she doing arguing with this convict? She would not be intimidated. Attempting to look around his pork-barrel belly, she observed, "The weather has calmed."

The Dutchman chuckled with a Neptunian wisdom that reached far beyond her limited comprehension of all things nautical.

"Do not be deceived, mistress. The captain is very goodt at what he does. That is why the ship flies like a pretty bird over the waves."

"Then why can't we come out?"

"Because if you or any of your men step out, he will throw you overboard." The portal slammed in her face.

"Mother Mary," she crossed herself, "rats have overrun the ship." She could only hope Miguel succeeded in ridding the ship of its entire powder stores.

Placing her ear against the wood, she listened.

What were they doing?

Finally, she gave up and went back to the hold.

Liandra sat cross-legged on the floor across from Alejandro and his grandfather. Together they split the last of the cheese. Liandra watched them eat the moldy concoction, and thought she might vomit. Staring at the chunk of fuzzy mess in her hands, she wondered how anyone could survive eating this kind of food.

"You must eat, *señorita*," Alejandro urged.

Above her, the deck vibrated with movement. Something heavy was being dragged to the center of the ship. She was more frightened below, not knowing what was happening above, than if she had just faced her foe.

Miguel and most of the crew were still below secretly disposing of all the gunpowder. The lower decks were flooded. There would be no forthcoming supplies. Her gaze again focused on the cheese.

The stench in the hold made her gag. Thirst parched her throat. Their last water barrel had been empty since yesterday. She met the grandfather's disapproving stare. Finally, his mere patience humiliated her into eating the cheese.

"Sometimes we do things because we must to survive," he said. "This is a good thing to remember when judging yourself or others."

She was so worried about her niece and the other children she could barely breathe. "I cannot in good conscience plead to my cousin to open that door, *señor*. I will not betray them to these pirates."

Liandra started to go back on deck. A hand touched her arm. "Stay below, *señorita*." The old man's voice held a hint of Spanish aristocracy that reminded her of Gabriel. Or Uncle Carlos.

And Liandra quietly yielded to his unspoken authority. Was she not forever impatient? She chewed the last of the cheese.

"*Señor* Marcus is no more safe than you are, *señorita*."

She brushed straw off her sleeves. "That's absurd."

"He must win the trust of those men."

"How could he not have the trust of pirates? He is the worst of the lot."

"This is not his ship, *señorita*. These are not his men."

"How do you know so much about this? Are you a pirate, too? Is that why you were in chains?"

The old man met the boy's gaze. Something unspoken passed between them. Something that excluded her.

He regarded her with Castilian eyes. "I only know that the *señor* has protected us when others have not. Alejandro would not have survived this past week but for him. We will stay below because he asked us to do so."

Liandra bristled at the very notion of obeying that wretched pirate—on her own ship, no less!

Behind her in the stall, the horses whickered.

"Where I come from, I have many horses," Alejandro said proudly. "These are very fine stallions. Are they not, Grandpapa?"

"Yes, Alejandro," the old man indulged the youth.

"What are their names, *señorita*?" Alejandro inquired.

Liandra stood. Dusting the straw off her pathetic gown, she walked to the stall. Her hair hung in tangles to her hips. "This is Sunrise," she proudly patted the white blaze on his muzzle. The other horse nosed in and she affectionately stroked his ears. "And this is Sundown. Thank you both for what you did helping to calm them."

"You are bringing them someplace special?" the grandfather asked.

"My mother's birthday is next week." She leaned her head against Sundown's muzzle. "It was important for me to be there."

"She does not live with you?"

Her heart slowed. "She lives at the Franciscan mission in the mountains outside Puerto Bello."

"You love your mother very much."

"I think . . ." Liandra felt her voice drop. She wasn't sure anymore what she felt. It shamed her that even at her age such issues should still dominate her heart. That her private pain was so visible to strangers. The storm, the Englishman, both had conspired to shatter her guard and notch the protective barrier that guarded her life. "I'm bringing her these horses." She brightened. "She used to love horses. She was once a great horsewoman. I raised them myself."

"And you wish to show her that you accomplished this?"

Liandra eyed the older man. A lump formed unbidden in her throat. "Is that wrong?"

"That you want your mother to be proud of you?"

"I wish to bring her joy." The way her brother did.

"Then maybe you should bring your mother home to live with you, *señorita*. A parent's joy comes from seeing their children. Watching their grandchildren grow. Not in horses."

Liandra turned to face her stallions. She rubbed Sundown's blaze. How could she tell the old man, who obviously loved Alejandro very much, that her mother didn't love her? That it was because of her that her mother had moved to the Franciscan mission before Liandra turned seven. Gabriel had raised her. But it was Grandmama who'd given her the courage to believe in herself.

Heavy footsteps sounded in the gangway. Liandra's breath suddenly came too fast. All heads turned as the big Dutchman and another equally appalling man, wearing black leather breeches and a red-striped canvas shirt, stepped into the lanthorn light. He had wild-looking red hair to match his height. Not in her whole life had she confronted so many tall men in one small place. Her exceptional height was insignificant among these foreign barbarians.

"Mistress," the Dutchman said. One hazel eye measured her bravado for the false melody it was. "You will come witht us."

Her heartbeat pounded in alarm. "I will not help you to open that door. I will not betray my people."

The Dutchman turned to the old man. His expression saddened with ominous eloquence, as if he would announce that his best hound had just expired. "It is better that you stay here, *compadre, ja*?"

Gripping her skirt to still her trembling hands, Liandra walked between them. Why couldn't the Englishman bring her topside? A strange sense of abandonment surged through her veins and squared her shoulders. Obviously, he was willing to abandon her to his crew.

Stand tall, Maria Liandra. Never let them forget who you are.

Her grandmama's words had never rung louder.

No one would ever know how afraid she was.

Chapter Four

Standing alone atop the forecastle deck, Marcus leaned with his shoulder against the foremast. Hunger and exhaustion chafed at his patience. He stood away from the proceedings, but not so far that he'd allow anything to get out of hand. A sword hung in a sling from the sash at his waist. The breeze whipped the tail of his kerchief.

His stance tightened. Dutch and the Scotsman led Liandra out of the hold. Heat rippled through the golden cross against his throat.

The bright sunlight hit her face. Dutch touched her elbow, whether to keep her standing or move her forward, Marcus couldn't tell. He realized she stared at the gauntlet of unsavory picaroons that lined each side of the deck. Her long dark hair fluttered in the wind. Bare feet peeked from beneath the tattered hem of her ruined velvet gown.

He crossed his arms over his chest. In the sunlight, she suddenly looked lost. Vulnerable.

Scared.

His jaw hardened on an oath. Her very unwillingness to bend had brought her to this farce.

Her gaze scanned the men as if searching. Slowly she turned her head and found him on the deck. His gut hurt.

Liquid eyes more brilliant than the Caribbean sky rooted his feet to the deck. The innate urge to protect her leapt to life with a ferocity that jolted him.

Blast it. His hands fisted. He didn't even like her, and already he wanted to save her.

"Mistress." The Dutchman jerked her gaze around. "The captain, he has spoken witht you. You know why you have been brought up here?"

Her shoulders squared. But her stance was like glass. She was ready to shatter.

"Will you now talk to your man, Ramón?"

"No," she said feebly.

Dutch appeared fearsome as he considered her lack of cooperation. "Do you know what pirates do to stubborn prisoners?"

"Pah!" Her small chin lifted. Skeins of silver thread in her gown glinted in the sunlight. "Everyone knows of the atrocities committed by your ilk. Are you all not a plague on the Spanish Main?"

The crew erupted into a fanfare of ribald laughter. Marcus grinned at her spirit. The proud beauty he'd faced last night paled in comparison to the gilded portrait she now painted facing this unruly bunch. Despite himself, Marcus felt unbidden respect as she confronted her barbaric-looking captors with defiance.

Dutch glared at them all. "Mistress," he interrupted, affecting a sterner stance. "Wouldt you prefer to be blindfolded before we start our tortures?"

Her face paled. She shook her head, nay.

Dutch motioned for a blindfold anyway. The girl gasped when the black cloth wrapped her eyes. "It is goodt thing you are brave. You will need your courage."

She remained stiff and silent. Her beautiful hair caught the wind and shimmer of sunshine.

"You see," Dutch continued, "three armed men are behindt that door. You choose us to die. When it doesn't have to come to that for any of our people. Talk to der men. Let them hear that you are well. That they will not be harmed."

"I . . . I cannot betray them. I won't."

Dutch turned his head and met Marcus's gaze. Damn her. His jaw tightened. A burgeoning spark of pride for her courage spilled through him. Earlier it had been a game to best her. His wit against hers. He suddenly wanted to get this unsavory business over with.

Reluctantly, Marcus nodded for him to proceed.

"Put your handt on der block in front of you, mistress."

"W-what?" Her hands curled into little balls behind her back.

"You still have a choice, Mistress," Dutch's voice barely carried. Even he was feeling the strain of his role. "You can speak witht your men or put your hand on der block."

Clearly, she was too frightened to speak. Rigging snapped in the wind. Marcus knew what such silence did to the soul. It drained you of the will to fight. Not a word interrupted her terror as her mind probably spun webs of imagined horrors that were about to take place. Would they apply screws to her fingers? Or just cut off her hand?

Marcus awaited her surrender.

Slowly, Liandra laid her hand on the block of wood that pressed against her hip.

He straightened. Disbelief filtered through the part of his brain that wasn't suddenly furious. She stood braced in front of Dutch like some bloody Joan of Arc. All Marcus had to do was light the pyre to cap off his whole macabre affair.

Like a shift in the trade winds, he began to feel a subtle mood change ripple over the crew. An hour ago, their ardent hate for all Spaniards had nearly led to bloodshed when they'd discovered Miguel emptying the powder stores. They were willing to lash her to the mizzenmast beside the ship's master.

In another moment, they'd be falling at her feet.

And the door still wouldn't be opened. The crew needed that food and water. Marcus needed those navigational charts and logbook.

If he sent men crashing through those rooms now, people could die. Including the children inside who Liandra seemed so desperate to protect.

It was such a simple solution to just open the damned door!

Marcus realized Dutch was looking to him for guidance. He left the forecastle. The men parted at his approach. Stopping behind Liandra, he resisted the urge to rip off the blindfold and shake her.

He did neither. Instead, he made her suffer a little longer for all the trouble she'd caused him. Above all, he realized his own hands shook.

"Liandra—" Patiently, he removed the shroud of darkness.

She swung around to face him. Sunlight glinted against her tears. Only a few minutes had passed since the Dutchman had covered her eyes. Clearly, she'd expected horrible atrocities to befall her. To be reprieved from the brink of torture left her bewildered.

"Just go to the door and talk to Ramón," Marcus beckoned her. "Talk to your cousin. No one has to get hurt."

Liandra wiped her face.

She felt the sting of sea spray against her cheeks, and blinked. Marcus stood before her looking more fearsome than the whole lot of buccaneers; yet, something in his eyes drew her to the safety of his presence. She reached up to touch him.

"Liandra?" His voice stilled her hand. "Go to the door."

Dazed, she did as he bid. Stopping in front of the door, she vaguely noted small holes pocked the wood. Worms had started to barrel through the oak. The ugliness haunted her.

And at once her wits returned full force. She whirled. "I will not betray them. You can't make me do this!"

"As captain"—the Englishman set his booted foot atop what appeared to be a pile of debris in the center of the deck. Clearly, Marcus Drake indulged the last of his patience—"I recommend that you talk your stubborn cohorts into coming out."

For the first time Liandra noted the wreckage littering the deck. Wind filled the sails in a magnificent arc. Lying slightly to starboard, the ship rode gallantly on the waves. Only the sound of spars and blocks banging in the breeze impaled the lofty silence surrounding her. All eyes were on her.

Her gaze stopped on Marcus. "I cannot."

A tic took up residence in his jaw. The breeze tangled in the full sleeves of his white shirt. He held her gaze. The hot sunshine bore down on her head. Suddenly his mouth tilted at one corner and she felt his eyes ease over her. Her heart raced. The cocksure grin was so much a part of his irksome character that she'd failed to take note of its absence until now.

"Then you leave me no choice, *gata*. Dutch?" he called.

Her gaze snapped to Marcus's left. The big Dutchman stripped the charred mainsail from the pile where Marcus set his foot. A cannon faced the door.

"I'll blow the door."

Madre de Dios. Her heart raced in panic.

The very idea she'd planted in his head!

Clammy hands twisted in her skirt.

The pirate's foot rested on the cannon's brace. He laid an elbow across his thigh. "Trust me, Liandra. I will do as I promise."

Trust. Promises. A sob caught in her throat. Those very words assaulted her. "You cannot do this." She almost collapsed. "It isn't decent. There are children inside."

"Dutch?" he called. "If our brave *señorita* doesn't move. Light the fuse."

She remained braced against the door.

The Dutchman turned to someone behind him and accepted a lighted punk. The breeze swirled and captured the deadly tendrils of smoke.

All courage fled. "I'll never forgive you for this.

Never!" Tears welled in her eyes. "You are a barbarian, *Capitán* Drake."

"Aye, Liandra," his voice carried ever so softly, "and I will do what it takes to open that door."

Her eyes moved in panic over the men: some without ears, without teeth, all scarred and thin. Foreign rabble.

Liandra did the only thing she could. She swung around and pounded on the door. She pleaded with Isabella. With Ramón. Anyone inside who listened. Seconds lapsed into long minutes. What if they didn't believe her? What if they remained hidden? Would Marcus think she wasn't trying hard enough? Would he blow the door? She beat the portal harder. For a wild moment, she thought she heard Isabella screaming. Masculine laughter muffled and blended with voices.

Then from inside, the heavy wooden bar slid across the door. The door latch clicked and the portal swung wide. Confused, she stood aside as Ramón emerged. Another ship's officer and the galley cook followed. Slung over the shoulder of one stalwart prisoner, Isabella shrieked as she was carried kicking and screaming out of the hold.

Liandra stared, disbelieving. How was it possible? Four pirates carrying muskets shoved at the slumped line of captives. Isabella lifted her head and saw Liandra. Black hair tangled in her cousin's beautiful face. Her chocolate colored eyes widened in fury.

"You!" she screamed. "They came in through the stern galley windows."

Isabella wore a bright scarlet dress with black mantilla lace collar and cuffs. Her red lips and cheeks bore the hint of distress. A ruby comb adorned her tangled tresses. Liandra noted she'd been smart enough to remove her jewelry.

Her heart pounded for the children. Her niece and the other two boys didn't emerge. "Where are the children, Isabella?"

"They are locked in the cabin with our dueña. This is your fault, Maria!" Isabella raged. Her captor whacked her on the bottom. "Your fault," she screamed.

Liandra blinked back tears. She faced Marcus.

"We needed a distraction, Liandra." The Englishman had the audacity to shrug. "I couldn't be sure they'd open the door for you."

"You-you tricked me! You would have blown me up!"

His eyes hardened. "Do you honestly think I'd have allowed you to stand in front of a loaded cannon?"

"I believe you would lie and murder to get your way."

Marcus stalked toward her. She leapt back and hit the bulkhead. Splinters dug into her back. His fury was like a living thing; formidable. "Lie, yes. But even I frown on murder, sweet *gata*."

"You played unfair."

"Aye," he hissed. "I would cheat the devil if I have to."

"You would kill children!"

"Would I, Liandra?" He braced his hands against the bulkhead. "Dutch?" he called without taking his eyes off her. "Light the fuse."

Liandra watched in horror as the Dutchman lowered the punk to the fuse. And watched again as the fuse sizzled to life.

Even Isabella stopped screaming to observe this change of events. The men around her stilled. The fuse burned and hissed like a nasty snake.

In horror and disbelief, Liandra swung her gaze back to Marcus, who still hadn't removed his eyes from hers. Her pulse screamed in her head. Her ears rang.

Behind him, the fuse spurted then coughed. A black puff of smoke the size of her fist mushroomed and soundlessly disintegrated in the breeze. The cannon remained dead, its single eye a pathetic shadow of black iron. A ruse. A vile trick to mock her stupidity.

"It took us an hour just to find a dry fuse," Marcus said casually.

In the next moment, Liandra's temper exploded. By nature, she refused surrender on any terms. It smacked of defeat and cowardice and all manner of vile emotions she'd buried for years. Grandmama would turn in her royal grave to see her so spineless.

The Englishman would pay for this evil trick on her person.

Her hand found the hilt of his cutlass before he realized her intent. Fury lent strength to her dire purpose. Blood pumped through her veins, feeding life into her limbs. She was as skilled a swordswoman as any man was. Gabriel had seen to her training personally, and had taken pride in her skill.

With one swing she stripped Marcus's cutlass from its scabbard and barely missed taking off his arm. He leapt back, saving himself, then ducked as she swung. He narrowed his eyes on her. That she caught the scoundrel unprepared gave her a sleek instant of thrill. She would skewer the no-account sea pirate.

"Here, Captain," a pirate shouted, "take mine."

Someone tossed Marcus a rapier. He caught the hilt easily and raised it in mocking riposte.

Her skirts flapped in the breeze.

"She is a treasure, Captain!" Dutch yelled.

A chorus of laughter followed as men encircled them.

Marcus eyed her. His silver gaze stripped her to the flesh and burned her naked skin. "Aye"—white teeth lethally flashed behind his beard—"a treasure indeed."

Liandra was suddenly afraid. If she quartered the pirate *capitán* before his crew, what would they do to her? Or the children? Her arm suddenly felt like lead. If she didn't fight—

"I am waiting, *gata*."

She thrust, and he parried, then feinted. And at once, she was on the defense. For all his barbarity, he fought with a finesse that shouted of expertise far greater than hers. But she possessed agility and used it easily, countering his skill. He backed her through the crowd. She hit the port rail. Breathing hard, she met his gaze.

"Give up your sword, Liandra."

Her chest rose and fell. Wisdom bid her to throw the

weapon away. Pride made her lunge again. He ducked her attack and dared to laugh. Fury rose in her chest. He was whipcord lean and strong despite his captivity. He made piecemeal of her offense, and with one swift blow shattered her grip on the sword. It swished end over end, chinked the rail, and tumbled into the sea with a trifling splash.

The reality that he'd merely toyed with her hit soundly enough to make her cry out. Liandra shoved a furious shoulder against his chest. And at once, the ship pitched. His boots tangled in debris and they both tumbled. His sword slid across the deck. Liandra was conscious of his hardened body, the sinewed grip of his arms shielding her fall. Her hair tangled his arms and torso. She landed in an undignified heap directly atop her foe.

The very timbers of the ship seemed to gasp in shock.

Time stilled.

His knee wedged between hers, and he rolled her flat against the dampened deck. She struggled. Burning silver eyes met hers. "Normally, I would take this as an invitation," he rasped against her ear. Sweet tendrils shivered down her neck. "But in your case, I'll give you until tonight."

"Pendejo!" She shoved at his chest.

Amidst the chortling of his crew, he captured her wrists. "Unless you wish me to make an example of your insolence here and now, surrender, Liandra."

She met the threat in his eyes. Knew he spoke the truth. But the idea of retribution terrified her and made her fight harder. She knew she could not demean him in front of this crew and be allowed to escape unscathed for the insult. His steel-muscled grip on her wrists tightened with bruising finality. With the agility of a cat, he stood and yanked her to her feet. Liandra swung her fist. He caught her arms solidly and threw her over his shoulder. Rousing cheers followed.

He ignored her pummeling fists. "Dutch," he called.

"Find the food stores. Issue rations. Empty the hold of everything else."

"Aye, Captain. And what of the other girl?"

The question alerted Liandra. Lifting her head, she met Isabella's terrified eyes. Her red skirt billowing around her, her cousin sat collapsed on the deck like a wilting rose.

"You know what to do," Marcus said.

"No!" Liandra screamed. "Don't you dare touch her."

The English pirate strode arrogantly through his men, through the open doorway, and down the gangway, which took him past the cabins. The stern gangway was stifling hot.

"You cannot allow those men—"

"You should be worrying about yourself. Which room is yours?"

She would have a pistol locked in her chest. Her heart raced. "That one." Near tears, she pointed to the large, ornately carved door to her right.

He went left. The *capitán*'s cabin. With a shove, the door slammed against the bulkhead. His body was alive and powerful as he held her solidly, his thin shirt a frail barrier against his flesh. Her hair draped her face and trailed to the floor. With every step, his muscled shoulder burrowed into her stomach.

The heavy mauve draperies billowed out from the stern gallery that stretched across the back of the cabin. Sunlight blazed through the leaden glass and spilled onto the mélange of papers and books that littered the floor. Three windows were opened to the rolling sea.

Her eyes narrowed in disgust. This was how the English pirates had defeated her countrymen. While she'd distracted her men, the snakes had come in through these very windows.

The Englishman stopped. With little ceremony, he tossed her onto the bunk. Bed ropes groaned. He kicked the door shut. Attempting to catch her breath, she struggled up onto her elbow.

Marcus wheeled to face her. "Strip."

She grasped a hand to her neck. "I will not!"

A fist slammed against the door. "By all that's holy, Liandra, I swear if you don't remove your clothes, I will tear them off you."

Defiant tears blurred his face. His features bore the threat home. He was surely the cruelest of men. Swallowing the lump in her throat, Liandra stood. Her hands shook as they found the laces on the front of her bodice. Her gaze followed him to the desk. His shirt was partially open, revealing a glimpse of his broad chest. In moments, she wore naught but her chemise and corset.

Marcus leaned against the desk, his long legs stretched before him. Sweeping his eyes over her body, he crossed his arms.

"Everything."

Ice settled in the pit of her belly. "You can not be serious . . . what kind of—" The glitter in his silver gaze stopped her. "But of course. You are an Englishman."

"All of your clothes."

She flushed. "I am sure a man of your—"

"Character?" he cordially supplied.

"Surely, even you have scruples."

His brow lifted dispelling any notion that he was remotely decent. Suddenly she remembered other rumors about this man's foul character. Seven years ago, while imprisoned in Puerto Bello, he'd been scandalously linked to Aunt Innes, who had the morals of a *puta*. Her aunt had oft invited prisoners who worked the cacao fields to her bed, and Marcus Drake had been one of those men. Before the attempted murder of his guards had him and his brother condemned to die on a slave galleon.

Liandra stripped the linen off the bunk and covered herself. She struggled beneath the linen to remove her underclothing. "I shall see you hang, Englishman."

"And forgo our precious bargain? Really, Liandra, I thought you were a woman of your word."

She could say no more in her defense.

She thought of the horrible storm and how frightened

she'd been. How the Englishman, at great peril to his own life, had kept her alive. Despite her damaged emotions, logic conceded certain heroism in his actions. Then he'd gone and tricked her. Nay, threatened to blow her up with a cannon . . . humiliated her, duped her into betraying her people, and yet his compassion had protected an old man and boy.

When she stood naked beneath the linen, she faced the sea pirate. His presence filled the room with portent ease. Sinful, she surely was, for the leap of her pulse was not wholly due to panic. She met his hooded gaze and eyed him rebelliously.

In a stride, he straightened and started toward her. Liandra's heart squeezed. Never in her life had any man touched her. She opened her mouth to scream.

Marcus hesitated. His eyes laughed at her. Pulling his gaze from hers, he scooped up her shredded clothing. In three strides he met the opened window and shoved out her clothes. She gaped in disbelief.

"You'll stay in this cabin until I say otherwise. If you leave, you do so at your own peril."

"That's what this is all about? I-I thought . . ."

"That I would ravish you?" His sight fastened onto hers. "On your word, you owe me much, *gata*. If I decide to touch you, it won't be rape. That I promise."

She flushed and quickly drew herself up. "I-I refuse to be kept your prisoner in this room."

He suddenly laughed. "Who said I wanted you as my prisoner?"

"Why . . ."

"You're too much trouble. I'd only end up throwing you overboard."

"Then . . . what am I?"

He affected a courtly bow. The red scarf around his hair framed his smirk with eloquence. "Why, you're the sister of the man who owns this ship, of course. Consider me your devoted servant, *gata*."

"Quit calling me 'cat'!"

"Indeed." He straightened and from beneath his dark brows, all pretense of humor vanished. "What would you have me call you? Hmm?"

Clutching the sheet, Liandra stepped back.

"Maria? Liandra? Highness?"

He stalked her. His height was forbidding. His boot heels clicked on the wooden floor. She heard the rush of blood in her ears. Her knees met the edge of the bunk and she sat abruptly, lying back as she attempted to escape him. She realized now, he'd never been anything less than furious with her. He trapped her flat against the mattress. To her dismay, he planted his hands on either side of her head. His shoulders strained his shirt as he held himself aloft. No part of his body touched hers, yet her skin burned. His gaze lifted slowly from the swell of her breasts to meet her eyes.

"Who are you, really?"

Clinging tighter to the bedsheet, she turned her face away from his probing stare. The scent of male sweat and sea spray molded her senses to his. His breath caressed the tiny whirl in her ear. His beard was surprisingly soft. "Where did you learn to use a cutlass like a man? Who taught you your courage, Liandra?"

He was mistaken. She'd failed Grandmama so terribly it shamed her. Stinging tears razed her eyes.

"Miguel tried to throw all the powder overboard, Liandra," he suddenly said with menace.

Her gaze flung around.

"Aye." His mouth edged to within inches of hers. "His obedience to you nearly cost him his life."

"Oh, please. Don't hurt him," she gasped out. "Or Isabella. And the children. You must not let harm befall them."

He pulled back. "Is there anyone on this ship you *don't* care about?"

"You! And I will never allow you to touch me."

He ran his insolent gaze over the fluttering pulse on her neck. "Despite your opinion of me, I've never taken any woman against her will."

"And you've had so many, *sí*? You would know the difference?"

"Would a list of my conquests suffice your curiosity, sweet?"

She groaned and tried to shove him off her.

"Or do you only want to know what it's like to bed a pirate?"

Her eyes flashed. "You are an offensive, furry sea rodent. A conceited oaf. And a liar. I will throw myself overboard before I ever so much as touch my lips to yours."

"God blast you, Liandra. But you would test a monk."

Ripping his gaze from hers, he pushed off the bunk. Shuddering, Liandra pulled back against the bulkhead. Already her skin chilled where the heat of his touch once burned. She watched him shove items around on the desk and pilfer shelves.

He was searching for the logbook!

Alarmed, she sprang across the bunk and sat on the edge. Everything would be written in Latin as Miguel said. Most Englishmen were ignorant enough of their own written tongue, much less another language. Still, it would be safer if he didn't locate the book.

Not finding what he was after, he stalked to the *capitán's* personal locker. 'Twas locked. Her heart cried for the old man who'd sailed this ship for years. He had a granddaughter who lived in Seville. He'd loved the New World. Now he was dead.

On the floor, he found the quadrant. With his other hand, he lifted the heavy trunk easily over his shoulder.

"What are you planning to do?" she asked.

He walked to the door. "I have a ship to run." His hand stopped on the brass latch. Silver eyes hardened on hers. "And if you're not a good girl from now on . . . I'll have your men fed to the fishes. Think about that before you defy me again in front of this crew."

"This isn't *your* ship." It was the worst she could think to say.

His smile peeled the sheet from her body. "It is now."

Before she could throw anything, the door clicked shut behind him. At once her gaze flew to the cluttered floor.

She bounded off the bunk and dropped to the compartment beneath the bunk. This was where Gabriel kept the logbook and charts on all of his ships.

Searching the hidden shelves proved successful. She found the navigational charts and what appeared to be the logbook. But did it hold the manifest? She opened the leather casing. Turning the pages, she attempted to read the scratches and scrawls. A wave of unbearable doubt bore down on her. She gnawed her lower lip. The letters never seemed to form legible words. She had trouble reading the very basics of script.

Slamming the book shut, Liandra padded to the window. The Englishman was free. At least that liberated her conscience. But now, he would steal her brother's ship, her virtue, raid her precious mission supplies, and threaten all their lives.

Pah! Holding the sheet clutched to her body, she shoved the logbook and all the charts out the window with the other hand. She would soundly defeat the rogue. They would not reach an English port with any help from her.

Satisfaction lifted the corners of her mouth as she stretched out the window to admire her handiwork. Her smile fell.

Ten feet down the stern of the ship broken ratlines protruded like a safety net. The logbook and charts had caught in her dress, dangling from the webbed mesh entangled with other debris.

The heat drained from her body and left her weak and boneless. She spun back into the room. *Dios!* Her head fell back against the wall. She was cursed.

The silver-eyed devil had put a hex on her life.

Outside the door, Marcus stopped. Glaring at the oaken timbers in the gangway, he gnashed his teeth. Thirty years old and he has to lust after the icicle from hell. "Aye, like a stripling lad fresh out of swaddling clothes, I am cursed."

Before going topside, he made a quick visual check of all the rooms. The children and the dueña were already on deck. Next to the captain's cabin, he found Liandra's room. Blue velvet curtains—the same blue color of her eyes—framed the lead filigree glass stretching across the back corner of the room. His gaze took in the ornate chamber with its Baroque-style narrow bed, rosewood armoire built into the bulkhead, and plush cerulean brocaded settee. Sunshine spilling through the windows embroidered the Turkish carpet with gold.

He'd once enjoyed such wealth. Ten years ago, his family's plantation in Jamaica rivaled their finest estate in England.

Setting down the captain's chest, Marcus walked into the expansive room. Mosquito netting shimmered over the rumpled bed.

The armoire was filled with gowns made for a shorter woman. She shared the room with Isabella. He found Liandra's clothes neatly folded in ornamented trunks that lined the wall. Her scent lingered.

Marcus abruptly quit the room. Downstairs, next to the passenger's dining room, the men had already emptied the hold. He took the narrow stairs back, grabbed the captain's trunk, and ascended the final pair of steps to the deck.

He was annoyed that he couldn't keep Liandra out of his mind for less than a minute's stretch of time. Especially since his tastes in bed were too discriminating for that haughty iceberg. It would take more than male lust to thaw what luxury he'd find between her legs. No, his agenda pointed north of that feminine pulchritude of trouble. More specifically, to what secrets lay between those two little ears of hers. The logbook would answer his questions.

Dutch met him at the door. His one eye crinkled in amusement. "You are in a most foul humor, Captain."

Marcus slammed the trunk on the deck. The cool wind snapped his sleeves. "Where are the Spanish prisoners?"

"We have done as you saidt. They are on der quarter-deck."

"Have you discovered who the children are?"

"Two boys about twelve andt a little girl. They say they are orphans and that your guest is taking them to their new home. *Ja*, they are glad to be free. The youth, Alejandro, has joinedt them."

Tapping the quadrant against his thigh, Marcus swung his gaze aloft, past men in the braces, to the crow's nest on the foremast. A swift breeze captured the sails. So, why was the galleon riding sluggishly? He set down the quadrant.

"Thank you, Dutch, for seeing to the boy."

"*Ja*—" he cleared his throat "—you were busy."

A sharp glance dissuaded Dutch from grievously pursuing the topic. "Will the Spanish crew take their oath to us?" Marcus asked.

"They swear their fealty only to your prisoner, Captain."

"God blast this Spanish honor!"

He knew better than to lose control, but Christ, he hadn't had a decent night's sleep in weeks, his stomach bitched with a gnawing hunger almost as fierce as the one in his loins . . . and he'd rather be anyplace else in the world than here.

Marcus snatched a hatchet off the deck near the tangled rigging. He climbed the stairs to the quarterdeck. His gaze met Miguel's widened one. The ship's master remained lashed to the mizzenmast. Standing tall with that damnable Spanish pride, he faced Marcus.

With one whack, Marcus severed the length of line that lashed Miguel's hands to the mast. Above him on the poop deck, the Spanish crew measured the ax in his hands with a wary eye.

They *should* be worried, he realized with mounting fury. Marcus held their worthless Spanish lives in his hands.

But it was the children, including Alejandro sitting a

few feet away, who stopped him from committing outright violence. Slowly, he turned. His gaze fanned over the girl, Isabella, sitting with her prune-faced dueña on a coil of line. The dark-haired temptress, who flirted with her eyes, was a mere shadow of her vibrant cousin.

Marcus snapped his gaze from the girl's face. "Dutch?" The big man climbed the stairs from the quarterdeck. "Slap irons on each man who refuses his oath of obedience to me and bind him to the prow. Without food or water, he'll be dead inside three days."

Marcus swept past Dutch back down the stairs to the main deck.

Dutch cleared his throat and followed. "Der girl, Isabella, demandts to speak to you."

"Deal with it. I've had my bloody fill of Spanish *señoritas*." He kicked the trunk away from the door.

Marcus bent his mind toward retrieving the logbook. He fixed his boot on the trunk lid. Then, rubbing an agitated hand over his bearded chin, he straightened. "Tell me, Dutch. If you were a comely maid, would you consider me an offensive, furry sea rodent?"

"*Ja.*" Dutch affected a serious frown. His eye twinkled. "You wouldt scare me to death, I think."

Marcus grimaced with wry humor. It was bad enough that he'd pirated a ship occupied by women, children, and horses. He'd be damned if he were going to bend for any wealthy ice princess. The fickle cousin, Isabella, seemed eager enough to appease him.

Scowling at the trunk, he smashed the paltry lock with the ax. The lid splintered. An odor of stale tobacco and perspiration swept over him. He felt uneasy rummaging through a dead man's belongings. Marcus wondered if Talon had been forced to do this with his trunk.

And what had his older brother found to show for the time Marcus spent on earth? The realization that a few paltry possessions measured the entire span of his life struck him solidly in the gut.

He had nothing. Not even his name.

Shutting his eyes, Marcus let the dark intensity inside slide away. He'd done such an asinine job running from his past, why torment himself over it now?

Marcus directed Dutch to dispense the clothing. When the chest was nearly empty, he realized what he'd been looking for wasn't there. Not a logbook, or navigational chart appeared to ease the growing lump of fury that built in his chest.

Resting an elbow across his knee, he glared at the portal. He'd been gone from the cabin long enough for Liandra to clean it out. He allowed her this victory. He had the quadrant, hourglass, and compass. The charts would detail the reefs in this region, but he would have to rely on taking soundings at regular intervals now.

Suddenly, fingering the necklace beneath his shirt, he wasn't thinking charts or logbooks. He was remembering Liandra's soft body swathed in that ivory sheet and her liquid eyes as he bent over her on the bunk. He remembered her talcum scent and the way her hair wrapped his fingers like silken pride, promising magic to the man who captured its essence.

Then he was remembering her promise after he'd saved her life.

The real prize was no longer this ship, the hidden silver, or his freedom. Aye, Marcus Drake, ignoble pirate and thief that he was, wanted a far greater treasure.

"Captain!"

Marcus lifted his gaze and peered at the redheaded Scotsman walking toward him. Bruises visibly wrapped his shins. Black gunpowder striped his bare chest. He'd just come from below deck. He carried a petticoat, a spindle of wet vellum, and something shaped like a leather book.

"There is no' enough powder left to wage more than one broadside," the Scotsman said. "We've scoured what we can a' the hold for weapons and anything of value. No silver."

Marcus stood. "And the ship?"

"Aye, laddie. Aside from needin' to be refitted, she's sprung more than one leak. She needs to be recaulked and patched soon, or I don't give her so long. There be oakum in the hold to do the job."

"Start heaving the cannons overboard. That should lessen some of the weight on board. Put men on the pumps full-time." He eyed the book. His heart thumped an extra beat. "What's this?"

"We were checking the stern gunports and found these hung up on broken rigging."

Marcus took the ship's logbook, then the petticoat. Liandra's scent still layered each thread.

"There's more charts but we could no' reach the rest."

Knowing that sea spray had probably ruined the ink, he didn't bemoan their loss. "Leave the rest." Grinning, he tossed the chart to Dutch, who caught it one-handed. "I wouldn't want to have the young lady who pitched this out entirely disappointed that her efforts were in vain. Now would I?"

Battling Liandra was like playing chess. Marcus learned long ago the strategic advantage of outmaneuvering an opponent piece by precious piece. Holding the logbook, he grinned. It was his move.

Having a Spanish mother who enforced the rigors of learning both English and Latin in all its grammatical beauty did have its advantages. Thumbing through the book, he proceeded to read.

Chapter Five

Liandra surrendered her vigil at the windows, praying that a huge wave would blast the loose rigging out to sea. Sweat beaded her upper lip. She paced the cabin. Where was her niece?

The sun had set hours ago. Matching brass lanthorns firmly mounted on either side of the bunk lit the room. Above her, on deck, she heard laughing and singing as the pirate crew celebrated their freedom.

She needed to know that little Christina was safe. At least her niece was very fond of their dueña and would not feel so frightened alone with the older woman.

Liandra smoothed the coarse sheet down her legs. Using the sash from the mauve curtains, she'd created a respectable, toga-style drape around her body. Any victory her cleverness achieved lasted five tiny minutes. A few hours before, the Englishman dared to slap a bolt on her door as if she were some nefarious criminal.

He'd refused to talk to her. Then proceeded to imprison her when he said he wouldn't. She didn't know what she'd done to make him so hateful. Her fingertips trembled across her lips where the memory of his breath lingered.

And to think she'd actually fantasized about kissing the low-down wretch.

Liandra shook herself. She was far too pragmatic to revel in such romantic delusions. She would not be a victim of her emotions. Her resolve strengthened, she furiously rattled the door.

Earlier, her cousin had rudely brought her a tray of cheese and bread. Protesting her servant status, Isabella had fairly dumped the cuisine on the desk beside a pewter flask of wine. Upon espying Liandra dressed in only a sheet, her cousin had launched into a score of insinuations that left Liandra's virtue in shambles.

She'd defended herself and, in a way, the pirate as well. He had been passably honorable. Even if he did lie and keep her prisoner. Instead of arguing the subject, Liandra asked about her niece.

"Christina is spoiled as usual. I told her she was not to call you aunt. Our *dueña* will not leave her side."

Relief welled inside Liandra.

"And our crew has taken an oath of obedience to the English *capitán* in exchange for their lives. If I go out, I must stay on the quarterdeck. Only the boy, Alejandro, and his grandfather are allowed anywhere near the pirate crew. The *capitán* permits the boy in the hold to care for your precious horses."

"I have worried about them."

"I'm surprised the English *capitán* thinks of you at all." Her cousin strolled to the windows. "He is very handsome, is he not?"

Liandra sniffed. Isabella would find any man praiseworthy.

"And, I think, his eyes tell me he is not such a gentleman, *sí?*"

"Of course, he is not a gentleman." Liandra lowered her voice. "He is dangerous, Isabella. And you cannot trust him."

"Even so, if one such as he touched me, I might not kill myself, either."

A weary exhale doomed Liandra's aplomb. Getting angry with Isabella would only exasperate her plight. "Have you asked where he's taking us?"

"What does it matter?" Isabella's elegant skirts swished the barren floor as she paced the small room. "We would never be in this predicament had you not overstepped your authority. I warned you not to leave that night. The English *capitán*, he thinks you will rile our men into a fight. That is why he keeps you here. He dies not trust you. He told me so. Whatever scandal you find yourself in is of your own doing."

"Better that we all have drowned? Is that it, Isabella?"

"*Sí!*" She lifted her prim nose. "Better that than be a traitor to your own kin."

"You locked the door on *me*, Isabella. I almost died out there."

Isabella's hands twisted. "Ramón said terrible pirates had overrun the ship. Besides, you know how dreadfully seasick I've been. I was too weary to think straight."

"I've known you for seventeen years, Isabella. You're only sick when it suits you." This was all beside the point. "The Englishman was set to murder poor Ramón. I hope you stood up for the man."

She shrugged. "The *capitán* has not harmed any of us. It is not so bad, I suppose, being the captive of our enemy. He has paid much attention to me. He supped with me. Alone. In the dining room."

Liandra walked to the window where the salt-scented breeze wrapped her in its cool embrace. She cared not one whit what the Englishman did with Isabella and said so.

Isabella came to stand beside her. "Did you know his father was an English earl? His family was murdered, Maria. He and his older brother are the only two still alive. They have spent the last ten years trying to clear their family name of treasonous crimes against the English crown."

"He told you all of that? Did you think that maybe he was filling your head? We both know what his family really is."

"He told me nothing. I heard the crew talking. The English *capitán*, all he wanted to do was talk about you," Isabella said nonchalantly, flicking a speck of dust from her lace sleeve. "He asked about your name."

Liandra clutched a hand to her chest. "What did you tell him?"

"Do you think me a fool? I gave him your poor mother's name. We both know that is the only real name you can claim, *sí*? So it was not a lie."

Liandra whirled from the window. "You can be very cruel. Sometimes I forget you are only a child."

"At your age, everyone is a child." Isabella patted her plaited coif. "The English *capitán*, he finds me beautiful. He said so."

"Can't you see what he is doing?" Somehow, he'd tricked Isabella into saying or doing something she shouldn't. The Englishman was very clever in that way. Look how he'd tricked her. He'd yoked outrageous promises out of her, stolen her pride, and swindled her out of her ship, all in a mere span of days. It would take longer than that to comb the tangles out of her hair. "You stay away from him, Isabella. 'Tis not a game, he plays."

"You are just jealous, Maria. You resent that men pay attention to me." Her cousin's mahogany eyes stabbed her. "Perhaps I will let him bed me, *sí*?" She laughed, but it was not glee that Liandra glimpsed in Isabella's eyes. "Do you know what my *precious* father, the esteemed *alcalde*, would do to him then?"

Appalled, Liandra could only gape as Isabella left the cabin.

Confusion still tormented her.

Uncle Carlos had once gelded a slave caught climbing into Aunt Innes's bedroom. Liandra knew about the horrible incident because she'd been a friend with the stable hand.

A strange impulse to protect the Englishman leaped from her heart. Liandra stopped pacing. The crank and rhythm of the bilge pump refocused her seditious thoughts.

Digging the perspective glass out of hiding, she leaned over the window ledge to scope the sea. A huge round moon hung suspended in the sky. Gabriel wouldn't know that his ship had been pirated. Yet, if she found a way to warn her brother, she would betray her vow to the Englishman to see him free.

The pirate equaled her brother in skill and courage. Should they meet on the sea, their match would leave no winners.

If only Grandmama were here to tell her what was the right thing to do. Throwing herself onto the bunk, she closed her eyes and tried not to weep foolish tears. She was terrified and uncertain, her nerves shattered beyond repair. She thought about the children on board, including Alejandro, and hoped Isabella paid as much attention to them as she did to the English pirate.

Liandra closed her eyes. Sleep cruelly evaded her.

What had she done to make the sea *capitán* despise her so? Long ago memories of her mother walking out on her threatened to evoke all the old horrors of abandonment.

Gritting her teeth, she sat on the edge of the bunk. And at once, Isabella's accusation came swirling back into her face.

Her cousin was right. Liandra *was* resentful.

But not because Marcus Drake paid attention to Isabella. Clearly, men could not be trusted to behave honorably. They'd proven that to her in the past.

And hadn't Aunt Innes often said that Liandra was too tall, too fair-haired to be considered an epitome of Spanish beauty? She'd been right. Liandra had learned that men of proper breeding didn't approach her. The few who dared, mostly merchants or officers, arrogantly forgave her deficiencies for the chance to wed into the family. As the sister of the vice admiral to the treasure fleet, she indulged men's appetite for power. They'd merely attempted to use her to get to the elusive Gabriel. She loved her brother with all her being, but grew to resent the name Espinosa, and had grown protective of her heart.

So, at sixteen, she began to follow scholarly pursuits that put her aristocratic male counterparts to shame. Though she could not read well, she could argue with the skill of an English solicitor—in four languages. She learned to sculpt beauty out of clay and sew her own gowns. She learned to shoot a pistol and use a sword. When she was particularly ornery, she'd done breeches and ride a horse astride just to shock her latest patronizing suitor.

Then one day she learned something else.

Being angry solved nothing and only defeated her with bitterness. She learned to accept herself, shortcomings and all.

Inadvertently, living half her life with Grandmama at the mission to care for her sick mother helped her find another calling, one that filled her life with meaning. She'd become a reformer, quietly fighting for a just cause: secretly funding the construction of Friar Montero's mission in the hills outside Puerto Bello. In some manner, she gave lives back to outcasts, the same way that Grandmama had done for her.

Sí, Liandra *was* resentful.

It took a terrible storm, and a man of no breeding or morals, an English pirate, to reawaken her to something other than her beloved mission. He made the blood hum through her veins.

Marcus Drake made her feel like a woman. An ember ready to ignite. 'Twas lust pure and simple.

Sí, Liandra resented that she would be anything like Isabella!

Marcus checked the compass heading at the helm. They were on a heading north-northeast to catch the trade winds before bending south again. He turned and nodded to the gaunt-faced man on duty, his cheek branded with a *T*.

A bucktooth smile greeted him. "Mornin', Cap'n."

Marcus climbed to the poop deck. The crew had jury-rigged the mainmast and patched the cracks in the hull with oakum. Neither fix would last long; in a few days, their situation would be critical. They were floating targets for some hungry pirate ship or mercenary Spaniard who happened on his sails.

He stared down at the book in his hands.

Marcus had let three full days pass since he'd first opened the logbook. He ceased pacing and stood at the taffrail high on the poop deck, staring out at the sea. Few whitecaps marred his view of the oily surface. Wind sliced through his hair and the sleeves of his shirt. He watched the brushstroke of light streak the horizon. Dawn.

He should have slept.

Canvas snapped. The sounds of the ship became his thoughts and throbbed beneath his feet.

The logbook became lead in his hands.

Except for the Spaniards on board, no one else knew Liandra's identity. If anyone learned her name, his reluctant captive would find her life suddenly disposable. With impunity, the man known as El Condor had nipped the freedom of most every male captive here. Gabriel Espinosa was the most despised Spaniard on the main.

Marcus, as much as any man alive, had reason to hate him.

And Maria Liandra Espinosa y Ramírez was the man's sister. So, what had Marcus done but lock the shrew in her cabin, out of his way, lest he throttle her, or worse, if he put a hand on her body.

In Liandra, he possessed the most lethal instrument for retaliation. Her worth alone would be a ransom worthy a king. If they survived. But there was another way: more fatal to Espinosa than any ransom. More fatal than facing him over a sword.

El Condor was a proud hero of Spain. Undefeated in battle. His bloodline pure as groundwater. Tarnishing his sister, stealing his ship and crew, struck at the heart of El Condor's honor. To blight his name would corrupt him in the eyes of the Spanish crown.

That it was he, Marcus Drake, who committed the deed,

would rub like sand in wounds that already festered between them.

Marcus gritted his teeth. Liandra was now fair game.
She'd promised him his freedom, looked him straight in
the face with eyes that could melt a man's soul, and lied.
She'd lied, knowing that as long as El Condor hunted him,
he could never be free. Not that he'd never been told an un-
truth, or that his profession wasn't warped with duplicity,
where best friends betrayed a man for gold, but she'd actually penetrated his instincts. He'd believed her to be honorable. She'd whipped him at his own game of deceptions.
Disappointed him.

Perhaps that was the crux of the problem.

Disappointment humanized him. Awakened emotions
he didn't want. Until now, he'd considered himself hardened against such sentimentally. Watching one's parents
die, and living for years in the dark horrors of a Spanish
dungeon, did that to a man. Pain gnawed like rats until
there was nothing left of a man's soul to chew.

Marcus gripped the taffrail. The cross against his throat
heightened his growing hunger for her. By right of conquest, Liandra belonged to him, to do with as he pleased.
By her own actions and deceit, she'd changed the rules of
the game.

Winding back his arm, he hurled the logbook and
watched it slap against the sea. In the predawn darkness,
the leather book remained visible for only a moment before it disappeared forever.

He breathed deeply of the rain-scented wind. Slowly, he
turned. His arms spread as he recklessly gripped the rail at
his back. The deck separated him from her cabin.

Visions of her on the captain's bunk, lying naked in a
wild tangle of her sable hair razed his thoughts. "You
called me a pirate," he voiced to the deck at his feet. "An
English sea rat."

It was time he lived up to the legend of his name.

•   •   •

Liandra sprawled in unladylike glee on her bunk. This morning it had rained. The room felt like springtime. She'd gathered water and washed her hair. Frowning, she sat up. Earlier, Marcus had seen fit to have her personal toiletries delivered. Wrapped in his red kerchief, they were! Hastily, she'd tossed the detestable scarf out the window, only to watch in disgust as it too spiraled into the net directly atop the sodden charts.

Before she could gather her indignant steam all over again, someone threw back the outer latch on the door. Isabella entered. Carrying a tray balanced on one hip, she immediately prattled in the most disgusting manner. Liandra stifled a groan. For fifteen minutes she was subjected to stories of *Señor* Marcus this and *Señor* Marcus that, until Liandra ached to pinch her errant relative.

"He even has our dueña giggling." A sigh accompanied this latest benediction.

Liandra rolled her eyes.

Isabella patted the wrinkles from her skirt. Today, she wore a red and gold satin creation befitting the finest salon in Spain. Black mantilla lace draped her glossy tresses.

"This morning he let Christina steer the ship. Then he took the boys with him into the crow's nest. Now everyone wants to be pirates."

"Did he not consider their safety?"

Isabella waved her hand. "You are not their mother, Maria. Sometimes you forget these brats are not yours."

Snatching her comb off the bunk, Liandra walked to the window. Staring down at the indiscreet splotch of red, Liandra yanked out the tangles in her wet hair. The net remained filled. Belaboring that calamity, she leaned further out the window. Strange, but it appeared as if the galleon rode lower in the water.

Isabella joined her at the window. "I have missed you, Maria." She fingered the drapes. "There is no one I can speak to during the days. Perhaps I will plead for your release. Would you like that?"

More than anything Liandra wanted to escape this

prison. But she'd rather be eaten alive by crocodiles than
be indebted to Isabella for any cause. Her cousin sighed.
"Miguel talked to me this morning. Christina has been asking for you. The boys miss you. Our men want to see you.
The *capitán* will have to bring you out soon enough, I
think."

Later, nearer dusk, Dutch carried in her trunks from her
room. "We have taken der liberty to remove your pistol
and knives," he announced. "The captain has decided it is
safe to speak to you now, mistress. He will fetch you at
sunset for dinner."

Liandra crossed her arms as she saw him out her door.
Sí, the English rat would stroll her around the deck like a
hound on a leash. Who did Marcus Drake think he was to
summon her with a snap of his depraved fingers?

"You tell his magnificence, if you please, that unlike Isabella, I prefer my own company to dining with pirates.
But if he wishes to escort me on deck, then he may ask me
personally."

"He will prostrate himself with der honor, I am sure,
mistress."

She shut the portal in his grinning face.

The arrogant oaf. He was almost worse than the Englishman was. She could not abide the one, much less the
other. Let Isabella suffer the both of them. Liandra had her
principles, after all.

Still, her less emotional half argued that it wouldn't hurt
to talk to the crew and let them know she was alive. And
she wanted so much to see Christina.

Unfamiliar excitement laced through Liandra. A quick
glance out the windows told her the sun was fast making a
fiery exit from the sky. The sea burned. A flicker of flame
shivered over her.

After her hasty toilette, she dug through her trunks,
scattering clothes. Long ago, she'd learned from the Indi-
ans at the mission the soundness of under dressing and regular bathing in this climate. Her feminine peers oft
snickered at her rebellious logic touting comfort over opu-

lence in this heat. Unfortunately, everything now seemed so perfunctory. She possessed not one, flashy, useless item.

Finally, she chose indigo muslin with a mantua looped over a white, ruffled underskirt. The simple indigo creation lacked the customary whalebone bodice and high neck. It laced up the front. The square collar and loose slashed sleeves marked the only fashion statement to her otherwise unconventional attire. Comfortable slippers amplified her lack of taste.

She tossed her hands. What was happening to her? The overwhelming impulse to outshine Isabella made her feel childish. She'd yielded such feminine fancies to more mature ideals years ago.

"I care not what the Englishman thinks," she vowed.

After plaiting her hair, she wrapped the thick length around her head and waited for what seemed like weeks before the sun finally dropped into the sea. She drank a glass of wine then spent the next hour laboring through one more paragraph of the book she'd tried to start reading days before—Cervantes's *Don Quixote*—finally giving up the quest to skip to the last page. She hated sad endings and this one looked to be transpiring in that direction. With an annoyed sigh, she finally closed the book.

Marcus was late.

The clank of the bilge pump drifted through her head. The breeze billowed the curtains. The room grew darker. Above her, someone paced the deck. He wore boots. Often at night she'd listened as that same man walked the deck. 'Twas a lonely sound, she thought idly, and her gaze followed the invisible click of heels back and forth over her head.

Sitting on the edge of the bunk, Liandra smoothed the wrinkles from her skirt. Darkness pursued the light across the floors and the wall of the cabin, slowly consuming the room.

Finally, Liandra acknowledged that Marcus wasn't coming for her after all.

•　•　•

Movement awakened Liandra from a sound sleep. The cabin was dark when she pushed up onto her elbow. Heart thumping, she was disoriented and afraid. She still wore her clothes. Blinking, she shoved a strand of fallen hair out of her face and sat up. What time was it?

Immersed in the shadows, a man sat in the *capitán's* chair in front of the desk. Awareness of his identity struck like sparks in her blood.

Moonlight sifting through the cracks in the drapes outlined the broad width of shoulders beneath his white shirt. His long legs were propped on the desk. Boots glimmered in the pale light. His ankles were crossed, his fingers twined around a book in his hand as he watched her.

"Since you didn't want to join me for dinner, I thought to join you." His gaze dropped to the book in his hands. "So, would you consider Don Quixote a true hero, or a romantic fool?"

She lifted her chin. The Englishman's lazy tone boasted his ease in her presence and something more. Hostility emanated from his being like an unseen entity threatening her with its presence.

How long had he been in the room watching her? Contemplating her murder, no doubt. She told herself that he couldn't know that she was Gabriel's sister.

Dropping the book onto the desk with a *thunk*, he stood and walked to the window. His head nearly touched the rafters on the ceiling. He stretched his arms the length of the curtains as he prepared to throw open the heavy drapes. Liandra was on her feet in a heartbeat, blocking his way. If he looked over the window's edge, he would see the net.

"No," she said. "I like the dark."

Mere inches from her, he looked down into her face. In the sharp blade of moonlight slicing through the crack in the curtains, she saw his brow quirk in amusement. She also saw much more. The man who filled her vision was not the pirate she'd seen only a few days before. Her breath caught in her throat. Marcus had shaved. His brown angular jaw, the aquiline bridge of his nose, bespoke a man self-assured, a man entirely too comfortable with his effect on women, a man impatient with the world. His dark hair was washed and tamed back into a queue tied with a leather thong. Moonlight touched a pair of silver eyes made more beautiful by the fringe of ebony lashes. She was terribly conscious of his masculine presence and of his mouth so near her own.

"Pray tell," the dark silken thread of humor in his voice only made him more lethal, "what does a young lady do in the dark with a strange man in the room?"

"You are calling yourself strange?" she queried. An interesting scent wafted from his clothes and mingled with the smell of ocean on his skin. She bent and sniffed his shoulder with unladylike marvel. "You . . . you smell like a flower."

Like a thunderous storm that suddenly dissipated into gently falling rain, the hostility she felt toward him faded.

He leaned back against the desk and crossed his arms. "We took advantage of your fine crate of soap and the rain today. I'm afraid the whole pirate crew smells like the finest Parisian strumpet."

Before she could catch herself, Liandra laughed. "That soap was smuggled from France. Isabella paid two month's allowance for that crate—" She clapped a horrified hand over her mouth but could not contain her mirth. 'Twas her worst trait to babble so indiscreetly.

Marcus grinned. "I've not seen you laugh before." His gaze dipped to her breasts, taking in her attire, and lifted slowly to her flushed face. "You have nice teeth."

The ludicrous compliment stole her guard. She found herself rallying behind anger that wouldn't materialize. His expression gave away nothing. Yet, she felt naked beneath his gaze.

Marcus found the flint box stored on the shelf above the bunk. He lit the lanthorns. Light illuminated the confines of the room. He seemed even taller as he turned to face her. He walked to the desk and picked up an amber bottle of wine she recognized from Gabriel's stock in the hold.

"Have you come to apologize for locking me in this cabin?" She watched him yank the cork from the bottle and fill two crystal glasses normally used in the passenger's dining room. "Or are you here to bring me on deck so that I may appease my troops?"

He presented her with a glass. "I apologize. Seriously," he replied to her skeptical look. "Even if it was a mutiny I was trying to prevent."

He didn't seem the least sincere.

"Is it true that you and Innes . . ." Her chin lifted. "When you were imprisoned in Puerto Bello . . . that she took you to her bed? The very same one she shared with the *alcade*?"

His mouth tightened into a frown. "Innes's passion for slave labor was . . . well-known among certain circles. But even I'm discriminating." He paused and looked at her carefully. "That was seven years ago. You would have been practically a child. How could you remember something like that."

"I was not so young that I didn't have ears," she said flippantly, aware that her heart pounded. "Why didn't you escape? You could have."

His finger ran over the glass rim. "My brother was still there." His gaze lifted and found hers. She detected the barest flicker of vulnerability before his mouth suddenly kicked up and whatever it was she'd seen vanished. "I may be a thief and a lot of other things I won't mention, but I do have my standards when it comes to women."

Despite the rapid rate of her pulse, she was suddenly starved. The soup on the desk smelled delicious. She took the proffered glass and, stepping around Marcus, sat in the *capitán*'s comfortable chair. The worn leather still radiated Marcus's body heat.

"I'm sorry that there isn't another seat," she said.

"We can always share the bunk."

"Eating bread in bed makes for a crummy night."

Dios. What was wrong with her? Averting her mortified gaze, she proceeded to eat. Isabella was always the first to point out that Liandra owned no sense of humor. Here she was spouting silly proverbs as if she were born to the task of entertaining men.

Lifting a bowl of soup, Marcus leaned a hip against the desk. "Maybe the company you keep needs improving, Liandra."

The bread she was chewing stuck in her throat. "I keep no company, *Capitán* Drake."

"Never?"

She squirmed in her seat. "We should not be having this conversa—"

"Have you ever kissed a man?" he persisted.

"Of course." Hastily she sipped her wine. How many men did a respectable twenty-two-year-old woman of virtue kiss in her lifetime? "At least . . . ten or eleven."

He leaned toward her. Her gaze focused on his hand splayed beside her bowl. Black hairs spattered his skin just below the ruffled cuff of his shirt. Her eyes traveled up the muscled length of his arm. In the shadows, his teeth shone white against his tanned visage. His silver eyes sparkled.

"Do you keep promises better than you lie, Liandra?"

"I always keep my promis—"

He'd tricked her. She knew the moment the words spewed out what he was about. The smile in his eyes brought her to her feet.

"You are an unprincipled pirate, Englishman."

His laughter surprised her. The anger that she'd seen earlier in his eyes had changed to something more powerful. Captured by his vigor and the beat of her racing heart, she stared like a starry-eyed maid.

"I propose a truce," he finally said setting down the empty bowl beside *Don Quixote*. "I do need you on deck."

"What kind of truce?"

He slid his finger across the book. "I won't remind you of your debt to me. You won't remind me of my chosen profession. I'll behave like the most cordial of gentlemen."

She crossed her arms and sniffed.

"For an hour. We'll walk the deck. And talk."

Laying her hand on the muscled curve of his arm, he led her toward the door. His flesh beneath his shirt warmed her palm. "An hour is hardly enough time—"

"It's beyond me how a woman can talk any more than that."

"You've never talked to a woman for an hour?"

He opened the door. "I'm usually not engaged for my conversation, Liandra. I have to admit, you're the first."

She sensed hidden peril in the grin that preceded her exit. Butterflies fluttered in her stomach. At once, she was suspicious of his scheme. He had tricked her once. She was not so daft as to allow him to dupe her again. While on deck, she'd find Miguel. She had to discover a way to regain control of the ship.

"And Liandra—" Marcus braced his hand on the doorframe trapping her next to his body. His voice, laced with warning, brought her gaze to bear on his. "Don't say anything to your men that will get them killed."

Chapter Six

Marcus leaned with his hip to the rail and listened as Liandra talked. Moonlight broke through a wispy ridge of clouds. The deck lifted gently in the swell. He was pleased to see how easily he could finesse his feisty captive. The late evening sortie had been a success. First, he'd surprised her with the second course of their dinner on deck: baked fish, a plate of sliced mangos, and again with a fine bottle of wine pilfered from her stores. Notwithstanding her obvious dislike at having her illegal stash raided, she drank and ate everything he'd offered, including his charming conversation.

They strolled across the deck. Not quite touching, but close enough that her skirts whispered against his legs. The stars invited discussion. She stood first at the larboard rail, then moved to starboard, talking about the weather and the constellations. Despite the insignificant topics, her voice carried with infectious excitement. She revealed enough knowledge about navigation to impress him. Most women thought a longitude was something one wore to bed.

He didn't divulge that Jamaica was his destination. A road that Marcus hoped would lead to Talon, and a score of other unfinished business he had there.

Idly watching the seductive twitch of Liandra's skirts as
she walked, Marcus half smiled to himself. He could se-
duce her easily. It was, after all, what he did best. She had
the hopeless innocence of a child. And clearly—his gaze
slid down the outdated dress she wore—she did not indulge any royal allowance in her wardrobe. He knew more
about women's fashion than she did.

"Do you and your cousin smuggle regularly?" he suddenly asked during a brief lull in her monologue. A splash
somewhere across the water had rushed her excitedly to
the rail. She'd told him earlier about porpoises in these waters.

At his question, her head snapped around.

He could have raised issues consistent with certain
facts: for instance, not one item in the hold was listed in
the ship's manifest. If there was silver on board, she'd hidden the cache. He had no doubt he'd find it. Tonight, however, he didn't particularly care if the galleon was laden
with treasure.

He wanted Liandra.

Lifting his gaze from her breasts to the flutter at her
throat, he wanted to put her against a wall, look into her
tilted-blue eyes, and drink her lips. He wanted to imbibe all
of her.

Marcus stopped beside the rail. "You said Isabella paid
two months' allowance for that crate of smuggled soap."

"*Sí,*" she admitted, "the price was outrageous."

Searching her blue eyes for some hint of guile, he
mused aloud, "Doesn't buying smuggled goods in your
country count the same penalty as smuggling?"

"Of course. But it only makes a difference if you're
caught. Besides, how can a king decree that we only buy
goods from Spain, at exorbitant prices, and then not de-
liver those needed goods? We do have to survive. The supplies on this ship belong to a mission."

He stared in disbelief. "So you risk your neck for some
church?"

"'Tis more than just a church! It is a whole world.

While my brother oft traveled, I lived there with my grand-mama. Friar Montero is her brother, my great-uncle. Much of my mother's family lives in the surrounding mountains. I have thirty-five cousins."

He choked.

"Isabella is my only cousin on my father's side. Mother had eleven brothers and sisters." She lowered her voice to a conspiratorial whisper. "So you see, I am not so noble. I too enjoy soap and cloth to make dresses."

"For you or your thirty-five cousins?"

She laughed at his silly joke. "In case you think I tell everyone this, I don't. It must be the wine."

"Or the company," he offered, knowing that she was definitely doing unexplainable things to his male psyche.

"*Sí*, I suppose. Tonight, I don't feel so much like a pris-oner. Perhaps if I ask, you will tell me where you are tak-ing us."

"Maybe I'd rather hear you talk more about your mis-sion."

The wine had surely made her relaxed. For without so much as a worried frown line to mark her thoughts, she talked fondly of the mission and of Puerto Bello.

"We have built two churches, a fine school to teach reading, and many *cabañas*," she continued. "It is a real town. This year we will build a mill to grind sugarcane. Or at least try."

Puerto Bello was a God-forsaken, mosquito-infested jungle and, frankly, Marcus applauded her futile efforts. For a long time, she chattered about the two boys that she was bringing to live in the mission. "Their parents died of fever last year. They worked for my brother at his home in Hispaniola. No one else in Santo Domingo would take them. Do you know how many children live on the streets? It is outrageous that so few people care."

Despite everything, Marcus found himself engrossed in her fervor. Her lilting voice rolled over his senses like warm cream, and he lapped it up like a hungry cat. The moonlight captured the vivid color in her blue eyes.

She possessed an innocent blend of sophistication and sensuality he'd recognized the first moment he saw her in the hold. And he admired the kind of courage it took to stand up for something. To see a wrong, and try to fix it in an age when it was easier to look the other way. It was the kind of vision he lacked. Not because he was a sheep, a follower, or that he accepted the status quo of New World atrocities, but because he didn't believe in the inherent good in people. For the most part, they weren't worth saving. Certainly not at the risk of his neck.

Where had she lived her whole life that no man would take notice of her rare beauty? Her laughter or her spirit? What was wrong with her that no man would have married her by now?

"You're not listening, are you?" she said suddenly.

Blinking stupidly, he realized he'd been staring at her. Her blue eyes scanned his with concern. Concern that he'd found her boring? It astounded him that he had not. "I'm only amazed that we've talked for almost three hours."

"*Sí.*" Her gaze hesitated on his face. Then moved to the velvet sky and the blinking morass of stars. "Dawn isn't so far away."

"What about your brother?" He suddenly wanted to know if Espinosa shared half her character. "Does he know how you spend your spare time and money?"

Her mouth tightened to a serious line. "The little I've seen of him through the years . . . he's been good to me. And I love him. But I fear his vision for the future does not match mine. He loves Spain too much. He is blind to reality."

"You do not like Spain?"

"She is my heart. But I do not agree with everything the king does. Grandmama taught me to do what is right," she said quietly, "to do what I must. I would never wish to disgrace my brother, but I must follow my conscience. So, I do what I can for the mission. What about you, Sir Pirate? You have not always sailed the seas as a freebooter."

Turning to the rail, Marcus leaned into the breeze. "A

long time ago, my mother filled my head with dreams of happily ever after. My father was a planter, when he was not a privateer sailing for Henry Morgan."

Her warm silence invited him to continue. Years seemed to fall away from his memories. They talked about trivialities he'd never even told his betrothed. Like being schooled two years at Cambridge University in England, only to be expelled for unruly behavior.

"I am a rapscallion by nature," he confessed not knowing how they'd reach this point in the conversation. "Maybe it's from being born the second son. Responsibility has always terrified me."

"But you captain a ship."

"I haven't always sailed a ship. My brother was the one who loved the sea and became a privateer with my father." They descended back to the main deck. "I wanted to be a planter," he said. "I loved the land. There was so much more I could do with my hands."

"Surely, you love the sea?"

"I'm not even a good swimmer."

"You?" She suddenly giggled. "I do not believe it."

"Aye," he admitted, watching the play of moonlight on her skin. Her whole face glowed. "I even get seasick."

She laughed. No, she guffawed, Marcus reconsidered as he turned to face her. Leaning a hip against the rail, he crossed his arms and observed her humor with the eloquence of a saint. Usually he had no tolerance for tea-party chitchat.

But tonight was different.

The moon and the breeze conspired to soften his mood, and rattle his composure. Watching Liandra, he tried for a moment to remember his past and the other women in his life. Being a practiced rake since the day his prim governess had undressed him in the barn and opened his life to a whole new realm of boyish-fantasies-come-true, he'd never much cared about the lives of the women who shared his bed.

He closed his eyes and tried to summon the image of his

betrothed. Her eyes were blue, much like Liandra's, but that was where the similarity ended.

Something about Liandra pulled at him. She was a contradiction. Part girl. Part woman.

She was a Spaniard.

Frowning, he realized he was beginning to like her.

She wiped a straggling tear from her cheek. "Is it really true that you're the son of an English earl?" she suddenly asked. "Isabella told me."

Marcus stiffened. Their truce had ended hours ago. He had no business discussing his past with Liandra. Again he walked, but no longer cared if she fell in beside him. He was taking her below deck, and it only mattered that she followed. "My brother holds that illustrious title now. For what it's worth."

"What happened, Marcus? To make you turn pirate?"

"One day the governor's henchman came and took it all away. My father's home. His life. Mother was murdered. And I grew up."

Her face paled. "And your brother and sister?"

"Talon grew up faster. Of Sarah?" His little sister had been nine. "Sarah is gone, too," he said. "That was ten years ago."

Liandra dropped her gaze when she realized he wasn't going to offer any further comment. He opened the door that led to the passengers' cabins and continued to walk her to her room. The narrow gangway was humid and needed a good airing. She stopped in front of the captain's door. Hesitating, she turned. The brass lanthorn set in the wall behind him cast a shadow over her face.

"I'm sorry," she quietly ventured.

Her compassion nettled him. "Don't you want me to go on?"

"Yours is not the only family to suffer in these times, Englishman." Surprisingly her voice was gentle. Her calmness contrasted poorly to his temper. "I do not understand the hate or the politics that make men commit atrocities against each other. But a man must choose his own path and cannot blame anyone else for who he is. You are a pirate because you choose to be."

The echo of her rebuke seized what remained of his charity. The lofty *señorita* knew nothing of the fate that had snatched his life. "Aye," he leaned a hand against the door, "and I choose never again to be another man's slave. I will die by the lash before anyone puts a rope around my neck the way they did to my father."

She backed against the door. Her hair whispered over his hand. "Why do you tell me this?"

"Because I would warn you now of the kind of man you bargained with. I do not forget anything. I am not nice. My enemies are few because they don't live long enough to annoy me. And I've no fondness for Spaniards . . . or liars."

Her chin lifted. "You are consumed with revenge."

"That is my brother's task. Mine is simpler. Unlike Talon, I *know* justice is a myth. There will never be any benediction for my sins. There is no such thing as impartiality or fairness. When the enemy is at your door, you destroy him any way you can."

"Perhaps you are this other side as well," she said quietly, "the planter. A man with kinder visions."

He laughed. "Don't bet your life on it, *gata*. I'm a pirate. The man you'll be taking to your bed."

Shock knotted her features. And something else.

"I'm going to kiss you, Liandra." He tipped her chin. "That is . . . if you know how."

She yanked her chin from his grip. "I think you will not find out."

"And you said you were a woman of your word."

Blue eyes flashed. "I will be free of my promise soon enough." She dismissed him with an audible sniff and started to turn.

Marcus blocked her escape with his other arm. He lowered his mouth to within mere breaths of hers. "You will be free when all your debts are paid, *gata*. Not one minute sooner."

Her hands splayed his chest. She smelled of fresh air and scented talcum that suited her well. "And if I choose not to kiss you?" The feverish words were breathless and tasted like wine.

Faintly challenging, he held her wide, blue gaze. "You could always scream instead," he suggested, before lowering his mouth.

Contact with her soft lips sent shock waves crashing through his chest. He tasted the potent wine and sweet honey of her breath, savoring her resisting lips, until he slipped his tongue inside and deepened the kiss. Her soft moan answered. Headiness encased him. He flared a greedy hand over her round bottom and pressed her against the hard hungry length of him. The other hand cradled the back of her head. Another deep groan joined his. She trembled. Slowly, her splayed fingers curled then climbed around his neck to entangle in his hair. The leather thong dropped to his shoulder and fell to the floor. His hair spilled over her face.

Like a flooding eddy, blood lapped through his veins feeding the fire in his loins. Jesu, but she was more potent than rum. The violent inferno raged through his body and scorched his skin.

Something inside crumbled. Some elusive barrier that had started to fragment the day she'd laid her hand on that block and invaded his dreams. He'd never known another like her. Simple and complicated at once. Hot. And it came as a shock to realize how much he needed her to want him.

A deep growl formed in his throat. He lifted her against his thigh until she straddled his leg in carnal surrender. His tongue circled the shape of her lips, teasing and thirsting, reveling in her willing response. Wrapping his hand in her silken braid, he dragged her head back, trailing his mouth over her jaw, down the smooth column of her throat to taste her. Her breasts strained the simple dress that had at once become an erotic and sensual barrier to her skin. Her wild pulse tattooed against his lips.

"Marcus," her throaty gasp moved over him.

He slid his kisses over the pale curves of her breasts, felt the swift intake of her breath, and knew he was dangerously close to losing himself. Sexual hunger consumed him.

"Ah, Christ, Liandra. You make me hurt all over."

"*Sí.* I cannot breathe. I will surely die if you stop."

"Tell me you have done this before."

"You were right," she said. "I have never . . . I have never kissed a man. You are the first."

The trembling words hung in the air between them. His head lifted, and he met the bright oval of her shining eyes.

The erotic beat of his pulse, his thoughts, the very depth of his conscience all conspired to defeat him. Reality crashed over him.

She had no business trusting him. In that fateful instant, he knew she didn't deserve to pay for Espinosa's crimes.

Marcus straightened. Reaching behind her for the brass door latch, he opened the portal and shoved her inside. Out of his reach.

"Did I do something wrong?"

"Lock the door from your side," he said briskly. "You've convinced me to release you from our bargain. Don't make me regret my decision."

She opened her mouth as if to speak. Tears mixed with the confusion that clouded her eyes.

Marcus shut the door.

For a long moment he braced his hand against the door-frame and bent his head in disbelief. Anger tangled with pride and a perpetual erection that threatened to collapse his restraint.

He shook his head and waited for the heat to pass. No greater idiot had ever lived than a noble pirate.

"*Señor Capitán?*" A small hand tugged on his shirt.

Looking way down, he gazed into the little girl's huge blue eyes. Her name was Christina. She often came on deck and bothered him and his men. She was a friendly thing. The door to her cabin swung with the ship's movement.

"What are you doing awake?" he asked, concerned that she might have witnessed his display with Liandra.

Black curls reached down the length of her back. Eyeing Liandra's door, she sniffed. *"Mi tía . . .* she told Isabella that I mustn't talk to you alone. But . . ." She shuffled her bare feet. Her white nightdress barely covered her thin ankles.

He knelt. "Your *tía?* Liandra is your aunt?"

"Sí." Her piquant face suddenly screwed into a frown. "Is that bad, *Señor Capitán?* I am not supposed to tell anyone."

His heart hammered against his ribs. "Your father is Gabriel Espinosa?"

She nodded.

Jesu. Gabriel Espinosa's daughter.

Caught by her beauty, he stared at the small face and bright blue eyes. There was some resemblance there to Liandra. "Aye," he quietly answered, "it is wise that this secret remain between us."

"My *dueña* is asleep, *señor.* And I'm . . . I'm hungry."

Marcus lifted the frightened girl. Wary blue eyes watched him back. She was small-boned and fragile in his arms. He could crush the life out of her with little effort at all.

Nausea accompanied the thought. The years had turned his soul to sludge. They'd made him into many things, but a butcher was not one.

His little sister hadn't been much older than this when the governor's henchman took her. Had she died looking into her captor's face as Christina looked into his?

His throat tightened. "Would you like some soup?" he asked.

"Sí." Her curls bounced with eagerness.

Marcus took Christina to the galley. The wind was calm and he didn't have any problem standing up straight even with the wine he'd consumed over dinner. Rummaging through that night's leftovers, he obtained a loaf of bread and some fish soup still sloshing in the cauldron. Under

Miguel's distant vigilance from the poop deck where he slept, they sat cross-legged on deck. The past week Marcus had watched little Christina with Miguel and knew there was quiet affection between the two.

While Christina ate, Marcus rigged up some line on a thick bamboo pole the crew often used for fishing, and together they fished. As he listened to her innocuous chatter, he met the Spaniard's gaze and grinned.

It wasn't a nice smile.

At that moment, he didn't feel nice, or particularly humane. Ten years of his life he'd spent in a cockroach-and-rat infested Spanish dungeon, the cacao fields, or on the sea fighting side by side with Talon to reclaim their lives. He wanted Miguel to see little Christina and know the helplessness of captivity. To know the pain and uncertainty of watching someone else hold a loved one's life in his hands.

So, why did his skin crawl with self-loathing? After years of running amuck in an amoral abyss, was he suddenly getting a conscience?

Christina's excited laughter pulled his gaze back to the pole in his hands. He'd caught a fish. For the next fifteen minutes he let her help pull in the fish.

When he deposited little Christina back into her room an hour later, his gaze fell on Liandra's door. A surge of animosity bent his thoughts.

Gabriel Espinosa, the Spaniard known as El Condor, had a daughter. A sister. A home. A whole family of extended relatives that surrounded him.

Did the bastard even recognize how fortunate he was?

Liandra lay curled in her bunk, staring at the knotty wall. The groans and creaks of the ship echoed the strange emptiness inside. All night she'd tossed and twisted until the sheets entangled her limbs. Shame was the purveyor of her wretched conscience. A reminder of her outrageous behavior in the arms of that . . . that sea rat.

She kicked the sheets off the bed.

Pah! She should thank Marcus Drake for the honorable eviction from his arms.

Stiffening with apprehension, she stilled as another thought struck. Men such as he, men that her brother fought to eradicate from the sea, did not possess honor.

So, he must have found her uninspiring, inadequate at best. Like her peers made her feel when she tried to fit into Gabriel's golden world.

Sí, she was not Isabella.

Trying to ignore the tight ache in her chest, she twisted to face the window. Sunlight pressed through the cracks in her curtains. Dampness already beaded her neck. She sat. Fretting over a problem never made it go away. 'Twas Grandmama's stately advice and warded off many a bout of self-pity.

Liandra tried the door and found it unbolted. Her heart raced. Peeking outside, she discovered the narrow hall clear. Freedom loomed. Just as Marcus had said.

She ached to check on her niece and the boys. They'd probably be asleep, but it didn't matter. She would see them with her own eyes.

After washing, she hastily dressed. The second ceremony of the morning would be to see her horses.

Then she'd find Miguel, her ally on this ship.

Fifteen minutes later, Liandra was back in her room. The Dutchman barred the cabin door with his body. Arms crossed over his massive chest, he regarded her sternly.

"*Ja*, the captain has certain rules, mistress," he explained again, as if thrice wasn't enough. "You are not allowed in der hold."

"But my horses are down there."

"As is der convict crew, mistress."

"He can't do that—"

"*Ja*. He is der captain. If you cannot be trusted to mind the rules, he will lock you back in this room."

"And what else does his splendor expect?"

"You do not speak with your crew. Not without one of us in presence."

She was tired of always losing. Liandra narrowed her eyes. "Are you his faithful watchdog?" she queried the muscle-bound oaf.

"*Ja*, I am."

After he left, Liandra tossed her arms. *¡Ay, yi, yi!* he couldn't even be counted on for a decent argument.

Knife clutched between his teeth, Marcus dangled high in the ratlines of the mainmast just below the crosstrees. The sun bore down on his head and shoulders. Sweat beaded a path down his spine. The red kerchief that bound his hair was the only head protection he had against the sun as he finished the last of the repairs on the mast.

Miguel sat in the ratlines across from him and grinned. "It is hot as the blazes, *si*?"

With the front of his forearm, Marcus wiped the sweat from his brow. Together they'd mended the main topsail. Two more men worked in the lines above them. Four more below.

Miguel admired Marcus's handiwork. "Not bad for an Englishman."

He sheathed the knife. "Especially when it's Spanish flotsam I'm working with. We're lucky we're still on top of the water and not a league beneath."

Dark eyes carefully assessed him. The Spaniard's black mustache twitched in amusement. "It is unfortunate our two countries cannot work and live in such continuous harmony. Do you see what we have accomplished in such a short time?"

Marcus studied the younger man. He had an honest face. For all that he hated character, Marcus was glad the man had kept his word not to rebel. "I'm relieved to be on the same side here," he agreed.

"That surprises you, *señor*? You do not trust easily."

"I've known friends with less integrity than you."

"And it is not my way to judge a man by rumors."

"Then let me reassure you that everything you've heard is probably true." He grinned. "I wouldn't want to confuse your loyalties. It might get you hanged."

Miguel shrugged. "I am your prisoner. What can I do, *sí*?"

The sweet melody of laughter lifted in the breeze.

Marcus's attention fell on the supple figure standing far below near the helm. Wearing a bright yellow gown more suitable to the child she held in her arms, Liandra conversed with Dutch. With her long black sleeves and black-tipped skirts, she looked like the bees that would flutter around his mother's flower garden and annoy him.

His mother had created the most beautiful miracles from the weed-infested earth his father had carved out of Jamaican soil to build their home. His little sister often wore lilacs in her hair. She possessed the whitest mane, like spun silk on silver-haired angels. . . .

His eyes refocused. He hadn't thought of his home and family in years. Not until he'd spoken to Liandra.

Frowning, he continued to watch her on the deck. A dozen uncouth knaves who didn't know the difference between fine porcelain and pottery loitered near her and Christina. Dutch must have told Liandra something amusing because she laughed again.

That she should look like some glorified bumblebee and appear radiant all at once irked the hell out of him.

"She is very beautiful. Is she not, *señor*?"

Marcus snapped his gaze back to Miguel.

"I have known her since she was a girl and she'd come with her grandmama to visit her mother at the mission."

"Her mother?"

"*Sí*, her mama moved to the mission when Maria Liandra was seven."

"Alone? Why would a woman leave her own child?"

He leveled a knowing gaze on Marcus. "Everyone must learn to live with ghosts from their pasts. *Sí, señor*?"

A shiver prickled his spine. Miguel could have been talking about Marcus's own past.

"Everyone knows that her mother deserted her. But the *señorita* is stubborn. Once given, she does not easily give up on her heart."

Marcus was not to be swayed by her foolish nobility. He didn't trust Liandra. Less now that she'd managed to get beneath his skin, like a thorn from one of his mother's roses.

Only Liandra was no rose. She was a Spaniard. Espinosa's sister. And he'd do well to remember where his loyalties lay.

With himself.

Liandra leaned against the ship's newly refurbished wooden rail. Marcus had just spent three days in calm seas to repair the failing hull and mainmast on this ship. Banded together by the fear that another ship would see them floundering, the men worked side by side. Over the week, she'd sensed a strange camaraderie growing.

Marcus Drake had done the impossible. He'd united the two crews.

The steady flap of sails all but lulled her into an easy peace despite Marcus's presence at the helm on the quarterdeck. She breathed the salt-misted air. After brushing and fashioning her long hair in a chaste plait around her head, she'd dressed that morning in a bright yellow muslin creation that she'd hand sewn herself.

Idly she drew a heart on the sea-dampened rail.

Miguel stood near the passenger's door beneath the quarterdeck overhang before vanishing inside. Alerted, she glanced around. The sky was especially bright today. No cloud marred the horizon. After spending the morning with her, the children had abandoned her when Marcus arrived on deck. The boys played swords with two lengths of wood Dutch had given them. Their laughter seemed out of place on the storm battered ship stolen by pirates.

Casually picking the hay off her bright yellow cuff, she moved closer to the door where Miguel had disappeared. Marcus allowed Alejandro and his grandfather, Pedro, to escort her to the hold morning and evening to feed the stallions.

Marcus called something to the men perched in the rigging. His voice loomed with a strange, intoxicating power. The ship began to cant over as the masts changed direction slightly. Liandra turned. A rainbow arced through the mist that hovered over the deck. Marcus measured the sun's angle with the quadrant. Even without the charts she'd thrown overboard, he seemed to know where he was going. Most likely he was headed to some pirate port. She had to find a way to change his mind.

Isabella and Rosa lounged in canvas chairs set on the poop deck. Her ridiculous cousin and their matronly *dueña* were relaxed doing needlepoint. Wearing a flowing, blue silk gown, Isabella looked the cornerstone of feminine grace and virtue. She thought of her cousin and the ease with which she dropped into her role with men. Twice she'd seen Isabella collar Marcus on the deck. He didn't seem to mind the woman pawing him, but Liandra noted he never touched her in return.

Despite her vow to ignore him, Liandra stared as he stood over the binnacle to read the new course. It became apparent every other feminine eye on deck ogled him, too, including five-year-old Christina. Her niece adored the Englishman. Even more so since he'd given her a doll a few days ago styled out of hemp and old canvas. A thatch of Dutch's blond hair gave the creation a certain struck-by-lightning look that obviously appealed to five-year-olds. Considering his care of Alejandro, it didn't surprise her to see that Marcus was patient with Christina, too.

Grandmama, who'd made it a habit of studying people, once told her that details formed the man. Pay attention and you will know his true heart.

But since the moment she'd met him, Marcus had done naught but wreak havoc on her well-ordered life. He'd maimed her logical mind. Her will. Her control. Now that she'd tasted the sweet waters of his passion, an unbidden desire lurked to know more of this sea pirate.

Her sense of fair play didn't allow him to kiss her to the point of melting, then leave her standing alone in her cabin betwixt confusion and moral annihilation. She felt sorely abused and possessed an irrational bent to prove that she was *not* uninspiring.

Instinctively, she knew the forbidden fruit he presented, and Liandra braced herself with the knowledge that at two and twenty, she could handle more than one taste.

Pah! It wasn't as if she could be attracted to the uncouth rogue. He was a breed, the lowest species of men who preyed on other men for profit.

Voices from the rigging roused her. The wind rushed past her ears. Breath catching in her throat, she realized with sudden humiliation that Marcus was watching her stare at him. Standing at the helm on the quarterdeck, talking to the Dutchman, he lifted his mouth in the barest hint of a secret smile. Her heart kicked her ribs and escalated. She was suddenly remembering his kiss, the way he tasted, like sunshine and wild, berry wine. She could never have another glass without thinking about him.

Dios. Not only was she severely attracted to the Englishman, suddenly her promise to him didn't seem so awful.

The single unspoken thought electrified the air between them.

"Señor? Señor?" Little Christina's voice moved his gaze away from hers. *"Tú miras.* Look, Alejandro has taught me the minuet."

While he was looking, Liandra quietly slipped through the door to find Miguel.

Chapter Seven

Darkness shrouded the narrow gangway. Liandra nego-
tiated the stairs leading to the dining room with detail
to every step. The wall felt smooth beneath her hand.
Damp.

Forcing herself to focus on the problem at hand, she
dismissed Marcus from her thoughts. Somehow, she had to
regain control of this ship. Maybe then she could go back
to her existence, her normal undisturbed self; before the
Englishman had marched into her life and ruined everything.

She walked into the dining room. Two small, crystal
candelabrum set in protective alcoves against the wall tin-
kled with the ship's movement. Every evening since Marcus had allowed her freedom, she sat at the appointed end
of this dining table opposite him and a dozen criminals.
The ludicrousness of sitting down and discovering she actually enjoyed these formal dinners with a bunch of pirates
emphasized her current level of insanity.

And who were these wild men anyway? Former orphans that no one cared about? Abandoned children? Like
the two boys she was taking to the mission? Liandra
vowed those boys would be loved. She suddenly thought

of Alejandro. Liandra was in the dining room before she realized the significance of Christina's declaration.

The minuet? Ordinary twelve-year-old boys didn't know the minuet. A hand reached out from the shadows and snagged Liandra's arm, pulling her around.

"Miguel!" Her heart jumped into her throat.

"Shh. You walked past me. The *capitán* will not go lenient on me if he finds me here talking to you."

"I'm so glad you are here." She slumped into his arms. He stiffened slightly at her scandalous display. Not since they'd been children had she breached the circle that separated their rank in society. But she didn't care. Miguel was her friend. And now they were allies as well.

"How is our crew?" she asked.

He hastily brought her up to date on the events since the pirates had stolen their ship. He didn't know whether the hidden cache of silver had been found. "We did pour most of the powder overboard before they caught us."

"I'm sorry that I made you risk your life, Miguel."

He placed a hand on the ornately carved high-back chair that matched twelve others set around the mahogany table. He stared out the opened, stern galley windows. Crystal rainbows shimmered over the oak ceiling. Liandra moved beside him.

"We took our oath not to mutiny." His quiet statement underscored his quiet worry. "In exchange for our lives . . . and yours."

"Then I have failed everyone." Her people. Her brother. She could not protect her niece. "Everything is lost."

"You have failed no one." Miguel took her back into his embrace.

"The Englishman will abandon us all in some wretched English port and we'll be imprisoned. Surely, it is better to fight."

"I will not wage war with you and Isabella to think about."

Leather creaked behind her. Liandra jerked away from

Miguel, and came face-to-face with her nemesis, leaning in the arched doorway.

Marcus casually crossed his arms. "It's fortunate at least one of you is a man of his word. I would hate to kill you, Miguel." His eyes glittered with promise as they fell back upon her. "Maybe we should keep the fight between us. Hmm? Fewer people will get hurt."

Liandra feared for Miguel's life. "It is not his fault that he's here. I asked him to meet me here."

"She is trying to protect me." Miguel stepped forward. "I brought her down here and take full responsibility."

Marcus remained silent. Annoyance flickered in his eyes. Then with a curt nod, he sent Miguel away.

Liandra watched the ship's master leave. Grateful that Marcus didn't threaten to have her friend tacked to the broken mainmast, she met Marcus's gaze. Arms crossed, he filled the doorway. She tried to be regal. How could he affect her so thoroughly, ravage her will, and not feel an ember of the heat that raced like fire through her veins?

The silver flecks in his eyes darkened. "I'm surprised it took you this long to break the rules, Liandra. I'm impressed."

"This is all a game for you," she whispered.

"Aye," his gaze moved over her mouth, "you've taught me a new meaning for chess."

"How much will it cost to set us free?"

"You wish to be set free out here in the middle of the sea?"

"Of course not in the middle of the sea." She paced. "I ask that you release us in some safe harbor."

His incredulous gaze locked with hers. "You want me to sail this heap of rotting timbers into a guarded Spanish port?"

"Take us someplace close to Puerto Bello. Old Providence. That is near Panama."

He snorted. "That place isn't fit for civil habitation. And it isn't a Spanish port."

"You aren't Spanish. I have family there." Frustrated by

his lack of response, she snapped, "Truly you cannot have anything better to do!"

"You're wrong." He straightened. "I have a brother somewhere in trouble, and I intend to find him. Those men on deck have lives."

She stopped pacing and glared at her foe. "And we do not?" Her hands clenched in her skirts. Liandra hated that she was feeling desperate and out of control. But she could not allow him to reach an English port. Spaniards were detested on the Main. Her peoples' lives would be for naught. And today was her mother's birthday. What if she never saw her family again?

"I want to go home," she said to the awful silence.

A shadow fell across her captor's face.

"What more will it cost us?" she demanded.

Marcus advanced into the room. His boots made little sound above her pounding heart.

"Liandra . . ." He raised his hand to touch her cheek but she stopped him from touching her.

"I can make it worth your while, pirate."

"Another promise?"

She wiped her cheeks and clasped her arms to her chest. "Everyone knows your family's penchant for stealing Spanish treasure. Being a Drake, you will be glad to learn it is silver that I offer."

"And what exactly do you know about my family, Liandra?"

"Your father was a pirate."

"A privateer."

"He was a captain for Henry Morgan. Everyone knows about the gold your father stole during Morgan's raid on Puerto Bello."

Marcus laughed, but his eyes were furious as he looked away. A muscle worked in his jaw. "Naturally. You and all of Spain knows everything," he said, punctuating his sarcasm with a bow. "Even if it did happen before you were born."

"I know what happened in Puerto Bello that day . . ."

Her voice was a bruised whisper before she snatched back her grief. "Will you take us to safety or not?"

The sudden mercenary flicker in his quicksilver eyes quailed her heart. Stubble marked the sharp contour of his jaw and sharpened her awareness of him.

"You do understand," he said, moving a threatening inch closer, "I would have to see this silver first. You haven't been one to honor your promises."

"What promise would you have me keep?"

His mocking leer made her knees melt. She backed up a step. Her thighs hit the table. "I think you know. And you can't stand the wondering." Placing his palms against the table, he leaned forward until his mouth hovered above hers. "I've made you perfectly noble and tedious life interesting. We've swum the seas of lust . . . and enjoyed it."

His breath whispered sweet promises against her cheek. She should run. "But you tested the water and found it shallow—"

He pulled back. "You? Shallow? I don't think so, *gata*."

Her anguish faded away from the single pinpoint of light standing before her. Marcus. "Then . . . I am not uninspiring?" she whispered the childish sentiment.

His stronger hand wrapped around hers. The calluses on his palm scraped the sensitive bend of her knuckles. Tendrils of fire shimmered through the veins in her arms. He drew her hand to his belly. "Do you have any idea what a woman like you does to a man?"

Eyes wide, she shook her head. She had no idea what kind of woman she even was. Men didn't dare respond to her carnally. Not like Marcus, who tempted her beyond her overtaxed imagination; who roused strange and terrifying emotions. Who *had* made her perfectly noble life shamefully interesting.

His shirt was damp and molded to his hard-ridged stomach. Watching the challenge in his eyes grow brighter, she allowed him to lead her hand downward. Her clammy palm splayed his hip. All the girlish notions she possessed about the male anatomy bounded past her racing pulse to focus on her palm. Anticipation sizzled and burned her fingertips. Her breathing quickened. He was daring her to gather her icy shield and retreat in shock.

Suddenly she knew she would not run.

"I too play chess," she whispered in breathy abandon.

Her eyes drifted closed. The delectable essence of wind and sea mingled to invigorate her. She yearned to taste his lips.

To her utter disappointment, his hand stilled.

"Aye," he murmured in strange torment against her mouth. Suddenly he placed her hand on his chest. His heart thudded against her palm. "You have been a worthy opponent. More than I had expected to find in a Spaniard."

The weight of his confession startled her. Languid heat still burned through her body. *"Sí."* She traced her finger around the silly ruffle that marked his shirt. The trite decoration was so unlike his formidable character. "I have never known anyone like you, either." She wanted to see him without the shirt. The way he'd been when she'd first confronted him in the hold. "It is unfortunate that you are English."

He clamped his hands on her wrists. "And therein lies my problem, sweet enemy of mine." The silky gravity of his voice belied the hunger in his eyes. "I don't know what to do with you."

His damning remorse struck Liandra like a blow. How many times in her life had she heard those heartless words?

The horrible irony of this second rejection brought her chin up. If she wasn't uninspiring, then what was wrong with her that he would not touch her? For a second time.

Fiercely, she blinked back the moisture that dared abase her further, and shoved away from him. "Will you take the silver then, pirate? And let us go free?"

His expression almost softened.

"Well, Englishman? Do we have a bargain?"

"Take me to the silver, Liandra."

Sweeping past, she yanked the width of skirt out of her path to avoid touching his leg. He was like the plague.

In the narrow gangway, she released a lanthorn from its inset in the wall and, finding flint, lit the lamp.

As Marcus watched her hands, he could still hear the pitiful bravado in her voice. He swore softly.

She continued to humble him.

Despite everything that she knew him to be, she still trusted him. He, who had cheated the devil to his face.

He felt like he was committing blasphemy against the Holy Virgin.

Marcus let his gaze go down the curve of her back. He fought the urge to yank her back into his arms, tear the pins out of her prissy coif, and bury his face in her hair.

Her path led down another half-dozen steps to the dank hold, where his men had pulled out a wealth of smuggled goods. Barrels remained tied against the wall.

"There will be safe haven on any island that borders Panama," she said with renewed determination. "I have family most anywhere you choose to land. I will get word to the mainland."

"Through one of your thirty-five cousins, no doubt."

Her eyes flickered with hurt that he should poke words at her family. "Or their many children," she snapped. "Some of them are even English bastards born after Morgan's raid on Puerto Bello. You should feel right at home."

He frowned. Perhaps because he did understand what the Spaniards had suffered during that raid, he allowed the insult to slide. Liandra walked to the back wall and began prying boards loose. The lanthorn wrapped her in a dismal halo of light that matched his mood.

Where the hell was his hungry conscience when he'd first laid eyes on her? Before she opened her haughty mouth and demanded he save her? Marcus felt no triumph that he must soundly defeat her to survive. Benevolence would only get him killed.

In a moment, she'd opened a hole big enough to thrust her hand into. She removed three more planks, then stood back and presented him with a bag of silver reales. "There are fifty more bags. Enough to make the lot of you wealthy if you choose not to spend it on debauchery."

"The seal of Spain is stamped on this bag." He lifted his gaze. "I've seen enough Spanish treasure to know this belongs in royal coffers."

"This ship was going to Puerto Bello. The silver belongs to the soldiers there. Now it is yours. Take us someplace safe. I will guarantee your safety in Spanish wat—"

"No."

"But . . ." Her fragile eyes searched his, battering him afresh. "I gave you the silver."

Ruthlessness seized him. Balancing one bag, he weighed her guarded expression with a deliberate smile. "The crew thanks you. You are very generous, *Señorita* Espinosa. Call it a ransom paid."

An audible gasp escaped her lips. He welcomed the look of terror in her liquid bright eyes.

"How long . . ."

"Have I known?" His eyes narrowed. "About five minutes after you tossed the logbook out your window."

"You let me go on about my brother. Myself. The silver. You . . . you are such a liar as I've never seen!"

"Count yourself as another beleaguered martyr, *Señorita* Espinosa. We've known about the silver. You merely saved us from torturing your hapless men to find it."

"Bastardo!"

She hit him. Jesu. A right hook to his jaw. The blow caught him unaware and he braced himself against the wall. With a cry, she tried to sweep past him out of the hold. He blocked her escape. She slammed against his arm. This time he was prepared when she raised her fists.

"I promised you freedom . . . and silver. And still you are heartless. Get out of my way."

He impaled her with his gaze. "You see. I don't trust you, *gata*. I don't trust this ship. Or these waters. Once long ago someone else asked me to put my life in his hands. He helped Talon and me walk straight into your brother's arms. Thanks to me, I condemned my brother to four years in a Spanish prison. I cannot order this ship to turn around."

"It is not I who is treacherous."

He looked down at the slim fingers pressed against his chest. A void stretched between them viciously sucking away at his will. He'd captured her prized galleon, robbed her pride to feed his, and countered her every move save one. Raising his eyes past the rise and fall of her breasts to her kiss-me pink mouth, he felt his burning thoughts continue their downward spiral to roost in the less rational part of his body.

He finally met her unsettled gaze. If he kissed her now, he would finish this madness between them. He would seal his own blasted fate. His tongue tasted like copper. "So far you haven't lost anything that can't be replaced, *gata*."

"*Sí*," she spat. "I still have my virtue."

He wiped the blood from his bottom lip. "You have your life."

"If I thought it would save my people, I'd gladly give you both, pirate," she rasped.

"I would not allow the sacrifice, Liandra."

"But you will, Englishman. By sailing into Port Royal, you condemn every Spaniard aboard the ship. Including Alejandro and Christina. Or don't you know what English soldiers do to little girls and women."

She shoved past him.

Plowing one hand through his hair, he clenched the other against the wall. The soft pad of her slippers vanished in the lonely shadows. Mulling over the dark implications of her words, he leaned his head against his hand and groaned. He knew she was right.

"Is it true, *Tía* Maria? Are we going home like the big palehaired man said?"

Christina's voice sounded so hopeful, Liandra joined

her smile with her own subdued excitement. "*Sí*, little one. As close as we can get."

That morning Dutch had announced over breakfast that a vote had been taken among the crew—the same crew who had terrorized her and threatened to cut off her hand—to change their course. She'd listened in silent awe as Dutch related the news. Marcus had not been present.

Liandra caught strands of her wind-whipped hair that battered her face. Standing on the poop deck, she lifted her gaze to the crow's nest where Marcus had climbed earlier to relieve the look out. Liandra noted the red scarf he wore. He must have pulled it from the safety net.

He knew everything about her. Yet, he'd said nothing to the crew. To them, she was Maria Liandra y Ramírez, the name Isabella had given him.

She thought of Dutch's announcement. Someone had recognized the Spaniard's plight and brought it up for discussion last night. Was it Marcus? Considering no nationality outnumbered the other, the dilemma in choosing a new destination was obvious. Where could an international pirate crew of thieves, convicts, and slaves land without coming beneath the gun of any stone fortress?

Because of its own precarious allegiance, Old Providence was chosen. Liandra knew Marcus's assessment of the island had been correct. 'Twas a pirate haven filled with skullduggery: the same place, over twenty years ago, where the wretched Henry Morgan had launched his attack on her people. If the wind continued to blow, the ship would reach the island in a week.

She would never see Marcus again.

"Alejandro says we do not have enough food to sail forever," Christina said.

"He is correct, *mi niña*. But soon we will be on land. I will ask Alejandro to come with us."

"Can we take the *capitán* home with us, too?"

"That can never happen, *niña*," Liandra said. "He is English and we are Spanish."

"But . . ." Her round eyes wandered the deck in

wounded confusion. "I do not care if I am Spanish. I like everyone, *sí*?"

Liandra didn't spoil Christina's outlook with her many prejudices against Spain's enemies. Friar Montero had tried to teach Liandra that there was good in all men. If Christina saw that, then who was she to cloud the little girl's heart.

"But don't you like the *capitán, Tía* Maria?"

"That is the question of the day, *sí*?" Isabella said, coming to stand beside Christina. Her eyes were swollen, as if she'd been crying. Gripping the rail with both hands, she gazed over the sea. Her fashionable red silk skirts flapped in the wind, boldly showing off her ankles. Gold lace tightly wrapped her coifed hair. "Did you think that some of us might not wish to go back to Puerto Bello, Maria?" Isabella's words startled her. "The English pirate must care for you to change his course."

"He did not do anything for me."

"You do not know men, *mi prima*, to be so blind. These fools look upon you as if you are a cross between the Virgin Mary and the queen of Spain. Miguel said that you are revered by all." She sniffed her tears. "Including the English pirate. But he is not yours, Maria."

"I never thought he was."

But she lied.

Secretly she wanted to claim Marcus for herself. He was not like the fops in her life, who didn't know their aristocratic right hand from their left foot. She wanted him to like her. More than that, she wanted him to touch her again.

"The *capitán* is a slave. He will die a slave if he is caught. You have forgotten the English pirate is a Drake. You have forgotten that his father killed yours. Gabriel has not," she whispered.

The truth of Isabella's words hit. She gripped the rail. How well she knew the history that began with Henry Morgan's raid on Puerto Bello. Marcus's father had been part of that attack. How many years had her brother been at war with all pirates because of that wretched day? The Drakes in particular?

Especially since their ship, *Dark Fury*, had decimated her family's wealth and that of many fine Spanish families over the last few years.

Liandra closed her eyes. The salt-scented wind washed over her face. Was it twisted to hate because of the past? She'd always feared what she didn't know or understand. She disliked the English because they warred on her people. The Dutch and French were even worse. But the man she'd kissed, the man who filled the sultry nights with such carnal promise, did not have the soul of the man who committed evil deeds.

Isabella's eyes rounded. "You can not possibly like the no-account rogue."

"I do! I do!" Christina blurted out, jumping up and down.

To Liandra's horror, she'd forgotten her niece's presence. Her cherubic face lit up like a golden sparkler Liandra had once seen at the fair.

"You?" Isabella's lip sneered. "What would you know, Christina."

"He let me steer this ship. And he carries me on his shoulders. He is nice. A lot nicer than you!"

Isabella's tear rimmed eyes narrowed on Christina.

"He made this doll." She thrust the ugly thing toward Isabella. "He said no one should ever have to be alone, so be made me a baby."

Isabella yanked the doll from Christina's gasp and sent it flying overboard. "I hate babies! Do you hear me? I hate them!"

An ear-piercing scream sliced through the wind. Liandra grabbed the child before she climbed the rail.

"How could you do that, Isabella?"

With a sob, her cousin whirled and ran from the deck past Miguel, who looked on helplessly. Liandra clutched Christina as she continued to wail. All around her, the crew stopped what they were doing. Christina's arms stretched and begged. She cried for her baby.

The doll bobbed on the dark surface of the water and grew smaller and smaller as the ship sailed farther and farther away. Tears filled Liandra's eyes. "I am so sorry, *niña*," she whispered into Christina's dark curls. "We cannot get her back."

"I want my baby!"

Holding the little girl in her arms, Liandra worried that the child would fling herself into the sea for the sake of a doll. It struck her that Christina loved that rope doll more than Liandra's own mother had ever cared for her.

The doll finally vanished in the ship's wake.

Amidst the worried stares of the crew, Liandra carried Christina below deck. She laid her in bed just as Marcus flung open the door to the cabin. Winded, hair tousled, a growth of stubble marking his handsome face, he filled the doorway to Christina's tiny cabin that she now shared with their *dueña*.

"What happened?"

"Isabella threw her doll overboard." Liandra quietly answered the unspoken worry in his eyes.

Christina sat up, her tear-streaked face furious. "She is a . . . a *puta*!"

Liandra gasped. *Dios*. This is what came from associating with foul-mouthed pirates. "Christina! You can not say such things."

She watched Marcus grin. Now that he realized nothing life threatening had occurred, he seemed to relax. "I'll make another doll, Christie. If you wish. Even more beautiful than the last."

Her tear-filled eyes widened. "You will?"

Watching Marcus bend over Gabriel's daughter and soothe her broken sobs, Liandra felt something inside pull.

Once when she'd been eight, Gabriel had given her a doll for her birthday. She'd carried it everywhere until its fancy lace clothes were in tatters. One day the doll bounced off the wagon she was riding in and the right wheel crushed its head. He'd never taken her in his arms for such a silly thing as that. Grandmama had soothed her tears, but it hadn't been enough to fill the emptiness, even when she'd quietly assured Liandra 'twas unseemly for men to cuddle little girls over lost dolls.

The Englishman did not seem less manly for his kindness.

Liandra remembered Marcus said he had a little sister. Was her memory the reason he'd fostered Christina's affection?

How had his sister died?

The sound of his soothing voice pulled Liandra from her thoughts. The dread pirate Drake, son of a murderer, had a whole past filled with hurt. Like her.

She suddenly questioned Gabriel's part in condemning Marcus.

Quietly, Liandra slipped out of the room and leaned back against the bulkhead. Splinters snagged her braid and pulled at her hair. Her heart unraveled the same way.

Marcus had given her something back from her past, before her mother had torn her life apart. He'd awakened the dormant part of her heart. The part afraid to love again.

Liandra knew deep inside that to love was folly. To love this Englishman would make her the biggest fool of all.

Christina's sobs quieted. Later Marcus emerged. Turning to shut the door, he stopped mid-motion when he saw her.

Her heart bumped against her ribs. Clasping her hands in front of her, she straightened her shoulders. "Thank you for what you did," she said awkwardly. Disdain flickered in his silver eyes.

"You know who she is, don't you? Did Christina tell you?"

Quietly he closed the door. "I'm not entirely a monster, Liandra."

"I know that." He seemed surprised by her easy admission. She fidgeted with her skirts. "Which makes it more imperative that you know how grateful I am."

"Save it." He started for the stairs.

"There's something else I want to say."

Slowly he turned. Impatience flashed in his eyes.

"I know how important it was for you to go to Jamaica—"

"Do you?"

He took up all the space in the gangway. She braced a palm against the wall and raised her chin. "You want to find your brother. You must care for him very much to risk your life trying to find him."

An eyebrow lifted.

"You are a pirate. You would be in as much danger as us if you were to be captured by your English governor."

"Your concern touches me. Especially since we're not headed to Jamaica. But I am not so easily captured."

The mockery in his eyes hurt her. "You were caught in Tortuga."

"Aye," he conceded with a grin. "You have me there."

Taking his grin as a small victory, she continued. "Obviously your usual charm did not work to save you? What happened?"

"I was injured during a fight and left for dead on the beach. A plump tavern wench . . . nursed me back to health. After I recovered, she exchanged my life for fifty doubloons and a bottle of black rum. I was very hurt. I didn't tell her I was worth a hundred times that."

Liandra sniffed. "She probably was glad to get rid of you."

He leaned a shoulder into the doorjamb. "Women are fickle. I have no use for liars or traitors."

"Yet, your brother left you in Tortuga."

The amusement left his face. "Talon doesn't know I'm alive. If he did, he wouldn't quit searching for me."

She folded her arms beneath her breasts. "How fortunate that you can be so certain of another person's love."

"And unfortunate that you're not?"

Her eyes lowered.

"What's the matter? Doesn't your brother pay attention to you?"

She stiffened her spine. "I want Alejandro and his grandfather to come with us. Tell them, *por favor*. That they will be welcomed."

"Your precious Spanish soil may not be safe for them. But I'll ask. Anything else?"

"Thank you for setting a new course."

He placed his fist near her head. His sleeve brushed her cheek and stirred the scent of the sea and sweat. "Those men voted to go to Old Providence because of you. Not because I told them to."

Confusion caught her by surprise. "I don't understand."

"Courage is a man's only true measure. They have not forgotten when you put your hand on that block. I have not forgotten."

Something warm settled in her chest. This was almost as important as being told he liked her. Her gaze focused on his mouth. The memory of his lips on hers strained her beleaguered will.

Lifting her chin with his finger, he snapped her startled gaze to his face. The silver flecks in his eyes darkened with something akin to desire. "I'm still a dangerous man, Liandra. And very close to doing something stupid to ruin both our lives. So stay away from me."

He turned on his boot heel and took the stairs to the deck in one bound. Her cheeks burned. As he opened and slammed the door in his wake, cooler air rushed over her face.

Her throat felt dry. She swallowed. What did it matter, this inexplicable attraction between them? He wasn't taking her to Port Royal. She'd finally won something against this sea pirate.

Then why did she feel like she'd lost another round to him? Again?

●　　●　　●

One hand wrapped around a bottle of rum and the other behind his head, Marcus lay in the hammock he'd roped between the rail and the mizzenmast, where he usually slept. He glared at the firefly-size stars. Dawn wasn't far away. One booted foot hung out of the hammock and rapped an annoyed tattoo on the damp deck. The ship's soothing rhythm did nothing to ease the fire in his groin. Dutch and Pedro slept a short distance away on the poop deck with some of the other crewmembers.

Above him, the sails lay flat against becalmed seas. Spars and blocks moved in concert with the gentle lap of water against the ship's hull. No hint of a breeze threatened the absolute stillness that surrounded him.

Liandra's laughter sounded again. This time he flinched at the unwanted intrusion. She and the three boys had come on deck an hour ago to fish and proceeded to wake him. He grunted. The woman could wield a sword as good as any man, brave her brother's wrath to help feed a mission, endure storms, and confront convicts . . . but she could not fish.

Jesu, could she not fish!

She'd already tossed one pole overboard, embedded two hooks in the mainmast sail, and nearly yanked off the helmsman's ear with the third. Worse, she wore breeches.

Breeches for Christ's sakes! On a Spanish noblewoman.

The soft buff leather limned her small waist and shapely bottom in a carnal vision of feminine flesh that would spur the imagination of a Jesuit priest. And he was no priest. She was every man's fantasy.

Swigging from the bottle, Marcus frowned. A moment passed before he realized no one around him slept. Oh, they pretended to sleep well enough. But it was a lie. They were all watching Liandra. Including Dutch, who was old enough to be her father. Only Don Pedro managed to find peace in this stygian hell of masculine deprivation.

"Maybe someone should go down there and teach her how to fish," a man's sleepy voice rumbled from the shadows. A round of quiet conjectures followed, but no one volunteered.

Perhaps because no matter the unconventional wrapping, unlike her cousin Isabella, Liandra was still a lady.

And even though they were pirates, most remembered mothers and sisters. Liandra was a reminder of a gentler, kinder time.

Her bright laughter resonated like fine crystal in a room full of glass. She wore her persona like a golden aura. Her bearing, the way she carried herself, her dignity, all transcended the boundaries that separated her class from his. She belonged in the finest parlors of Spain bedecked in silks and satins. Not to this broken-down galleon.

Not to him.

Marcus swigged the rum. Liquid sloshed in the half-empty bottle. She'd opened the door to his past and reminded him of the more civilized self he'd chosen to forget.

His plight had never troubled him before. Indeed, being the second son, he'd welcomed living in Talon's shadow, following in the dark wake of his older brother's quest to regain their stolen lives.

For the first time, Marcus looked at his life without anger to cloud the view. Talon had understood that without their name and honor restored, they would die traitors to their country. They could never be anything more than pirates forever branded by the lies that condemned his mother and father. They were nothing.

Even if Liandra wasn't a Spaniard, worlds like hers were forever closed to him.

Liandra's laughter joined the boys' as Alejandro pulled a Neptunian blunderbuss on board, sending the huge fish flapping across the main deck. The wind began to pick up. The ship rocked. Marcus shifted his gaze. Holding her pole, Liandra leaped out of the creature's path. Awash in moonlight, she became more than a shadow in the night. His heart quickened its pace as his focus narrowed to her animated profile. The light picked out the feminine curves and swell of her breasts beneath a boy's pale blue shirt. She couldn't help it; her body just naturally did things to a man. He no longer thought of his betrothed. At the moment, he couldn't even remember her name.

He saw Liandra's gaze slide back to her pole then to the water. She jiggled the pole. He could tell she wanted a fish.

To hell with honor.

Marcus set the rum bottle down on the deck and rolled out of the hammock. After tomorrow, he'd never see her again.

What could be the harm in teaching her how to fish?

Chapter Eight

Liandra jiggled the fishing pole in hope that the hook would latch on to anything. Rain scented the pungent, salt-misted air. She stared expectantly over the rail. It wasn't as if she could see anything in the darkness. She just wanted a fish.

"Are you coming, *Doña* Maria?" Alejandro's voice joined the other two boys as they lined up behind her. Each boy proudly displayed his catch. "The moon has already gone behind the clouds. It is too dark to see. Soon it will rain."

"Are you sure cook will fry those fish for you?" she queried the three eager faces. She'd been asleep when the boys beat on her door. Carrying poles and enthusiastic smiles on their youthful faces, they'd talked her into joining them. "It is terribly early."

They exchanged confidence glances. "Cook will do it as long as we share half."

"You've done this before?"

"*Sí,* many times. When the wind is calm and the moon is out we always fish. *Señor* Marcus usually joins us. He catches *mucho pescado.*"

Liandra narrowed her eyes. Dignity was no contest

against the competitive bent that took hold. Immediately, catching a fish became the most important thing in the world. "Does he now?"

Emilio, the tallest of the three, slapped Alejandro on the back. "Alejandro never fished either before last week. *Señor* Marcus, he showed him well. Now, he wishes to fish every morning."

They hurried off to rouse the cook out of his hammock. Liandra smiled to herself as they disappeared beneath the forecastle door. Who could have guessed they'd been frightened young boys not so long ago? She wasn't the only one who'd changed since leaving Hispaniola.

Liandra gripped the thick bamboo pole tighter and turned back to the rail. Marcus's strong arms came round her as he placed his hands over hers on the pole. His hair fell over her shoulder and touched her breasts. "Easy now, *gata*." Every nerve in her body throbbed with the touch. He moved her deeper into the shadows beneath the quarterdeck overhang, to a place of exclusion. "Don't jerk."

Her bottom pressed into his groin. She'd seen the physical anatomy of rutting stallions often enough to know 'twas no sword or pistol that rubbed her backside.

Her palms grew moist. "The pole is heavy," she whispered.

"Aye, it is big. Huge." His breath touched her ear and moved forward to caress her cheek. "Think of this pole as an extension of . . . me."

Her heart pounded in her throat. "Pah!" She tilted her face and glared at him through her lashes. Dark stubble emphasized his unscrupulous character. All he needed was a gold earring in his ear to complete the picture. "You are showing your conceit, Englishman."

An unholy smile underscored his complete lack of shame.

"Go away." She squirmed. "I want to fish."

Ignoring her request, he boldly flattened his palm against her lower belly. "Begin by placing the pole here."

Through the thin layer of her skirt, the heat of his touch scorched her flesh. He shifted the pole nearer to her pelvis.

"Feel the rhythm of the sea, Liandra."

Instead, she felt his heartbeat and the rush of his breath. His body wrapped around hers like warm bread. The tips of her breasts grazed his biceps. *Dios*. This surely is what it must feel like to be butter. All hot and melty down to her toes. Slick.

"Be gentle. But firm with the pole." He slid his palms over her hands, guiding them along the staff. "Take control."

She smelled rum on his breath and felt her eyes glide shut. "Are . . . you sure we're talking about fishing here?"

His laughter vibrated against her back. "What else would I be talking about, *gata*?"

Not quite sure, she swallowed.

"I never imagined fishing could be so . . ." She hesitated. "Is this how you teach all your students?"

"Except Alejandro."

She didn't want to think of him enjoying other women in this way. Or that she totally lacked the experience to compete.

Or that she cared.

"Perhaps I should feel insulted."

"You shouldn't." She felt his crooked smile against her hair. "No other woman is like you."

"You . . . find me attractive?"

The rough edge of his cheek scraped hers as he bent over her mouth. "Aye, *gata*." His words shivered over her temple and down her spine to settle in her loins. Somehow, he got his hand beneath her shirt. "Exceedingly so."

Her breath came harder. "I'm not too . . . tall?"

His muscles tightened. "Not for me."

"Ugly?"

"Who would tell you that, Liandra?"

Measured her whole life against Isabella's perfection, she'd grown up feeling ungainly. Grandmama always said it didn't matter so much what was on the outside as what pulsed beneath. But for a young girl who wanted so desperately to fit in, those were only words. It had hurt to hear Aunt Innes talk about her imperfections as if she were a cow.

"Whatever they said," he whispered with such promise her heart stopped, "it's a lie, Liandra."

She closed her eyes. The fishing pole grew slack in her hands.

"Don't let it go," he whispered. "It's bad luck to lose two poles in the same day."

She straightened the pole. Her forearms began to burn.

Beneath her shirt, his callused hand moved over her ribcage. "You make a man crazy for wanting you."

Her breathing shortened to quiet, restless gasps. "I do?" She should have hated his touch and what he did to her body. She should have shoved him away. Struck his face for taking liberties.

A knuckle caressed her nipple.

Her knees nearly buckled. She did not want him to stop.

"You're perfect, Liandra. Perfect." His lips touched her neck. "God. I shouldn't be doing this."

"*Sí.*" Her voice was breathless. Her body hummed. She laid her head back against his shoulder, reveling in the hardened plane and masculine textures of his body. "You should stop."

Her voice mingled with his deep-throated groan. "Tomorrow, you'll go back to your world. I'll return to mine. We don't fit anyplace else, Liandra. This shouldn't be happening."

"I know," she breathed.

His hands razed her breasts, stroked the length of her waist and hips. A bulkhead was at Marcus's back and he leaned against the wall, molding her to him. Rain scented the air. Liandra could see very little in the misty darkness, but she felt safe from prying eyes in the tiny alcove she shared with Marcus.

She tilted her face sideways and met his eyes. They glittered sharply in the fractured moonlight. "So what are we going to do about it?" she asked.

His stark gaze ran over her face, down the length of her body, burning everything along the way.

He kissed her.

Shoving his fingers through her hair, he made love to her mouth with his lips, his tongue, and the softly whispered word that was her name. It was the hushed sound of her name on his lips that sent her sailing into the abyss of no return. Passion. Lust. Both were foreign threads of emotions so powerful they unraveled her insides.

All the while she gripped the pole.

It's magic was potent and real, and she wasn't about to tamper with luck. Good or bad. Her heart burst. Surely, this crushing feeling could not be anything less than love for this wild Englishman, who'd mastered her heart as capably as he did her body.

He'd done other things to her as well. Like touching her soul.

His compassion for her crew riddled her heart. He'd saved her ship, fashioned dolls for another man's child. And made Liandra feel more beautiful than a blue moon against a velvet sky. He made her feel wanton and whole at once. She wanted to wiggle her naked toes in sand.

All of this and he had yet to take anything for himself. He wanted to find his brother, and she ached that he had not just gone on to Jamaica.

Sí, she acknowledged in a haze of passion. She could love this sea pirate: all the way down to the soles of his borrowed black boots.

He broke the kiss, but only to torture her neck as he slid his wet mouth down the pale curve of her shoulder. "Jesu, Liandra. I want you."

"*Dios,*" she breathed hoarsely. An explosion of nerves corrupted her good reason. "*Sí, por favor—*"

Marcus growled and kissed her again. Drawing the breath from her lungs and a mewling cry from her throat, he slid his tongue along the sensitive rim of her gums, deepening the kiss, ravaging her mouth with soul-searching need.

Still holding the pole, she couldn't move in the tiny space shared between them. Thick lines entangled her feet. His delicious hands kneaded her breasts and raked the swell of her hips as if devouring her body. He edged one hand beneath her breeches. She moved her hips in rhythm to his powerful body. The first drop of rain splattered on her forehead.

His fingertips probed her navel then slipped deeper into her breeches, heightening every earth shattering sensation that streaked through her body. "I can give you more, Liandra," he promised against her mouth. She tasted rum. "Do you want that?"

"*Sí.*" She nodded, then felt him sink a finger deep inside her wet center. He swallowed her cry with his hungry mouth, lapping up her wordless pleas. She writhed against him.

"God. You feel so tight."

Liandra remained speechless. She'd surrendered to him completely. He sucked her earlobe and did fancy things with his tongue. She wanted to touch him back. Anything but hold this pole.

But dropping the pole might shatter the magic spell between them. All the while he dug his hips into hers, he moved his hand and did things to her body that were surely forbidden by God's law.

"Do you like this, Liandra?"

"You need . . . to ask?"

Grateful for the darkness, she could no longer make out his profile. Only felt his hot breath against the corner of her mouth. The wind rocked the ship as it began to bring the limp sails to life. Creaks sounded and mingled with her quiet groans. Rain pelted her face and lips. His finger delved inside her body, and moved in carnal tempo to her raging pulse.

"What . . . are you . . . doing?" Her words came out in a

pathetic whimper of wanton abandon. All around her rain pelted the deck of the ship, the sails, her face and body.

His teeth nibbled the flesh on her throat. "Let it come, Liandra. Let it come."

She could not respond. Her breasts rose and fell. Her breathing quickened. Her grip on the pole slackened.

And Liandra shattered.

Her voice, her woman's musk, her utter surrender stripped Marcus of the last of his restraint. Grabbing the pole with one hand just before she dropped it, he drank in her cries, sultry and wet against his tongue like a hot monsoon rain. Then she went limp against him, giving herself completely over to his strength. Her vulnerability touched him. He held her protectively against him. A quick glance in the shadows told him that the mizzenmast rigging shielded them from the eyes of any crew that might be waking up. The angle of the quarterdeck overhang protected them from the lookout.

A wave of heat gripped his loins. He was so hard and on the edge, he was close to ripping her clothes off.

Her blasted breeches would not make it easy to enter her. In fact, the manly contraption made it impossible.

"Liandra."

Her eyes opened in dawning wonder. His breath snagged in his throat. She swallowed him in her gaze like he was some bloody hero. Took him in and chewed him up.

He didn't want or deserve that look.

After all, they weren't even on the same side here.

He inhaled a gulp of salt air and anchored himself back in reality. Then Liandra turned in his arms. The rain had plastered her shirt to her flesh like a second skin. She said his name, feathered her small hands across his chest, and reality splintered like so much shrapnel in his chest.

With a groan, he dropped the pole. It tilted and flipped over the side of the ship. A splash sounded.

Liandra's gaze leaped to his. "Marcus. The pole—"

"Forget it." He kissed the tender whorl in her ear, trailed

his lips down her throat and feasted on each nipple through the wet cloth of her pale blue shirt. Somehow, he managed to untie the laces on her breeches. "Who believes in all that superstition anyway?"

Mindless, incoherent words answered him.

"Jesu, Liandra. I can't promise this won't hurt."

"I know," she answered in breathless anticipation.

Backing her a short step to the rail, he laved her swollen lips. "Christ. You know how to tie a man in knots. Someone could see us."

"*Sí,*" she agreed. Her full breasts pressed restlessly against him. Every inch of her soft feminine body melded to his.

He didn't know why he bothered with these discussions. Perhaps that older, respectable part of himself encroached too much on the man he now was. But he wanted to give her a chance to back away.

Easing her breeches over her hips, he grabbed her bottom with both his hands bent slightly and lifted her. He pushed for entry.

"Liandra . . ." An oath clenched his teeth. "This will hurt."

"Of all the consideration to come out of your mouth, pirate. Why now?" she panted.

With a quiet laugh, he thrust into her. She was so wet he slipped through her maidenhead and buried himself deep inside her. He hadn't meant to take her. Not like this.

Or had he?

"God, Liandra." His clasp tightened on her hips to still her movements before she sucked the life out of him. She was incredibly hot and tight.

Her hands wrapped in his hair. "It's all right," she whispered against his mouth. "Don't stop. Never . . . stop."

He looked into her passion-filled eyes. It suddenly dawned that he was seeing color. Beautiful colors. Her sapphire eyes, her rich sable hair loosened from the strict braid that wrapped her head, the color of her plum-hued nipples outlined against the wet shirt.

They were no longer shrouded by complete darkness.

He lifted his eyes. The squall had passed. A thin line of pearlescent light hovered over the glassy sea. Dawn highlighted the sky. His muscles froze.

"Bloody hell!"

Silhouetted between heaven and hell were the masts of three Spanish galleons.

Chapter Nine

Liandra sat in the dining cabin dressed in a sophisticated gown of formal black velvet trimmed in white lace, which she usually wore to mass. Or funerals. A black mantilla lace headdress covered her hair. She'd gathered with the others in the dining room to await the arrival of El Condor. A thrill of foreboding hovered.

Moments ago she'd glanced out the windows and seen her brother's bloodred banner flying on the stately foremast of his ship. The ornate, sun-gilded galleon was befitting the *Almirante* of the treasure fleet. Brass cannons loomed from three decks of the galleon. Men with shiny brass buttons on pristine blue uniforms lined the deck, ready to open fire. She didn't have to see the other two ships to know they posed an equally ominous threat to this ship.

And to Marcus . . . and the thirty-seven men who stood with him.

Despite the heat, her hands and feet were ice cold. She stared at the bright yellow slippers she wore. Blinking, she numbly realized she'd grabbed the wrong pair.

The sound of Isabella's weeping filled the room. Liandra's gaze first touched on Christina, a new rope doll wearing a canvas dress clutched to her chest, sitting primly with their *dueña* beside her. Her niece wore a velvet gown of robin's egg blue: attire becoming Gabriel's daughter. Then Liandra settled her gaze on the boys sitting in the high-back chairs at the table. Alejandro, wearing borrowed breeches and a linen shirt, watched her. His grandfather stood at the stern, galley window, legs braced against the ship's movement, his hands behind him, one fist resting in the other. At the other end of the table, Isabella would not cease with her tears.

Liandra glared at her cousin, prostrated over her arm on the table, and wanted to pinch her.

A bump jolted the ship. Nearly thrown from her seat beside the windows, Liandra gasped. Grinding wood resonated through the wooden frame of the ship. Grappling hooks scraped the deck, where the crew's movements, the scattered sound of voices, drew her gaze to the ceiling. Blood drummed against her ears.

Marcus was up there now.

She fought down the choking urge to sob. Dread threatened to topple her courage. He was lost to her.

She would never know more of that unrequited glow that started with his touch and ended too soon. The alchemy between them had shattered with the sighting of the galleons. With only the soreness between her legs to remind her of their passion, he'd been quick to dress her and deposit her back in her cabin.

"It's been interesting, *gata*." He'd brought her palm to his lips. "My only regret is that we'll never finish what we started."

In the hold, while still in chains when she'd first set eyes on him, he'd stood before her wearing that same fatalistic indifference. His actions returned her to the hopelessness of their plight. He was an English pirate. She, a Spanish *Doña*. Forever on opposite sides.

"Marcus." She clung to his shirt. "Will you surrender?"

"Would you?"

She swallowed raw tears. The odds of survival if he did

fight weighted her response. She knew he had little gun-powder to wage a war. His fate was sealed. But there were children on board.

"I promised you your freedom once. I will not let you down."

His gaze dropped to her hand, then raised slowly to her face as if searching out her heart.

Then he'd turned and raced up the stairs. The door to the deck opened, allowing a wedge of bright sunlight to touch his face.

And suddenly he was gone.

"Thank you for what you have done for my grandson, *señorita*," Pedro said from his stance at the window. His voice drew her back from the dregs of her thoughts. "I will not forget this."

Liandra's gaze fell on Isabella wiping her eyes with a lace handkerchief. Whatever happened, Liandra would not allow the boy to be enslaved again. She'd made Alejandro one of the children she brought from Hispaniola and, wherever her horses went, she made sure Pedro would be allowed to follow.

Turmoil twisted her insides. If only she could command Marcus's fate and that of the pirate crew with as much cer-titude. She could not pull her worry away from what might be happening on deck.

Noise in the gangway, one deck up, alerted her. Every head turned as footsteps quickly approached. Starch in-fused her veins even as apprehension filled her heart. Lian-dra vowed to meet fate head-on.

Gabriel, in defiance of proper protocol for his station, was the first man down the stairs. Liandra's breath caught. Black hair carelessly swept his brow. Over the striking white and cobalt blue velvet waistcoat of his high rank, a golden braid attached a short cloak carelessly strewn over one shoulder. Dark eyes scraped the room, settling first on Christina, then lifting to her. The concern in his eyes trapped her panic. From out of nowhere, tears swelled. Emotions confused and overwhelmed her at once.

Liandra had never seen her brother with so much as a hair out of its proper place. The shadow of a beard even marked the angular plains of his handsome face. Too tall for the ceiling, he carried his feathered hat tightly clasped in his hands. In knee-high leather boots, he was as tall as Marcus.

Until this moment, she hadn't been entirely sure his ship had survived the storm. She wasn't sure of anything anymore.

Slowly, she stood. Her velvet gown rustled in the silence.

Christina stood beside her like a porcelain soldier at attention, her small mouth trembling. Then Gabriel knelt, his Spanish saber scraping the floor, and Christina ran into her father's strong arms. His fierce reaction was as close to outright emotion as she'd ever seen in Gabriel Espinosa, the infamous El Condor. Not since his brief marriage had softness encroached on his fierce pride. Even Grandmama's funeral had not cracked his carved-in-granite heart, although he'd been as close to her as Liandra had.

He was an Old World man who lived by the biblical principle of an eye for an eye. That message was repeated over and over in dealing with Spain's enemies.

He and Marcus would kill each other.

"You are all safe." Her brother's somber voice inserted itself in her thoughts. His eyes lifted from Christina's face, and Liandra found herself the recipient of his dark, enigmatic gaze. "That is good, *querida*. I missed you in Hispaniola."

"You were three days late, Gabriel. I didn't think you were coming."

Gabriel lifted his daughter in his arms and stood. "I was delayed. I thought I had lost you both in the storm—"

"If not for those men on deck we would have perished."

"—so what madness do I find but my crew paying allegiance to pirates. Has the world changed or is it just me, Liandra?" His gaze raked the boys, hesitated on Pedro, then fell on Isabella before finally sweeping over the room. "Is this not a galleon of Spain?"

Ten years Liandra's senior, Gabriel was much like her parent. And she'd never felt more like the errant child. She knew he'd feared for her safety. Worried to the point of disrepair. And now that he'd found her, on the heels of his relief came wrath.

She'd experienced such fury once before when she was eight. A traveling fair had grabbed her attention and she'd wandered off with the beautiful ladies and singing minstrels. For two days they'd fed and clothed her. She'd only been a little afraid. Gabriel found her three villages away, and after calmly thanking her benefactors for seeing her cared for, he had the audacity to spank her for her disobedience. As if she'd gotten lost on purpose.

Behind him, Miguel and two other officers nervously shifted. Turning away, Gabriel asked one of his men if the ship was secured.

"Take my family to the flagship."

Later in private, Gabriel would yell at Liandra for leaving Hispaniola without escort. Then he would throttle her for letting pirates overtake his ship.

Not literally, of course. Her brother, for all his dark bluster, had never hurt her. But she'd endangered Christina's life, and for that, Liandra knew he'd probably banish her to some convent for a lifetime.

"Gabriel. This is *Señor* Pedro," she rushed to introduce the older man. "He has been caring for my horses." She moved to stand behind the boys. "And this is Alejandro, Emilio, and Luis. I'm taking them to the mission."

Her brother's gaze moved over the youths. She knew he was seeing them only as street rabble. His patience with her charity had worn a thin line years ago. "They can stay on this ship," he said.

"No. They cannot."

Gabriel's dark eyes narrowed only perceptibly.

"What is going to happen to those who were sailing this ship?" Liandra asked.

"Their fate is out of your hands. Carlos will deal with them."

Isabella gasped. Her eyes flew to Miguel. "Papa is on this ship?"

Something kicked Liandra in the stomach. Hard. "Marcus Drake and those men saved this ship from sinking."

"This is not the time, *querida*."

"When is the time, Gabriel? Next week? Next month? Next year after you return from another one of your trips to Spain?"

Her brother handed Christina over to Rosa. "Take my daughter to my cabin, and don't allow her out of your sight."

With a harried glance at Liandra, Rosa instantly obeyed. A tall man, dressed splendidly in the blue uniform of the flagship's master, led her away.

"*Señor* Miguel." Gabriel didn't take his eyes off Liandra. "Take my cousin and these . . . young men to my ship. They can sleep in the hold. Pedro will stay here with the horses."

"*Sí*, Excellency," Miguel murmured. Sliding past Gabriel, Isabella moved after him. Liandra started to follow.

"Not you, sister. You stay. And Miguel? On your way back, bring Drake down."

Finally, Gabriel turned, and her mouth felt suddenly dry. She could barely endure the silence that followed. His presence overshadowed everything in the room. As a little girl, she'd felt so protected by that sweeping impression. While other men trembled, he'd made her feel safe.

She needed desperately to feel safe, now.

Little by little, as Gabriel watched her, his ebony eyes softened. "This has been hard on you, *querida*."

Liandra tried to be strong. Standing before him, she lifted her chin. But tears glistened in her eyes and blurred his face. "I promised those men their freedom, Gabriel. I gave my word."

He set his hat on the table. His boots clipped on the

wooden floor as he took one step and then another toward her, and suddenly she was wrapped in his arms. Strong arms. Secure.

"I know why you left Hispaniola," he whispered into her hair. "And I'm sorry I wasn't there to take you to our mother."

She wiped at the tears. That he would remember something so important to her melted the barriers of her defense. "I've never missed her birthday, Gabriel. Not ever."

"You brought your stallions? You love those horses."

"What is joy without sharing it with others?" she quoted their grandmama. Liandra felt his arms tighten. He stroked her hair and touched his mouth gently to her temple.

"You have a soft heart. Too soft for an Espinosa, I think."

And she loved Marcus. She loved him with her whole heart. "There are so many things I don't understand, Gabriel. Things about you and . . . and *Capitán* Drake."

"What has he told you?"

"That you imprisoned him and his brother. That he was betrayed to you. His family murdered. He hates Spain."

"Did he tell you that his mother was once betrothed to Father? That he comes from a long line of murderers and adulteresses?"

"Gabriel . . ." She lowered her eyes. She did not know this.

"Everything he said is true. But he and his brother were criminals before they were ever handed over to me. His own government convicted them both of treason. I did not. *Sí*, I had him imprisoned. He and his brother were delivered into my hands and I was very eager to do my job."

"Because of what his father did to ours?" she asked miserably.

"The English pirates destroyed our parents' lives. Stole our wealth. You know what they did to our mother." He started to say more and hissed a vicious curse. "Please, *querida*, don't make me say any more. You ask that I dishonor Spain. You ask that I dishonor you."

"Is not a man's life more valuable than honor? Even mine?"

"Not his."

Liandra buried her nose in his collar. He smelled of sandalwood and security. "The men on this ship are brave, Gabriel. Not like what I thought pirates would be."

"You mistake their motives for courage, *querida*." His voice lowered in frustration. "If they let this ship sink, they would have died, too."

"Marcus Drake saved our lives. He saved Christina. No matter the past, we owe him his freedom. You are El Condor. Is your word not law?"

"*¡Ay caramba!* You are the stubborn one. It is not in my power to free all the men." She felt more than heard his reluctant groan. "Tell me, *querida*?" He tipped her chin. "You fight for this because you are grateful? And nothing else?"

She dabbed at her wet eyes with the back of her hand and straightened. "I fight because it is the right thing, Gabriel."

A scraping sound in the doorway turned her head. Her heart hit her ribs. Marcus stood beneath the archway.

Stance relaxed, hands chained in front of him, he watched her beneath thick lashes. She could feel the predatory strength of his powerful body coil in tension. A red kerchief bound his hair. His torn, white shirt bore the marks of a fight. Blood from a cut on his lip spattered the torn ruffle.

An unsteady breath marked her alarm. Miguel and three men at arms stood behind him, as if one chained man could hold such a threat. She ached to run into his arms and put aside this pretense.

Marcus slid his hooded gaze to Gabriel. A ghost of a reckless smile hovered over his mouth. "Espinosa," he acknowledged. "You look like shark bait. Had a bad couple of weeks?"

His midnight eyes seething with hostility, Gabriel stepped out of Liandra's embrace. The two men faced each other across the short distance that separated them. The ship listed slightly in the wind. Liandra caught herself on one of the chairs. Marcus and Gabriel, legs braced against the swell, rode out the movement. A storm brewed.

"For the sake of the lives that I owe you, I won't string you up where you stand, Drake."

"I can't say that I'm pleased to see you either, *compadre*."

"Gabriel." Liandra caught her brother's sleeve. "Please . . ."

Beneath the fine cloth, his tense muscles relaxed. "If I set you free, you will only raid my ships."

Marcus didn't attempt to dispute that fact. "What about the other men on this ship?"

"I will not let loose a shipload of pirates on the Main. It is bad enough that I consider your freedom."

Liandra bit her lower lip trying to stay calm. Gabriel would set him free. She chanced a nervous glance at Marcus. His expression was unreadable. Was his heart not beating with the same ferocity?

She turned her head and at once Liandra realized her error. Her brother pinned her with bleak eyes, a strange expression on his face.

"Did any of his men touch you, *querida*?"

"No," she gasped.

"Did he?" Gabriel nodded toward Marcus.

Her gaze clung to Marcus only a heartbeat before she looked away. Thunder rolled like an angry drum across the sky.

"Did the English pirate put his filthy hands on you?"

"He saved our lives, Gabriel!"

Gabriel flung his gaze into the crevices and shelves that held the ship's china. He stalked to the last cabinet, swung open the heavy doors, and withdrew the Bible kept there for daily mass, something she had not attended to since the storm. Her heart beat a bleak pattern of trepidation as Gabriel approached.

"Swear, Liandra—" Gabriel tossed the Bible on the table—"swear he didn't touch you."

Flinching, she stared at the black leather casing. The Latin holy words carved on the front spun around her head like fiery dervishes. Liandra swung around to find Marcus watching her with a naked intensity that frightened her to the core of her being. Only a short time ago they'd shared something beautiful.

To save him she would have to deny him.

To lie—*Dios*—to lie condemned her soul to hell for blasphemy.

To lie freed Marcus.

Liandra laid her trembling hand on the Bible.

"Don't." Marcus's voice snapped her gaze up with a startled gasp.

All around her, the light seemed to fade as a storm cloud eclipsed the sunlight. Hope faded. Marcus didn't move. Looking at her, his silver eyes caught the withering brilliance, like candlelight seized by the wind, before flickering out.

And in that horrible moment, Liandra knew that whatever had been between them was gone: buried by oceans of hate and an irreconcilable legacy handed down by their parents.

"Please do not do this." Her voice trembled. "You don't understand."

Marcus shifted his gaze to Gabriel. The arrogant flash of his white teeth did not veil the ruthlessness in his eyes. "It wasn't her fault. She never had a chance to defend herse—"

"Stop it. You didn't do anything wrong."

He met her horrified gaze, his expression perfectly blank, as if an artist wiped the life from his eyes. "I wanted to see the great hero Espinosa squirm with his medals and iron crosses when you told him a lowly pirate bedded his only sister and ruined the proud family name. It was business, *gata*. Your brother understands, I'm sure."

She could not understand his words, or why he would

say these things. She had done something wrong. But what? Didn't he see that she would fight for him?

"No"—Liandra clawed a frantic hand through her hair—"what we shared . . . meant something."

"To whom? You?"

Outside the wind pulled against the ships. Hulls scraped.

Liandra desperately probed the sardonic mask that shielded his eyes. To be used. She would not believe it of him. Yet, there it was in his insolent stance, the faint lopsided curve on his beautiful mouth as if he might be ill. A look tinged with indifference.

"Do you mind?" He flicked an annoyed gaze to Gabriel. "I'll be returning to my own men now."

"You cannot do this."

"I just did, *gata*."

Liandra exploded. She could not believe it of him. Yet, there it was in his face. *"Bastardo,"* she whispered. Eyes brilliant with unshed tears, she came around the table. Gabriel wrested her arm, spinning her around into the protective custody of his embrace.

"Shh, *querida*," Gabriel whispered into her hair. His black gaze pinned Marcus. "He is a bastard like you said."

Wiping her eyes with the heel of her palm, Liandra glared miserably over her shoulder.

Without waiting for dismissal, Marcus pivoted. His bravado reeked of self-contempt for the stupid sentimentality that for just a moment before dawn made him forget who and what he really was.

Espinosa's outrage followed. "We're not finished, Drake!"

Marcus flicked an obscene gesture over his shoulder that didn't do justice to his anger as he stalked past Miguel and the other open-mouthed guards. The manacles on his fists rattled in the humid darkness of the corridor and he furiously snapped them taut. He'd barely restrained the urge to wrap his chains around Espinosa's throat. He ached to tear Liandra out of the man's arms and sink his face onto her shiny hair: hair that smelled of talcum and rainwater, of promises and magic.

He'd never be able to touch her again.

Christ, the air seemed to squeeze out of him.

Miguel closed the distance between them. "You take the blame, *señor*. I think what you feel for *Doña* Maria is not business after all. You broke her heart."

"She'll thank me tomorrow."

Marcus would not allow Liandra to lie for him on the Bible. Not when he knew what that lie would cost her.

Not when his life would be spared at the expense of his men's.

It seemed ironic somehow that he would see her now as Espinosa's sister: a feminine icon of sainthood. While he was an utter fool with no future: a taunting parody of his own impotence.

He would never be more than what he was now. Nothing.

Maybe the truth hit him when he'd walked down the stairs and saw Liandra in her brother's arms. The gilded portrait of sibling domesticity struck him like a blow in a belly already tender with abuse. He'd stood without speaking in the arched doorway terrified by her love for a man who'd helped destroy the very fabric of his existence. Liandra loved her brother, perhaps as he loved Talon.

His hands went to the golden cross he wore. It shaped to his palm, and he closed his weary eyes.

He didn't want to remember that for one instant this morning amid the colors of eternity, before the world awakened to find him, she'd almost made him feel worthy. She'd almost made him believe life held more than betrayal and broken dreams.

Almost.

Now, he just wanted to forget that she ever existed.

Miguel stopped at the top of the stairs, his expression grave. "The *alcalde* is awaiting you on deck. It will not go well for you once the *Almirante* leaves."

Marcus looked down the dark gangway. The silence

coming from the direction of the dining salon tore a hole through his gut. Liandra's wounded expression just before he turned to leave remained frozen in his memory.

"Look on the bright side, Miguel," he shoved a shoulder against the door, "in Carlos's care, I won't live long enough to be miserable."

With that, he walked out onto the deck just as it started to rain.

Gabriel dropped into a chair. He yanked the gloves off his hands and tossed them on the dining table beside his hat. He was bone weary. Already he was two weeks overdue returning to the fleet in Havana. A reprimand from the Captain-General would be the least of his problems. Men of honor did not put personal business above the king and expect to live long in his chosen profession.

Muffled voices filtered through the planked floor and ceiling as Carlos's men searched the rest of the ship for prisoners. Two had already been found hiding in the bilge deck and dragged to the main deck. Behind him, the stern galley windows were open. Wind lashed the heavy curtains. Liandra stood watching him with bright liquid eyes.

Only twice before in his life had he ever seen her cry. Her black velvet gown fluttered at her ankles. The mismatched shoes only made her more vulnerable.

His mouth tightened. Wearing discordant attire was exactly the sort of innocuous act that too often drew hurtful snickers. Yet, it was because he loved her that Gabriel had long ago ceased trying to hide her away like she was some shameful anomaly. His sister was too stubborn to be anything but what she was. He'd accepted that she was not like other Spanish aristocracy. She didn't believe in the same ugly politics. She didn't dress in the same fashions. Nothing ever quite balanced, including her childlike belief in humanity.

He saw it in the way she continued to care for their mother, in her work at the mission, her devotion to Friar

Montero. She was always on some ridiculous quest to save lost souls, whether they belonged to wayward orphans or pirates.

And Gabriel was loath to spare any man who harmed her.

But his hate for Drake was more than the pirate's incursion on El Condor's territory. Marcus, of the two brothers, was always the more dangerous. Reckless and foolish, he defied life with a challenge to anyone brave enough to take it from him. Many had tried.

Raking a hand through his hair, Gabriel looked away from his sister. Just thinking of Drake with his sister made his blood run hot with anger. The man belonged to a breed who, years ago, had savaged his mother and his innocence; who had plundered his people. Drake's father had killed his. It wasn't enough that two decades had yielded his revenge as he'd hunted down every man responsible for the attack on his family. Another twenty years wouldn't be enough to forget what English pirates had stolen from him and his mother.

Gabriel lifted his head. Miguel stood in the doorway awaiting his orders. "Take my sister to her cabin," he said.

The worried glance exchanged between this ship's master and his sister told him that he was alone in his condemnation of Drake. Between the two, he felt like a serpent.

"Gabriel." Liandra knelt at the chair; her fingers clutched his sleeve. "No matter what he's done, I still gave him my word."

"Just do as you're told, Liandra. *Por favor*. Please."

She wouldn't like what he was about to do anymore than he did. But that didn't take away the seriousness of her offense against the Church. What he was about to do would protect her.

"Gabriel—"

"Just go, Liandra. I'll summon you when I'm ready to take you on board my ship."

• • •

Marcus sat with his knees braced against his chest. The day progressed with little hope of sunshine or comfort. Salt spray cut through his clothes. He stared at Espinosa's flag-ship.

"Many here think you should have told us who der girl was."

Manacles dripped from Dutch's wrists and connected him to the rank of other half-dressed, barefooted men that sat against the rail.

"And would she have been spared, Dutch? Tell me I had a choice."

A shrug of his huge shoulders conceded the point. "Perhaps if I wore your boots, I would not have walked from der freedom the girl offered."

Marcus turned his head and glared at Dutchman.

"This ship is not so big. Voices carry." Silence filled the narrow space between them. "We are all in a pan of shit now, *ja*?"

Dutch confirmed the mood of the rest of the crew. Marcus felt their eyes on him as if he alone and not the Creator had the power to save them. Resentment crawled through him and he leaned his forehead against his knees. He didn't want that job now, anymore than he'd wanted to captain this ship.

A whip wielding guard approached—as if that pathetic whip protected him. Normally, Marcus would have wel-comed the chance to fight. One sweep of his feet, he could flatten the guard to the deck and snap his neck before the bastard took a breath.

Ignoring the paunchy Spaniard, Marcus found his gaze straying to the wooden portal that led to the passenger's cabins. Liandra had yet to be brought topside and trans-ferred to Espinosa's flagship.

His gaze stopped abruptly. Espinosa stood on the deck.

"*Ja*, you are dead," Dutch concluded. "He has der look of killing in his eyes."

A few minutes later, the guard brought Marcus back to the dining room. Espinosa stood with his back to him in front of the galley windows, one hand fisted in the palm of the other.

Expecting an ax to fell him, Marcus surveyed the room, impassively checking for an ambush. A square sheet of vellum lay spread out on the polished table. The ink was still wet. Inside a squat jar of black ink, a white-feathered quill swayed drunkenly with the ship's movement. Espinosa didn't move.

Marcus wanted to know where Liandra was. But didn't ask. His gaze went back to the document. He froze. "You want me to sign this?"

Espinosa turned. "My foolish sister has no idea the consequences of her actions with you. Or the kind of man you are."

His eyes narrowed over Espinosa. Black hair swept across the Spaniard's dark eyes. "Better wedlock to a traitorous dead pirate and widowhood than eternal damnation. Is that it, Espinosa?"

Black eyes flashed. "You're lucky I've let you live this long."

"Lucky? I don't think so. I'm well acquainted with Spanish hospitality from my last visit to Puerto Bello. Carlos's brand in particular."

Espinosa slammed the flat of his palms on the table. "You were tried and legally condemned, Drake. My mistake years ago was in sending you and your brother to a Spanish slave galleon to die instead of hanging you both when I had the chance."

"Answer one question." Marcus leaned forward on the table. "Did we know each other in some past life? You've hated my family with such personal Spanish eloquence that I've felt cheated not ever knowing the reason."

Barely concealed malice flashed in Espinosa's dark eyes. His shoulders and arms strained the seams of his uniform, a sure clue that he drilled every day with the cutlass hanging at his waist. Still, if it came to a fight, Marcus would beat him. Espinosa possessed a handicap Marcus himself didn't suffer: value for his own life.

"I've done my job, Drake. But you've always managed to be in my way."

"Ah, yes. A by-the-rules Spanish hero to his Catholic majesty. Your nobility daunts me." Marcus flicked the document. "I wouldn't marry an Espinosa if she were swathed in frankincense and presented to me on a silver platter."

"Do one honorable thing in your life, Drake. As much as I dislike you, I don't want to see her pay any more than she already will for what happened between you. Excommunication from the Church would kill her."

"You wouldn't be doing this if there were any thought that I might survive my stay in Puerto Bello." Marcus leaned his head down. The muscles on his shoulders bunched. Espinosa was correct. The hypocritical righteous would crucify her. Bloody hell. He hadn't even gotten the pleasure of finishing what they'd started. There truly was no justice in this world. "Have you told Liandra about this?"

"I'm the one who wrote up the marriage contract and signed it. I don't need her permission."

Marcus laughed and shoved away from the table. "That's bloody rich. If you don't mind, I'd prefer marrying her. In the flesh. I've never done this before. I want to know what it's like looking someone in the eye when I vow to spend the rest of my life with her. What will that be? Thirty seconds, maybe?"

Espinosa stared at him. Shoving away from the table, he walked to the door. Boot heels rapped on the floor. He told the guard outside to bring down his sister. "For her, the union will be blessed by a priest. I'm bringing one over now from my ship."

"One more thing." Marcus leaned his hip against the table. "The Spanish crew who sailed this ship are to be spared punishment by your whip-wielding butchers. I am solely responsible for everything that has happened here. I forced your sister to release all of the prisoners, and then I took the ship."

Espinosa narrowed his eyes, as if trying to assess him

and unsure of what he saw. "I don't beat my prisoners, Drake."

A knock sounded. Miguel led Liandra forward and quietly left the room. When she entered, her reddened eyes widened with a smile that made his breath catch. Her beauty was ethereal. After everything he'd said and done to her, how could she still look at him as if he were sunshine on a stormy night? Clenching his jaw, he turned his back on her and stepped away from the table. The chains scraped the floor.

"Sit down, Liandra," Espinosa bid.

She did as she was told. Folding her hands in her lap, she looked askance at her brother. Espinosa pushed the sheath of folded vellum beneath her nose. "Sign this, Liandra."

Hands trembling, she unrolled the intimidating sheath. Swirls of fancy characters greeted her query. Her gaze lifted back to her brother's face. "I do not understand."

"Just sign the document, *por favor.*"

She stared back at the manila parchment, seemingly lost as to how to proceed with her brother's bidding. It was as if she didn't know what the document was. Clearly, she couldn't read Latin.

She turned her shining eyes and caught him watching her. Annoyed with the lack of control on his emotions, he straightened and reached across her for the quill. His heart hammered. The chains touched her arm. Dipping the pen in ink, Marcus signed his name at the bottom of the page. The civilized task felt awkward, foreign to his hand, which was more adept at hefting a cutlass that penning fancy script.

Handing the quill to Liandra, he had to take her hand and put it on the vellum. Clearly confused, her eyes held his. "Your name, Liandra."

A glance at her brother confirmed his request. Her tongue darted nervously over her full red mouth. Her brows drawn together in concentration, she formed each letter where he'd told her to write. The childlike scrawl looked odd and out of place on the document.

She spelled her name wrong.

"Will this free you?" she quietly asked him, glancing over her shoulder when the priest entered the room.

"Only in hell, sweet *gata*. But it will free you."

Chapter Ten

W hy does *Tía* Maria not want to be with us, Papa?"
Christina buried her nose against the coarse fabric of
Gabriel's uniform.

With his daughter firmly in his arms, Gabriel turned
with her to the poop deck, where Liandra stood. Looking
more fragile than porcelain, his sister continued to stare
across the water at the majestic curves of the single Spanish galleon silhouetted against the sunset.

Liandra had lost her mantilla lace headdress when
boarding his ship hours before. The combs in her hair no
longer held the thick length of her hair. She hadn't spoken
to him since coming on board.

Narrowing his eyes, he pulled his gaze from Liandra's
profile to the aloof galleon half a league away. The sun
burned the sea a brazen gold, the same color that touched
the distant stern and painted the sails.

"Papa?"

Louder now, Christina's voice ventured through his
thoughts. He bent his gaze and encompassed his daughter's worried face. Staring at the hairy, doll-like creature
clutched in his child's arms, he was annoyed that she cher-

ished something so utterly ridiculous. Something that Drake had made.

Even El Condor had one weakness, and Drake had found it as capably as a shark closes in on the kill. The sea bastard had succeeded in usurping both his sister's and daughter's affections.

Could they not see the man for what he was?

Women, even young ones, possessed no sense. He now knew why the whole sex should be married off young. Sentiment and a pretty smile moved the feminine mind to commit senseless acts that a man would never consider. He'd made a bad mistake with Liandra, allowing her to roam free.

"Papa?" Christina tugged on his bristly jaw. "Can I?"

Gabriel realized he hadn't heard a word his daughter said. "Tomorrow, *ratón*. Little mouse. Right now, it's your bedtime." Over Christina's shoulder, he found Rosa standing nearby. "It has been a long day."

"But I don't want to sleep," she pleaded. "I want to fish with Alejandro. We always fish, Papa."

"Who would teach you such a thing, Christina?"

"*Señor Capitán*. He showed us. We eat them, Papa."

Gabriel snorted his disgust. "Young ladies of breeding don't fish, Christina." Handing her to Rosa, he said, "Sleep outside her door if you have to. She's not allowed to roam this ship."

His daughter burst into tears. "But I always fish, Papa."

Gabriel stared aghast at the emotional display of his once well-mannered child. She wailed all the way down to her cabin. He'd even heard a questionable word mixed in with her tears. Glowering at his crew, Gabriel silently threatened any man who took notice. At length, he made his way up the stairs to the poop deck, where his sister stood.

Without turning to look at him, she murmured distantly, "You should try fishing. It's quite enjoyable to . . ." she waved her hand about as if searching for the exact words. "One uses a pole and string, and you put a hook—"

All patience snapped. "*Dios.* You live in the clouds, Liandra." He glared at the distant ship. "That man humiliates you. He used you to get to me. And all you can do is spout nonsense about fishing?"

He expected outrage. Instead, Liandra lowered her lashes.

"Ah, *querida*," he whispered against her temple. "It will soon be over. You have been taken in by his charm. But Drake will not hurt you again."

Her wet eyes encompassed his. "What are you saying?"

"I was late getting to Hispaniola for a reason," he said. "Two months ago, I received a missive from New Spain. It seems the new viceroy did not arrive at his destination, and I was ordered to search for his ship. I captured the *Dark Fury.* She's sitting now in Puerto Bello. Drake will see what remains of his brother's ship. It's a victory for Spain."

Naked despair haunted her expression. "You mean for El Condor!"

"The Drakes are convicted pirates, Liandra. Do you forget that we have lost family and friends beneath their guns?" He raked a furious hand through his hair. How could she continue to champion the bastard? "This is the way it must end and you know it."

"Not every man in the Caribbean sailed for Henry Morgan. Must you go on hunting and hating for something that happened long ago? Can there never be peace in your heart? Can there never be any forgiveness between our families?"

"Forgiveness?" The hideous word choked him. His sister regarded him as if he were the monster. "You will not fight this, Liandra," he warned. "Do you understand?"

She swept past him. Gabriel grabbed her arm and spun her around. Her skirts swirled around his legs like a typhoon of velvet. "*Sí*, Gabriel." She yanked her arm from his grasp. "I understand family honor. You made him marry me, your poor ruined sister, knowing I would soon be a widow. But after he learns what you have done to his brother, you will not be able to hold him. He will kill us both."

She walked away, her slippers making no sound on the damp deck. Night had descended and the shadows snuffed out his sister's bright presence.

His foolish sister still had no idea of the consequences of her acts and the suffering he'd saved her. Excommunication from the Church would have been the least of her problems for what she'd done.

But something far more insidious than the marriage contract plagued him. He found the distant sails, a ghostly specter on the horizon. A terrible feeling shaped itself into a fist inside him.

He was responsible for condemning his sister's husband to die.

But Gabriel's world held no place for doubt, even where Liandra was concerned.

Thrust across the slippery deck of the galleon for the second time that day, Marcus was shoved through the narrow door and down the steep stairs to the captain's berth. Miguel followed closely behind, but was shut out of the room when the two guards pushed Marcus through the door. Manacles wrapped his ankles and wrists. For a single, black-tempered moment, he stood framed by the dying light of day in the room where Liandra had once slept and tried not to count himself a fool. His glance briefly touched the bunk then slid to the stern, galley window. Moonlight bathed the sea silver. In the distance, he glimpsed the tall white sails of Espinosa's flagship.

Liandra was there.

His wife.

Movement near the desk stirred his attention and brought him back to the matter at hand. *Comandante* Carlos de Vincente y Morales, serving his esteemed title as *alcalde* in Puerto Bello, sat on the desk, leaning forward with his arms crossed over his chest. Surveying Marcus and his distinctive height in the low-ceilinged room, Carlos straightened. An imperious gesture to the pair of guards snapped the men to action. They dragged Marcus to the chair set opposite the desk. Hampered by his chains, he stumbled but did not go to his knees. He gave the guards a murderous look as he dropped into his chair.

"Drake," Carlos said pleasantly, slapping a pair of black leather gloves against his thigh. "Nice to see you again."

A faint stirring of dread mingled with the copper taste of blood in his mouth. "Cut the shit, Carlos. We both know you didn't bring me here to chat. What do you want?"

The man laughed. "A confession will do."

"And what would you like for me to confess today? Murder? Thievery? Piracy? All of the above? I confess."

"I could kill you."

"Stand in line, you bastard. Your precious government has prior claim."

A sinister smile hovered just beneath Carlos's thin mustache. "I'm relieved the years since I have seen you last have not robbed you of your sense of humor." One at a time, Carlos slid his hands into the gloves and worked the smooth leather down his fingers as he walked around the desk. "But it is unfortunate your wit has not improved with age. I will take great pleasure in cutting out your tongue . . . and other more vital extremities before my nephew has you hanged in Puerto Bello."

"Go to hell, Carlos."

Carlos hit him. Blinding lights flashed through Marcus's skull. His head snapped back with the impact. Slowly, he returned his narrowed gaze to the small, insignificant spec of humanity, and spit blood on his shiny black boots.

Carlos moved closer. "Tell me. What was it like bedding Espinosa's virginal sister? Was she tight? Like a glove?"

Marcus came out of the chair. The guards jerked him back. "For Chrissakes, she's your niece."

"My niece?" Carlos laughed. "In name only. Maria

Liandra is no more than the by-blow of one of the late Henry Morgan's men. There were many such brats born in Puerto Bello the year after Morgan's attack. Why do you think Espinosa married her off to you, a worthless pirate? Because no one respectable would have her as a wife. Don Gabriel was too much of a weakling to put her in a convent where she belonged."

An ember of respect for Espinosa briefly flared within Marcus before Carlos hit him again. Marcus lifted his head. "He was right. She . . . doesn't belong . . . in a convent."

"No man has ever been able to get between her legs. Do you have a secret we mere mortals lack?"

A faint smile curled his bloody lips. "I heard long ago you were no man at all."

"Ah, yes, you and my dear Innes. My adulterous wife. She fancied a man in chains." He turned his back and poured a glass of wine. The sound of liquid sloshed in the crystal glass. "As I recall, all those many years ago, she was not to your liking. No matter." Eyeing Marcus carefully over the rim, he casually drank. "Where my wife failed with you, I will not. You will be on your knees soon enough."

Marcus measured the thin man with unveiled contempt. He would die a thousand times over before he went to his knees in front of any man. A knot of loathing lent strength to that vow.

"But, alas, my pleasure will have to wait." Carlos set down the glass. "It seems I have a slight matter of missing silver to contend with first. You will sign a confession that you threw it overboard rather than see it fall back into our hands."

"I have no doubt whose hands it fell in—"

Carlos punched him in the stomach. The guards held Marcus in the chair by his shoulders. "You see, it belongs to my soldiers," he said casually. "They anxiously await payment for services rendered in his most Eminent

Catholic Majesty's army. It will go poorly for you once they learn they will not be paid."

"You don't care . . . a frog's ass for your men. Why . . . all this pretense? What . . . do you . . . really want from me, Carlos?"

The Spaniard perched on the edge of the desk and waved his gloved hand negligently. "I can save your life . . . if you tell me what you know about the treasure of Puerto Bello."

"Oh, this is bloody rich."

"I know for a fact that you have seen a map," Carlos said.

"Christ . . ." Marcus laughed between bloody teeth.

He should have known. His hands tightening into fists, the truth hit with the force of a blow; he and Talon could fight injustice for a thousand years. He could hide from his emotions, his heart, his very self, and still never escape the sins of his past.

Carlos was no different than the hundred other bastards who'd hunted him in an attempt to snare the golden fable. Who'd put a bounty on his head. Men who would do anything, including murdering little girls and destroying his family. Men like Carlos, who cared nothing for human life.

The treasure of Puerto Bello was a myth framed in greed: born when Henry Morgan and a thousand other English pirates had raided that city over twenty years ago. For whatever reason, millions of doubloons in gold and silver were spirited away from the Spanish domain, yet only half of that wealth had made it back to Port Royal. Through the foolish years of his youth, Marcus had believed that his father, who had been Morgan's trusted captain, knew the truth.

God in heaven, that mistake remained to haunt Marcus forever.

No longer protected by indifference, Marcus prepared now for his fate at Carlos's hands. Perhaps because his life had been such a dismal failure, he wanted only to die with more courage than he'd lived. It was all he had left. He spared a moment to think about Liandra, and another to regret that he'd been unable to see Talon again.

Then he grinned—and told Carlos exactly in which part of his anatomy he could shove his promise.

Carlos hit him in the mouth. He could not endure this agony for long. "More . . . Spanish hospitality?" Marcus slurred the words.

As if reading his mind, Carlos bent over his ear. "I'm not going to kill you, Drake." A wormy chuckle eased over Marcus's temple. "But I swear you will wish I had."

Carlos dined and drank after each bout of abuse. Aye, the *alcalde* wanted him alive. For what, Marcus didn't know. But as the night grew colder, and the wind sang in the rigging, he could not quell the foreboding that there was something else awaiting him in Puerto Bello far worse than death.

Liandra was vaguely aware of the whispers that followed her as she climbed from the ketch onto the verdant shores of Puerto Bello and walked past the gathering crowd. Word of her indiscretion with the English pirate had spread in the colorful ranks stationed ahead of her like a disease. The few people who lived in the swamp-ridden town this time of year had gathered along the beach and dusty streets for Gabriel's arrival. Sunshine glinted off the whitewashed walls and red-tiled roofs of buildings that lined the steep incline. Liandra adjusted the black veil covering her face.

"Poor foolish girl." The whispers followed her. *"So desperate for love. What with rumors about her mother."*

"He'll hang in three days at the Almirante'*s order."*

"What if there's a child?"

"Her poor brother. And after losing his young wife so many years ago. He must be devastated."

With regal disdain, Liandra met their pious stares. Weariness reached all the way to her bones. All her life, she'd born the brunt of derogatory gossip. They'd always made her feel ashamed.

Liandra slowed as two stout, white carriages rattled up to the walkway ahead. Heat filtered through the soles of her slippers. The carriages would convey them to her brother's stone residence, stretched along the bay, where Carlos and Innes also lived. Twisting her reticule nervously in her gloved hands, she focused on the bright coat of arms emblazoned on the door: a bloodred shield and black bird of prey with wide-spread wings. The sign of the conqueror. To her, the once proud insignia meant only death.

Isabella caught up to her as they reached the row of soldiers patiently gathered at attention to pay respects to the *Almirante*. Head cast down, her cousin slowed her pace to a walk. Questioning Isabella's strange behavior, Liandra looked back over her shoulder. She knew Isabella was terrified of her tyrant father.

Carlos had yet to appear. Instinctively, Liandra stared at the galleon. Silently, she prayed for a glimpse of Marcus or any of the others that remained behind. The absence of life on the ornate decks frightened her.

Nearer to the beach, Gabriel was inspecting the troops lined nearer the shore. Brass glinted in the sunlight. Flies buzzed in the heat. Standing behind Gabriel, Rosa remained with Christina, who was contentedly playing in the white sand. The three boys walked up the street, stirring dust with their feet.

Liandra gave the boys an encouraging smile, and their faces brightened. "You will ride with us to the house," she called, and dared anyone to argue with the order. The boys piled pell-mell into the carriage behind Isabella, rocking the conveyance with their zeal. Her cousin squealed.

One final, stolen glance at the galleon before turning, Liandra looked again for any sign of Marcus. Longing rushed through her veins, and she shivered, suddenly remembering her last morning with him on board, loving him as the golden sun crested the sea.

Hot tears sprang into her eyes. She was married to her black-hearted pirate.

And soon to be widowed.

Since last night, she'd come to the slow realization that
Gabriel could not have forced Marcus to marry her. Perhaps it wasn't an act of vengeance that drove Marcus to
make love to her, but it had certainly turned into that. The
proud name of Espinosa was now linked to Drake.

With a heavy heart, Liandra's gaze slid past the other
listing masts in the harbor. One ship pulled her attention.

Drawing back her veil, Liandra shaded her eyes and
stared at the insolent, thirty-four-gun frigate riding anchor
in the turquoise sea. Her infamous black sails furled tightly
against the huge masts, *Dark Fury* was a mocking tribute
to the gaudy elegance of the Spanish galleons that reefed
the bay. Liandra could not help but admire the black
frigate's sleek lines and curves. Even in captivity, the
ship's commanding essence could not be ignored. She was
indeed a proud trophy, equaled only by the powerful men
who'd sailed her.

A lump caught in her throat. Did Marcus know his
brother's fate?

"*Tía* Maria? *Tía* Maria?" The small voice roused Liandra from her languor. Cheeks flushed, curls askew,
Christina ran up the dusty streets. "You were not at our
morning meal. I wanted to see you."

Liandra knelt beside her niece. "I missed you, *niña*. I'm
sorry."

Christina touched Liandra's swollen eyes. "Why do you
cry?"

She hadn't realized she was crying. "Remember when
you lost your doll? That is how my heart feels."

Christina bent her troubled gaze in the direction of the
ship. "Is *Señor capitán* there?"

"*Sí, niña*, he is."

Clutching Liandra's sleeve, Christina leaned closer. "Is
he a bad man, *Tía* Maria? Like they say?"

"What does your heart tell you?"

"He is good at fixing things. Maybe he will fix your
smile if you ask." Then she wiped at a sniffle.

"What is it, *niña*?"

"*Señor Capitán* and the others. They rescued us. Who will rescue them?"

Liandra tightened her arms around Christina. "Does your papa know you are up here with me?"

"*Sí.* He told me to give you this peach."

Taking the gift, Liandra lifted her head. Dressed in the full uniform of his station, Gabriel stood at the end of the docks talking to his men. Listening with head bent, he was watching her from beneath the cocksure hat resting at an angle on his head. She had not spoken to him since last night.

"Will you eat dinner with us tonight?" Christina asked.

Tears burned behind her lids. "You must go back to your papa now, *niña*. He is waiting." Liandra kissed her niece. "Tell him thank you for the peach. I will see you later at the house."

She watched Christina return to her father. No matter how she tried, Liandra could not escape the horror that she had betrayed both Marcus and Gabriel. By loving one man, she dishonored the other. By respecting her promise to Marcus, she had deceived Gabriel.

Liandra gripped the carriage wheel spokes and pulled herself up. Her knees were weak. Her jaw ached with the effort it took not to cry. Then, like a mother's gentle touch on a beloved child, the breeze caressed her face and whispered through the sable tendrils of her fallen hair. She'd not felt that touch since Grandmama died except in the solitary communion she shared with nature. She often spent hours sitting on the grassy knoll behind her brother's house in Hispaniola watching the sunrise, or in the mountains here that surrounded the mission, listening to the wind in the trees.

As long as Marcus lived, hope remained.

Nothing else mattered but doing the right thing.

"Where have they taken him, Pedro?"

Four hours of frantic waiting had passed since Liandra

had arrived at the house and quickly made her way to the stables. Outside, an afternoon shower cleansed the dust from the air and brightened the sky to a stark dome of blue.

Pedro clutched a strawhat in his gnarled hands. "It is rumored Carlos has him locked away in the dungeons beneath the fortress. I am told that the guards know you. You nursed two of them back to health last winter during an epidemic of dysentery. They agreed to speak to me, but could only say that he is not well."

Her heart beat faster. "What have they done to him?"

The fingers around the hat worked the rim. "When he saw his brother's ship in the bay they could not restrain him, *señorita*. This man Carlos took the whip to his back until *Señor* Marcus went to his knees. I have never seen such an evil creature as the *alcalde*. If the English *capitán* lives to be hanged now, it will be a miracle."

Liandra pressed her palms against her temples. In a nearby stall, her horses whickered. "Where is Miguel? Why hasn't he come to me?" Pedro looked away. Her heart skipped in panic. "What is it?"

"I am sorry, *señorita* . . ."

"Sorry?" She gripped his sleeve. "What has happened?"

"He tried to save the Englishman. Carlos shot him. He is dead."

Miguel dead? This could not be!

"Nobody told me."

"Many of our Spanish crew threw down their swords and chose to take their place with the pirates. Your brother is furious at Don Carlos, but there is nothing he can do here on land without a royal decree."

Liandra swallowed her tears beneath a veil of rage. She paced, her skirts dragging in the straw. She'd ripped her hem only an hour before on a rusty hinge in the barn awaiting Pedro's return.

Suddenly, she felt lost. "Why did Marcus have to be so stubborn? He could have had his freedom."

"At what cost, *señorita*? He would not leave his men.

Not after changing course and sailing directly into El Condor."

Liandra clasped her arms to her chest. "But he said the men voted."

"They voted. After he brought it up. There were rumblings that he betrayed them because of you. Then there was talk among the crew that he was also responsible for the death of his parents and sister. And also for leading his brother into El Condor's trap many years ago that caused them to be imprisoned here."

She swallowed painfully. "But he would not do such a thing."

"Not on purpose, *señorita*. Nonetheless, it happened."

Liandra would not believe it. She'd felt the honor inside him, touched his heart, and sensed the vulnerability behind the careless veneer he flaunted to the world. Surely a man who had sheltered the daughter of El Condor was not capable of the atrocities of which he'd been accused. And Marcus hadn't taken anything from her that she'd not willingly given.

The unbidden reality of it all scattered her courage. Marcus had trusted her to free him and his men.

He'd needed her to fulfill her side of the bargain!

Everything made sense now. That was why he'd lashed out—one of the reasons anyway. It was his way to go down with the ship of broken promises. She should have known he'd not abandon his men.

She should have fought harder. Miguel would still be alive.

"Marcus must hate me," she whispered.

"You do not know him, *señorita*, to say that."

"You are wrong." She glared at the rafters above her. A huge black spider with a single white dot on its back had built its web among the cracks. Liandra wrapped her arms against her to ward off the ugly premonition of death. "Marcus is like Gabriel in so many ways. I should have known what he would do."

Impulsively, she hugged the older man. His skinny

shoulders pressed into her collarbone. "We must find a way to get you home, too." He seemed shocked that she would consider his plight at all. She was offended that he, too, would think so little of her. "I sent Alejandro and the boys to the mission with the supplies. I have asked Friar Montero to come. If anyone can help us, he will find a way."

But they were fast running out of time.

Later, Liandra confronted Gabriel in the library.

"Why didn't you tell me that Carlos had killed Miguel?"

Gabriel stood with his hands clasped behind his broad back, staring out the opened verandah doors. The crash of waves on white-sanded beaches lifted her gaze past her brother. Red cascading flowers dripped from the wrought-iron balustrade outside and framed a picturesque country-side so unlike anything that belonged to Gabriel. She hated this house with its proud Spanish conquistadors lining the hallways in shining statues of armor. The rooms filled with heavy baroque furniture were dark and uninviting. In the distance, the white stone fortress that housed the militia stood as a bleak sentinel against pirates. Marcus was there, buried in the caverns below the citadel.

"I was told your man Pedro tried to visit the English-man."

"You were told correctly."

Her brother turned to face her. The fading light etched his handsome face in shadows, rendering his expression unreadable. She felt his gaze go over her in disapproval. She had yet to change her rumpled clothes from yesterday. Only her long hair retained some semblance of order.

"Why didn't you go to the mission with the others?" he softly questioned.

In the awful stillness between them, Liandra knew Gabriel loved her. He'd made people accept her. He'd shown patience in his infinite tolerance toward her. But he didn't truly understand her.

She lifted her chin. "I demand that you spare Marcus's life. I want him and his crew freed."

"*Madre de Dios*. Let it go, Liandra. I cannot protect you if you do something unlawful. This is Carlos's jurisdiction."

"Carlos is a murderer."

"I know Miguel was your friend, Liandra. I've sent for Friar Montero. He'll be here tomorrow to claim Miguel's body. He'll be buried next to his parents at the mission."

"Is it so easy to dismiss what has happened?"

"Miguel is fortunate that he will be buried with honor. He interfered with a *capitán*'s decision to render corporal punishment. Such a crime is punishable by death."

"Will the others die also?"

Clearly reading her panic, Gabriel answered, "The others did not follow orders. Their sentence will be given after a trial. It could be months before their fate is determined."

Marcus did not have months. His nights numbered three. Three. Such an insignificant number, like her third birthday, which she had celebrated alone, or the number of orange cats she had, or the seconds it took a rope to snap your neck.

"Liandra?" Gabriel called as she started to turn. "Did Drake ever mention anything about a treasure?"

"Do you chase Carlos's obsession for wealth now, Gabriel? I thought you only chased vengeance?"

He slammed his fists against the doorframe. "Do you think there aren't questions here that need to be answered? I don't wake up every morning of my life and count the Englishmen I want to slay!"

"Then let Marcus and his crew go."

His dark eyes pinned her. "You know I cannot."

Swinging open the door, Liandra turned in a whisper of rumpled velvet. As she looked across the room at her brother, one fierce vow etched a path across her heart: she would sever their relationship forever if he hanged Marcus.

She made sure Gabriel read the promise in her eyes.

Once outside the door, Liandra stared numbly at the tiled floor. Her throat tightened. With a muted cry, she ran from the house, her slippered feet carrying her past gaping servants and gardeners, who worked the immaculate grounds. Reaching the stables, she threw open the wide doors and ran inside. Wearing only the same wretched gown she'd worn since yesterday, she mounted Sundown bareback. The stallion balked. Gripping the mane, Liandra galloped out of the stables, leapt the fence, and gave Sundown his head. Without benefit of a chaperone, she blindly rode toward the fortress.

People here were used to her eccentric behavior. When forced to stay at Gabriel's house in Puerto Bello she'd oft ridden horses along the beach alone at dawn. No *dueña* could keep up with her. Nor would they go with her when she'd nursed ill soldiers at the citadel, where decent Spanish señoritas would never step. In the past, she'd intentionally flouted society, pretending that she didn't care what people thought of her. Liandra wasn't immune to the pitying stares or the whispers that hinted she was as deranged as her mama.

She wondered suddenly what Marcus had ever seen in her.

Watching barefooted children play in the ditches along the beach, Liandra thought of her own life. She'd spent years carving out walls from the stone around her heart, sculpting turrets and gates from a lifetime of loneliness. In reality, holding the world at bay only succeeded in keeping her prisoner in her own castle. By fearing pain, she feared life. What did she have to share with anyone but a nest filled with foolish dreams that no one in her family cared about? Only Grandmama had cradled her face and kissed her tears. And she'd died a year ago. Gabriel remained hard and unbending. Else he would not allow the man she loved to die.

Today had been a lesson in grim fact. The only person in town who'd changed was she.

Liandra slowed Sundown in the sand. The wind caught

her hair and lifted her skirts. Her fingers shook in Sundown's thick, red mane. Numbly, she stared up the rocky slope at the imposing stone fortress that overlooked the city. Triana they called it. Spain's enemies would go inside those walls and never again see the light of day.

Cold anticipation coiled in her chest. Short of a miracle or a fortune to bribe the masses, what could one old man and a woman do against a fortress of heavily armed soldiers?

How was she going to free Marcus in three days?

Burying her face in her hands, Liandra hopelessly realized that only an act of God would save him now.

Chapter Eleven

"D id you hear, Maria? Did you?"

The sun had barely made its morning debut. Liandra shoved the herbs she'd just gathered beneath her skirts. Brushing the dirt off her hands, she lifted her gaze to assess Isabella, who'd rushed breathlessly from the house.

Liandra had been waiting for news. All night, she'd waited to hear from Friar Montero. Her heart slowed in dreadful anticipation.

"He escaped. The Englishman escaped. No one knows how. But he's gone. Papa is livid."

Raising her face to God, Liandra said a thankful prayer. It was enough to restrain a yelp of excitement. Tears of relief welled.

"Maria?" Isabella's voice lowered to a scandalous whisper. "You weren't involved somehow, were you?"

She wiped at her face. "I've been here all night, Isabella."

"*Sí.* Since Friar Montero arrived."

He'd arrived late last night. Liandra and Gabriel had gone with him to the little chapel at the edge of town where Miguel's body had been wrapped and prepared for transportation back to the mission. After the service, Liandra had followed Friar Montero outside, where he and Ramón loaded the coffin onto the back of the cart that would take him home.

Liandra had poured out her story. Begging her great-uncle for help. She'd given the Englishman her word, promised him safe harbor, she told her Uncle Montero, for he would understand about such things as vows and integrity.

He considered her carefully before finally replying. "I once knew Marcus's father," he said. "Perhaps it's time to put those ghosts to rest, *sí* little one?"

"Then you can help?"

"I will try."

Unable to stem the tears, Liandra dropped to her knees and kissed his robes. He snorted at her display and pulled her to her feet. She'd wanted to ask him more. But there would be time enough later, and Gabriel awaited her inside the chapel.

And now Marcus had escaped. He was alive!

Friar Montero had pulled off a miracle.

But Liandra knew that all was not safe. Carlos would be hunting Marcus. Scouring the countryside for any sign of the Englishman.

She had to get to the mission. Foraging the garden for the last of the medicinal herbs, Liandra carefully stuffed them in her small canvas tote and slipped the string around her wrist before returning to the house. Many years ago, she'd learned the value of medicinal plants. Every summer epidemics plagued the coastal communities. It was a time Liandra took Christina and went to live in Hispaniola or with her grandmama in the mountains. If not for the mission and her mother, Liandra would have left this dreadful place long ago.

"Maria," Isabella fell in beside her. "You will take me to the mission with you. Will you not?"

Liandra stopped. She noted the dark circles beneath Isabella's eyes. "You will not enjoy it."

"I know what I said before . . ." she started after Liandra. "But this is different."

"No."

"Maria . . ." Isabella lifted her thick skirts and ran after her. Her petticoats swished as her feet pedaled up the slope. "I do not wish to stay here. I'll help with Christina."

"Gabriel has Rosa for that. Besides," Liandra turned, "Christina still hasn't forgiven you for throwing her doll overboard."

Isabella grabbed her sleeve, nearly ripping the thin cloth from her arm. "Maria. I do not want to stay here. If you don't take me . . . I'll tell Papa that Alejandro and Pedro are slaves."

Liandra whirled. "I wondered why you have not already."

"Papa never found the ship's manifest." She shifted and stared down at the small golden slippers peeking from beneath her walking dress. A small sniff sounded. "I did not have anything against the old man and boy."

"So you decided to suddenly be generous with their lives?"

"I was going to ask that you take me to the mission."

"You mean blackmail me." Liandra threw up her hands. "I don't have time to coddle you, Isabella. But if you have one kind and decent bone in your body, you will say nothing to anyone."

Isabella followed Liandra up the stone steps that led to the main yard. A verdant landscape surrounded them. "I heard Papa talking to Ramón about our time spent on the galleon. Ramón and Miguel were friends. Papa is already suspicious of all of us, especially since the silver was found missing. Now, he will even be more so since the Englishman escaped. They say *señor* Marcus could not even walk. That he could not have escaped on his own. Papa will close off the streets leading outside the town. Everyone will be searched. He has already gone to the mission. If I go with you, the soldiers would not dare search us. They will not find your herbs and wonder who you are going to go nurse."

Liandra came to an abrupt halt. Isabella hit her from behind and they both stumbled forward. Standing at the top of the stone walkway, Gabriel watched her. Beneath his hat, the sun touched his obsidian eyes. She nervously swallowed. Everything about him was polished from the tips of his shiny boots to the immaculate brass buttons that adorned the blue-gray jerkin. Liandra flicked the dirt off her sleeve and dared him with her eyes to comment about her appearance. But deep inside, her heart beat a frantic pace as she considered all the awful reasons why he must be standing there glaring at her like some powerful demigod. He was not so far away that he couldn't have missed hearing Isabella speaking.

"I need to talk to you, Liandra," he said. Ignoring Isabella, he punctuated the command with a stark, "*Now.*"

Fifteen minutes later, Liandra sat with her hands tightly folded in her lap. Gabriel had bypassed the decorative salon for the verandah. Clearly, he didn't want Liandra traipsing dirt inside. A white-clad servant appeared carrying a silver tray filled with fruit and cheese. After he scurried away, Gabriel spun around.

The salted breeze whispered through the red and blue flowers that cascaded from clay pots hanging from the iron grillwork.

"You can dispense with the docile act, Liandra."

Lifting her head, she narrowed her eyes.

"The temper can go, too. I'm just in the mood to lock you up." He paced, his boots furiously clicking against the tiled floor. "A convent would do you good. One in the highest mountain regions of Spain, where you would never have to pull your head out of the clouds." He whirled on her. "I hope they don't find the Englishman. Do you know why?" Liandra flinched against his fury. "Because somehow I'd learn that you are involved. I no longer want to know. Do you understand? I don't want to find out what you might have done. *Dios*. Carlos could hang you. And there's nothing I could do to save you."

Liandra closed her hands around the herbal bag. Gabriel saw the movement. "I still have a job to do, Liandra. The *flota* is gathering at Havana. Already I will have to explain my delay. One doesn't make excuses to the *Capitán-General* or to the king."

Liandra lowered her gaze to her lap. He was right, of course. Men had been stripped of far more than their power for not fulfilling their honorable duties to the king.

"Though I cannot repair your reputation, I did my best to protect you. Now, I see, I made a mistake making the Englishman wed you. If he somehow survives, which he can't without help, I will make you a widow and have you wedded to someone else before summer's end."

"Gabriel!"

"I've had my fill, Liandra. It is time for another man to be saddled with you. You will remain at the mission with Friar Montero until my return. I am taking Christina back to Spain with me."

"But why?"

"Her mother's sister lives in Seville. I don't have to worry about Christina's other aunt chasing after orphans and English pirates. She is a decent Spanish noblewoman. At least she can be counted on to provide Christina with the proper upbringing a child of her station should have."

He turned to go. Liandra was so shocked she couldn't speak. Gabriel suddenly stopped. He turned to face her again, and his gaze lingered on her face. A breeze carried the hint of lavender and soap, and the bittersweet scent of regret.

"You cannot save him. If you knew where the English pirate was, you could turn him in. And be finished with all this pain." His voice was gentle, filled with understanding. Pleading. She knew he wanted to protect her. A lone tear splattered on her hand. His hands twisted around the wooden latticework on the chair. "No one would ever have to know what you've done."

When Liandra didn't reply, her brother's exhale lifted her gaze, "Drake will never appreciate what you're sacrificing for him."

Liandra's fingers worked the edge of her tote. Gabriel would never understand her heart.

With an oath, her brother turned and walked away.

So it was that Liandra said good-bye to her precious niece.

Marcus hadn't dreamed in years. He drifted in scented currents. He saw his mother's beautiful face, heard his sister's laughter as if it were yesterday and nothing in ten years had ever changed. Kneeling, he cupped a tender bloom in his hands: a flower on a grave. A single yellow rose.

And the memories spilled over him.

The long ago nightmare began with a careless word, a moment of drunkenness shared between two friends.

The soldiers had come in the yellow haze of dawn. Men like Carlos, chasing legends of gold. And in less time than it took to scream, his mother was murdered over a handful of misspoken words and a generation of greed. Later, they would hang his father for treason. His mother was Spanish, and his father had spent the whole of his married life protecting her. He went to his grave knowing he'd failed her.

Yellow was the color of gold.

The treasure of Puerto Bello was a lesson in avarice. It was a time Brendan Drake had never discussed. The only treasure his father said he'd ever taken from Puerto Bello was marked on the map of that venture he'd given as a gift to his wife. He'd told Marcus that one day, he'd understand about what that treasure had meant to his life. He'd said some riches were more valuable even than gold.

But Marcus had been nineteen and filled with the omnipotence of youth, the romance of unconquered dreams. Nothing was more valuable than gold. Judas, he'd been a fool.

Yellow was the color of cowardice.

Too many times in his life since that fateful dawn, Marcus had cursed the devil who'd kept him alive when the soldiers came. But as much as he despised himself, he'd loved the brother who never let him give up fighting. . . .

Marcus suddenly stirred.

He lay with his eyes closed in thick straw, his cheek pillowed against his arm. Far away voices, muffled by the thick stone walls, alerted him and with consciousness came pain. His skull ached with the movement. Muscles burned where the iron manacles had torn into his flesh. Wounds festered on his injured back.

His eyes opened. The room smelled old with mildew and the faint remnant of death. A lone candle provided light. The walls were wet with algae, and the steady drip-drip of water engaged his ferocious thirst. Turning his head, he spied what looked like iron tombs placed against the walls. He'd seen this often in the dank catacombs beneath most churches he'd visited as a child.

Finding the direction of the voices, he peered into the darkness and watched the light grow outside the iron grill-work gate that separated this room from the passageway. Roaches scattered from a trencher of gruel someone must have brought him earlier. He moved his filthy hand to his neck. The golden cross was still there.

Marcus forced himself to stand. Purpose alone kept him on his feet. During the last two days as he'd labored with the decision to die, taunted by the memory of *Dark Fury* and a past he could no longer escape, his thirst for blood replaced ambivalence.

Now that same hate underscored the very fabric of his being. It had sought to destroy him. Then it became him.

Not even Liandra was spared his growing wrath as she continued to haunt his fevered dreams. She'd weakened him. Because of her, he'd gone noble in the first place. He'd struggled to understand the insanity that drove his actions to protect her and knew that whatever she'd awakened inside him, Carlos had effectively butchered with each inch of flesh he'd stripped from his back.

Marcus was glad for its demise. Never again would he be so weak.

Standing just this side of the iron gate, he steadied himself. Blood caked his face from a deep cut on his temple.

Still in quiet communion, as if conversing in secrecy, a Spaniard entered through the iron gate ahead of the others. Marcus was quick. Despite his injuries, instinct bred by years of constant fighting moved his hand over the hilt of the man's cutlass. A single burst of strength brought the sword to bear on the next poor fool who'd entered. Marcus's raspy breathing filled the stunned silence. His gaze lifted to the brown-robed figure standing in the doorway.

"A man of God." He grinned. "You're in your element, padre. But you're wasting your prayer beads on me. I'm still alive."

"No prayer is wasted, *hijo*, my son. Not even on an Englishman."

Marcus considered the padre. There was no fear in his dark eyes. He was tall for a Spaniard. His face bore a faint resemblance to Espinosa. But then in his state, all Spaniards looked the same.

"Come," Marcus beckoned, weaving the cutlass in a slow arc before the friar's eyes, "all of you. For your sakes one of you better have the keys to these shackles."

Two shorter men flanked the padre. The fire from the torch crackled in the silence. Marcus recognized Ramón from the ship. There was no animosity in the man's dark eyes, only a strange sense of purpose as he handed the torch to the other guard and entered to unshackle Marcus. The other man also belonged to the galleon. These weren't the normal guards he'd had while jailed at the fortress.

"What do you plan to do? Walk out of here?" the padre demanded.

"Aye. Then I'm going to pin Carlos to the wall and rip the little maggot's throat out."

"Men all over the city are hunting you."

Marcus nodded to the flask in the padre's hands. "What is that?"

"Fool's poison." Despite the sword pressed to his throat, the benevolent padre appeared amused. "Wine."

In no mood to listen to the sanctimonious poppycock, Marcus grabbed the flask. He could barely move, much less think coherently. His whole body burned.

The wine tasted warm and bitter. Still, he drank, desperately trying to assuage his thirst. Shifting his gaze over the padre, Marcus wiped his swollen mouth with the back of his tattered sleeve. The man's calmness alerted him that he was not reading the situation correctly. Marcus drank again, swished the wine in his mouth, and spat out the liquid.

"Who are you?" he asked.

The friar nodded to the filthy canvas sack the size of a man's body crumpled beside the straw. It was the same morbid contraption used to wrap the dead before they were buried. "We got you out of Triana, but getting you out of town will prove to be more difficult. Don Carlos has patrols along all of the roads."

"You broke me out?" He looked carefully at each man. The sword grew heavier in his hands. "Why?"

Ramón removed the manacles and stood. "Just as all Englishman are not *bastardos*, not all Spaniards lack honor, *señor*. You will discover that we are not so different in what we believe to be right. For me, I am indebted to you for sparing my life on the ship when you could have killed me for my cowardice. I left Doña Maria to perish in that storm," Ramón said. "And Miguel was my friend."

"What the hell are you talking about?"

The padre quietly said, "Miguel died trying to save you from the whip."

Jesu. The sword lowered and Marcus fell against the stone wall. Sweat beaded on his forehead. "I didn't know." He asked about the other men from the ship and discovered they were all imprisoned. His chest ached. Then he asked about the crew of *Dark Fury*.

"We do not know, *señor*," Ramón said. "We only know that they are not here in Puerto Bello."

"My brother was on that ship—" Dizziness assailed him. He pressed his palm to his skull. Lifting his furious gaze, he impaled the padre with it. "Jesu, you *did* poison the wine."

The padre's eyes were compassionate. "My niece believes in you, Captain Drake, but alas, you're still an Englishman and notoriously uncooperative in matters regarding your own life."

"Liandra? Keep her the hell away from this."

"You'd have more luck roping the wind, *mi hijo*. She's been very distressed worrying about you." The padre laughed a fatherly sound that told Marcus in more than words that this man would never allow Liandra to come to harm. "She'll be joining us at the mission."

His insides gave an odd twist. He couldn't say what was happening to him. He crumpled to his knees. Bathed in the torchlight, a coffin sat against the wall a short distance away.

"Miguel"—the friar crossed himself—"will not mind if he does not get home yet. We buried him in this churchyard. You will go to the mission in his place."

Marcus lifted his gaze. "Who are you?"

"A friend."

"Here? In Puerto Bello?"

"From what I've already seen, you have many friends."

Friends. The concept was as novel as snow. People used him for what they could get out of him; they didn't befriend him. Not in a world that coveted wealth over a man's life. He was suddenly afraid of his emotions. Where had this kind of loyalty sprung?

It was his last thought as they banged the coffin lid shut.

• • •

The hour was nearly midnight when Liandra's carriage finally rolled into the mission village. Warm winds sent clouds scuttling across the moon. Ramón flung open the door.

"Is he . . . safe?" she asked before descending. "Carlos's *soldados* are everywhere."

"They have already searched the village and the mission. The *capitán*, he did not come willingly, *señorita*. Friar Montero is with him now."

Liandra's skirts caught on the steps and, impatient to be near Marcus, she nearly fell face first out of the carriage. *¡Ay yi yi!* She would break her neck. She tightened the string on her reticule.

"See to Isabella, *por favor*. She is asleep."

Ramón's expression turned incredulous. "Doña Isabella? Here?"

"It's a long story, Ramón. I don't want her coming to my house. Uncle Montero will give her a room at the mission with the other sisters." Behind her, Pedro eased out of the carriage. She made quick introductions. Her horses stomped impatiently, and Liandra bid them a silent farewell as a sleepy young lad wearing a wide-brimmed strawhat gathered their reins. They would be safe at the stables.

"Where is my grandson?" Pedro asked Ramón as she hurried off.

Thunder grumbled overhead and Liandra lifted her black veil to search out the sky. The air smelled of rain. She tore the black veil away, slowing only briefly as she reached her house near the southern edge of the small mission town.

The small two-story whitewashed structure marked the edge of the mangrove forest. Passionflower vines covered the front porch overhang and, untended during her absence, scurried along the red-tiled rooftop over the second-floor verandah.

This was her small piece of paradise: her real home

since Grandmama had died and left it to her. She closed her eyes.

Nothing bad could happen here.

Her hand braced on the door, Liandra suddenly turned to look down the long empty street toward the pale pink, shuttered structure overlooking the oval plaza where Pedro stood talking to Ramón. A shadow lingered in the top-floor window, watching. Lightning filled the sky and the wind rushed through the trees behind her house. The small flowerpots hanging from her roof creaked in the wind.

Liandra swung open the door and ran inside. Her house was in a shambles. She gasped. Friar Montero came from the other room. Light from a single pewter lamp framed him in the doorway. He was not as tall as she was. Gray feathered his once thick black hair. To her, he'd always been much larger than life. No mere mortal to suffer the ravages of time. Tears filling her eyes, Liandra ran to him and fell into his opened arms.

"I could not spare your small home from Carlos's men," he said.

"They did not find him . . ." She could not finish the words.

"Did you doubt I would keep him safe?" he admonished. "I had him at the cemetery while the *soldados* went through the village. Your Englishman is alive. Though not so happy to be in the debt of a Spaniard, I think."

"I will never be able to pay you back for what you have done."

Wiping her tears, Liandra stepped past him into Grandmama's old room. Surrounded by yards of mosquito netting, a mahogany bedstead filled the center of the room.

With a cry, she flew to Marcus's side. He lay on his stomach, a sheet entangled around his narrow hips, one arm flung to the side, the other hanging slightly off the bed. The light sculpted his powerful muscles where deep wounds gouged his flesh. Bathed, with his hair washed and combed off his face, his chiseled profile looked pale in the amber light.

Shoving aside the netting, she knelt and touched his hand. Fever cooked his body. "Carlos will burn in hell for this."

"Maria Liandra!"

She whirled on her uncle. Yanking her gloves off, she tossed them onto the yellow threadbare chair beside the nightstand. Rain furiously drummed on the tiled roof, drowning out her heartbeat and every unholy thought that crippled her restraint.

"Isabella came with me," she said. "Something is wrong with her. She hasn't clung to me in a long time. Not since she was a child and used to crawl into my lap to wait for the storms to pass."

"You were hardly more than a child yourself, then."

"*Tía* Innes is not back from Spain. Isabella is afraid of her father." Liandra opened her reticule and, dumping the contents onto a nearby desk, she went to work. "*Sí*, I am afraid of Carlos, too. I am glad he does not come here. I don't know how Gabriel can abide him."

Hurrying into the main room, she went to the small glass hutch where she kept her medicinal supplies.

"With your brother gone, you must never be alone with Carlos."

Her hands paused. "You know that Gabriel left?"

"Gabriel took Christina away this time," he said. "I am sorry."

Liandra couldn't bear to confront her fragile emotions on that subject. Not now. "I will visit her in Spain one day."

She pulled her gaze back and, wiping a hand across her cheek, fumbled in the cabinet. Nothing looked the same. Everything jumbled in her head when she was upset. Flustered, she squeezed her eyes shut. Friar Montero touched her arm.

"Breathe, Maria. Or I will be picking you up off the

floor as well." He handed her two bottles, a bowl, and a spoon from the shelves.

With her precious bundle clutched tightly to her chest, she lifted her chin. "Thank you. . . ."

"Maria." His kindly brown eyes touched hers. "If your Englishman lives, he will not stay. You know that, don't you?"

Her eyes fell to her hands and the small bowl she clasped. Deep inside she knew there could never be a union between her and an English pirate. There was no utopia safe enough to hold the world at bay.

"He is alone now. He needs me."

Uncle Montero started to say something; then his expression softened. "Go"—he nodded toward Marcus—"make your Englishman well."

Numbly, Liandra turned into the bedroom. The rain still pebbled against the roof. Kneeling beside Marcus, she lined her medicines along the nightstand beside the lamp. Carefully, through her tears, she fed him syrup that she'd made from the bark of the cinchona tree.

Marcus stirred. His eyes slid open.

"This will lower your fever," she softly whispered.

Confusion etched his face. He touched the tears on her face. His callused hand lingered with infinite gentleness before his eyes closed. Something glinted around his neck. With delicate fingers, Liandra followed the chain to discover a cross.

Her necklace! She'd thought it forever lost during the storm.

"Thirsty . . ." he rasped.

Friar Montero brought a ladle of water and Liandra helped Marcus drink. Mumbling something incoherent, he again succumbed to his feverish tossing. Liandra couldn't move as she stared down at him.

Her heart beat faster. He wore her necklace.

Why?

Later, she washed his face and shoulders with cool water.

He'd been whipped before. Formidable scars branded his back. Scars that bespoke a life of violence and turpitude, befitting an English pirate, marking his soul as surely as they marked his flesh.

What had happened in his life to make him turn from everything he knew? Remembering Pedro's words, she stilled.

What if Marcus *was* to blame for his ill-fated path in life? She touched his left hand, and he stirred.

His hand was large and strong, capable of taking a life.

And just as capable of tenderness. Could two such opposing forces survive without killing the man?

Liandra cradled his fingers against her cheek. He was her husband. She tried not to cry, but her overpowering fear for him consumed her and she quietly sobbed her grief into the bedding. She didn't know when her uncle finally left, or when Pedro entered to take his place. She'd fallen asleep with her head resting on the bed. When she looked up again it was dawn, and Pedro was standing at the end of the bed.

They worked through the next two days to stave off Marcus's fever. She fed him soup that she'd made and cold liquids freshly chilled from the nearby lake. The rain grew heavier and kept visitors at bay. Liandra attended afternoon mass and left a candle on the altar for her Englishman. Her husband, though she had yet to think of him as that. She prayed that Carlos's soldiers would not come again. She didn't visit her mother. Nor did she see Isabella.

By the fourth evening, Marcus became delirious, his strong body ravaged by fever. She cut dead skin away from the wounds. In the cooking house outside, she boiled the stained rags. It was the only way she'd ever learned to rid the rags of the smell of infection.

Liandra finally removed her traveling dress and changed into a clean chemise and cotton floral dress. Sprigs of violets matched the curtains and, in a moment of madness, she laughed at the absurdity of wearing window hangings. It had seemed so logical last winter, when she'd bought the cloth, to use every inch of the precious commodity. She was always so practical.

Liandra was beginning to hate practical.

Exhaustion poured through her muscles and she crumpled to her knees beside the bed. Her fingers ached with the meticulous effort it took to clean Marcus's wounds. She finally fell asleep, awakening when Pedro brought her hot soup.

"You must keep up your strength, *señorita*."

She sipped the soup and grimaced.

"*Sí*, it tastes awful," he agreed. "I cannot cook."

Smiling, she drank the bowl and licked the lentils from the rim. "You are not like other servants, Pedro."

"I think, I am not like anyone you know, *señorita*. Go upstairs to your own room and sleep. I will stay with him."

"No. I cannot leave."

He watched her with watery eyes, as if he too knew that she loved this man, and it would end in naught but heartache.

It didn't matter.

She wiped the tangled hair out of her face. Nothing would change her deep down desperation to heal him. Her vow to him gave him his freedom, and it mattered little that he was an Englishman, a pirate, or even a Drake; she would keep that promise.

"You will not die," she told Marcus the seventh night.

The laudanum bottle was nearly empty. She knelt beside the bed. Spooning another dose, her hands shook.

Marcus's palm moved slightly over her arm. She dropped her gaze to find him watching her. Her breath froze. Dark lashes framed the liquid brilliance in his silver eyes as he stared at her. Two weeks' growth of beard only emphasized his rakish, attractive looks, and her heartbeat raced seeking that now-elusive port that was his mind.

His hand tightened around her wrist. "No more," he rasped, shaking the spoon from her grip.

"Marcus—"

"No more opium. Or you *will* kill me."

His lucid eyes held her gaze suspended.

She dared not move. She didn't breathe. He eased his hand over her pale shoulder, edging aside the wrapper. Her breasts strained against her chemise. His eyes slid lower over her body then closed.

"Where am I?"

"Valle de Angeles. The mission village."

"Valley of Angels. . . ." His mouth crooked in self-contempt. When he opened his eyes again, they were nearly black. "Then I must not be dead. No God would send me to heaven."

His fatalism frightened her. "You're in my house."

"Alone?" he rasped.

Liandra stood. Her heart began to pound in earnest. She didn't answer as she considered Pedro asleep in the parlor and what the older man could do if Marcus decided to become violent.

Acting on her thought, Marcus suddenly moved. Wearing only the single gold cross around his throat, he rolled to his knees like some mythical phoenix. The sheet fell away from his hips. Liandra's startled gaze snapped to the manly juncture between his thighs. Heat soared into her face. Pedro had handled all Marcus's personal ablutions. Her eyes shot up the length of his muscled torso and slammed into the full threat of his eyes.

"What are you doing?" she demanded.

In one swift movement, surely born of instinct and no more, for his injuries were much, he wrapped strong fingers around her throat and pulled her onto the bed beneath him. "I asked if you're alone?"

Liandra couldn't breathe. Braced against his strength, she looked helplessly into his eyes, her movement marked by the tiny flutter of panic that healing Marcus was akin to letting a lion loose among a flock of sheep here in this valley. He did not have a fondness for her people. Not even for her.

She clawed at his fingers. "You'll tear your woun—"

"Answer me." Eyes wide, she nodded. He lent his full attention to her breasts. "You take too much for granted, *gata*."

"Stop it!" She shoved against his shoulders.

His grip lessened. Liandra flew from the bed. She spun around, prepared to thrust a fist toward him, her only weapon, if he made one move in her direction. "I am not afraid of you, Marcus Drake."

Watching her pitiful show of force, Marcus laughed softly. A laugh that didn't reach his frigid eyes as he studied her disheveled form. The realization that she could not hold him if he chose to leave underscored the need to retain control of her panic.

"Where is your brother?" he asked.

"Gone."

"With the *Dark Fury*?"

"No." He seemed to want for no explanation and trusted that she told the truth. "You are safe," she whispered.

Strength spent, he collapsed back against the pillow. Thick hair fell over his temple as he turned his head to look at her. "How long . . . have I been unconscious?"

"Eight days. You are still very ill, Marcus."

"Am I a prisoner?"

"Are you in chains?" she countered.

He tried to bend his neck to glimpse his surroundings. Pain seemed to shoot through his skull. He flinched.

"You must let the healing poultice on your back work."

The lone pewter lamp flickered on the table beside the bed. Outside the shuttered windows, it was dark. A breeze pulled at the lavender curtains and filled the room with the smell of cooking fires. Soon it would be dawn.

Marcus touched her with his gaze. She wondered if he saw her as his wife or a mistake he'd made. "You're a fool to be here with me."

He *was* dangerous.

Even now, she felt his power. It filled the room and surrounded her until she could barely breathe. Like a moth, she moved closer to the flame. She could burn for eternity and not feel the pain.

She slid her gaze across his torso, barely covered by the modest sheet. Watching her, his eyes grew wary, and her mouth lifted in a grin. As far as she was concerned, he deserved her shameless gawking.

Plunking her fists on her hips, she tossed her head. "We are no longer on the ship, Englishman. Here, *I* am the *capitán*. And if you try and get out of bed again, I will tie you to the posts."

His mouth cocked into a grin, a blatant challenge to try. Clearly, he didn't know whom he was dealing with. Her mood grew bolder. "And this time, I do not need fishing lessons to finish what we start, pirate."

Chapter Twelve

Fishing lessons.

Hell. He'd be ancient and decrepit before he ever picked up a pole in Liandra's presence again.

Drifting in and out of another restless night, Marcus kicked at the clammy sheets that wrapped his hips and thighs, but could not dislodge their grasp on his flesh. The opened window near the bed allowed more than the fragrant breeze to enter. Outside, birds chattered. Grinding his teeth, he shoved a pillow over his head.

Liandra had at one time built some absurd birdhouse out back. A red-gabled roof and blue trim brightened the yellow monstrosity. Birds by the droves nested in the lap of luxury while he was forced to endure their ungodly racket.

A rustling movement alerted him and at once Marcus came awake. He didn't move, not even to push the hair out of his eyes.

Liandra was tidying the room again. He noticed that about her. Something he hadn't seen when they were on the ship. Everything had its place, including her implacable patience with him.

She turned and caught him staring. "Good morning." She smiled.

Annoyed with her cheer, Marcus frowned. He'd done nothing but sleep and eat for the last two weeks—fourteen days of misery trapped in the same house with this blue-eyed ptarmigan amidst lavender ruffles, bright enduring sunshine, and carnal urges enough to drive a snake to molt.

She was his wife.

Wife!

Shivers rippled all over him. Surely she was rational enough to recognize that he couldn't stay married to her.

"Why hasn't Carlos searched this place?" he asked.

His voice pulled her closer. "His men have already been through here. And a week ago, not too far from the church where Uncle Montero took you, Carlos recovered a body dressed in your old clothes. He thinks you are dead."

Marcus considered this and frowned. "Who was the body?"

"He was a man imprisoned as you were. Uncle Montero used his death to get you out of Triana."

Marcus recalled the canvas bag that night in the crypt. Then he thought of Miguel. Two men had died to give him life.

"Carlos buys that ancient ruse?"

"I don't know." She nervously stroked the sheet. Marcus followed the slim fingers. "The roads are all flooded. No one can get in or out of the village. Some families on lower ground have had to seek shelter here at the mission. Even if he wanted to, Carlos can't get through at the moment."

"If he wanted to? What's that supposed to mean?"

"Carlos has only set foot here once."

"Why?" He laughed. "Is this holy ground or something?"

"Marcus Drake!" Her eyes flashed a brilliant blue. "You should take these things more seriously."

Her passion surprised him. But then Liandra was passionate about the act of breathing and walking. She lived daily to save souls, especially unworthy ones. He lay back against his pillow, exhausted. "You should have taken care to save my crew, instead."

"First, I will save you, Marcus Drake."

Her quiet conviction tightened his chest. "That, *gata*, will never happen." And he meant it.

She didn't know him.

Liandra sat on the edge of the mattress, her luminous gaze alighting on his. "Your fever is down," she pronounced.

When he didn't reply, she leaned forward to brush the hair off his face, her movement nearly pushing the curves of her creamy breasts past the physical endurance of her bodice. Jesu.

Oblivious to his torment, she rambled on about fevers and herbs, and stuff he didn't give a frog's ass about. She smelled of talcum and starch. Her hair was washed and braided in one of her prissy coronets. She'd stuffed little red flowers in her hair. She looked like a happy poppy for Chrissakes.

With a groan, he clamped a hand around her slender wrist. "I want some clothes, Liandra."

"*Si*, we are working on that." She reached for a shaving mug and bristle brush and immediately went to work lathering the soap.

"What are you doing?"

"You need a shave." She smiled with perfect equanimity. "You must be terribly uncomfortable in this heat."

He took the appliances from her hand and firmly set them down on the nightstand. Her meticulous row of little green medicine bottles rattled. "I can shave myself, Liandra."

"Very well," she said, then reached for a comb. He snatched it from her hand.

Her blue eyes settled on him. "I am sorry bed rest does not suit you, but I told you yesterday this is the way it has to be for now."

"Is the *Dark Fury* still in Puerto Bello?"

The abrupt change of subject startled her. Surely, she
lived in fairyland subsisting on amnesia to forget why he
was here in the first place. Unbidden images swirled in his
foggy thoughts. He thought of his brother, ashamed that
while he'd been romancing Espinosa's sister, El Condor
had found retribution in Talon's demise.

"I want you to find out what happened to my crew,
Liandra."

"I will try."

"Don't try. I want to know."

His anger hurt her. Marcus knew he was acting boorish
and ignoble and all manner of other disreputable names he
called himself. He claimed them all under a flag of war.
She was the enemy. He didn't want to see pretty flowers in
her hair or that sparkle in her eyes he recognized as the
first throes of unrequited love.

He didn't want to be married to her.

She stood between him and escape.

Not in the physical sense, he'd realized long ago. He
could easily overpower both her and Pedro with his thumb.
Her threat to him ran far deeper—all the way to the core of
his being. He battled more than illness, more than emotions. He battled his heart.

And it was a fight for his life.

When he left here, he intended to sail out on the *Dark
Fury* and blow Carlos's defenses to hell. And if the bastard
died with his city, all the better. It would save him from
coming back later to finish the job. But it was Gabriel Espinosa Marcus aimed to destroy. His very escape would
make a mockery of Spain and her mighty hero. Then Marcus would hunt down Espinosa and make him pay for what
he had done to Talon.

"Uncle Montero." Liandra closed the rectory door behind
her. Palms braced against the solid oak, she gripped her
nerves. The room smelled of soft leather and ink. Volumes
of books lined every wall on great mahogany shelves. A

lone lamp sputtered light over the desk. Her uncle looked up from behind a pile of thick leather-bound books. Upon seeing her, he smiled.

"You're back from Puerto Bello," she said. "Did you see Carlos?"

Her uncle snorted. "His temper has not improved. At least he has temporarily disbanded his search for the Englishman."

Movement startled her. She hadn't seen Pedro at first. He lifted his head from behind the same pile of books. He and Uncle Montero were sketching a diagram.

"You are working on plans for the mill?" she asked timidly, aware that she'd interrupted something important.

"*Si.*" Her uncle folded his hands on the desk. "As poorly drawn as they are. But that is not why you are here."

"I will leave." Pedro stood.

"No." Liandra stepped forward. "That's not necessary. Please stay." Twisting her hands, she hurried across the forest green rug. The carpet muffled her slippers. She sat in a stiff, comfortless, oaken chair better suited for the Inquisition than the homey comfort of this room. "You have not been by to visit today," she told the elderly man.

Pedro grinned. "I think that you are a braver physician than I."

She was not brave at all.

"Uncle," she spread her skirts, "did you find out where Carlos imprisoned the crew that sailed with Marcus?"

"I know." Crossing his arms, he sat back and sighed. "It will take a king's ransom to buy back their lives from the labor fields where Carlos sent them."

"Marcus will not understand. I fear he is so angry."

"You must have patience, Maria. It is not easy to survive the lash. And he has done so with courage."

Marcus *was* fortunate to be alive and she thanked Providence for his strength. "Uncle . . . a few weeks ago you told me that it was time to put ghosts to rest. Tell me what you meant."

"You are in love with the Englishman."

"I love him so much, my heart breaks, Uncle Montero," she whispered past the tightness in her throat. "He is alone. He needs me whether he sees this or not. I am his family, now."

"You wish to convince him to stay?"

"I do not know. I only know that I must find a way to mend the rift with Gabriel. Gabriel can help him."

"And you think the Englishman will take your brother's help? After everything that has happened between them?"

She cast her gaze from his probing one. "It is his only chance against Carlos."

"Ah, *mi sobrina*." Her uncle shook his head. The hood of his brown woolen robe fell back against his shoulders. "There is so much to say, I do not know where to start. Your Englishman, he has much to hate Gabriel for. If this is about Gabriel . . . you cannot mend the rift. Your brother is a proud man, Maria. It will take more than your want to heal his heart."

"But he hates Marcus. Marcus did nothing to him."

"In a sense that is true."

"Then tell me, Uncle Montero. What happened? I have to understand . . . I have to know what made my brother the way he is."

He sighed in frustration. "This is very complicated . . ."

"I know that long ago Marcus's mother was engaged to our father. Is that why his father killed ours during the raid on Puerto Bello?"

"No."

"Was it for treasure like everyone says?"

"Who is to say that there was ever any treasure. At least not in the way Don Carlos thinks."

"Then what?" she whispered. "You must tell me."

"Brendan Drake was a good man," her uncle quietly replied. "Your Marcus looks very much like him. The resemblance is striking."

"You knew Marcus's father? Personally?"

"*Sí*. I married him to Mary Francis. She was your

mother's best friend and she stood up for the couple as their witness." His gaze drifted. "Brendan had been brought here as a captive. He was wounded in an escape attempt, and Mary found him. She nursed him. They fell in love. But it was ill-fated from the beginning. She was engaged to another very powerful man."

"But . . . she married her Englishman anyway."

"Her family disinherited her. The Church excommunicated her."

"She gave up everything."

"It is because of that kind of love that I married them at a small church in Puerto Bello. Fourteen years later Brendan came back here with the pirate, Morgan. The English butchered our countrymen from here to Panama. Morgan put out the word to gather up all the townsfolk. He wanted gold, and he didn't care how he got it. His men killed our women and children." His voice faltered.

Liandra's heart hit her ribs. She'd heard the story of her mother's incredible courage during that raid. Henry Morgan had ordered her placed in a vat of gunpowder and tortured for the whereabouts of any gold her family had concealed away. She'd heard other things as well. Liandra herself was born nine and a half months after that raid.

"Brendan saved your mother. He'd tried to help others. He took her to safety. And that's when Gabriel's father found them. A fight ensued. Carlos could have stopped it but didn't. We could do nothing. Gabriel watched his father die. He'd already . . . endured more than any child should at the hands of Morgan's men."

Liandra sensed the unspoken horror of what her uncle left unsaid. The undercurrent shivered over her.

"The death of his father was like the death of your brother's soul. He would never be the same again. None of us would."

Frair Montero would tell her no more.

"Surely twenty-three years is long enough to forget," she rasped.

"I am sorry, *mi sobrina*. Without faith, forever is not long enough to forget."

Hot tears burned behind her eyelids. How did a man replace an angry heart with faith? She knew Marcus remained scarred, too.

Drawing in a ragged breath, she shifted her gaze to Pedro and changed the subject. "I visited with Alejandro yesterday," she said. "I hardly even recognize him."

Pedro laughed. "He is growing fat. I think he will not want to leave this place."

"Are you leaving?"

He looked around the room and his shoulders lifted in a sigh. "Like the *capitán*, I, too, do not belong here."

Liandra stood. "*Sí*. Sooner or later everyone leaves . . ."

"Know that I am doing all I can to help your Englishman. But it takes time," Pedro said.

"You cannot help." She gathered her skirts and whirled to the door. "Not unless you have connections to the king of Spain himself."

Liandra stared at the solid-oaken portal of her mother's residence. She'd been driven here by some internal need she could not name. Her fists clenched but it was more an act of cowardice than anger that kept her immobile. Voices carried up the stone staircase from the village square below. Her mother lived on the second floor of the sandstone quarters built just outside the main gate of the mission. The church had first been erected here almost thirty years ago. The village had grown up around the mission and thrived in these hills away from the politics and disease that plagued Puerto Bello.

Warm sunlight behind Liandra cast her lone shadow on the door. Festive clay pots of red geraniums splashed bright color up and down the stairway and along the porch where she stood. She'd come here often with Grandmama and the memory lifted her courage.

Heart pounding, she started to knock. The courtesy was

merely habit. There was something inherently rude about invading a person's privacy. And no matter the years, Liandra always felt like an invader.

"Maria!"

Isabella's voice made Liandra flinch. Gripping her heavy skirts, her cousin hurried up the narrow, stone staircase. She wore a pale blue gown devoid of lace and the feminine frippery that usually adorned her fancy clothes. "Maria, you haven't returned any of my messages." Winded, she showed to catch her breath. "That dreadful Pedro person would not let me see you."

Liandra carried a canvas bag filled with fresh flowers, bread, and her mother's favorite fruit. She'd shopped at the marketplace just before arriving here. The bag suddenly seemed too heavy. "I've been ill, Isabella."

"*Si,* you have." Her cousin sniffed, offended by the obvious lie. "The whole village speaks of the English pirate's escape from Triana. And I know you well enough to suspect that you are protecting him."

Liandra gripped Isabella's arm. "You will watch your tongue. Do you understand? Uncle Montero has risked his life."

Tears filled her cousin's brown eyes. "You do not trust me."

"Of course I don't trust you."

Clasping her hands, Isabella lowered her lashes. "Friar Montero said I should be patient with you." Her voice lowered. "I'll tell you, Maria, all the young girls are positively swooning for a chance to glimpse the pirate's face."

Liandra's heart lurched at the miserable thought of sharing Marcus with other women. And that he might be amiable to such attention. "They are just silly girls. They don't even know him."

"Some of the men who were on the galleon have families here. They all knew and loved Miguel. They hate my father more than they fear your English *capitán.* How long do you think you can keep him a secret?"

"Why are you here, Isabella? At the mission, I mean. You don't even like me."

"I told you." She scraped a slipper against the clay pots of geraniums. "I didn't know where else to go."

"Your father scares you so much?"

"Just today Friar Montero arrived back from Puerto Bello. He visited Papa."

"*Sí*, Uncle Montero is still searching for someone to build a mill that will crush the sugar cane." Liandra didn't tell her he'd been seeking information about Marcus's men.

Isabella sniffed. "Papa didn't even know I was gone. He has been so obsessed with finding the Englishman that I have been gone three weeks and he did not even know. Mama is still in Spain."

For the first time in many years, Liandra began to feel some compassion toward her cousin. Friar Montero had said she was adjusting slowly to her small room at the mission.

A moment's guilt passed as she reconsidered asking Isabella to stay with her at the house, then quickly regained her senses.

"I'm sorry, Isabella."

"Don't be. Papa wasn't going to hang the Englishman at Triana, Maria. You don't want to know what he'd planned. It is too . . . horrible." Isabella lifted her chin. "I'm glad your pirate escaped. So will you tell me how he is?"

Liandra brushed lint from her yellow skirts. Her hands trembled. "He's recovering," she managed to sound positive. "In a few more days he will not be so weak."

Isabella looked at the oaken door. "I have been here every day to visit your mother." She flung open the door, leaving Liandra numbly standing on the threshold. "Come inside," Isabella softly encouraged.

Dressed in a black gown, her mother sat on a slatted, high-back rocker staring out the verandah doors. Black lace decorated the thin waterfall of silver curls that flowed down her back. Her balcony overlooked the busy square. Past the village rooftops, verdant fields of sugar cane shimmered in the breeze. A thunderstorm darkened the distant mountains purple.

Liandra walked into the richly furnished room, her slippered feet making no sound on the floral carpet. Tiny blue veins were visible beneath her mother's skin. She looked old and so much more fragile than when Grandmama was alive.

"Hello, Mama." Liandra kissed her cheek.

The floor creaked with the methodical rocking as her mother continued to stare out the doors. "*Doña* Estella," Isabella greeted with a perky peck to the cheek. "Look what Maria has brought."

Liandra stared at her mother, then started when Isabella nudged her. "Mangoes." Liandra stepped forward. "They are your favorite."

Her mother's gaze lifted. Deep violet eyes flickered. "Bananas are my favorite, Maria. Isn't that right, Bella?" She reached out to take Isabella's hand. "You look lovely today, dear. Bella has come to live here at the mission, Maria."

Ignoring the sudden tightness in her chest, Liandra looked through her bag and pulled out the few items she had purchased from the market. Last year her mother hated bananas. Looking at Isabella, she dropped her gaze to her mother's hand then looked away. "I know."

Until recently, her mother had seen Isabella twice in her life and didn't recognize her as her niece. But then her mother hated Carlos with a savage passion, so wisdom bid Liandra not to remind her.

Setting her bag down on the rosewood sideboard, Liandra glanced around the room. Thanks to Gabriel's generosity, the appointments were as rich as those that belonged to the queen. A silver lamp and a gold-bound book sat on a cluttered stand near the rocker. Gauzy blue curtains draped the windows. Fancy tapestry covered the chairs and sofa. Her mother's bedroom connected to this room.

"Where are the servants I hired for you, Mama?"

Her mother waved a ringed hand. "I dismissed them. I have found someone from the village who will let me do as I please. I am not a criminal to be locked up, despite what you and my son think."

"We only care about your welfare."

"Why have you waited so long to see me, Maria?" her mother asked without turning. "Where is Gabriel? And little Christina? I have missed them so terribly."

"Have you been to the stables, Mama?"

She waved a hand. "Nobody here knows anything about horses." Her mother gazed up at Isabella. "I have tried to tell them, but they will not listen. When I was a girl, we had the most magnificent horses. No one in all of Spain could rival my father's stables . . ."

She rambled on and on, as she usually did, for over an hour, reliving the past. Liandra had heard the incoherent string of stories many times, but she listened anyway, tidying her mother's small compartments as she did so. She sliced up the fruit she had purchased at the market, and together they all shared lunch.

As Liandra listened to her mother's voice, she wondered if there had ever been a time when they were close. Perhaps it was when Liandra had been a baby. She couldn't remember her mother's touch.

"You have not angered your brother again, have you?" her mother chided, snapping Liandra out of her reverie. "She was always such a difficult child, Bella. *Dios.*" Her eyes drifted closed.

With a sick stomach, Liandra recognized the dreadful signs of her mother's incapacitating headaches when they appeared. She stood.

"Rub my temples, Bella. You do such a good job, child."

"*Sí, Doña* Estella," Isabella whispered, her gaze seeking out Liandra's in sudden apology.

As a child, Liandra had listened helplessly to her mother's tears, rubbing her mother's head until her fingers ached. But she could do naught to ease the pain, and to a child who so wanted love, or that precious glimpse of a mother's smile, that was everything.

"Read to me, Maria," her mother's rasp arrested her gaze. "I would hear your voice, child."

Liandra's hand slithered into a clench. Voices from the village square mumbled like the low sound of thunder in her ears. Grandmama had always done the reading for her. Liandra had sat curled beside her and listened to the wonderful stories her voice brought to life. Something Liandra would never be able to do.

With a heavy heart, she lifted the book from the stand beside the rocker. The gilded pages were beautiful, with flowery script and yellow roses drawn at the bottom of each page. Shame filled her as she stared numbly at the first page.

Isabella touched her arm. "I would be honored to read, if you don't mind?"

Liandra's grateful gaze held her cousins'.

"Thank you," she finally murmured. Isabella smiled as Liandra handed over the book. And from the bleakness in Liandra's heart, a sense of camaraderie was born.

Chapter Thirteen

Standing before the mirror, Liandra rearranged the flow-ers in her hair. She wore a simple, bright blue, forget-me-nots silk dress. No matter what she did to her appearance, Marcus didn't notice anyway. And today she didn't care. A scented bath had aided in her mood, and she felt delicious.

A breeze swept through her opened verandah doors and touched the mosquito netting that draped her bed. The house smelled of beeswax. She'd methodically scrubbed the walls and floors in her house, polished the furniture, and washed clothes. Not a dust ball or spider web re-mained when she'd finished.

With a final glance at her room, Liandra took in the faded lace pillows and counterpane that Grandmama had made when Liandra was six. Everything from the wardrobe to the wash stand was in its place.

Her slippers made no sound on the stairs. In the parlor, she heard Pedro and her uncle Montero conversing.

"You don't know how to read this thing," Pedro said.

Her uncle's reply grew surly. He and Pedro had battled constantly in one form of contest or another since she'd in-troduced them. Last night they'd fussed over a game of cribbage. Before that, it had been chess. They leaned over the dining table, a sketch spread between them. Her uncle bent forward on his palms. His long brown robe brushed the floor.

"Turn it right side up and it would make more sense."

Pedro switched the diagram back. "You make this too difficult, Friar. If you build this your way, the mill will be upside down."

"*Buenos días*," Liandra interrupted from the doorway.

They both turned at her greeting. "*Señorita*, I hope your uncle did not awaken you with his yelling."

"Pah!" her uncle snorted, offended by the accusation.

Liandra glanced at Marcus's room. The door was closed.

"Your Englishman had a restless night," her uncle replied. "We thought it best that you both slept."

"I did the cooking today, *señorita*," Pedro said. "I was just on my way to bring the *señor* lunch." With a superior glance at her uncle, he left the room.

"*Sí*, and you cannot cook," Friar Montero called after him. After Pedro left, he chuckled. "He thinks he has made mutton stew."

"You are like two lion cubs, Uncle."

He sniffed. "When he beats me at chess, he has the audacity to laugh."

"Only because you bragged to everyone at the mission that no one can beat you. *Sí*, Isabella told me yesterday how you boast."

"Ah, *mi sobrina*, she told me that you visited your mother."

Liandra toyed with the loose edging on her sleeve. "Gabriel should not have left before seeing her."

"Your brother may strike fear in the hearts of his enemies, but he lacks your strength. He would rather not see her than face what she has become."

"These are the plans for the mill?" Liandra asked putting an end to the subject. Staring down at the large parchment, she studied the scratches. The lines made no sense to her—no matter the direction of the vellum.

They talked about the sugarcane fields, and soon Pedro appeared, carrying a wicker tray, topped with a steaming bowl of soup, bread, and a glass of goat milk.

Her uncle rolled up the diagram. "If we are to make our sugarcane profitable, we must begin this project soon. Our first harvest is in two months. I brought this diagram here hoping Pedro might know something of this planting business."

Liandra spared Pedro a surprised glance. "You know about mills?"

"Clearly, he does not," her uncle rebuked.

Smiling at the both of them, Liandra took the tray. "I'll bring this to Marcus."

Her uncle caught her sleeve. "Your pirate has had a difficult time. Be patient."

"Please, Uncle, he is not *my* pirate. And I am always patient."

Perching the tray on her hip, she opened the door.

Marcus was asleep. The room was a mess, the windows closed. Blankets had been draped over the curtains to keep out light and sound. At once, Liandra stripped the horrid things from the wall and threw open the windows. Birdsong greeted her, and she smiled on a big inhale. She loved the sound of life.

A pile of clothes had been laid out at the end of the bed. She recognized Gabriel's black breeches, white shirts, and a pair of boots. Uncle Montero must have brought them back from Puerto Bello.

When she again looked at Marcus, her pulse leapt. He was glaring at her from beneath a rebellious wave of black hair. A dark growth of beard lent a thrilling edge of danger to his silence. With one look, he still had the power to turn her knees to powder, even if that look did test her confidence.

"Do you know how long it took me to get those blankets to stay?"

"You need fresh air, Marcus. And the sun is out."

"A full broadside with forty cannons makes less noise than what's outside that window."

Scooting aside the tray, she sat next to him on the bed. "Grandmama loved birds," she announced, leaning over to test his forehead for fever. He pulled away and refused to let her touch him. Sitting back, she folded her hands in her lap. "I helped her build that birdhouse. It needs to be repainted, don't you think?"

"It needs to be chopped down. The thing's a bloody nuisance."

"It's pretty," she said stubbornly, wiping at a spot of liquid where the soup had spilled. "You just don't see the colors, Marcus. Or you would notice the beauty of things around you—"

"Liandra," his quiet voice lifted her chin. "I appreciate what you have done for me here."

"I am not after your gratitude."

"Then what do you want?"

She stood, wounded that he could not see her heart, that he did not feel the same toward her. Neither she nor Marcus had broached the subject of their marriage and an attack of pride prevented her from doing so now. "I have done naught but keep my word to you, Englishman. You are free to leave anytime you choose."

He was thinking she'd capitulated too easily, perhaps. Or that her offended pride would rebel. But he didn't know her at all if he thought his leaving could make her stop loving him. 'Twould be like telling the sun to go away or the moon not to shine.

"Where have you been the past few days?" he suddenly asked.

"I do have a life here."

When he realized she wasn't going to add any depth to the explanation, he grew silent. Averting her attention to the tray, she retrieved the bowl of soup. Marcus's hand joined hers.

"I can feed myself," he gently reminded her, easing the

bowl out of her uncertain hands. Without removing his gaze from hers, he sipped.

"Jesu!" Spewing the contents back into the bowl, he glared at the soup in horror. "This tastes like horseshit."

"Marcus Drake!" The leash Liandra had managed to keep on her temper these past weeks snapped. "You eat all of that soup. And quit being such an infant. Pedro made it. You'll hurt his feelings."

"Get it away," he gagged, "before I puke."

"*¡Ay yi yi!*" She slammed the bowl on the tray. "And maybe the bread will also make you puke, *si*?" Marcus barely dodged the missile. Her cheeks blushed furiously. Her eyes looked like streaks of blue fire, and he stared in awe at her magnificent wrath.

"Or maybe this milk, hmmm?" She held the glass aloft, wobbling it threateningly. "Perhaps it is not chilled enough for your royal palate. Tell me, Marcus Drake? Is there nothing any of us poor Spaniards can do right?"

With that, she upended the milk over his head.

Whirling away, she walked toward the door. She wore no petticoats. Leaning slightly to better glimpse her furious flight, Marcus found refuge in the sway of her skirts and the shapely bottom beneath before he caught himself and frowned.

"Where are you going?"

"Fishing!"

Milk dripping from his hair and eyelashes, his dignity sorely battered, Marcus could only glower as Liandra slammed the door and left him to his own rancid bent.

The evening sky had barely breathed a cool sigh of relief when Liandra washed and undressed for bed. She'd spent the last few afternoons with Alejandro at the pond, and tonight she had attended supper with Isabella. Anything to take her out of this house.

Outside a man's raspy growl pulled her chin around. Alarmed, she threw back the lavender counterpane and padded across her floor to the verandah. Marcus stood below her in the grass, stretching, bending, and lunging. She pulled into the shadow of a hanging vine.

Purple twilight whispered through the blanket of leaves overhead touching the chiseled ridges of muscle that framed his arms and chest. A sleek mist dampened his body. *Mi cielos.* Heavens. She swallowed, stretching onto her toes a little more to peer over the verandah rail. He wore naught but a flimsy pair of canvas breeches. His chest was bare and flecked lightly with dark hair. The golden cross at his neck flashed in the fading ribbon of sunlight.

Her emboldened gaze traveled down the length of his ridged belly to the line of dark hair that disappeared just beneath the thin tie at his waist. He stretched his arms and leaped for the thick tree limb at least an arm's length above his head. Gritting his teeth, he threw back his dark mane of hair. He was in pain.

Breathlessness gripped her. Her first panicked thought was that he'd rip his wounds all over again. But they'd healed to red scars and were in no danger of reopening. With a driving vengeance only he understood, Marcus pulled himself up. Rigid tendons sculpted his neck and measured the effort it took him to touch his chin to the branch. Once. Twice. Liandra watched his fight, unable to comprehend the mercurial force behind his strength. Sheer will kept him from dropping. He didn't quit as he pulled up one more time.

Biting her lower lip, Liandra cursed Carlos with all her being. That whip-wielding monster had brought Marcus to this.

Finally, he dropped from the tree to his knees. His ribs expanded as he drew in air. Retrieving a cloth from the grass, he blotted his face. Suddenly, his hand stilled. He lowered the cloth, and she found herself trapped in his silver gaze.

Heart pounding, Liandra let him stare. His slow gaze went over her before he bent and snatched up his things.

"*¡Ay yi!*" she boldly whispered. Watching him walk away, she leaned against the wall. 'Twas hot as summer and it was only April.

Marcus tossed down the last melon slice Pedro had brought with his meal and went back to staring at the door. Sunup barely interested him. Stretching the stiffness from his shoulders, he fought the urge to drop back into bed, cursing this infernal weakness. For the past week, Pedro had brought Marcus his meals and held the mirror while he shaved. Marcus glared at the empty tray of fruit.

Even the racket of birds outside failed to distract him.

The front door shut.

He was out of bed and to the window in time to see Liandra leave the yard. He'd been waiting for this. Wearing an old, baggy pair of canvas breeches, a shredded leather vest that Pedro had found in some ungodly place, a battered strawhat, and leather sandals, Marcus stepped out of the room.

Curiosity about Liandra's life, her unwillingness to talk to him, all spurred him to follow her. It was time that he learned the mechanics of this village and worked on a plan of escape for he and his men. He didn't trust his new bride. He didn't trust these Spaniards. He trusted only in his ability to ferret out the weaknesses of his enemies so he could escape.

A glance around the empty room told him Pedro was visiting Alejandro. Liandra's house smelled like beeswax and lemon. A sign of the perfectly insane who found it impossible to function in daily life without first cleaning and scrubbing every living space around them. He restrained the temptation to smudge his fingerprints on the furniture. It occurred to him that as her husband, he owned everything around him. Gilt-leather wallpaper colored the parlor a soft gold. With its damask floral-pattern settee, wing armchairs, and burgundy needlepoint pillows, the room was the epitome of feminine quintessence. A mahogany cupboard braced the farthest wall, and contrasted to the otherwise frilly order of things.

Espinosa would suffer to realize the control Marcus now wielded over his precious sister's life.

Stepping out of the house, Marcus scattered cats. Someone had set out seven bowls of cream. Where he came from, a coddled cat was about as useful as a three-legged hound or a flock of squawking birds outside one's window. Clearly, Liandra had a soft spot for all God's creatures.

The stone-paved street looked like some quiet backwater alley in Seville. Liandra wasn't hard to pick out among the peasants and whitewashed exteriors of the buildings. She wore her bumblebee dress today. The bright scrap of yellow turned the corner. And Marcus darted off.

It wasn't long before he felt the effects of nearly eight weeks confinement. Still, he managed to follow his quarry. She disappeared up the stairs of a row of pale pink dwellings.

Marcus found himself studying the busy square. He attributed the village's fortune to the presence of the mission. Adorned with lofty bell towers, the imposing adobe structure hemmed in the town plaza. Brown, barefooted children played a game of blindman's buff in the street. Soon their laughter intruded with his concentration and, surrendering his vigilance, he shifted his gaze. He and Talon had played that game as children. For a while he lost himself in their laughter and smiled.

Liandra suddenly appeared. Sunshine brightened her dress and warmed the color of her hair to rich sable. Annoyed by the poetic bent of his heart, he concentrated on keeping distance between him and his wife. She moved among the vendors, purchasing an armful of flowers before she entered the mission yard and headed to a long wooden building that he surmised housed the sick. Watching her through the window encasements, he saw her tend to the patients.

Marcus found a grassy spot shaded by a poinsettia tree. A scrawny mongrel plopped next to him. Two men slumbered farther down the wall. Absently, scratching the hound's ears, he settled back against the adobe wall and watched her through the window casements as she bent and talked to patients.

Hours later, she left the infirmary. Gnawing on a blade of grass, Marcus adjusted the brim of his hat and came to alert. She glanced at the dark clouds. Another storm brewed over the mountains: one that mirrored his growing tumult. A single gust tossed her skirts.

Children's laughter drew her across the lawn to the mission school at the far end of the compound. From this distance, Marcus almost didn't recognize Isabella. She sat in a chair, a book patiently folded in her lap. Liandra's arrival excited the children gathered outside in the grass. They crawled all over her lap, touched her face and hair, and shared her musical laughter.

His gaze shifted back to Isabella. Her presence here in the valley interested Marcus, but not as much as the realization that she and Liandra seemed friendlier than he remembered.

How loyal was Isabella to her father?

After the children disappeared back inside the school, Liandra walked the short distance to the cemetery behind the church. She laid a single yellow rose in front of a black headstone and, for a long time, stood with her head bowed.

After she left the cemetery, Marcus walked to the black headstone and stared down at Miguel's name. An inexplicable tightness gripped his chest. For a long time he didn't move. Then he knelt. Bracing an elbow against his thigh, he lifted the rose to his nose. Slowly, he turned. Liandra had gone inside the church for mass.

Marcus returned to the house. Kicking off his sandals, he tossed down his hat and dropped into the faded chair next to his bed. He was no closer to escape than when he'd started this morning, nor to figuring out a way to free his men.

Marcus closed his heavy eyes, bolting upright when **thunder crashed. Running a hand through the sweep of his** hair, he looked around him. The bedroom door banged softly in the draft that swirled around his feet. Darkness reached beyond. No one was home.

Alarmed, he started forward when a sound outside stopped him. He pulled back the curtains on his front window.

Rain sheeted against the house. He didn't see her at first, the solitary shadow amidst the thrash of bushes and tree limbs. Lightning flashed and reshaped the darkness into the body of a woman.

Liandra stood in the middle of the yard, her face lifted to the sky. Opening her palms to the night, she twirled. The banshee winds whipped her long hair and molded her sodden skirts to flesh. She drank in the storm, letting the rain wash over her with a child's love for life. She stopped his breath.

For centuries, such a vision had crowned the bowsprit of great ships. She was hope and death. Memories born and lost. She was every man's reason for going home again.

Suddenly, as if sensing the darkened house for the first time, she swiped the drape of wet hair out of her eyes and searched his window. He felt the kick of his pulse, the rush of his blood, feelings that clawed at the abandoned layers of his life. Liandra's image burned into his head, reaching lower and lower until he felt her hand touch his heart.

Marcus dropped his hand from the curtain. Turning, he squeezed his eyes shut. His palm opened, and he stared at the pinprick of blood where he'd crushed the rose in his hand. The rose he'd taken that afternoon. A flower on a grave.

A single yellow rose the color of sunlight.

The house was deathly silent when Liandra shut the door. She stood in her small entryway and listened. Only the sounds of the wind and the storm filled the emptiness that suddenly surrounded her. Heart pounding, she took a deep, fortifying breath, and walked into Marcus's room. Would he leave without saying good-bye?

Her hands fumbled along the bedside commode searching for the lamp. Somewhere flint scraped, and the lamp hissed to life. Marcus sat in bed holding the lamp. His eyes held hers until it took all of her effort to speak.

"Did I wake you?" she asked.

"No." He eased the lamp back onto the table. The mosquito netting shimmered. He hadn't pulled it around the bed.

"I see Pedro brought you dinner."

They both studied the tray of food left at the foot of the bed.

"You haven't eaten. I'll warm the food." She bent to retrieve the tray.

"Leave it. I'll eat."

His gaze ran over her body assessing the wet garment. Despite the chill, heat suffused her skin. She grew flushed. "Grandmama and I used to play in the rain," she felt compelled to explain. Smiling, she glanced down at the sodden gown and noted the puddle of water building beneath her feet. The carpet absorbed the mess. "At night, she would wake me up. We'd strip down and stand beneath the eaves to wash. It was an odd thing to do, I know." She glanced beneath her lashes to see if he was listening or if his silence measured only boredom. He watched her in that intense way of his that set her blood on fire. "Grandmama never did things in the normal way."

"You loved her very much."

"I wish she were alive today to meet you." Dropping her awkward gaze, she fidgeted with her wet skirt, wondering what had suddenly come over her. "I thought you'd left, Marcus." She retracted an uncertain step. "It's late. I didn't mean to disturb you."

"You haven't disturbed me." No longer hooded, his gaze tenderly alighted on her.

Reluctant to leave, she straightened his bedside commode, gathering two glasses and a silver spoon—the color of his eyes as they continued to hold her gaze. And for a long moment, they were both caught in something inexplicable. Her mouth dried up. There didn't seem to be anything else left to say and with her fleeing wit, so went her nerve.

She backed a step off the carpet. "I'll let you sleep," she murmured.

"I'll see you in the morning then."

At the door she stopped and found Marcus still watching her.

"Good night, Liandra."

Her heart began to sing. And suddenly she smiled. Perhaps deep inside he did like her a little after all.

Chapter Fourteen

Marcus wanted to know whom Liandra visited in the pink house. The next morning, she beat him out of the house by fifteen minutes and, as he stared across the busy village square, he realized a sense of disgust. He'd lost her.

All around him in the main plaza, colorful tents boasted an array of goods. Green and red produce shared the stands with pottery and fresh flowers. A young doe-eyed woman with small breasts wiggled past with her laundry-toting mamma. Crossing his arms, he leaned back against the building that sported a wooden cantina sign and smelled of smoking beef. The girl peeked over her shoulder and boldly met his assessing gaze.

"Enjoying yourself?" The lilting voice came from behind him. Marcus turned. Arms crossed, slipper tapping, Liandra surveyed his attire with a sparkle. "Really, Marcus, if you wanted to follow me out again this morning all you had to do was ask."

His narrowed glance took in the alley behind her.

The color was high in her cheeks. "I have my spies," she boasted, clearly too pleased with herself. "Three young ones as a matter of fact. They told me that you'd been out yesterday."

"It seems there's a lack of trust between us, *gata*. I am merely out enjoying the scenery. You did say I wasn't a prisoner."

Blue eyes probed the marketplace. Her search halted on the dark-eyed temptress who even now continued to ogle him. Liandra's eyes, oft the window to her gentle soul, took on a wrathful look. "You have eyes for all scenery in skirts."

Marcus studied Liandra, a half-smile curving his lips. Something about her jealousy endeared her to him. He had no desire to look at anyone but her. She smelled of sweet talcum and a hint of wildflowers. Today, she wore her thick hair unbound and free to catch the breeze. His hands itched to trace the sunlight in her hair.

She snapped her gaze back to his face and caught him staring at her. Ruefully, he rubbed his chin. "I have eyes for only one skirt in this town. And that one vexes me to no end."

Her gaze studied him. "How so?"

He shrugged. "I understand so little about your life here."

"What you really mean is that you've been living on a pirate ship for so long you have no ken as to how the rest of the world lives. Very well, if you're going to spy on me, then you'll have to keep up, pirate."

Liandra swept past him, skirts swishing in the dust. Marcus followed. He didn't know why. He was free to roam as he saw fit.

Clearing two paces for her every one, he caught up to her quickly as she stopped at the nearest vendor. Blue and green pottery filled the shelves beneath a square of red canvas tent.

"Doesn't my being seen with you in public put you in danger?"

Running her finger across the rim of a red bowl, she shrugged as if indifferent. "Most people consider me abnormal in some way. Shielding an English pirate is something they'd expect of me. Last year I went into Triana and treated sick soldiers and prisoners. The ladies were aghast and tired to make Gabriel marry me off."

"Your brother seemed eager enough to do just that."

"No, it only took you to accomplish that miraculous feat." She moved to another stall that sold fruit. Drawing a coin from inside her skirt, she paid the vendor for two papayas and tossed Marcus one. "I, too, felt trapped. But had I known what Gabriel wanted me to sign, it still would not have mattered to either one of us. He didn't need my signature." Her mouth gently curved. "Only yours."

He looked away from her. "I thought learning Latin was a prerequisite for all Spanish ladies of breeding."

"Women are not widely educated no matter their breeding. But my daughter will be taught as well as any man."

Her daughter. A bittersweet surge of emotion stirred his blood. She'd probably have dark curls and bright blue eyes like her headstrong mother. Like little Christina.

His jaw clenched. It hit him that after he left, Liandra would go on with her life. One day she would be another man's wife; she'd lie in another man's arms; her daughter would be another man's child.

He bit into the yellow peel and spit it out, tasting the bitterness on his tongue. "So what other social crimes have you committed?"

"Many." She laughed, bringing the papaya to her lips.

Small white teeth probed the yellow first layer. His gaze riveted on her pink tongue sliding over the juicy flesh in delicate ecstasy. Succulent droplets rolled down her chin. Her lips wrapped around the fruit, sucking the sweet flesh dry.

Jesu. Marcus closed his eyes and looked away.

"Before Triana—" she licked her fingers "—I accompanied Friar Montero to Panama to help with financing our sugarcane."

"Scandalous. What did you do, steal the money?"

They walked past the next booth without even looking

at the wares. "Two years ago, Friar Genero"—she launched into a lengthy explanation about his being one of her thirty-five cousins—"he donated an altar for our church. He'd pulled it from the rubble of an old church that burned many years ago. The altar was scarred and painted black, but the most beautiful angels had been carved along its legs. They turned out to be gold."

"Probably left over from the days of Morgan."

"Uncle Montero said that the older priests used to use clever means to disguise valuables before an attack." She eyed him smugly. "It is good to know that pirates have not ravaged everything."

He watched her devour the rest of her papaya. Another luscious droplet rolled down her chin. This time, he caught it with his finger. Her wide-eyed gaze followed that droplet to his lips. "So this place is financed on plundered gold." He sucked his finger. And laughed. "Poor Carlos. Does he know where such a treasure went?"

She turned away abruptly. The marketplace was all but forgotten. "Carlos is a man who measures life against cold metal and colorful rocks. I detest such men who fall beneath its lure."

"It's a fact of life, Liandra." He finished the last of his fruit and tossed it into a ditch.

"Have your years of pirating made you affluent, Marcus?"

"Alas," he smirked, annoyed with her already, "everything I own in the world used to belong to you." When she stopped abruptly, he spread his arms in supplication. "Or had you forgotten that, *wife*?"

Sidling up to him, she flicked the leather ties on his vest. "If you stick around, you might even be able to spend some of it."

He rubbed his jaw feeling the bristles on his face.

"Come, I will show you. Can you ride a horse?"

He lifted a brow. "I haven't forgotten that much, sweet *gata*."

They crossed the square. A stable loomed before him. "So tell me, am I safe here?"

"I would not let anyone harm you."

He took her arm, spinning her to face him. Her mouth was ripe and wet with papaya still lingering on her lips. "That wasn't my question."

"You are safe here in Valle de Angeles. Most of the villagers have had family sent to Triana. Besides, Friar Montero is very beloved. The people will not betray him to Carlos to see him hanged."

"And you?"

She grinned. "I am beloved, too."

His mouth lifted at one corner but he pursued the subject. "Why does Carlos hate you and your brother?"

"He detests everything that he cannot control. Despite his *alcaldes mayores* position, he depends on Gabriel for his wealth."

"I doubt that."

"We've had differences in our family." Her gaze drifted to the pale pink building farther down the road. "The last time Carlos came here, my mother tried to kill him."

So, it was her mother she visited, and not some secret tryst. "I like your mother already."

"My mother is very ill," she quietly stated. "If it weren't for Gabriel, she would have been condemned. As it is, she can never leave here even if she wanted to."

"I'm sorry."

"For what?" She looked at him in surprise.

Marcus didn't know what prompted the apology. Maybe because he found he was acting like an ass again or that he just plain enjoyed her company and didn't want to run her off. It wasn't her fault that he had an erection from hell. He looked up the street, past the children playing in the dirt, past adobe buildings, toward the mountains, and thought about being alone. Not liking it at all.

"I'm sorry that she was never much of a mother to you."

"Mama is the bravest woman I've ever known. It is I who has failed her."

"You?"

"*Sí*, I was born."

She turned and left him staring. He caught up to her at the end of the street.

"Doña Maria," a skinny man, wearing a brown shirt and baggy breeches, hurried out of the stables. Twisting a strawhat in his hand, he regarded Marcus warily before turning his attention back to Liandra. "You will ride today?"

"Is Sundown still limping?"

"You will need to let him rest another day. I will bring out Sunrise for you."

Marcus caught her elbow. "You still haven't answered my question."

"Are you truly safe anywhere, Marcus Drake? Carlos can do nothing to you if he doesn't catch you. You are safer here than anywhere."

The little Spaniard led a red stallion from the stable. "This is Sunrise," she introduced.

"Aye," he stroked the long muzzle. "We've met. He looks to have survived his ordeal."

Grabbing a handful of mane, she leaped atop Sunrise. Marcus caught a fleeting glimpse of petticoats and slim ankles. "I don't ride with a saddle," she announced, bending over to secure the reins. Her long hair framed her face as she surveyed him from her superior height. "Saddles are restricting."

A moment later the Spaniard returned towing a stubborn burro shorter than a ten-year-old. "This is all we have left, Doña Maria."

White teeth flashed at Marcus. "That will be fine. I'm sure she won't be too hard for this Englishman to handle. He is so good with the ladies."

A slow grin answered the challenge in her eyes. "If she should throw me, I'll be crippled for life," he said.

"Then ride her gently, Englishman."

"Is that how you like it, Liandra?" He lowered his voice. "Gentle? Like the wind?"

Her jaw dropped open.

He moved closer, running his roughened palm up her leg and boldly claimed her thigh. "Or hard like the pounding rain?"

Swinging a leg up onto the stud, Marcus settled against her nicely rounded bottom and nuzzled his mouth to her ear. The rise and fall of her chest drew his gaze downward over her shoulder. He took the reins from her hands and wrapped his other arm around her waist. "I can give it to you both ways, sweet *gata*. If I was so inclined."

With that, he nudged the stallion and set him into a smooth gallop out of town.

Five minutes out of town, Liandra threw her leg over the stallion's neck and slid off. Her bottom smacked into the dirt. At once she planted her knuckles on her hips and faced her antagonist.

He held up the reins, a portrait of innocence. "What?"

"I will not be fondled. Especially since you've made it perfectly clear that you will have nothing to do with me."

"I was not fondling you—"

"Nor will I be subjected to"—she wiggled a finger at the blatant evidence of his carnal designs on her person—"that!"

Silver lights danced in his eyes. "What do you expect when you insist on riding in front?"

She found his lively interest diverted to her legs. With a small gasp, Liandra snatched her skirts down. "Is it my plight in life to be the object of your boorish behavior, Marcus Drake?"

"That is solely your discretion." He smiled pleasantly.

With a frustrated groan, she started walking.

"I would trade places," he said with such deep concern she almost amended her opinion about him. "But I'm sickly."

Liandra glared at him, looking ripe with masculine vigor and as perfectly at home on the back of her stallion as he had on the deck of her ship. Beneath the shadowed brim of his silly strawhat, his silver eyes sparkled. His muscled thighs hugged the stallion's sides, keeping her horse easily in check.

His power surrounded her.

She was suddenly completely and utterly miffed at him. Everything about him was wrong: his calm, his ability to annoy her, his rakish good looks. The fact that women ogled him openly only added to his sins. She picked up her pace.

"Where are we going exactly?" he asked when she stopped to pull a pebble out of her slipper.

"Less than a league down this road."

He looked around. The road they traveled had been built on a hilly ridge dividing the valley. A gradual slope led away from the route down into a valley. Nothing but green fields of sugarcane swayed in the breeze.

"Exactly what is down this road?"

"When my grandfather died everything here went to Grandmama and Gabriel. When my brother came of age he gave this whole mountain valley to Grandmama." She bent and slid her slipper back onto her foot. "Half a league is the measurement of the land that now belongs to me."

She watched the expression change on Marcus's face. "You own all of this for half a league?"

"Everything north of this road Grandmama gave to the mission. Everything south"—she tented a hand over her eyes and proudly surveyed her small sugarcane empire—"is mine."

After a moment, she turned expectantly to find him watching her, a frown on his face. "Well?" she asked. "What do you think?"

"How is it you've been able to run wild all these years? Your brother should be shot."

"Pah!" She lifted her chin. "I've decided that after I am very wealthy that I *will* marry a Spanish don just as you suggested. Only I shall be free to choose the man myself this time. And he will be nothing like you or Gabriel."

"Your brother and I aren't anything alike."

"You are both insensitive, stubborn, and have no ken of the kinder, gentler things life has to offer."

"For instance?"

She started walking. "Birds for one. They make beautiful song. And all *you* hear is the noise. Then there is the feel of rain on your face, or the wind in your hair. Have you ever just sat and listened to a child's laughter?"

She stopped again to empty dirt out of her slippers.

"I've lain naked in the sunshine," he offered.

She snapped her gaze up to confront his mirth. "Alone?"

His eyes smiled. "Laundry days on board a ship can be fraught with excitement. The only clothes most men own are on their backs."

"I have never lain naked in the sun," she conceded, thinking secretly that such an outrageous ritual sounded rather exciting.

She met his gaze and knew he read her thoughts. Giddiness intruded on her composure. The heat suddenly pressed in on her.

Holding out his hand, Marcus beckoned her to climb back onto the horse. "Your feet aren't going to make it two miles."

As usual, he was right. Attempting to appear casual, Liandra latched on to his wrist. He swung her effortlessly behind him. She wrapped her arms around his chest, tightening her grip when he urged the stallion to a trot.

They rode in mutual silence. The narrow road met up to a river, which it paralleled north until the road forked. A waterfall thundered over the distant ridge into a churning river. White-water rapids foamed on the surface, running the gamut of boulders and logs as the water made its way down the hill. The sound was nearly deafening.

"There," Liandra pointed to a gently rising knoll away from the power of the river. "We want to build our mill on that hill."

Marcus slid off the horse. Before she could move, he

wrapped his hands around her waist and lowered her to the ground. He walked the short distance to the edge of the field. Resting an elbow on his thigh, he crouched as if to study the layout of the land. His gaze climbed the giant sugarcane stalks that reached over twice his height. "This is your first harvest?"

"We have waited almost thirteen months for this moment."

"You think this sugarcane will buy you your freedom?"

Something in the tone of his voice alerted her. "It's a start."

He dug his hand into the dirt and sifted it through his fingers. His expression told her he was impressed. "Freedom from what?"

"I want to be in charge of my life without answering to Gabriel or Carlos . . ."

"Or a husband? Or the king of Spain? You live in the clouds."

Marcus surely possessed the same mettle as her brother to be so exacting in his descriptions. "I want to be free to roam the world."

"You want to be a man."

"I want to be . . ." Loved? Cherished? Valued?

He twisted to face her. "Everybody answers to someone, eventually, Liandra. Even me. At least you have a family."

Her heart raced. Liandra felt shame for bewailing her plight when he'd lost so much.

He stood and brushed off his hands. "When your next planting arrives you should start spacing this cane at least five feet apart. I suggest that in another six to eight weeks you burn these fields."

"Burn?" She stared aghast. "As in a fire?"

"You'll save yourself labor. Burning gets rid of the leaves and the poisonous insects. It leaves only the cane to harvest."

"And the mill?"

"The mill should be built nearer the river. You can harness the power of the water to work the wheels that grind the cane. That too will save thousands of hours in labor."

Liandra walked past him and stared in wonderment at the spot where he'd envisioned their mill. Trees lined the riverbank.

"They would have to be cut down," Marcus said from beside her. "But the wood could be used to build the mill."

She turned to face him. "Then it will all work?"

"Aye"—he tapped her chin—"and you, my sweet, will indeed be very, very rich."

The low murmur of voices came to him from far away. Marcus picked out Friar Montero among the vicarious whispers, then Pedro's. Turning into the pillow, he was reluctant to give up any part of the dream still clinging to his senses. Liandra's presence had become more than a misty image in his head. The room smelled of her: talcum and starch, lemon and beeswax, all things clean and pure.

He opened one eye. Six brown-robed men stood around the bed chatting as if they were at a wake. They spoke Spanish with an educated flair he'd oft heard in university-schooled men.

"I *am* alive," he grumbled, "if it's all the same with you." Shoving hair out of his eyes, he glanced briefly at the window. A pitiful breath of light squeezed past the curtains. The sun hadn't even debuted in its entirety.

Liandra stood at the end of the bed wearing a happy smile that matched her happy, yellow bumblebee dress. Somehow, she'd skillfully managed to salvage the thing after its drenching. Her cheeks possessed that lustrous glow of excitement he recognized every time they shared the same space. He wondered if he too possessed some telltale emotional remnant on his features.

His gaze took in each man, but something about her expression told him she was to blame for this quaint gathering. "What are you doing here so early?" he asked her, sounding as irritated as he felt.

"It has been a long time since they've seen an English pirate. And never one so famous. They want to know if you are useful for anything. Or if they should just lop off your head, like you deserve."

There was a chorus of muted chuckles. Impatient with her humor, Marcus glared at her. Her eyes laughed and, despite himself, he felt something inside his chest kick.

"Don't worry, I will not let them cut off your head. Not after I've gone to all the trouble to save you."

Returning her gaze, he smiled. "I wasn't worried."

"These are the men trying to build our mill. I told them you were a planter before you took to freebooting."

A bad feeling formed. "I don't know anything about building mills."

"You know about sugarcane." Her voice lowered. She trifled with her bottom lip. "Marcus, you would only have to look at our diagram and tell us how to build it."

In Jamaica he'd designed but never actually built a mill to crush the sugarcane. His father never did appreciate the smaller gifts Marcus had tried to give his family. Or the amount of work it took to design a mill. Liandra continued to hold his gaze. Warmth seemed to settle in his loins.

God blast it!

He held out his hand. Friar Montero handed him a wide sheet of vellum. It crackled when he unfolded the parchment. The sketch was not complete. The diagram was nearly worthless to someone who didn't know what he was reading. "Where did you get this?"

"We bought it last year at a fair," Liandra supplied.

"You mean you bought it from pirates. This is English."

"Old Providence holds an annual fair bigger than Puerto Bello's in June. We buy many things. The cost is cheaper."

He looked up at Friar Montero. "You allow her to go to Old Providence?"

"She is most stubborn. Besides, she is safe enough. I have seven nephews who live there. They would not allow anything to happen to their cousin."

Marcus rolled his eyes. He should have figured her network of thirty-five cousins stretched beyond the boundaries of Puerto Bello. "Jesu. I've landed in a nest of rabbits."

"You needn't make fun of my family, Marcus."

"How can I make fun of your family? I don't even know them."

At once, she began to remedy that situation. She introduced the two robed figures standing on either side of Friar Montero. "They live farther south in the valley. When you get out of bed, I will introduce you to Franco and Estephan, who are waiting outside. The are my overseers. You can take them to the sight where you said that the mill should be built."

He groaned inwardly.

But these people had saved his life. The least he could do was help them in this one endeavor.

"As long as you know that I don't intend to build this mill."

The day taxed his vow.

And as the warm balmy night quietly unfolded, Marcus's displeasure deepened, for his restraint, once pliant, began to crack.

After washing the day's grime off his body, he changed into a pair of charcoal breeches and a black silk blouse that he suspected belonged to Espinosa. The dark attire fit his mood. He tied the breeches at his waist with a black sash then, shoving his feet into a pair of expensive boots, he turned and gathered up the things he'd pilfered from various drawers in his room.

In the parlor, Friar Montero and Pedro didn't see him as they argued over a game of cribbage. Alejandro had joined them for dinner and stood behind his grandfather, watching the game. Marcus smelled pork roasting from the cook house out back.

Clutching inkwell, quill, and the lone sheet of vellum, he set the paper on the dining table. Soft light from a serpentine candelabrum spread shadows over his splayed fingers as they moved across the coarse paper. For a long time, he stared at the blankness.

He should be concentrating on a way to free his men.

But today, when he'd visited the mill site with Liandra's family, something had happened. Ideas churned in his head. Ideas he'd once visualized when he'd been a wet-eared kid fresh back from the university. Ideas that had died with all the other things in his life.

Other things . . . like family.

Later, he'd spent lunch with Liandra's cousins, and imbibed in a bit of foolishness with the boisterous lot. He'd sat on the outskirts of her family, sharing their rum and their excitement as they'd probed him for his ideas, anxious to learn what he could teach them.

Without knowing anything about him except that he was married to Liandra, they'd accepted his presence, and his allegiance. They'd accepted him as family.

The concept of family snagged at something so elemental inside that his chest tightened.

Jamming the quill into a bottle of black ink, Marcus poised the pen above the paper. Sometime later, when he heard Liandra setting the table, he'd already drawn the backside of the mill with its custom machinations: river-powered wheels that moved the grinders and cutters. A surge of excitement filled his veins. He'd never actually engineered such a mill before.

"Marcus?"

Liandra stood behind him. She clutched five plates to her chest. The lamplight illuminated her eyes. "I have never seen anything like this," she said, laying one hand across the vellum. Her eyes roamed all over the diagrams and did things to his gut he didn't expect. He liked the approval in her eyes. That validation of his worth.

The realization that his current state of mind was due entirely to Liandra's meddling pressed against his thoughts. Had she known what she was about when she got **him involved with the mill?**

He edged the diagrams away. His gaze fell on the pork roast she'd labored over for most of the day. She'd rolled up her sleeves to her elbow. Flour dotted her cheek and nose. Biscuits, corn, and baked apples served on the finest porcelain crowned her sterling efforts. He knew she'd created this feast for him. A celebration of sorts.

His vision of her in bright silks and satins didn't meld with doing manual labor. "Why don't you have servants to do this work?"

"It didn't seem prudent to have others underfoot while you were ill. Besides," he detected a hint of a boast in her words, "this house isn't so big."

Nothing she couldn't handle. Her energy was infinite. Her determination boundless. Her optimism addicting.

Marcus fidgeted with the quill feather.

The friar plopped down in the chair beside his. "Perhaps you feel disloyal because you are beginning to question what it will be like to stay with us," Friar Montero quietly said.

Marcus withdrew his gaze from Liandra's. "And have you taken up mind reading, Padre?"

"I know that you like the family you married into, *sí*?"

Aye, he liked them. He was beginning to like many things here. His hands closed around the vellum. "If you'll excuse me—" he bowed to Pedro. Why he did that, he didn't know. Such an action was redolent of the past, of a man he no longer was. "I need to walk."

Liandra flinched when the front door quietly shut. She turned and, without meeting her uncle's gaze, finished setting the table.

"You cannot save the whole world, Maria." Her uncle wrapped his hand around hers. His palm was warm. She was startled by the little girl inside who wanted to crawl into his lap and weep. "Promise me, when the time comes, you will let your heart go."

Chapter Fifteen

Marcus looked up from his drawing when he heard the heavy rectory door open. A shaft of amber light preceded Pedro as the old man stepped into the room. Shadows wavered over the shelves of books that lined the walls.

"You are still in here?" Pedro asked.

Marcus set the quill down. He'd been here all night, drawing. He slid the lamp away from his eyes. Pedro approached with a clay jug in his hand. "Mind if I sit awhile?"

"Who is staying with Liandra?"

"We have all left. Dinner was excellent. You're almost finished," Pedro observed, pulling a chair up to the desk. Liquid sloshed in the jug. Marcus surveyed that vessel with a wry look. In his youth, he'd spent more than one night well into his cups, and possessed a hankering to do so now. Pedro set down the rum. "Your sketches look very good. The artist is as talented as any Spaniard."

Marcus shoved the drawing aside. One by one, he closed the textbooks he'd pulled from Friar Montero's shelves. He scraped his hands through his hair and sat back. "It's been a long time since I've done anything . . . intellectual."

"I've seen many a buccaneer in my day. You do not fit. What happened to you, *Señor* Drake?"

Gripping the jug, Marcus brought it to his nose. Black rum. "Appearances can be deceiving, Pedro." He swigged and let the fire slide down his throat. "For instance—" he wiped his hand across his mouth "—you've done a poor job at passing yourself off as a servant."

Chuckling, he conceded the point and took the jug Marcus offered. "I am very wealthy, very titled, and very lost. Like you, I think. Until the French pirates took my ship and killed my brothers, I was set in my ways." He swigged a lusty drought of rum. "You have unset them, Englishman."

"Why didn't you tell anyone who you were? Despite my opinion about Espinosa, the man would have helped you."

He shrugged. "You were the only man I trusted with my grandson's life. Then I saw what Carlos did to you and decided I must stay to learn for myself what is happening here. Carlos is a *bastardo, sí*? I will see him fall." He edged the jug back at Marcus. "But that is enough of me. I want to know about you."

Closing his eyes, Marcus found temporary solace in the rum. "I'm an English pirate, Don Pedro. Nothing more."

"I never did thank you for my grandson's life," Don Pedro said after a while. "You saved our lives more than once on that ship."

"Trust me, I was thinking about my own more than anyone else's."

Don Pedro sprawled back in the chair. "If you insist."

The room swayed and Marcus suddenly felt as if he were back on the deck of a ship. He didn't want to be on any damn ship. He shoved the rum away. Focusing on the older man's face, he wondered if the man's stomach was made of lead for him not to be affected by the rum.

"I could drink you to the floor, son," the old man chuckled, clearly reading the query in Marcus's eyes. "I grew up on this stuff."

"You're from the West Indies?"

"My father was an ambassador to every court in Europe before venturing here. I knew your mother when I lived in Panama. Of course, she was younger than I was. *¡Ay Carumba!* She caused such a scandal when she married your father and went to live among the English."

Marcus fidgeted with the books. "My father was wrong to take her away from here. But then he was wrong about a lot of things."

"You forget that she chose her life. Your father loved her enough to take a chance."

"She was ostracized." Marcus sat back. "Nothing has changed between our people in all those years."

Don Pedro leaned forward in his chair. "Go to your wife."

"Did you hunt me down to harass me, Don Pedro?"

"She needs you. You need her. Who else do you both really have?"

Marcus stood. The room careened, and he caught himself on the desk. "You're mistaken." He wrapped the sketches in oilskin. His hands trembled. "I don't need anyone."

Just as Marcus reached the door, the portal opened. A wedge of light spilled across the forest green carpet. The friar stood framed in the doorway like a celestial headache. The room swirled in a mini tailspin. "Save your sermon, padre. I didn't come here to confess my many sins." He crooked an insolent grin and pretended he was past caring what anyone thought about him. "Not today, anyway."

Friar Montero sighed when the outer door slammed shut. "Youth. I never remember being so foolish."

He padded across the carpet, his robes swishing slightly with his gait, and dropped into the chair Marcus had just vacated. "He is a man consumed with much anger. Perhaps I have overestimated him."

Don Pedro snorted in disagreement.

"You did not see his eyes just then. I fear, he will break my niece's heart."

"What can two old men do? We cannot work out their problems for them. At least he is still alive."

"Are you up for a game of chess?" Montero pulled a marbled board and carved, wooden pieces from a shelf behind him.

"*Sí.*" Don Pedro slid the nearly empty bottle of rum across the desk. "But I already own all that you have."

Friar Montero sniffed. He set the pieces on the board. "Perhaps, we should have told him everything."

"We must wait until I hear back from my man in Havana."

"Don Gabriel will not be a happy man when he learns what was in the letter I gave him." The friar chuckled. "What will happen if you cannot get a pardon?"

"That is why we must wait. I would not wish to break *Señor* Drake's heart when there is so little of it left to go around."

Marcus walked the empty streets in darkness. Two rangy black mutts kept him company, chasing up and down the street barking at shadows. A brisk wind rushed through his hair. Another rainstorm brewed. It rained every damn night in this place.

Dizziness slowed him. More than dizziness, he realized. He ached to run like those dogs, to feel the blood pumping in his veins, anything but this self-doubt and want burning through him like the second plague.

The first drop of rain hit him in the face. Reaching Liandra's house, he braced a hand on the small picket gate and leaped the fence dividing her colorful world from the street. Flowers batted at his ankles. Stooping to pick one, he sniffed the petals, disappointed that it lacked perfume. What did Liandra feel about a flower that lacked scent?

Below the flower, a tiny bud shared the same stem.

Life.

A shiver passed through him, stoking his nerves, beckoning with promises that stole beneath his guard. He felt that elusive spark inside grow and wanted to grab onto it with every ounce of his being.

He followed the cobblestone steps around back. A huge tree loomed in the shadows before him and he leaped for the first branch, pulling himself up. He pulled himself up over and over, fighting the burn in his arms and shoulders. Thunder clapped across the sky.

Dropping to his knees, he sucked in air. Slowly, his heart quit pounding; the world came back into focus. Rain and earth misted the air. He passed his hand over the grass. Then tearing off his boots, he curled his toes in the thick wet blades, squeezing and exploring the coarse texture. He let the rain roll off his eyelashes.

It had been so long since he'd felt alive.

The rum had breached his defenses. Defenses Liandra had already plundered with her golden faith, idealism, and hope.

She may as well have committed murder against him.

With a sigh, he opened his eyes, and froze.

Liandra stood on the balcony outside her room, shrouded in the mist, her meager nightdress no barrier against his hungry gaze. He stared up at her, willing himself to leave. "If it isn't her highness in the flesh." He swept into a gallant bow, nearly toppling as he stumbled. "Most sensual flesh it is, too."

"What are you doing out here, Marcus?"

Somewhere in her house, a clock chimed twice. He lifted his hands to the sky. "Playing in the rain?"

Liandra wrapped her arms against her chest and took a step nearer to the rail. Frogs hopped across the long grass into the cover of the noisy woods. "You've been drinking."

"Aye, my beautiful Spanish wife. That I will not argue."

"Come inside, Marcus. You are soaked."

"I cannot." He placed a hand on his heart. "I am a knight adventurer on a quest."

"What is a knight adventurer?"

He laughed, clearly incredulous that she would not know. "Why he is a most miserable and needy being, so sayeth Don Quixote himself. I am compelled to agree."

"Indeed," she grinned. "And what quest is this most needy and miserable being on?"

He walked beneath her balcony. Lightning flashed in the distant hills. "A very dangerous one."

"*Sí*, I am listening," she whispered.

"I will come to your room."

"No, you will speak first."

He leapt the tall distance to her balcony and grabbed the rail.

"Don't you dare!" The slick bars lent him no purchase and he fell back to the grass. "Marcus!" Liandra leaned over the iron-slatted rail. "Are you all right?"

He lifted himself up on an elbow. "No, I'm not all right."

"You will kill yourself."

"You have already done that for me, *gata*. I lay here mortally wounded with an arrow through my heart."

"Pah! I see no arrows but the ill-aimed ones coming from your tongue."

"You are a witch, Liandra. My curse."

"And you are cruel."

"Aye"—he stood and kicked at the bushes—"if not for you, I would find succor in another bedchamber and be content with my lot. I am married and do not wish to be so. You have ruined me."

A hot flush burned her cheeks. "I'm going downstairs to let you in. Go around. Or sleep out here and die of lung fever. I don't care."

Liandra spun into her room. Her gown was soaked, but she gave no heed to her discomfort as she flung open her bedroom door and slogged downstairs. She shoved back hot tears, determined not to cry. "You refuse my kindness. You refuse my love and throw it back into my face," she muttered aloud.

Her house was dark. The wind battered the bushes

against her outside walls. Shadows jumped at her from all directions. Bracing her hand on the door latch, she rested her forehead on the solid oak panels. She needed to gather the fragmented edges of her composure.

A hand came around her head.

Liandra spun around. Heart pounding, she gazed helplessly into Marcus's face. He pressed his other hand against the door trapping her within the iron fortress of his arms.

"How did you—?"

He placed a finger against her lips. His stark silver gaze encompassed her face. "I'm sorry for what I said to you out there. I had no cause."

A heartbeat passed; then he wrapped her to him. "I have been such a bloody fool."

Relief made her foolish. The tears just at the surface began to fall. She couldn't help it. She laid her head against his shoulder. He held her like a lover or a friend. For a while they stood listening to the storm. She tightened her arms around his back, memorizing the feel of his heartbeat with every ragged breath.

Her clothes were wet and she began to shiver. He moved his hands up the curve of her spine and cupped her neck. His palm was hot. "You're cold," he said against her temple. His mouth became more insistent moving lower to her cheek.

"Only . . . a little."

He placed a finger beneath her chin, tilting her face. "What do you see in me, Liandra? I don't understand your faith."

Steel laced his query but did not conceal the underlying hint of uncertainty. Her eyes searched his, but they remained hooded. "I have seen the goodness in your heart for a little girl that was not yours and a boy who would have died if not for you. I have seen your courage in the face of brutality and your loyalty to your men. These are not the traits of a coward." She grazed her knuckles over his chest. The golden cross was warm against her palm.

"You are my husband. And no matter what you say, I don't want to marry another. I only want you, Englishman."

"But I have no future, Liandra."

Her hands cupped his jaw. "What man can see his future, Marcus?"

"Aye, except through the devil's eyes." He tangled his hands in her hair, and tilted her head back. His gaze dropped to her mouth. "You have me beaten, *gata*, at every turn I make. I can't think straight. Right now, I'm so damn hard, I'm not thinking enough to consider the consequences of what I want to do to you."

He claimed her mouth. The kiss was long and sensuous, a mating fraught with tenderness and dark promise. Thunder rattled the sky and spiraled through her senses. She had not expected this from him. Every scrap of sanity she possessed warned that nothing had changed. Yet, here he was tenderly exploring her mouth, holding her in his arms. A groan vibrated deep within his chest. He traced his lips down her throat to the swell of her breasts. Stubble scraped her tender flesh, arousing brazen sensations: delicious, and shameful. Her body hummed with life, the elusive ornament of light that spread like liquid honey over her soul. Her head fell back beneath the onslaught of his moist mouth. 'Twas lust, pure and simple.

Marcus broke their kiss. Pressing a muscled thigh between hers, he moved his hands over her breasts. "You'll need to get out of this nightdress."

"*Sí*," she managed as he edged the wet gown off one shoulder.

Lust was not so bad.

Breathing in his scent and the virile heat of his body, she felt the warmth of his fingers. His hot mouth replaced his hands and he caught one nipple between his teeth, suckling her through the sheer fabric of her nightdress. Wind lashed the door at her back. Her breath came in gasps.

Sí, lust was good. Very good.

"Wait!" She pressed a desperate hand against the wall

of his chest. His heart pounded against the sensitive tips of her fingers.

"Is that what you want?" His voice was husky against her cheek. "Tell me now. Or it's too late."

He confused her. She needed to think, at least a little. Liandra ducked beneath his arm and whirled to face him. "We need to talk."

"No more talking."

Removing an oilskin sheath first, Marcus pulled his shirt over his head and let it drop. With a gasp, she bent down to retrieve the sodden garment. "Leave it," he said kicking the shirt away.

"It will ruin the floor."

"To hell with the floor." The play of light flashing through the windows sculpted his shoulder and arms bronze. Swallowing, she stepped backward onto the stairs.

He followed, touching her only with his eyes. "I want to make love to you, Liandra. Tonight. Now."

She climbed the stairs. Her hand gripped the banister. "You do?"

"Why does that surprise you?"

"Because . . ." Her voice faltered. "You have run from me for months. You don't . . . like me."

"You're wrong." He continued to track her slow flight up the stairs. "I think about you constantly. I think about how you taste, how you feel beneath my hands, your fragrance, and your smile. You're the last thought before I go to bed at night and the first when I awaken. I haven't been able to keep my hands off you since we met."

Her tongue slid over her dry bottom lip.

"I've a yearning to see you . . . all of you, Liandra."

Hesitantly, she fingered the folds of her dampened nightdress. Barely breathing for want of dissolving before him, she raised the silky gown over her head. He caught the whisper of cloth and, pulling it through her fingers, dropped it behind him. Her wet hair fell over her shoulders to the top of her thighs.

"Now . . . what?" she whispered, taking another step up.

Without moving his eyes off hers, he worked the laces on his breeches. "Now, it gets good."

A delicious tremor coursed through her. She reached the top stair. She stood taller than he did.

Stopping below her, Marcus reverently brushed aside the wet length of her hair. Her heartbeat quickened. She held her breath as he took her into his gaze. "You're so beautiful," he whispered.

The words were like a rainbow in the darkness, filling her with joy and desire. Her hands trembled on the polished banister.

Stepping out of his breeches, Marcus continued his slow, determined pursuit up the stairs. In the silvered flash of lightning, he stood before her in primal glory, chiseled in shades of stark light and darkness. Gold glimmered from the cross at his throat.

Her eyes slid slowly, possessively downward over every perfect inch of sculpted flesh. Dark hair shadowed his chest, tapering in a narrowed line past his ridged stomach to the ebony thatch at his groin. His arousal riveted her gaze. Her mouth grew eager and dry.

A gentle forefinger to her chin snapped her jaw shut. "You make me blush, *gata*."

"You?" Her voice was breathy, barely audible above the storm. Or was that her heart singing in her ears? She lifted her chin. "You have never blushed a day in your life."

White teeth flashed wickedly. He kissed the moist hollow of her collarbone. Stubble scraped her flesh. "But I make *you* blush. If it were daylight you'd be red as a pomegranate."

"You . . ." Her head rolled back on her shoulders. *Dios*, he was doing such sinful things to her body. His kisses slid up her neck and over the curve of her jaw. "You think too much of yourself, pirate."

"No, *gata*." His gaze locked onto hers. His breath was husky against her lips. Vulnerable now as something inexplicable shaped his voice. "I think only of you. I want you. I need you." He wove his fingers in her hair and held her face between his palms. "More than I've ever needed anyone or anything. I don't want to hurt you."

The fires of purgatory could not put out the forbidden flames he ignited. She wrapped her knee around his leg to better touch him, to know the wildness he made her feel. Her cloak of hair fell forward as she buried her face in the bend of his neck. "I told you before, I am not afraid, Marcus Drake."

She only feared losing him.

His mouth claimed hers in a burning kiss, awakening her flesh, caressing her nerves with liquid fire, and Liandra kissed him back, unable to get enough of the velvety heat, wanting more, so much more. He slipped his hand between their bodies, stroking her inner thigh, dipping one finger, then another, between her legs.

"Marcus . . ." She arched her back.

His strength alone kept her from melting into a boneless heap. He tightened his grip around the back of her head, holding her firm while his hand and mouth did wonderful, thrilling things to her body. Outside the tempest vibrated through her flesh. Like the storm on the galleon. It seemed appropriate that she would now draw passion from the very forces that brought them together.

She clung to his corded arms as he lowered her onto the floor. The smooth wood was cool against her flesh. Beeswax mingled with the redolence of hot, male sensuality and a musky scent she vaguely recognized as hers. He nudged her thighs apart. His ragged breath, husky with want and passion, whispered over her. "Look at me. Let me . . . see you." Her eyes snapped opened.

He pressed into her body and Liandra's voice melted. She wrapped her legs around his thighs, wanting all of the hot pulsing length of him. He was incredibly hard, hotter than flame.

With an oath, Marcus stopped. "Not yet, sweet," he said against her ear. "Not . . . yet."

Liandra felt her heart catch. "Are you in pain?"

"Aye, the sweetest kind possible. You're killing me."

Bracing his palms on the floor, he moved against her, his powerful body rocking slowly at first, as if savoring the sweet ecstasy like one savored the rare taste of rich chocolate. A whimper escaped. Her head fell back. She could not keep her eyes open. Her name touched his lips, and then he was kissing her deeply, catching her trembling cries until she was drowning in his arms.

It mattered little that tomorrow would come, and the storm would be gone, the sky would be blue. Now there was thunder and rain.

There was Marcus.

She sobbed his name. Her blood sang with the consuming force spiraling through her, sweeping her with him into the night.

A ragged inhale resonated in his chest. "Liandra, sweet Jesu—"

Tension stiffened his body. His hot searing release pulsed through her. Finally, he collapsed against her.

Minutes passed before she floated back to the flesh and blood of her body. The floor was warm and slick against her back. With a groan, Marcus rolled to her side. Her eyes fluttered open. He was looking at her, his gaze hooded.

She knew every honed muscle, every inch of his body intimately. But she knew nothing of his thoughts. Or his past. Or what drove him past the confines of human punishment.

He was two men: the knight-errant who'd stood outside her balcony tonight waxing poetic, and this one.

A man of darkness.

He was having a nightmare.

Gasping for breath, Marcus came awake with a start. His heartbeat staggered against his chest. He forced himself to breathe, and slowly the haze of terror faded, but did not retreat. It never retreated. Never completely abandoned its hold on him.

Liandra lay against him, her glossy hair tangling around him like a silken net. With an unsteady hand, he mapped the length of her bare arm and brushed the strands of hair from her face.

The pleasantness of the rain outside the opened verandah door had given way to the silence of an approaching dawn. He felt the world poised on the brink of awakening. His muscles relaxed, he eased back against the soft down of the pillows strewn around him.

"Marcus?" Her warm breath stirred the tiny hairs on his shoulder. She brought her sleepy hands to his face and cupped his bristled jaw. "*Te amo.* I love you, Marcus Drake." She put a finger across his mouth. "I would take away your nightmares if I could."

"Liandra . . ." His throat tightened. He could drown in her soul and never care that he didn't breathe again. "You just don't know."

"Whatever you have done in the past does not change who you are now."

Jesu, he wanted so much to let go of the past, to see it scraped from his memory. He wanted to trust. But he'd lost his innocence years ago. He didn't believe in the inherent good of humanity. He didn't believe in happy endings, especially in a world that weighted survival on a man's cunning and not a man's heart. People lied. Everyone had his own agenda and everyone else paid the price.

He didn't believe in anything.

Until he'd come here. To the Valley of Angels.

Marcus gripped the counterpane in his fists, marking the seconds as his voice gathered in his throat. Maybe it was time to tell someone. He realized he trusted her. No one, not even Talon, had ever come close to knowing his darkest secrets. Would she hate him then?

"You asked once if I believed in the lore of gold." He scraped his palms over his face. "When I was nineteen, I thought gold was everything. I thought it could free a man. Make him important."

Marcus raised on his elbow to look down at her. Liquid eyes watched him back. "After I was expelled from Cambridge, I'd wanted a chance to prove to my father that I was worth something. Compared to Talon, I had failed miserably. But my father didn't trust me with any part of our planting business; he didn't trust me in the fields. I had visions for our land. But he didn't see them. It wasn't long before I started drinking heavily. You name it; I did anything to rouse the old man into a fight."

"Is that so different from other young men?"

He lay back against the pillows. She followed closely and pressed into his body as if she understood the hunger for such affection. "One night, I found a map in his study. It was more than a navigational chart. My father had drawn it. He was a very talented artist and I stared in awe at what he'd done. I never even knew at that time that he could draw. Holding that map was like touching a part of him that he would not share with me. Something I hungered for. It also held the lore of treasure. I knew that he'd been a trusted captain to Henry Morgan. I'd grown up on the gossip of buried riches like everyone else. In a moment of insanity, I stole the map."

Her arms tightened around him. "You thought it would lead to the treasure of Puerto Bello."

"Aye. I took it with me that night to a friend's house and showed him. Harrison Kendrick's stepfather was the chief high justice in Jamaica. Respected. I knew this friend from Cambridge. I trusted him. I didn't know at first the portent of his excitement or the evil of what I'd done."

"This friend betrayed you . . ." Her voice broke.

"He played the part of my friend, even when the soldiers raided my parent's home. My mother . . . and little sister were murdered that day. I couldn't save them. Father and I were taken into custody and thrown into prison on charges of treason. The chief justice accused my mother of being a Spanish spy. He said we conspired with Spain to raid Jamaica, that we favored his Catholic Majesty. Being Catholic weighed heavily against us.

"Later that week, Talon came home, and was arrested for piracy and thrown in prison with me. The authorities in Jamaica took his letters of marque, then accused him of piracy. Within a week, we were all condemned to hang."

"How could any man do that to you and get away with it?"

"The chief justice wanted no witnesses to his crimes."

Marcus closed his eyes. God, he remembered like it happened yesterday instead of ten years ago.

"He came to my father with the map I'd taken and told him if he shared the secret of the treasure, he would spare us all. I saw my father's face when he recognized the map. He knew that it had been me who'd betrayed them. His gray eyes, so harsh and condemning my whole life, touched me with nothing but forgiveness. I'd betrayed him, and he forgave me."

"You didn't betray anyone, Marcus."

"He told them there was no gold. He swore on a Bible. . . . And they hanged him anyway. Henry Morgan, who was lieutenant governor at the time, tried to get us a pardon. He arranged for our deportation to England to face a tribunal there. But my *good* friend had arranged another meeting. He didn't want us getting to England. Not after what they'd done to my mother and sister. The Spanish were waiting for us. He gave us over to your brother's arms. El Condor had religiously hunted any Englishman who was involved in the raid on Puerto Bello. He couldn't get my father, so he took us. Talon and I were taken to Panama and handed over to the Inquisition."

Her gasp told him in more than words that she understood the horror.

"Eventually we ended up in Puerto Bello. During that time, I survived because Talon had the will to live for both of us. When we finally escaped, I survived because Talon could sail a ship and taught me all he knew. We soon became everything they said we were. Pirates, thieves, and murderers. We raided the slavers Kendrick brought over from Africa. We attacked the Spanish. We plundered the Main with a vengeance. My brother was not after wealth or fame. He was after honor from those who stole our name and killed our family."

"And what were you after?"

"My death."

"And now?" Her small voice faltered.

"Now, I'm not sure what I'm chasing."

"Revenge?" Her voice was a whisper. "Against those who have betrayed you?"

"Years later after the chief justice had died, my *good friend*, Harrison Kendrick, went on to become the governor of Jamaica. He was injured during a sea battle we had with his ship some months ago. While I was in Tortuga, I'd heard that he'd lost his leg to gangrene. No one knows for sure if he survived the surgery. I would rather leave the bastard alive and suffering than do him any favors by killing him. May he rot in his living hell for his deceit."

"What about . . . Gabriel?" she suddenly asked.

He closed his eyes and forced air into his lungs. "If we meet again, Liandra, I won't be in chains."

She turned over and gave him her back. "You make me fear for your life," she said quietly. "You are still so angry."

"Aye, I am angry." He twisted on his elbow. "I need to find out what happened to Talon. He would be here for me if he knew that I was alive. I need to free the men who sailed with me on the galleon. But more than anything . . ." He placed a hand on her jaw and turned her head to look into her eyes. For an instant in time, he wanted to tell her that he'd begun to dream of a future with her.

"I owe you more—"

Kicking the sheet off her legs, she dislodged herself and rolled to her knees. Her thick hair was tousled. His gaze fell to her lovely breasts, eased over her flat stomach to the gentle flair of her hips. She looked like a woman who'd been thoroughly loved. His erection pressed against the sheet. If she tried to escape him, he was prepared to grab her.

With a toss of her hair, she straddled his lap and sent his pulse spinning. "You owe me nothing, pirate. We are even. You and I."

"Not quite. . . ." He pressed her back onto the bed, kissing her, tasting her, loving her. She was everything that was honest in his life.

Aye, he was in love with his Spanish wife.

Pounding on the door downstairs stopped him. "Doña Maria?" Alejandro's faint voice sounded.

Groaning, Marcus lifted his head. "Have you missed mass?" he queried.

"No, I have not."

Pounding again. "You must both hurry. Don Carlos is here!"

Chapter Sixteen

Carlos's laughter echoed through the rectory, halting Liandra's hand on the door. Hesitating, she sucked in a deep breath and entered. Conversation stopped. Carlos sat comfortably in Friar Montero's leather chair, with his ankles resting on the fine, oaken desk. Hands clasped behind his head, he didn't bother standing. He merely looked at her with dark eyes that made her shudder.

"Maria Liandra. My esteemed *niece*." He smiled. "How nice of you to join us. Care for some wine?" His hand moved over an amber flask set near his booted feet.

Liandra's gaze moved to her Uncle Montero and the other robed figures standing ill at ease near the bookcases. She'd left Alejandro and Pedro with Marcus. "What is happening?"

Carlos sat up. "Can't I visit your valley and this peaceful church, Maria Liandra?"

"Clearly no one is in more need than you," she rejoined.

Friar Montero hurried beside her. "Maria," he took her arm and led her to the wretched Inquisition chair. At least it felt that way as she stared across the desk at Carlos. "He has come to see his daughter."

"Among other things," Carlos replied, narrowing his eyes on her. "You have changed since I saw you last."

Her dark hair was hastily pinned in a coif around her head, but tendrils had escaped and she'd forgotten her headdress and veil. Looking down at her attire, she realized her red sash did not match the avocado-green gown she wore. Flinching, she knew she should have taken better care. Carlos did not respect her anyway, but seeing her so unfashionably attired only added to his perception of her station.

She lifted her chin. "Then why have I been summoned here?"

Carlos wore his black gloves. He saw where her eyes rested and chuckled. "Don't worry. I haven't come to serve any warrants. Unless you have something to hide, Maria Liandra."

"I have nothing to hide."

"That is good to know." He sipped a glass of wine and relaxed in the chair. "Have you enjoyed your widowhood?"

Liandra had the distinct impression she was being tested. Something else was happening here. "What woman would enjoy being a widow? Except maybe Aunt Innes," she qualified. Montero choked. She continued. "She still has not returned from Spain?"

"Isabella's mother is a whore. It matters not if she ever returns."

"Maybe it does to Isabella."

With a wave of his gloved hand, Carlos dismissed everyone except Uncle Montero. While the room emptied, Carlos poured another glass of wine. "You are insolent as usual, Maria Liandra. But there is something else about you . . ."

Leather creaked as he set his ankles back on the desk and let the silence lengthen. Liandra forced herself to relax. What was she doing? Baiting this monster? Sweat moistened her palms.

"Did marriage agree with you?" Setting the glass down,

he stood and walked around the desk. "Though, it looks like Drake is less than a man, after all. He did not leave me to contend with his brat."

Her gaze flew to Uncle Montero. He stepped forward. "This is inappropriate, Don Carlos," he said. "I have told you, your suspicions are ungrounded. Marcus Drake is dead."

"Suspicions?" she asked trying desperately to keep the panic out of her voice as she swung her gaze back to Carlos. "Marcus would have had no loyalty to me. Not after what Gabriel did to his brother."

Carlos laughed. "Talon Drake was never on the *Dark Fury*."

"What did you say?" Uncle Montero rasped.

Liandra paled. Carlos tipped her chin. "You didn't know that he is on Martinique?"

Uncle Montero stepped between her and Carlos. "How is it that you do?"

"I have my sources, Friar." Liandra heard Carlos whisper. Her eyes closed as she gathered her thoughts. "Obviously better sources than Don Gabriel. He thought Talon Drake was killed by the crew sailing the *Dark Fury*."

"Why would an English pirate be on Martinique?" Liandra finally whispered. "That . . . is a French port."

"Why would I care? He is their problem, not mine. Had I caught Marcus Drake, I would have sent the older brother a special gift. One that your Englishman prized. Unless you would have wanted it as a—" he seemed to search for just the right word "—a trophy."

Liandra slapped him. "You are a vicious animal."

Carlos backhanded her. Then grabbed the back of her head, twisting a fist into her hair. Hot tears stung her eyes. "You do that again, Maria Liandra," he kissed the blood from her lip, "and I won't stop at a slap. I don't care whose sister you are."

The door opened. Two blue-uniformed men entered. "We have searched the house," the taller one said.

Friar Montero wrapped his arms around Liandra's shoulders.

"We found only her servant and a boy. One of the orphans she brought from Hispaniola."

Carlos turned his gaze on her. "Nothing at all?" he asked his men.

"No, Excellency."

"Why would you search my house?" she demanded. "Your men have already been through here twice before."

"It is always wise to follow-up, Maria Liandra. Especially where you're concerned." Carlos lifted his gaze to Uncle Montero. "Teach her obedience, Friar. She'll live longer. Now, if you two don't mind, I wish to see that bitch daughter of mine. Since she didn't bother to find me, I'll find her."

After the heavy door slammed shut, Liandra met her uncle's compassionate gaze. He touched a sleeve to her mouth. "You should not have said those things, Maria. He is not to be trifled with."

"I must go to Marcus."

"Stay here until Carlos leaves." His voice was a command. "Carlos must suspect something. Or he wouldn't have come here."

"How could he? People here wouldn't betray you."

"It only takes rumor, Maria."

"Talon Drake is alive," she said, burying her face against the comfort of her uncle's strong shoulders. "Marcus's brother is alive." She was no longer her husband's only family. He was no longer alone in the world. He never had been.

"Why would Carlos tell us this, Maria?" her uncle asked. "He does nothing without a purpose. And if he came here, today, then something has happened to make him suspect that Marcus is not dead. Everything he said could be a lie. A ruse. What is the first thing your Englishman will do with this news?"

"He will leave," she whispered. Nothing would hold

him here, she realized. "He might try to find some way to get the *Dark Fury* back."

"Perhaps that is what Carlos wants. He knows there are many men who would jump at the opportunity to sail with your Englishman."

What better way to lure Marcus out of hiding and into a trap? What better way to kill him than to dangle in front of his nose the very carrot he values most in the world? His brother's life.

Carlos could not have shattered her paradise more effectively.

"I have . . . I have to tell Marcus."

Uncle Montero's grip on her arm tightened. "If you tell your headstrong husband what Carlos said, you will kill him, Maria. Let me do some investigating." Her uncle cupped her face and gently kissed her swollen mouth. "Let me find the truth. If your Englishman risks his life, let it be for a good reason. When the time comes, I will make him understand why we didn't tell him at first."

But instinctively, Liandra knew Marcus would never understand.

"I'll kill him," Marcus hissed.

The parlor was dark, and Marcus fumbled through the debris littering the floor to light the lamp. How could he for one minute have ever dreamed he'd had a chance here? How could he have been such a blundering fool?

Liandra gripped his shirtfront. "I swear, it doesn't hurt."

"No man strikes you."

"Please, Marcus." She wrapped her arms around him, clearly terrified that his anger would get him killed. It probably would. He wanted to strangle that bastard Carlos. "This isn't your fault," she whispered.

That Liandra was subjected to the same ill treatment that almost killed him nearly tore the heart from his chest. He wrapped her to him. "I'm sorry about your house," he said against her hair.

"It can be cleaned. This is not the first time Carlos's soldiers have come through here."

Marcus sat and pulled her to his lap. He'd waited all day for her return. When the soldiers had come to the house, he'd evaded them easily. Pedro and Alejandro had cleaned up any hint of his presence. Then remained behind while he went into the woods.

It was dangerous to Liandra if he stayed in this house. Dangerous to everyone in the village if he remained here. But he didn't know where else to go. His gaze fell on the diagrams he'd drawn for the mill. They lay on the floor in a violet ribbon of moonlight, thrown there by a careless hand as soldiers tore up Liandra's house.

No one else cared whether he lived or died. Except here. Here in the one godforsaken part of the world he couldn't live.

Nor could he take Liandra away. Not if he wanted to keep her safe. 'Twould be like slow murder; the way he'd watched his mother suffer. He had nothing but his name to call his own, and even that was small pittance. The name Drake lacked honor. She must understand there was no future for them. She must be made to see the truth.

His eyes moved back to the mill plans. "He'll never be able to hurt you again, I swear."

He touched Liandra's beautiful mouth, now swollen by Carlos's abuse. Then closing his eyes, he buried his nose into her hair and kissed the silken waves. Her perfume was like a brand on his skin. Tonight she would be his. He would leave her tomorrow at dawn.

Mass was ending when Marcus entered the church. Strawhat pulled low over his eyes, he stood in the shadows. The bells tolled. Somber voices filtered through the cavernous hall. Liandra never missed these morning services, but today he'd left her sleeping.

Turning away from the inquisitive gazes of those who walked past, he came face to face with a small granite statue of Mother Mary holding the baby Jesus. Candles flickered below the image. Marcus shoved his hands into his pockets and cast his gaze aloft, only to confront a colored-glass window depicting a silver-haired cherub reaching toward the cerulean sky.

His sister had hair the color of moonlight. Once, a long time ago, he'd listened to his mother spin heavenly tales of silver-haired angels. She'd had a minstrel's gift for weaving stories, and invited his imagination to take flight among the stars. Liandra had done the same, only her touch had gifted him with peace.

Marcus turned away. Across the chapel, Friar Montero bid farewell to a young dark-haired mother. Two children clutched her red skirts. Brushing a hand across their dark heads, the friar watched them leave, pausing his gaze when he saw Marcus standing off in the shadowed alcove. Their eyes met.

As the friar approached, his brown eyes lifted to the glass cherub. Sunlight laced her silver hair. "She reminds you of someone you used to know?" he asked, his voice rife with the same tone Liandra often used when she'd read his thoughts.

Marcus withdrew the oilskin packet from inside his vest. "I'll build the mill, Padre," he said, slapping the sheath of vellum against the friar's palm. "On one condition."

Marcus grinned at the man's brief flash of uncertainty. He would quickly relieve the friar of the notion that he was some Good Samaritan. "Those are the names of my crew. The ones Carlos imprisoned. Franco and Estephan manage the field laborers. I want the men who served with me on the galleon brought here as laborers."

"We are not a rich mission—"

"Will silver ducats work the needed miracles, Padre?"

"You know where to find enough silver to free your men?"

"I do."

The friar frowned. "You will visit our esteemed *alcalde*?"

"What's a thief robbing another thief? The silver isn't his."

"You are mad. Carlos will catch you and hang you."

"He can try, Padre." Thrusting his hands into his baggy pockets, he awaited an answer.

The friar's inquisition ended on a sigh of surrender.

Marcus spun on his heel and stopped. "One more thing. I'm building the mill on my wife's land. I want your reassurance that her brother or any of her thirty-five cousins cannot take it from her."

"Gabriel gave up his rights to his sister when you married her. And he gave up that land to her years ago."

He looked away. "Will you do what is necessary to protect her, Padre? I don't want her involved in what I'm doing. If Carlos goes after her she must know nothing."

The friar's eyes became sad. "You will leave her after you have finished the mill?"

"I've left her now. I'll be staying with the laborers in the fields. When the mill is finished, I'll take my men and leave here for good. There's no more reason for me to stay."

"Isn't love reason enough?" the friar said.

Marcus swung away. He was a stranger to nobility, and this act reeked of benevolent stupidity. He was beginning to think like his wife.

"There!" Liandra pointed to the tall figure nearly hidden by the mist from the waterfall. The mill site was marked with colored rope. With a nervous smile, she handed Alejandro two pieces of eight and a rose. Yesterday it had been a hibiscus, the day before, a yellow violet with a little purple center. "Tell *Señor* Drake my message."

"*Sí, Doña* Maria," he pursed his lips as he recited off his fingers, "you want him home, you miss him, you love him very much—"

"Don't tell him all *that*, Alejandro." She cut him off before someone overheard. "Just the part about dinner, *por favor*."

"It is always the same message," he complained.

"Go, Alejandro," she beckoned. "Tell him."

Liandra sat atop Sundown. Readjusting her bright fuchsia skirts in a way she hoped caught the light, she watched the activity on the hill. A low blanket of clouds hovered and thickened the air with humidity. Up and down the valley, sugarcane caught the sunlight in a verdant burst of color. Despite her heartache, excitement sizzled inside her, surpassing the roar of the river, and pinned Liandra's gaze to the masculine figure directing the progress.

A month ago, their mill was but a vision. Today, the reality had taken the shape of their dream. Pride for her Englishman enveloped her. Wearing nothing but canvas breeches, vest, and sandals, he looked no different from the other workers, except that he was tall and glorious bathed in the golden light of another dying day.

She fidgeted with the leather reins. Metal rattled. A restless sound.

In the month since they'd made love, he'd changed her world.

Then he'd left her.

She loved her mill. But she loved him more. And she refused to allow him to throw their love away. Not because of his misplaced honor. If he could not stay here, then she would go away with him.

On a sigh, her eyes lifted to find Alejandro. He continued to bob up the steep hill on the back of his brown burro.

"*Señor* Marcus!"

Alejandro's hail was faint against the roar of the river. A score of men looked up at him enquiringly. In the distance, Marcus set the ax on a severed log and straightened his back. A wagon filled with cut lumber was being hauled up the hill by oxen and heavy rope. Liandra watched him wipe his forehead with the back of his hand and yank his hat lower against the harsh glare of the sun.

Everyday this week Marcus had turned away her mercenary force of youthful couriers and told them never to come back.

As if sensing her stare, he lifted his head and scanned the road. His strawhat shaded his eyes, but she knew that he'd found her. Her heart took flight.

He brought the yellow rose to his nose. And then he said something to Alejandro.

Marcus let his hungry gaze travel over her face, taking in her uncertain smile. In her bright clothes, she looked like a rare, plumed-orchid sitting on her stallion. From beside him, Franco took a dirty kerchief from his pocket and wiped his bearded face.

"She is very stubborn, *sí señor*? I tell her everyday that you are busy. She does not know where you go at nights."

Men had stopped their work to gawk at his wife. His hand tightened around the rose stem. Liandra had no business out without an escort. The very least, she should have the decency to cover her hair. "Tell her not to come to the fields again, Alejandro," he said, "it's too dangerous for both of you."

"But she pays me money," the boy protested.

"I will pay you more money not to come." He reached inside his pocket and slipped him a shiny silver ducat. "Go. Tell her."

"*Sí, señor*." He gaped impressively at the new silver coin. "You will make me rich."

Marcus watched Alejandro's brown burro pick its way back down the hill to Liandra.

"*Mi prima*, my cousin is in love with her husband, I think." Franco chuckled at the notion, and Marcus wondered why the errant relative should find that so amusing.

Gripping the stout ax handle, Marcus heaved the blade into a tree stump. Nearly as tall as Marcus, Franco was the only man in this valley Marcus didn't tower over. "Tell the men to get back to work. And remind anyone who has forgotten that Liandra is my wife."

He strode away from the work site. Kneading the hard

knot from his neck, he considered the time he had left here. After learning that his own men were scattered in cacao or canefields from here to Panama, he now awaited their release. Friar Montero was still trying to locate the Dutchman.

Out of necessity, he'd stayed away from the house. From Liandra. He'd stayed hidden from the townspeople. As far as the people in this valley knew, it was Franco building the mill.

Marcus watched his wife conversing with Alejandro. A few moments later the little burro bobbed back up the hill and stopped in front of him. "The *señorita* says that no matter what you pay me, she will pay double."

Marcus looked over Alejandro's shoulders. "Did she?"

"*Sí, señor.* She said any money that you have is either hers or stolen and that I should not take it."

A grin pulled at Marcus's mouth.

"She also said that she would give away her part of the mill before she let you leave the valley without her. I heard her tell Grandpapa that only yesterday."

"Alejandro"—Marcus leaned forward—"never get involved with a woman. No kissing. No nothing. It only leads to disaster."

The boy grimaced as if kissing was akin to sucking mealy worms from bread. Glancing back at his cavorting men, Marcus climbed over a pile of rocks and scrabbled down the hill. Liandra watched his approach. He was glad to see her wary. He didn't like being defied.

"I know what you're doing, Marcus," she told him when he reached her.

He doubted she knew anything, but he smiled and pretended shock. Patronizing her was the fastest way to annoy her. "You are too clever, wife."

Her eyes flashed. She lifted her gaze and encompassed the mill. "Staying away will not change what has happened between us."

"Why aren't you at the infirmary, or the school, or putting flowers on people's graves?"

She looked startled that he would know her schedule so well. A leisurely smile pervaded his revelry, and did all manner of impure things to his body. "I've come to bribe you, pirate."

Despite himself, he leaned closer. "Aye? With what?"

Her fingers nervously entwined the reins. "Dinner." She bent and touched her lips to his ear. "Dessert. Succulent sweetmeats. Chocolate. Me. Won't you come home, tonight?"

"This place is not my home, Liandra."

She withdrew. Hurt-filled eyes moved him a step closer, into her skirts. He regretted the impulse that had made him so callous. But her stubbornness waylaid him at every turn. "It's better that you stay away. I'll be in the hills for the next few days. Don't come back out here. It's not safe."

Without a word, she wheeled the stallion. Marcus watched her bright presence disappear over the last ridge. Rubbing the rose between his thumb and forefinger, he brought the yellow bloom to his nose, but it was the redolence of talcum that he was remembering.

Someone had declared war on Carlos!

Rumors of a notorious shadow bandit circulated through the valley mission all week.

Two weeks ago, the nefarious robber dared a raid on the *alcalde*, breaching the sanctity of his bedroom and escaping with untold wealth. Fortunately, the *alcalde* was not at home. A few days ago, the miscreant had acted again. If Carlos was angry over Marcus's escape from Triana, he was enraged with this latest insult. The *alcalde*'s *soldados* descended on the valley mission, searching houses and posting a reward for the capture of the man Carlos dubbed Night Shadow.

"Isn't this exciting?" Isabella plucked the poster off the town square wall. "Ramón said Father is actually afraid for his life."

An inexplicable fear jolted Liandra. She watched the

sky. A low blanket of smoke hovered and thickened the air. Marcus was burning the sugarcane fields. It had been weeks since she'd been to the fields to see her husband. She'd finally quit going for all the good it did.

"Who do you think the bandit is?" Isabella asked.

Liandra regarded her sprite cousin with a frown. "Aren't you even worried about your father?"

Isabella sniffed. "I've seen the scars on Marcus's back."

"Indeed. When?"

"When he lived here. He is not exactly *modesto* about his physical attributes. And why should he be? He is nice to stare at."

Liandra resented her cousin's odious adoration for Marcus. "It's going to rain soon. Let us go see Mama. I brought a new book from Friar Montero's library."

Isabella dropped her gaze to the book Liandra held. "*Don Quixote?*" Raising an inquisitive brow, she sighed over the poster in her hands. "Do you believe in knight-errants and brave crusaders, *mi prima?*"

Liandra snatched the placard from Isabella and crumpled it into a ball. "A thief is not a crusader."

"Now that depends on who he is stealing from, *sí?*"

A stiff wind swirled the dust and lifted the dead leaves. Isabella's pale blue skirts flapped, and if Liandra hadn't been looking at her cousin, she wouldn't have seen the tell-tale signs of an expanding waistline. Her gaze snapped to Isabella's.

Their eyes met.

Her cousin's chin shot up a notch. "*Sí*, Maria. I am pregnant. You can say the awful word." Isabella must have seen the pain flash in her eyes for she immediately looked contrite. "Friar Montero knows. I would have told you soon."

"You didn't think I would care?"

"Why should you? I have not been so nice to you."

Shame welled with guilt. Neither had Liandra behaved kindly. "Who is the father?" she quietly asked.

Isabella studied the lace on her sleeve. "I would rather not say."

"Isabella—"

Brown eyes snapped up. "He cannot help me, Maria. You brought me here and, for that, I am grateful. But I am not ready to talk about everything that has happened. I must deal with this in my own way."

Isabella's grit surprised Liandra. Perhaps because her courage sprang from such a leaky vessel. "Then you are never going back?"

"I will never go home again. Nor will I be forced to marry a man who doesn't love me!"

Her cousin spun in an angry flurry of skirts, leaving Liandra to follow slowly behind.

Liandra sat straight up in bed.

Pulse racing, she sliced her gaze first to her bedroom door then to the verandah. Outside, crickets and frogs solemnized the night. Somewhere a dog bayed at the full moon.

Nothing seemed out of the ordinary; yet, something had awakened her. Throwing back the counterpane, she waded through yards of mosquito netting and padded to her bedroom door. Moonlight shivered in a puddle at her feet. She drew in a nervous inhale. The sword and pistols Gabriel had given her were in a leather trunk downstairs beside the settee. Here, in this village, she'd never had use for them, and brought them out only occasionally to refresh her skills.

Hugging the wall, Liandra crept down the stairs. A gust of wind pushed against the house. She stepped into Grandmama's room. Easing open the wardrobe, she pushed aside Gabriel's clothes, which she'd placed inside for Marcus. Her husband's leather and spice scent enveloped her with such intensity that Liandra pulled away.

When had Marcus worn these clothes? He hadn't lived here in months. Unwilling to think about that right now, Liandra closed her fist around Grandmama's old walking stick. The stout weapon clutched behind her, she walked into the parlor.

A whisper of movement by the window froze her.

Dios! Someone *was* in her house!

Moonlight slanting through the curtains silhouetted a dark form, his hand braced on the glass. The floor creaked beneath her foot.

The shadow jerked around. Heart pounding, Liandra swiftly raised the wooden cane—"Marcus . . ." she gasped his name, a mixture of profound relief and shock.

He wore no shirt. His hair was wet. He'd been swimming in the pond. Moonlight outlined a bottle of wine in his hand. She could feel his awareness of her, the way the pale light molded to her flesh beneath her gown. Nervously, she stepped out of the light.

"What are you doing here? It is not even morning," she asked.

Clearly he hadn't expected her presence. His gaze hesitated on her breasts and eased over the flair of her hips. He set down the wine bottle. A glance at the table told her he'd raided her food stores. Bread crumbs, cheese, and part of last night's soup were all that remained of his meal. A black shirt lay over the chair.

"What can I say," he followed her gaze, "your cousins cook as badly as Pedro."

He didn't look like he was starving. Indeed, his body had hardened with new strength. He seemed harsher, more sculpted. A man who would no longer have trouble lifting himself onto tree limbs and verandahs. "How did you get in here? The doors are all bolted."

Somehow, he shortened the distance between them, his predatory grace suddenly alarming. "Does it matter?" Stepping into the circle of moonlight that embraced her, Marcus edged the tip of the cane away. "You don't want to run me through."

"You're right." She tossed the hair out of her eyes. "I want to bash you over your thick skull for scaring me to death. For making me miss you. I know why you are staying away from me."

"I have been suffering my choice."

"However much you hurt it is not nearly enough." She stared down at her feet, so vulnerable next to his black boots. A fingernail traced the thin scar on the ridge of his ribs. "But then maybe you are not really here." Without raising her eyes, she stepped a little closer. "Maybe I'm only dreaming."

"Then please, Lord, wake her up before I do something stupid."

She snapped up her eyes. "Sometimes I don't like you," she sniffed. "You stay gone for months. You cannot be seen outside. Carlos has men here in the village. Now you think you can enter my house and do as you will. You are more trouble to me than you are worth."

He gazed down at her lips. "Then what am I, love?"

"Nothing. You are poor and stubborn. You are English. I think you are worthless, *si*?"

Marcus stared at Liandra's upturned face, willing himself to move away, to leave before he touched her. He ached to run his fingers through her hair. There was something very selfish about wanting her when he knew he should not. But he was past redemption. Moonlight bathed her in a touch-me vision of white silk and lace, soaking up the last remnants of his will. How many times had he come to this house and watched her sleep? A dozen times?

"How is the mill going?" she asked.

He touched her hair. "We finished the second floor."

"Uncle Montero lights a candle for you at mass every day. He thinks you walk on water."

"You're right." He laughed. "One of us must be dreaming."

"It is not light outside." A fingernail traced the thin scar on the ridge of his ribs. She feathered a kiss against his shoulder. "Tomorrow is not yet here. Perhaps I can go on with the dream, *si*?"

It was still such a wonder that she could want him at all.

"Christ, I've missed you," he whispered.

Her head fell back. The cane clamored to the floor unheeded. "I've missed you, too."

Then she was in his arms and he was kissing her deeply. He didn't know how it happened; hadn't intended anything to happen. Reason abandoned him.

Marcus carried her into his room. Lifting her gown from her body, he explored her breasts, her throat, trailed his mouth down her belly, tasting all of her before burying himself inside her. Passion filled the hot space between them. He listened to her cries.

She was heaven and earth. She was everything that was honest in his life, and he wondered how in God's name he'd stayed away from her for so long.

A cacophony of birds drew Liandra out of bed and to the verandah. Lately, her sense of adventure lent her new daring and a well being that stretched beyond the mere portal of tomorrow. Life had blessed her with a future and a husband who loved her. Leaning her head against the doorframe, she saw as if for the first time the wild red hibiscus, poinciana trees, and vines that climbed the trees in her backyard. No human hand tamed the splendor of this savage paradise. Marcus was like that, wild and free; sometimes like the wind that brought down the mighty trees, changing everything in its path. She was more like the rocks. Immovable. Stuck. What mighty adventure do rocks have?

She wanted to soar! To be like him!

Wiggling a toe in the light, she remembered his long ago words. She'd never stood naked in the sun.

Drawing in a ragged breath, Liandra moved aside her curtain and boldly stepped onto the verandah. Warmth infused her and soared through her blood. She lifted her hands. Her heart pounded in exhilaration and the sunny momentum carried her higher.

She giggled, discovering an odd source of courage in her shameful behavior. She was surely mad.

"Nice, Liandra, Very nice."

"Marcus!" She dropped her arms but did not cover her breasts, feeling utterly shameless in her abandon.

Arms crossed, he leaned against the tree watching her. He laughed. "I did remember to warn you about others watching."

"No, I don't remember that part." And she didn't care. She loved his laughter. "You can look all you want, pirate."

"You're wicked." His expression softened. She noted he bent and lifted a cloth bag of shaving soap. He'd been working at the tree again. "I'm going swimming." His mouth crooked into a wicked grin as he stepped into the sunlight. "Join me. We'll swim naked."

Heart soaring, Liandra disentangled her gaze. Laughing, she threw on a chemise and gown and hastily joined him.

In the weeks that followed, Marcus secretly came home to her almost every night. Their marriage had become a truce, an affinity more fragile than rain. They'd made love in every room. Sometimes at dinner or beneath the lamplight afterward as he worked on more drawings for the mill, she'd watch his hands stroke the vellum, daunted by his ability to bring it to life. Then she'd look over to find his gaze on her. And for the first time in her life, she knew that she belonged to someone. Marcus shared her life on every level.

Her husband had great talent, a future as a planter; new purpose. She was proud that she'd somehow helped to give him that gift. Her hand went to her belly. She was proud of something else as well. The possibility of a child filled her with awe.

Lately she'd suffered vague signs that her body was changing. She had not had her menses in nearly three months. But then she'd oft skipped months at a time in the past, and it was because of that she didn't say anything, yet. That and something else.

How would Marcus feel if such a thing were true?

For her husband possessed another side: one that she'd seen when he didn't think she watched him. When he'd labored at the tree or in his eyes when they'd watch the sunset. A darkness that eclipsed the light. One filled with quiet vengeance. And lately, when he'd spend days away in the hills, she'd begun to worry. She could not bear that he would return to the life of a thief or a murderer or an English pirate. Not when he'd gained so much. If he went back, he would die.

But her conscience curled around a double-edged sword. One that would not survive the lie still between them. For Friar Montero confirmed that Marcus's brother, Talon, was indeed alive on Martinique. And Liandra had said nothing. Nothing at all.

Chapter Seventeen

Liandra made her husband supper, packed it carefully in a canvas bag, and wrapped it with a scented blanket. Marcus had spent the last few days in the fields. She would surprise him with a picnic. Packing a bottle of her brother's finest wine, she bought some flowers, and hurried to the stables.

One of her horses was gone. The boy who cared for her stallions told her that *Señor* Marcus had taken Sundown three days ago.

"Marcus did not go in the cart with the others?"

"No, *señorita*. But usually he does not. He often takes one of the stallions when he leaves for more than one night."

She'd been so busy with her mother and working at the mission, during the days that she hadn't even noticed. Eyeing Sunrise in his stall, Liandra rubbed his nose. "Are you lonely, boy?"

She looked at the bundle in her hands. Mounting Sunrise, Liandra rode to the mill site with her dinner. Trepidation began to edge over her. She'd been warned to stay away from the fields. Surely, Marcus would not be angry with her when he saw what she had brought him.

But he was not there. Franco told her he'd ridden higher into the hills. "When will he back?"

"Who is to say, Maria? He is a busy man."

Her gaze alighted on the mill. The massive two-story log structure dominated the hillside. "The roof is on," she said completely awed. The mill was almost completed. "It looks magnificent, Franco. I wish to see the inside."

Her cousin flatly told her to go home and sent for Estephan to escort her back to town.

"Go home, Maria. *Por favor.*"

Liandra looked over his shoulder. He was hiding something. Fires pocked the hill with orange. Woodsmoke settled like a cloud over the fields. Two men lounged indolently in the shadows. Vaguely familiar in baggy canvas breeches, they seemed to be watching her.

"Maria," Franco snapped her around.

Estephan arrived and escorted her back. Later that night, Liandra awakened. Sweat moistened her chest. One of those men had red hair: the Scotsman from the galleon! The other was the man who'd spoken to her so crudely that night during the storm.

A shiver rippled up her spine. What was Marcus planning?

Liandra forced herself to admit there could be a reasonable explanation for Marcus's secrecy. He was loyal to his crew. He meant to see them free.

And then what?

They would all live happily ever after in the Valley of Angels? Humbled with forgiveness for their brutal captors?

The mockery, so like the Marcus of old, slapped her. Hard.

Building the mill was the perfect cover. Liandra desperately attempted to pull her thoughts together. She loved Marcus. Still, he had told her nothing of his plans and that frightened her.

The next morning, she donned a lime green dress with black lace trim and went in search of her uncle. He wasn't in the rectory. Drawing in a ragged breath, Liandra ran a hand through her plaited hair. She clasped her hands. Frowning, she stared down at her skirts. Isabella had once said that the dress made her look like a tropical fish. Suddenly, self-conscious, she brushed the wrinkles from her skirt. The urge to cry hit her. She didn't want to believe Marcus capable of harming anyone in the village.

Desperate to find Friar Montero, she rushed outside. There, he was heading back from the schoolhouse. But seeing her, he abruptly turned east toward the infirmary.

Alarmed, she chased after him. "Uncle Montero!"

His shoulders stiffened. Turning to greet her, he laced his fingers in front of him. "Maria," he hedged.

"Uncle, I must . . . talk with you." She did not comprehend his strange mood. "I fear . . . I fear I have discovered something."

His brows lifted in concern. "You are upset."

She took his hands into her own. Tears filled her eyes. She could not bear to accuse Marcus of anything. "I don't think Marcus is up to any good, Uncle. I went to the mill—"

"I know what he is about, *mi sobrina*."

Relief spilled through her. "You know his plans?"

"*Sí*, Maria. We talked about it long ago." Friar Montero scraped his fingers through his graying hair. "When the mill is completed, I know he is leaving here."

Liandra clutched a fist to her heart. She'd suspected, but to hear it so blatantly as if it had always been so, almost made her laugh at the absurdity. Her uncle was mistaken. Wasn't he?

"He told you this?"

"Many months ago, Maria? I warned you—"

"No . . ." A deadweight dropped in her belly.

Marcus had swept her off her feet, told her he needed her, made love to her like tomorrow was forever, and all the while he'd been planning to leave her?

Her uncle's touch startled her. "I am sorry, Maria."

"Is that all?" Her voice squeaked. "Did he say anything about . . . about taking me?"

"No, Maria. He is not taking you."

Ashamed by the tears filling in her eyes, she turned away.

And then she saw them.

Marcus and Isabella!

They were beneath the spreading branches of an aged Poinciana tree, near the river. Sundown was tethered just out of sight. Marcus talked and skimmed rocks across the water as if he were angry. He wore black. Even from this distance, she could see that his shirt fell away from his chest in a vee. Shiny boots molded to his legs and added height to his already tall form. Hardly field attire. Clearly enjoying the society of his company, Isabella was touching his arm.

Unbidden, Liandra's jealousy turned toward Isabella's pregnancy. She remembered those first days on the galleon when Isabella and Marcus—she would not believe it!

She wouldn't!

"That is why you were running from me just now," she whispered.

Her uncle's touch did not stem her panic. "You don't believe there is anything between them, Maria."

Liandra snatched her arm away. The vicious tear in her emotions struck like a blow to her knees. Marcus was very clever. Ruthless. He had found a way to defeat Carlos.

"He has been gone for three days, Uncle . . ."

She could say no more. Liandra wheeled away and ran from the mission grounds. She didn't want to hear any part of her uncle's bid for prudence. He wasn't the one Marcus would forsake. Uncle Montero didn't have the slightest clue what it felt like to watch the world blindly pass you by, then one day look up and discover you're no longer alone. Only to learn it was a lie.

Uncle Montero didn't understand because he didn't lack for love.

Halfway home a stitch in her side slowed her to a walk

and she swallowed sudden nausea. By the time she reached her door, she'd spent her silly tears, but her stomach had not ceased its roiling.

Standing in the parlor, she stared around her. A figurine from the leather chest beside the settee lay upended on the floor. Gabriel had given her that chest. A ragged breath escaped. She picked up Marcus's discarded shirt. His scent pulled her nose to the soft silk.

She'd thought the last months had changed the world between them. But he'd made her no promises.

Not really. And needing wasn't the same as loving.

Gently folding his shirt, Liandra laid it on the chair. She climbed the stairs to her bedroom, closed her door, and slid the bolt home. Then crawling into bed, she curled around the pillows and shut her eyes.

"Liandra?"

Marcus's voice filtered through the fog in her head. He was knocking on the door. Twisting in bed, she shot up. Her gaze flew to the verandah. She was surprised to see the clouds rippled with red and looking bloody. The sun had gone down.

"Liandra?"

"Go away, Marcus."

There was a long pause and Liandra scooted to the edge of the bed.

"Open this door."

"I said go away."

"I talked to Friar Montero."

She stared at her feet. Noting for the first time that she wore one white slipper and one yellow. She threw them at the door in disgust. Marcus had turned her whole life upside down, inside out. She couldn't even think straight.

"If you don't leave, I will"—she sliced her gaze around the room. Short of a few pillows and precious mementos Grandmama had given her, her weapons were limited—"I will scream."

"Yea?" His voice had become ominous. Threatening. "How loud?"

She jumped to her feet. "Mock me, Englishman. That is what you are good at. That and bedding senseless women. But did you not warn me?" Gripping her bright, lime green skirts, she paced, stopping abruptly when she glimpsed her reflection in the long mirror. Her hair was lightning-struck frazzled, her cheeks red as if she'd been slapped. And her gown—she choked. Pride lifted her chin. She did not care if she looked like a tropical fish. She did not care if people talked behind her back. Or felt sorry for her. The only person who'd mattered didn't love her.

Pah! She didn't care about that, either!

"Do I listen?" She continued her tirade. "No! I am a foolish woman. I have to hear from my uncle that you are leaving us soon. I have to see you with Isabella and wonder—" her voice choked "—if you're the father of her baby!"

Silence.

"I should be grateful that you have consented to build our mill first, before you resume your fight with Carlos. And Gabriel, too," she added. "Will you blow up our city when you try to leave?"

No answer.

Heart pounding, she ran to the door and, pressing an ear to the panel, listened.

"Open the goddamned door, Liandra." His whisper shivered over her. She could feel him pressing against the door, feel his restrained fury. It was as if he could see her through the wooden panels. As if he felt her breathing so near to his words.

She leaped back.

"Go to the devil." Her voice trembled.

The door splintered. Another kick sent it smashing into the wall, where the latch remained lodged. Appalled, she stared at the damage to her door and beautiful wall.

"Look what you have done." Narrowing her eyes, she swung her furious gaze to Marcus.

His hands gripping the doorframe above his head, he watched her with eyes the color of tempered steel. Stubble heightened his easy strength. Dressed in black from the tips of his shiny boots to the black scarf that bound his head, he looked like a winged shadow of the night singed into her doorway.

Night Shadow.

Catching her breath, she took an involuntary step backward and hit the bed. Impossible! Her eyes roamed the length of him until she met his gaze.

At once, she hated her cowardice. Snatching up the object nearest her, she hurled the pillow at his face, then another, and another. "Out! Out! Out!"

He swatted the missiles aside. When his silver eyes came back around, he looked every inch the fearsome pirate. "You have a temper, Liandra. I didn't know that about you."

She knew he was laughing at her.

Scrambling over the bed, she reached the talcum jar on her dresser and turned to hurl it at him just as he caught her wrist. Powder exploded over his head and rained down on her gown in a fragrant plume of dust.

"God blast it, Liandra."

They both coughed. Powder scattered over her dresser, her bed, her carpet, her hair.

Their eyes locked and held. Her heart stopped. He backed her up against her wardrobe and pinned her hands against the armoire. Powder peppered her face.

"There's nothing between Isabella and me. I was on my way home today and stopped when I saw her walking beside the back road."

"Don't, Marcus." She shoved at his chest. Liandra did not trust a man who dressed like a thief in the night. "You are too close."

He put his warm mouth near her ear. "I didn't tell you I was leaving when the mill is finished because I thought you understood how things were between us."

"I thought the last few weeks had changed things between us."

"Aye, too much has changed," he rasped.

"Take me with you when you leave."

"To what end? To be the wife of a pirate? A man *wanted* by England and Spain? They would hang you with me."

"Then stay."

"I have remained as long as I dare. I've tried to stay hidden. But as long as I'm here you and your village are not safe."

She knew he was right and wanted to scream her frustration at him. "You . . . you lied to me."

"Look at me and tell me I ever lied to you about anything."

She could not. He'd fulfilled his every obligation to her. He'd saved her life, her ship, her land. He'd given her his name.

And destroyed her heart.

"You are not going to attack the village?"

"Your village is safe from me."

She didn't entirely believe him no matter what Friar Montero thought. He was an English pirate, with naught but vengeance on his mind. She crossed her arms.

With his hand, he tilted her face back. His eyes were no longer hooded. "Don't push me away, Liandra."

His mouth slanted across hers, his body pressing her backward into the smooth wood of her wardrobe. His hands caught her upper arms and crushed her to him. "Tell me you want me." His lips pursued her jaw down the curve of her throat. Hungry, caressing, alive. His careful words had softened her heart and made her forget that she'd seen him with Isabella today, that he wore black. That she didn't trust him.

She slid her palms under his shirt. She wanted to shake him. To beat her fists against his chest. "I want you to stay," she whispered, wrapping her knee around his hip.

He began to pull up her skirts, his hands bunching the

fine linen cloth. He kissed the whorl in her ear. "I'm not going anywhere tonight."

She closed her hand around him, feeling the hardened length of him, hot between her palms. With a deep-chested groan, he kissed her, plunging his tongue inside her mouth, lifting her against him. "*¡Ay Marcus!*" Trembling, she buried her face against the cords in his neck, her hair a cloak around their bodies, an erotic cocoon of forget-me-not silk.

His breath ragged against her ear, he carried her to the bed where they fell onto her rumpled covers. He looked down at her in awe, her hair spread around her like a velvet cloud of smoke, as if he would memorize her forever. "You do bad things to me, *gata*." Removing her drawers, he knelt between her legs. "You have no idea how bad."

Disbelief underscored her shock. Lifting her bottom, he kissed her gently on the thigh. But his eyes weren't so gentle when he raised his head to look at her. They burned into her like a bright silver comet, hotter than sin. Hungry. He plunged his tongue deep inside her, nibbling, caressing, and loving her with his mouth. She cried out. Every muscle leaped and thrilled to the touch of his tongue probing deeper. Surfacing and probing again. She thrashed. Her fists wrapped in his hair to push him away.

She held him there. "*¡Marcus!*"

Waves of searing pleasure washed over her, bathing her, stripping her of her will to move. Marcus raised above her. Opening her eyes slowly, she realized she wasn't going to die. Holding her gaze, he pushed inside her. What control he possessed vanished.

Swallowing her groans, he kissed her and began to move. She tasted herself on his lips; on his tongue. He drove her with his tumult against the headboard, his deep-chested groan rumbling through her senses in a broken litany of Spanish and English until she could not tell one from the other. Night had descended and filled the room with shadows. With him.

Their frenzied mating ended when his body arched and

she felt his life pulse inside her. He fell against her. His ragged breath moved over her ear. "You make me forget who I am, Liandra. And that is very dangerous to both of us."

"Who are you, Englishman?" She heard the anguish in her voice. "Murderer or savior? Pirate or gentleman? Or thief?"

He gathered her into the strength of his arms, kissing her, loving her mouth as easily as he had her body. "I am Marcus Ryan Drake. Born to English aristocracy. Husband to my Spanish wife. Confused as hell."

Sometime later, after Marcus had drifted to sleep, Liandra continued to stare at the canopy. She eased out of bed. Marcus didn't awaken, didn't even stir. An arm rested over his forehead as if exhaustion had claimed him before he could turn to the pillows.

Quietly, she descended the stairs. A lamp had been lit in the parlor. She found her leather chest stored beside the damask settee. A lace cloth draped the engraved leather. All the porcelain figurines were set upright. Perfect.

Heart pounding, she set them aside. Hastily, she flung open the lid. The cutlass Gabriel had once given to her lay in its place. So did her two pistols. Nothing had been moved.

Yet, she felt Marcus's presence all over her things.

"Oh, Marcus," she closed her eyes, "your secret is no worse than the one we've kept from you. Will your hatred be any worse for us than against Carlos when you learn the truth?"

Liandra no longer trusted her English husband enough to find out.

Garbed in his customary canvas breeches, sleeveless jerkin, and sandals, Marcus stood in the cavernous doorway of his creation with naught but the pungent scent of rough-hewn lumber and tar to remind him that his job here was finished. Expectant silence echoed between the clay pipes that would carry the hot water during the grinding process of the cane and iron vats that would hold the syrup.

A slow smile formed. His father might have clapped him on the back for this one. The thought stopped him.

Even after so many years, he still pursued some internal need to impress his father. Marcus leaned his head back on his shoulders and closed his eyes, letting the silence overtake him. Could a man ever truly redeem himself from his past?

A clatter of reins and horses' hooves drawing up the road preceded the announcement of approaching visitors. He glanced over his shoulder and bent his attention to the small entourage that just arrived. Today the village celebrated the unofficial completion of the mill. Families ventured to the mill in carts and wagons.

"Friar Montero has paid the silver ducats for the Dutchman's release." Franco came to stand beside Marcus in the doorway. "He will be brought to the appointed site in two days for you to pick up."

Marcus nodded.

"Your friend Don Pedro is leaving for Panama tomorrow," Franco added. "You've given him proof that will strip Carlos of his power."

Watching a carriage approach, Marcus rubbed his thumb across a splinter in the wall. Condemning Carlos still didn't clear Marcus's name, but it would protect Liandra when he left.

Franco looked around him. "You have done a good job here."

"Thank you." It felt good to say the words.

Hidden in the shadows, Marcus leaned with his arm against the doorway. Friar Montero helped Liandra out of the carriage. Dressed in bright aqua, she matched the seamless dome of blue sky. He watched in captivation as she turned a slow circle. She'd been acting strangely all week. But he didn't feel it now as she surveyed the land and the mill in full.

A sense of pride underscored his achievement here.

Most of these fields belonged to his wife. The mill would make her wealthy in her own right. He was glad to give her this before he left.

Not that he'd come to grips with the reality of leaving her. He hadn't. But in his way, he'd ensured that she would never lack for anything. No one would shame her over her relationship with him.

Liandra lifted her gaze just then. Shading her eyes from the blinding glare of sunset, she found him, and something warm passed through him, something that had nothing to do with the heat of day. She waved.

"I'll leave you in charge up here, Franco." Marcus clapped the younger man on the back and jaunted down the hill to join his wife.

For the past hour, Marcus sensed that he was being followed. He slowed once to listen. He had no idea the hour. He glanced at the sky. A splatter of stars greeted his query. Dawn was not far away. He needed to get as close to Puerto Bello as he could before taking refuge. A distant wicker sounded and Sundown answered.

A bad feeling engulfed him. Wheeling his horse into a copse of trees, he meandered among the shadows and backtracked until he found a hidden place to await his quarry. A full moon lit the rugged landscape. It wasn't long before his prey came into sight.

Dressed indecently in buff breeches too snug to hide her feminine form, Liandra trotted her horse near enough to him that his stallion shifted restlessly beneath him.

Startled by the noise so close to her, his wife yanked the reins and twisted around. A feathered hat plopped over her eyes. She shoved it back, searching for him in the shadows. Riding boots hugged her shapely legs and, as he trailed his astonished gaze up her body, he found himself getting angrier until he finally met her gaze with full-blown fury in his eyes.

"What the hell are you doing here, Liandra?"

Her eyes narrowed defiantly on the sword hanging from the sash at his waist. "What does it look like, Marcus? I won't allow you to endanger my people. I would see what you are up to."

Gritting his teeth, he glared at the sky through the web of tree limbs crisscrossing over his head. Something scampered through the leaves. He would never make it to Puerto Bello now. "Christ, Liandra. You're worse than the wrath of God. Are you His avenging angel? Or just my personal curse?"

"Do you deny you are this Night Shadow thief?"

"I deny everything."

"What are you doing?" she demanded when he pulled the reins out of her hands. Her hat fell to the ground.

"It's dangerous out here. Even for you, my blue-blooded snooping wife. I'm taking you back before you get us both caught."

"I can hide as well as you can, pirate."

"Perhaps." He leaned forward and with little effort plucked her out of the saddle. "But not today. And not in that outfit."

"Let go of me." She cursed at him. Even muffled against his shoulder, he recognized the impressive word. "Another time, sweet. But not now." He kissed her nose, thinking how much he loved her at that moment.

"How dare you mock my concern." She hit him in the chest. "I have been so worried about you. And whether or not you will bring Carlos down on us."

Tying the reins of the other horse to his pommel, he settled his arms around her. He could feel her heart pounding against his arms. "How did you follow me for so long?"

"I gave Sunrise his lead. I was frightened for a while that I had lost you. There are wild animals in these hills."

"You're a fool to be out here."

"Are you the Night Shadow, Marcus?"

"Whatever that is," he grunted, clearly unimpressed with the moniker.

Liandra surged out of his arms, and before Marcus

could yank her back, she slid to the ground. "Enough! You will tell me the truth."

"My patience is not unlimited, Liandra."

"What are you planning to do?"

He pinned her with his gaze. "I plan to find a place to go to sleep. It will be dawn soon."

Framed in moonlight, he looked like he belonged to the night, his eyes fired with the silver of a fast approaching dawn. His gaze fell on her breasts outlined against the shirt.

With just a look, he always turned everything around to his advantage. Tonight, Liandra would not allow him the upper hand. She would have her questions answered.

"You have raided Gabriel's house. You stole from the *alcalde*! People just don't look the other way. How can you justify this?"

He brought a knee around the pommel and leaned forward. "Do you remember the silver on the galleon?"

"The silver Carlos said you threw overboard rather than see it fall back into Spanish hands?"

"Aye. The same," he snorted his disgust.

"You did not throw it overboard?"

"Not hardly."

Liandra paced, moving farther away. Leaves crackled furiously beneath her boots. "How did you get into the house?"

"Getting into the house isn't difficult. I'd been there before."

"Under Innes's invitation?" She crossed her arms. "*Sí*, you have told me. It was seven years ago to be exact."

"She brought many men from the fields into her bedroom, Liandra. She did this beneath Carlos's nose. Through the cellar. Unfortunately for Carlos, I still remembered where that entrance is."

"How did you know where to go once you were inside?"

Marcus studied his hands.

"How?" Her voice was a painful rasp.

His gaze lifted and found hers. "Isabella drew me a map."

She gasped. "Isabella is in this with you? How could you, Marcus?"

"Because she doesn't have your moral fiber, *gata*."

"Why would Isabella do anything for you?" she whispered.

The horses were growing increasingly restless. Marcus gripped the reins, suddenly wary. He peered around the wooded copse.

Having caught the scent of something, the horses whinnied again. Liandra glanced over her shoulder.

"We'll talk about this later, sweet." Marcus lowered his voice. "Let's go."

Just as he held out his hand to her, a flock of jewel-hued birds nesting in the trees scattered in a mad flight.

Both horses reared. Their giant hooves barely missed Liandra's head. She stumbled backward.

Marcus hit the ground flat on his back.

Liandra struggled to sit. Her gaze flew to Marcus. Leaves covered his head and arms. He twisted in time to see the horses dive through the underbrush, stirrups flapping, and disappear.

Panicked, she scrambled over to him. "Are you all right?" She tested his ribs and chest. "What frightened the birds?"

Gasping for breath, he shoved her hands away. "I . . . don't know. Stay down." He turned over onto his hands and knees. The cutlass scraped the ground. "Do your horses . . . come when you call?"

She shook her head.

"But they won't go far," he said. "There is a creek just over the next ridge. We'll get them there."

He sat back on his heels and shoved the leaves off his legs. His hands slowed and, as he continued to watch her, something dangerous flared in his eyes. Alarm quickened her pulse. Without intending to retreat, she scooted backward.

"Oh, no you don't." A hand clapped around her ankle. Before she could gasp, Marcus yanked her across the dew-ridden ground to him.

"What do you think you're doing?"

Marcus gripped her flailing wrists and flattened her to the ground. His hardened body pressed her into the leaves. A smile twisted his sensuous mouth. "A mind reader. I like that about a woman. What am I thinking now, *gata*?"

There was a threatening quality to his voice and Liandra felt a thrill of excitement drive through her. His hungry gaze dropped to her mouth. "Are you insane?"

"Very." He pinned her hands.

"Get off me!"

"Miguel is the father of Isabella's child, Liandra. Not me. When Carlos killed him, she realized what a monster her father really is. That's when she ran to you for help."

She stilled. "Miguel and Isabella?"

"He'd wanted to marry her, but she was afraid of her father and tried to protect him by breaking it off with him. He never knew that she was pregnant."

"She told you all of this?"

"I didn't trust her either. If she was going to betray her father, I wanted to know why."

"Does Uncle Montero know? About everything, I mean?"

"He knows."

The rattle of harnesses drifted over the predawn terrain.

Marcus rolled to his feet, then dropped to a crouch at the edge of the copse. With an oath, he tore the scarf from his head. "This is just bloody grand."

Liandra crawled to his side.

"Get down." Marcus took her to the ground. An edge of steel, as strong as the arms that surrounded her, laced his voice. "That shirt stands out like a white flag. Stay low."

He parted the brush and together they glimpsed out. On the distant hill, a platoon of eight soldiers sat atop their horses.

Her pulse throbbed. She closed her eyes fighting the

dizzying sensation of panic, keenly aware of the pungent scent of decaying earth, sweat, and her own fear. This wouldn't have happened if she hadn't followed Marcus. But he didn't say that. He didn't say anything. Only his heartbeat against her ribs revealed any sign that he was alive at all, so still was he.

A man with a perspective glass quartered the trees.

"*Dios*! Why aren't they moving?"

"They're wondering what spooked the birds."

Her muscles bunched. "My horses—"

"You better use your divine connection to pray those studs of yours make it back to the mission, Liandra."

But even as Marcus said the words, Liandra heard a man's shout. She saw him pint to a place just over the hill. Immediately alerted, the soldiers kicked their horses into a gallop.

Chapter Eighteen

Gripping Liandra's hand, Marcus tore through the undergrowth. Daylight penetrated the thickest part of the jungle. All around him, birds chatted. Monkeys screeched. The jungle cacophony hid their noisy flight. Liandra stumbled to her knees again. Her staggered breathing pulled at him. She wasn't used to this kind of activity, much less the terror of being chased by Carlos's soldiers.

"I . . . am trying, Marcus." Her braid had unraveled, leaving her hair a tangled mess filled with tiny branches and insects.

Marcus dropped beside her. He swatted a spider away. "I know."

"I . . . swear, I will scream . . . if you pick another one of those things off me. I hate spiders!"

He cupped her face. Her skin was flushed. They'd run over a league, almost five miles. "You picked a hell of a place to live then, sweet."

The ground vibrated with the thunder of hooves.

Liandra's head snapped up. "They're still looking for us."

"Shh." Taking Liandra into his arms, he settled into as small a target as possible.

The soldiers had divided into pairs and spread out. He glared through the trellised patchwork of branches. The greenery provided some cover but not nearly enough. "They're heading north toward Puerto Bello," he said against her ear. "That's good."

The platoon passed barely twenty feet away. Marcus could smell the sweat on the horses. They'd been ridden hard.

Liandra's heart pumped in her chest. His arms tightened around her as if he had the power to keep her safe. He didn't. Again, because of him, someone he loved might die.

The notion of love appalled him. Perhaps because he hadn't considered himself capable of the sentiment. He'd lived in the darkness for so long, he'd grown roots. Or maybe because love made a person helpless, and he resented like hell that Liandra crippled him.

He turned his face into his sleeve, away from her hair. Away from her essence. The minutes ticked by in his head. Sunlight harpooned the copse with glittering rays. Puerto Bello was hot as Hades during the summer months, and it was already June. Coming out of the mountains was like stepping onto hot sand.

He looked up just in time to see Liandra's stallions towed by two soldiers. The horses were lathered and looked in bad shape.

"I have to get you back to your village somehow. You could say the horses were stolen. At least they couldn't prove they weren't."

"What about you?"

Wiping the sweat from his brow with his sleeve, he said, "It's too dangerous for all of you if I go back, now."

"Marcus . . ."

"No, Liandra. Don't speak. Don't say a thing."

He yanked her up. She attempted to stand without his help. This was another example of her stubbornness. She would pass out before voicing one word of complaint. He needed to find water.

Marcus lifted her and started running. Surprisingly, she didn't fight him. Her head fell against his shoulder. "I should never have followed you."

"You never should have done a lot of things, Liandra."

He was being unfair, of course. This was his fault for not being more careful. For staying long past the time he should have left. But being angry with her took the bite out of his self-contempt.

An hour later, they reached an abandoned windmill bathed in the shadows of towering trees. Marcus lowered Liandra to her feet. They half-slid down a steep hill, their feet swishing in the dead leaves.

Suddenly shadows swarmed him. Marcus clapped a hand over Liandra's mouth as she started to scream. "It's all right," he said against her hair. She shrank against him. His arms tightened around her, as much to reassure her as to warn anyone that Espinosa's sister belonged to him. "These are my men. They aren't going to hurt you." More lay in blankets on the ground and stirred now, twisting to face him.

"We've had a change of plans," he told them all. "Is *Dark Fury* still at anchor?"

"They moved her out of the shallows three days ago, Cap'n. She's been scraped an' cleaned of barnacles just awaitin' our arrival." The speaker chuckled. "Took 'em near a month to do it."

Marcus realized Carlos must be expecting Espinosa back sometime soon to go to all the trouble to prepare *Dark Fury* for duty.

"Do we have horses?"

"No, sir," someone mumbled. "Nothin' but an old burro what draws the cart that come yesterday with our food."

Turning with Liandra in his arms, Marcus strode with her to the windmill, instantly kicking the door shut behind him. Sunlight seeped through the cracks high above his head. Birds shifted restlessly in nests on the rafters. Liandra stood alone in the middle of the room, a halo of dust motes floating around her head. The ethereal vision stilled his heart. She looked so fragile standing there like some bedraggled imp.

"They won't catch you," she said, her voice small and determined, as if her passion alone could save him.

He blinked in disbelief. "You should be more worried about yourself, Liandra." She presented him with her profile. Marcus yanked her face around. "Don't you know what will happen to you if I don't get you back? Carlos will make you into an outlaw. He might even claim that you're in league with the Night Shadow. Who else but Isabella knows the layout of your brother's house?"

He shoved both hands through his hair, only to jerk when he felt her wrap her arms around him. "You should have told me what you were doing," she said.

He brushed the hair from her dusty face. Insects buzzed in the sleepy warmth of the room. "Would you have sat idly by doing needlework while I raided Carlos's house? And if Carlos had asked you what you knew about the Night Shadow? What would you have said?"

She closed her eyes, but did not relinquish her grip on his shirt. "See?" he said. "Your principles make you a poor liar."

"You're the one who found evidence against Carlos, aren't you?"

"Don't lay anything heroic at my feet," he whispered into her tangled hair. "If it weren't for your Uncle Montero, I wouldn't give a monkey's ass what Carlos's crimes are. He's been stealing from your Spanish king for years. I merely brought your uncle the proof in the silver I lifted from his precious belongings."

He felt her shiver in the heat. "You used the silver to free your men?"

"We're picking up the Dutchman tomorrow." He didn't tell her that ten of his men remained unaccounted for. That it was too soon, yet, to leave. Jesu, he was bone weary. The beginnings of a headache throbbed in his temples. "You need food and water—"

"I have been wrong about so many things. I am sorry."

She wept silently. Hot tears bled into his shirt. "I can't seem to help my emotions. I'm not frightened, really." She wiped a grimy hand across her face and left a streak. "I've done my best to protect you. I have." She swayed. "I'm glad I followed you. I'm not glad that I've put you in danger. But there are . . . things we must talk about."

Lifting her into his arms, Marcus carried her to the stack of hay in the corner. He'd spent many a night the past month sleeping here. He shook out his blankets and laid them down for her.

"I'm staying with you, Marcus. I will learn to fight like you."

Marcus stared down at her dirt-streaked face and felt a helpless surge of anger. He didn't want her to be like him. "Go to sleep, Liandra," he said. "We'll talk about this later."

Within minutes her body surrendered to exhaustion.

Burying his forehead into his palms, he groaned. Damn her stubbornness. What was he going to do with her? He had nothing.

Concealed behind a wall of greenery, Marcus studied the crystalline bay below. Tiny, diamond-marked ripples glittered in the sunlight. *Dark Fury* bobbed languidly in the sea. Inviting. Dangerous. The scene had trap scrawled all over it.

Marcus didn't turn when Ramón crouched beside him. "It will not be easy sailing her out from beneath the cannons of the fort."

"Carlos doesn't intend us to make it that far."

Ramón handed a water skin to Marcus. "We will make the rendezvous with the Dutchman tomorrow morning, *Señor*," the Spaniard said. "Friar Montero is bringing him to an old mission church at the edge of town."

Marcus swished water in his mouth and spit. "What about the others?"

"I am sorry, *Señor*. We needed more time to find them."

He scraped a grimy hand across his bearded jaw. Leaving now condemned them to die here.

With a soldier's practiced eye, Marcus returned his gaze to the scene below. Sunbaked hovels lined the beach. He let his eyes adjust to the distance. From this high advantage, he glimpsed not only the harbor where *Dark Fury* pulled at her anchor, but also Espinosa's house spread out like a miniature palace against the backdrop of the white, adobe town. He watched the small, sticklike figures run across the lawn. Another detail of soldiers had been called to the house.

Marcus had forty-five men at camp. Barely enough to sail *Dark Fury*, he realized in disgust. Not enough to man the guns. That was if powder was stowed on board. But with the activity below him, it became apparent that any move Marcus made would have to come soon.

A black beetle scurried between his boots and, idly, he watched it burrow into the dirt. Marcus knew that if he could just close his eyes, he would sleep forever. But his mind would not leave Liandra.

Boots crunched in the gravel as someone approached. Bracing an elbow on his knee, he twisted to look behind him. The windmill sat in a deep valley between the hills, an hour's walk through the meanest brambles if a man didn't know the path. A dozen of his men approached. He recognized the sentry he set to guard his wife.

"What are you doing here?"

"Yer wife is askin' fer you, Cap'n." The boy glanced warily at the thick copse of trees and bushes as if afraid of being set upon by soldiers. "She was real upset ta find ya gone when she awoke. Said she had something to tell you before you left. That it were important."

He stood. "Is she all right?"

"Who can say with a woman?" The towheaded youth shrugged. "Maybe she doesn't like her quarters."

"You left your post to tell me this?"

"Someone else is watchin' her, Cap'n. I thought you'd want to know that she's askin' fer you."

Inexplicably annoyed with Liandra, Marcus felt a surge of anger. "Make sure she's fed and has ample water to clean up with," he ordered the youth. "She wanted to be a part of this, she damned well better get used to life's inconveniences. And on your life, see that she doesn't leave."

Watching the youth scurry away, Marcus snatched up a stick. He motioned for his men to approach. "We have to move up our plans," he said. "Carlos has already sent men to the mission valley. It's only a matter of time before he discovers Liandra gone. He'll know that we were there."

A murmur of conjecture greeted his words.

Looking at the sky and the darkening clouds, he faced his men. "We can try to walk out of here. Through mosquito infested swamps. Take a chance on finding a ship." His gaze moved to *Dark Fury* as he spoke. "Or we go after the bigger prize. Here."

"God love you, Captain," someone said. "Ye know we'll be followin' you. But what about the cannons on those forts?"

"Leave that problem to me."

Ramón's dark eyes became speculative. "You are going after Don Carlos, *si*?" Something like admiration shone in his gaze.

"Aye. But tonight, we go after the ship."

Liandra's head snapped up at the sound of muffled laughter. Until now, it had been quiet outside. Hay rustled with her nervous movements. Perspiration beaded on her face. She sat with her legs drawn to her chest. Resting her cheek on her knees, she hugged her legs tighter, rocking slightly. She'd not been allowed to light a taper, so she sat in the darkness waiting for Marcus to return.

Rats were in this place. She was sure of it as she listened to noises around her. But she was more afraid of Marcus's men than the varmints in here. She'd seen the looks on their faces that afternoon. They all knew she was

Gabriel's sister: the sister of El Condor. And Carlos's niece. Marcus was the only reason she was alive now.

Squeezing her eyes tight, she forced herself to breathe. She was made of sterner stuff. But the day had taxed her strength. Her head ached. She hadn't been able to keep down her food. Her clothes were filthy, her hair an unmanageable ruin.

She needed to talk to Marcus.

Dios, he must be told about his brother.

The windmill creaked. A stiff breeze pushed against the wooden structure stirring hay and dust. Liandra hurried to the door. One hand on the frame, she looked out. Across the camp, she picked out four shadows hunched over a small fire. A small kettle bubbled. Their voices were low. Although they spoke in English, she recognized Carlos's name on the same breath as Triana. Where were all the men?

"Get back inside." A man loomed before her.

Liandra started but did not retreat from the scowl on his face. On closer inspection, she saw that he was a boy, barely older than she was. "Where is the *capitán*?"

"I told you, he will be back later."

She looked at the sky. It was at least two hours past midnight. "Did you tell him that I needed to talk to him?" she quietly asked.

"Obviously he didn't want to see ye."

"Leave her be," a man's gravelly voice interrupted.

Liandra met the eyes of the old man who'd spoken: the same man who'd terrified her in the hold of the galleon so many months ago. The one she'd seen on the hill at the mill.

Coming toward her, he offered her a tin plate of fried beans and bread. "You best be eatin' something, Duchess. Captain's orders. It be safer inside."

"No," she whispered. "I won't go back in there."

Something suddenly set the birds flapping in the trees and Liandra instinctively stepped back into the shadows. From the corner of her eye, she saw one of the men beside the fire stand. Slowly, the others followed. For a heartbeat no one moved. No one breathed.

"Carlos has found us," someone whispered.

The old man beside her dropped the plate. "Get inside, Duchess."

At once, a flaming arrow flew, barely missing her head; then another slammed into the windmill, and another. A horrendous swoosh. And fire caught the straw. Everything inside the windmill flared up like dry kindling. "Jesus, Mary and Joseph!" The old man shoved her out of the way. An arrow hit him between his shoulder blades. He slammed against Liandra, and they both fell through the door.

Thick smoke swirled around her. Heat singed her hair. Kicking wildly, Liandra screamed over her panic. She shoved the dead man off her chest and rolled to her knees. Her eyes fell on the cutlass at the old man's waist. Outside, musket shot thundered. Instinctively, she dropped. Soldiers had descended on the camp swarming over everyone in a furor of clashing steel. Coughing, she gripped the hilt of the sword and, sliding it from the scabbard, ran from the burning windmill. Marcus's men lay sprawled on the ground.

Soldiers filled the clearing. Her fingers curled tightly around the hilt of the cutlass. Heart pounding, she backed farther into the woods, away from the burning inferno, away from the soot-covered faces. Even if she were not out-numbered, she could not fight them. They were still her people.

Tongues of flame shot up the windmill, licking greedily at the structure. With a cry, she spun, and ran directly into a man's arms.

"Don Carlos!"

"Maria Liandra. Consorting with English pirates, I see."

His dark eyes sent terror down her spine. Liandra leaped away. Sword raised, she barely blinked before his cutlass slammed against hers. Pain shot up her arm all the way across her shoulder blades.

Fire burned in his eyes. A dark goatee framed his leer. "My men found your horses."

He drove her backward. Brambles tore at her arms. "That . . . proves nothing."

"And Gabriel's hat. What will he say when he discovers that you have been using his clothes for a disguise?"

With a sob, Liandra fought harder. Desperation alone fueled her strength. Their swords came together, slid until she stood shoulder to shoulder with Carlos. "Maybe if you give me back my silver . . . and show me how sorry you are, I won't hang you."

"That silver . . . was never . . . yours." She swung the blade and sliced through his sleeve.

Disbelief ruined his placid composure. "Only one person knows that. And I don't believe that you are the Night Shadow." Carlos swiped his leg against her ankles, knocking her flat. The air slammed out of her chest. Pain sliced through her abdomen. "There were two horses, Maria Liandra. Two!" He stepped on her wrist, and she cried out. Reaching down, he tore the cutlass from her grip. "Which means someone else was with you last night."

"No," she groaned. Stabbing pain gripped her insides.

"A particular Englishman, maybe? Who isn't dead, after all?" He grabbed a handful of her hair. "You are beaten, bitch."

"Never by you!" She spat in his face.

He was upon her like a beast in the night, pinning her against the hot, baked earth. Trapped, she fought like a leopard, horrified that he would suddenly rape her. He tore open her shirt.

"You cannot do this, Carlos!"

His mouth cradled her ear, his hand her breast. "Ah, but I can do anything I want, Maria Liandra." His fingers crawled around her throat. "You are a criminal now. A pirate's whore."

"He will . . . kill you . . . Carlos," she rasped.

"Maybe I'll throw you in that burning inferno." His grip

on her throat tightened. "Have you ever smelled flesh burn, Maria Liandra?"

She tried desperately to fight and, despite her will not to scream, she did. He choked off her voice. She could not pry his fingers from her throat. Her struggles lessened. A strange sense of lethargy settled through her limbs. Behind her she heard the burning windmill cave in upon itself.

Her final thought before she lost consciousness was that she would die and Marcus would leave without ever knowing the truth about his brother . . . or his own child.

Friar Montero stepped into the chapel and hesitated, allowing his eyes to adjust to the darkness. A stained-glass window over the main entrance provided the only source of light. Fingers of scarlet and amber stirred the shadows. Marcus sat with his head in his hands in an empty pew at the front of the small adobe church. A black scarf wrapped his head. On the wooden altar, a candle sputtered in the final throes of life. The acrid scent of burning wax lingered.

Marcus had arrived here this morning covered in soot, exhausted, knowing Friar Montero would be waiting with the Dutchman. Four of the captain's men were dead, the windmill where he'd taken Maria, burned to the ground. Montero looked at this strong man made so vulnerable by his obvious love for Maria, and felt a sudden tightening in his chest. He'd grown to care for his niece's English husband and regretted the secret between them. Though, in the beginning, it had been necessary to keep him alive.

At his approach, Marcus lifted his head. He took in the Friar's expression, and seemed to brace. His silver eyes looked stark against the hard planes of his unshaven face.

"She's alive," Montero said at once. "The *alcalde* has arrested her. He claims that she is the person he calls Night Shadow."

Marcus stood, the power of his rage clearly amplified by his height and darkness. "He must know that she's not."

"The charges will stick. Her feelings toward Don Carlos are well known. On more than one occasion she has denounced his policies toward the citizens here. He hates her and her brother. Don Carlos will use this to bring them both down."

"Christ . . . I should never have left her last night."

"Carlos still does not know that you have taken back *Dark Fury*."

"Aye. And my men on board will be used as target practice by the fort's cannons if he finds out before I catch him, Padre."

Montero clasped his hands behind him to keep them from shaking. "If you go after Don Carlos now it will be the excuse he needs to kill Maria. The compound is too well guarded. Not even Night Shadow can get through that armed gauntlet now."

Something told Montero that a mountain of fire could stand betwixt the Englishman and Carlos, and it would make no difference to this man. But he would not risk Liandra's life for anything. The captain possessed an inordinate amount of courage. Yet, his very strength was his greatest weakness. He feared for the lives of others, but did not fear for himself.

He was so like his father, from his height to the breadth of his heart.

"What do I do then? Sit around like a two-legged dog while Carlos destroys everything I hold dear? I won't be so helpless!"

"There is another way, *mi hijo*. My son. Last night Don Carlos sent men to the mission to retrieve Isabella and anyone else associated with Maria. Including her mother and me. They will be on their way back by now. They'll have to change horses. That is where your men can overtake the soldiers. I will go with you to the place."

Marcus shook his head. "Don Pedro will not be back from Panama in time to save you if you are caught."

"If I get caught, it will not matter who I am with, *Capitán*."

"Very well." Impatience clipped his words. "It's your bloody neck. Let's go."

He stopped Marcus from leaving. "There is one more thing."

"Jesu, Padre. Can't this wait?"

Montero turned in a slow circle, taking in the crumbling ceiling, the water-stained walls, thinking how time ravaged more than men's souls. Yet, once, long ago, love had found a way.

"Did you know your parents were married in this church?"

The words seemed to jolt Marcus. He turned.

"Spaniard and English. The unity was a good one." Montero carried on casually, realizing now with a sick heart how much he'd erred in not telling this man the truth about his brother sooner. "It still is," he said on a long exhale. "Don Pedro and I were hoping that we would be able to give you a gift before you left. Long before it ever came to this. Maybe change your mind about leaving us. I know as things stand now, it is impossible for you to stay."

"Forgive me if I'm not following you—"

"A letter went out on Don Gabriel's ship. Don Pedro is an emissary from Spain. A year ago on his way to Cartagena, pirates attacked his ship, killing the viceroy and most everyone on board. He is related to his Catholic majesty. A distant cousin of sorts. Nevertheless, they are acquainted. Don Pedro is seeking your pardon."

Marcus shook his head in disbelief. "Espinosa would never stand for it, Padre."

"Do you know why my nephew . . . why Don Gabriel hates your family?"

"No. And I don't have time for this—"

"During Henry Morgan's raid on Puerto Bello, your father killed his. To a boy who'd already endured too much, that is everything."

The expression in Marcus's eyes remained unfathomable and no less impatient, but he no longer looked ready to jump the gate.

Friar Montero turned away. "My niece has always known this. She loved you still. And whatever she has done these past months is because she would die herself rather than see you hurt. As would the rest of us."

A hand on Montero's arm drew him around. "What are you saying?"

"Your brother is alive, *señor*. He is on Martinique."

Marcus stared at him, as if the friar had grown horns and a tail, as if he still couldn't comprehend. For several seconds he did not speak. "Talon would never willingly give up the *Dark Fury* to another captain." His voice was a rasp.

"Don Gabriel knew this as well and considered him dead. He deported the crew he brought in to New Spain for trial. Most were sent back to Port Royal. Carlos didn't tell you anything because he wanted you to suffer. Later he found out where your brother was."

Hands on his hips, Marcus paced one step, then two, as the obvious tumult became hope. "You mean Talon might be in a French prison? How long? When did you find this out?"

Montero found his tongue caged by his thoughts. Something in his eyes must have betrayed him. He knew the moment Marcus read the truth. And as he watched the final remnants of life drain out of Drake's face, the thin veneer of civilization Drake carried like a glass shield shattered as if hit by a fist. For the first time since he'd known the Englishman, fear braced Montero's spine. He understood enough about violence to be afraid.

Marcus grabbed him by his robe. "Sonofabitch. How long?"

"Carlos told us that day when he came to the mission."

"And you said nothing when I came to you about the mill? Nothing? Did . . . did Liandra know?"

"You were in no condition to leave. We were trying to protect you until we could—"

"Or maybe I was just too damn convenient to have around, is that it? While my brother is rotting away in some prison, your outcast niece manipulated her precious sugarcane mill out of me. This is bloody rich." With a shove, Marcus pushed away. He kicked the bench and sent it scraping across the wooden floor. Then rounded on Montero. The cutlass hanging at his side lent an ominous portent to his presence. "You knew what Talon's life meant to me. Liandra knew—and she didn't say anything."

Montero watched him walk away, his boots rapping a grim tattoo on the floor. "What are you planning to do?"

"Find my wife before it's too late. Then I'm going after my brother." At the door, he suddenly stopped. His hand curled into a fist. "Whatever you thought you were doing, you had no right to make that decision for me, Padre. You had no right. Not for any reason."

Chapter Nineteen

The first shout came ahead of them. Ramón pounded on the carriage top twice. Marcus felt the carriage slow.

"We've reached the gates," Friar Montero said in a voice that rang like a prayer.

Isabella's small hands fisted in her lap. Marcus felt his jaw tighten. He didn't need to be worrying about his passengers. He extended his gaze to the pewter-haired woman on Isabella's left. "If there's trouble, both of you get out of my way."

"Quit fretting about us, *Capitán.*" Isabella's smile trembled. Despite her youth, she was determined to meet the challenge head on.

She'd grown to be like Liandra in that way.

Liandra.

His thoughts whispered her name, and fear fell on him like a pack of mongrels chewing and gnawing him with visions of her torture. Unbidden, it rose like hot bile in his throat.

Clasping his hands over his robes, he lowered his head slightly to keep his face in the shadows. The cutlass pressed against his thigh like a comfortable friend.

Isabella raised the leather window covering. The

grounds had grown lush with manicured trees and gardens. He could not see the house. Heart pounding, he listened to Isabella chatting with the sentry. Friar Montero made his greeting.

Marcus forced himself to breathe. The robe the friar found for him reeked of garlic and onion. It could not have been a more unpleasant place to hide, but it eased his torment to focus on something else.

His gaze fell on the woman sitting across from him. Liandra's mother. Her gloved hands were folded in her lap in a gesture of feminine serenity. Despite himself, he felt his gaze go higher. Her black lace mantilla headdress touched the carriage ceiling. She had not stopped staring at him since he'd climbed into the carriage hours ago. She was beautiful, with her dark enigmatic eyes and a full mouth shaped so much like Liandra's it hurt to stare. She was smiling. Just slightly, like someone who knew a secret. He met her eyes.

The carriage suddenly lurched forward.

"We're in," Isabella said.

"Find her!" Carlos's rapid Spanish bore the hint of rage. A slap. Some poor servant maybe. All was silent except for a girl's soft whimper. "She can't have gone far in her condition."

Hidden behind the cellar door, Liandra listened as the servant scampered away. Palms against the cool, stone wall, she turned her cheek against her hand to still her throbbing temples, to ease the weight of her senses. She no longer wore her wretched smoke-scented clothes. Someone had changed her into a clean nightdress. Free of blood. Her feet were bare. She hadn't had the strength to make it out of the cellar where Carlos had put her yesterday. It was only a matter of time before they found her again. Then Carlos would surely finish what he'd started to do to her last night. In front of his men.

Before the bleeding started.

"Your daughter's carriage is here." A man's voice sounded at the top of the stone stairwell. "I put them in the library, Excellency."

"Them?" Carlos's voice was further away now.

"She came in with Friar Montero. And another woman."

Her heart leapt. Uncle Montero was here.

A door slammed.

Liandra remained pressed to the wall. She'd been clever to escape the tyrant. A giggle suddenly pulled at her throat. She turned her back to the wall. Closing her eyes, she felt herself sliding down to the floor. The opiates they'd fed her took away her fear. And her pain. A part of her brain knew she had to reach Uncle Montero for something. But she couldn't quite remember what had been so important.

Marcus tore off the friar's robe and stepped behind the library door. Carlos's tirade rumbled the length of the house.

"Here he comes." Friar Montero sat opposite Liandra's mother as she applied herself to one of a pair of high-backed chairs.

"He is furious," Isabella whispered as she doffed her gloves.

She stood forlornly in front of the giant mahogany desk that dominated the dark, baroque-style room. Gilded books lined the shelves on three sides of the room like trophies of conquest, not mementos of pleasure. Marcus doubted a single book had ever been touched, except by the one who placed them on the shelves. The verandah doors remained opened. Outside, Ramón casually stood guard. Dressed in the garb of Carlos's soldiers, eight of Marcus's men had ridden in with the carriage and were now someplace within this house.

The rest of his men were waiting for them on the *Dark Fury*.

Dusk sat on the distant horizon in the form of a hazy orange ball. They still had nearly two hours of daylight, which was all he needed. Tonight they would all sail out of Puerto Bello.

Or never leave at all.

An angry voice came from just outside the door. "Send for me the moment she's found."

Whatever had set Carlos off made him careless. He stalked into the library. Marcus slammed the door shut. Carlos wheeled and Marcus smashed a fist into his jaw. It wasn't planned, but he couldn't take a chance on the little man raising the alarm.

"Papa!"

"Get away from him, Isabella." Marcus dragged him up by his pristine uniform and sat him in the chair behind his desk.

"But you promised not to kill him."

Marcus shot her a glare. "Take Liandra's mother and go find my wife. Friar, lay out the vellum and quill."

Isabella swung away in a flurry of skirts. Dazed, Carlos lifted his gaze. His teeth were red. "*Basta ya!*"

"Ramón, send a man to get the *alcalde's* launch ready."

"*Sí, señor.*"

"Where is Dutch?"

"He has rounded up the servants, *señor*. They are in the kitchen feeding him. He said to tell you that everything is under control."

Carlos snickered. "Perhaps your men are not so competent after all, Drake."

Marcus drew his cutlass. He leaned his dusty boot on the chair and stared at the hated Spaniard. "You keep telling yourself that while you write the orders that will free my ship."

"I cannot do it."

"Do you honestly want to know how *can't* feels, Carlos?" Marcus laid the edge of the cutlass over the man's hand. "I guarantee that after I finish with you, you will own a whole new understanding."

"You will die, Drake. I swear El Condor will hunt you down."

"Aye, maybe. But it won't save you, *Excellency*."

With a furious hand, Carlos wrote out the orders. After the ink dried, Marcus handed the papers to Ramón. He returned a few moments later. "It is done, *señor*. It will take at least half an hour to reach the officers in charge of the forts."

Two men carrying a leather chest between them entered the room. "Captain we have found everything of value. Carlos is a very wealthy man. The men will appreciate his generosity."

Carlos' mouth dropped into a savage line. "Sedition!" he spat at Ramón. "You are a traitor. I will see you gutted—" Isabella entered the room and he glared his fury at her. "Along with that Judas daughter of mine."

"Papa!"

Carlos suddenly raked her belly with his cold black gaze, and his eyes widened.

"*Sí*, Papa. Your eyes do not lie. You murdered Miguel. He was the father of your grandson. And to think I was worried because he was not aristocracy." Tears filled her eyes. "He was a better man than you many times over." Deliberately she turned her back and spoke to Marcus. "We cannot find Maria."

"Maybe I put out the reward for the wrong bitch, *sí*?"

Isabella lifted her nose. "If I had half my cousin's courage, I would have stood up to you sooner. You do not know what I have endured because of you."

"You?" Carlos scoffed. "Maria is no true cousin of yours, you spineless slut."

"Gag him," Marcus told Ramón.

"I don't care what you've always said," Isabella whispered. "She *is* my cousin."

"She lost your child, Drake," Carlos choked out.

Marcus's heart stopped for what seemed half a lifetime before his pulse kicked again.

"She's been bleeding like a throat-cut lamb. My hope is that she'll save me the trouble of a trial and die on her own . . ."

Something in Marcus's expression froze Carlos. Maybe it was the murder in his eyes, the shadow of the beast he could be when provoked. His hands started forward to grip the man's throat, but he did not move or touch the *alcalde*. If he had, he would surely rip the man's heart out. With desperate strength, Marcus pulled back.

"Isabella." Friar stepped between him and Carlos. "Find Maria," he ordered. "And get the Dutchman in here now."

Carlos leaned against the chair, his leer white against the pointed goatee. A line of gold buttons marched down the front of his jacket in perfect military precision. The *alcalde's* white uniform was a spotless mockery to the bloodred haze Marcus saw.

"Backing away from me?" Carlos jeered. "You're softer than your brother, Drake. He would have gone for my throat."

Montero wheeled. "*Dios*, but you tempt fate."

"Aye." Marcus slammed a fist into Carlos's jaw, sending the Spaniard tumbling over the chair. "But it's your lucky day, you bastard. I need you alive. Dutch?"—Marcus commanded as that one filled the doorway—"see that His Excellency is not made too comfortable."

Then Marcus was out of the library.

Time had no meaning. An hour could have been a month or a day. Liandra's eyes fluttered open. She must have dozed. Bits and pieces of her dreams drifted over her.

For surely, her eyes lied.

A long figure, dressed in black, sat in silent vigil beside her. Liandra's head rested in the woman's lap. They were on the floor.

"Mama?" Her voice broke. It hurt to talk.

"*Sí*, I am here." A taper flickered and caught the wet glitter in her mother's dark eyes, lucid now as they studied Liandra. A hand, wilted with torment, touched her cheek. "You were always like a doll," her mother's voice whispered, so soft, so beautiful. A dream. "They think that I would stay alone while others searched for you."

Liandra's gaze probed her mother's beautiful face. "How did you get here?"

"Bella brought me. We had to leave the mission. She said that you needed me."

"*Sí*, Mama. I am frightened."

"Nonsense. You are your mother's child. You are strong." She stroked Liandra's hair. "You will not forget that strength when you leave here. Even now, your husband is with Don Carlos."

"Marcus is safe?"

Her mother smiled. "He will not let you die. He is like his brave father."

Liandra blinked back the rush of tears. She could only stare at her mother in confusion. This was a dream. Not in fifteen years had Mama spoken more than ten coherent sentences in a row. Never had she spoken about the man who'd killed her husband.

"His dear *madre* was my best friend," her mother said, reading her mind. "It is God's blessing that my daughter found her son. Perhaps there can be forgiveness after all, *sí*?"

Liandra closed her eyes. "I love him, Mama."

"Then follow your heart, sweet Maria."

"*Sí*, Mama." She curled closer to her mother's warmth, the familiar scent of citron, the security of her voice, and wept.

"Liandra?"

Marcus's voice came to her from somewhere. His hand was cool against her face and she turned her cheek seeking more of his palm.

"Christ, what did he do to you?"

Strong arms lifted her as if she weighed no more than a babe. She stirred, but didn't have the strength to open her eyes.

"We have to get to the ship. Get the men together."

"Is she alive, *señor*?" A man's voice followed.

"Do it, man!"

Marcus carried her out of the room.

Then he was patting her face. "Liandra?"

Her eyes opened. His dark hair was pulled away from his face in a queue. The shadow of a beard framed his jaw. He wore the blue and white attire of Carlos's guard. Beneath one full sleeve, she could feel the corded strength of his forearm.

She grinned. "You look like an English lord."

His palm cupped her cheek, as he checked her eyes. "Not too English. Or they'll shoot me. The uniform is borrowed, sweet."

A laudanum-induced sense of peace swirled through her senses. Liandra touched his cheek. "You're alive."

"Aye. And we're leaving here. But you have to walk out of here. If I carry you, Carlos's men will stop us. It would not do for an officer in his guard to be seen carrying a friar. Do you understand?"

She nodded as he dropped a robe over her head. It smelled like garlic, and she wrinkled her nose. Uncle Montero never smelled so badly. When she straightened, she felt the rags between her legs shift, but they stayed in place.

Isabella threw her arms around her. "I will miss you."

Liandra's eyes flung open. Across Isabella's shoulder, she caught Marcus's gaze. The touch lasted no more than a grain of sand in time. Whatever flickered in his eyes vanished.

Liandra hugged her back. "What . . . will happen to you?"

Uncle Montero hugged her. "We will take the carriage back to the mission and await Don Pedro. Captain Drake is taking Carlos to our family in Old Providence for safekeeping. He will not hurt us again."

"Uncle . . . will you see my horses cared for?"

Liandra's mother cupped her face with hands of velvet. "They will be safe."

"Mama?"

Marcus came up behind Liandra. Estella's gaze found his. Then, as if she no longer knew where she was, she allowed Friar Montero to lead her away.

"We have to leave, Liandra," he said.

Somehow Liandra walked.

Always Marcus was there. His hand lightly bracing her elbow, his strength holding her erect. They walked out the back through the library door. Liandra was barefoot. They were almost to the beach before she saw the men standing around the launch. Carlos was unbound, but looking livid.

"What's it look like behind us, Dutch?" Marcus's tone was quiet.

"Der carriage has reached der sentry gate. Der guards are watching us."

Liandra closed her eyes. Keep walking. Keep walking. She said the words over and over again. A song and a prayer. Marcus seemed in no hurry, though she felt his tension as he kept to her pace.

Finally, they reached the beach. Lifting her, he set her in the launch and rushed to climb behind her. The heat was stifling beneath the robe she wore. Dutch sat beyond Carlos, who watched her with hateful eyes.

"Now I know what moves the pirate Drake."

"Then be really good, Carlos, and I might let you live."

Carlos slitted his eyes on her. "No matter what they do to me, Maria Liandra, you still have to answer the charges against you."

Burrowing beneath the hot cowl on the heavy woolen robe, Liandra pressed against Marcus's chest. Arms enfolding her, Marcus leaned forward. "And I promise this. You will never hurt her again."

"You won't get far, Drake. Not in the condition those sails are in. Not without enough men."

The skiff rose and fell over the surf as Dutch set his back to the oars. Liandra did not look behind her at the beautiful mountains of a home she would never see again. She did not glance at the forts guarding the bay, or the giant cannons on the ramparts.

The oars slapped the water and, as the boat drifted away from shore, *Dark Fury*'s Cimmerian shadow loomed across the water like an enormous bird of prey. Her breath caught. Three masts stretched gracefully toward the sky. Liandra tented a hand over her eyes to see the ribbons and flags that hailed from the top. The bright sunlight hurt her eyes. Already someone was lowering the sling that would take her to the deck.

"The officers commanding the guns at the forts received the *alcalde*'s message," Ramón said once they were on board.

Marcus did not set her down or give her over to someone else. "Raise the anchor," he said sharply.

She could hear his voice against her ear, overwhelmingly in control—so out of contrast to her racing pulse—as he called orders to ready the ship. Scurrying along the braces and ratlines, men answered his commands. She felt him descend into a narrow gangway. Then she rested her head against his heart.

He kicked open a door and ducked with her into a stern cabin. The window framed the entire back wall of the room. Filigree panes reflected the orange glow of the dying day on the Turkish carpet that covered the wooden floor.

Shattered delft littered the floor with other expensive debris. Empty bookcases shared the wall with the desk. A massive square-poster bed built into the bulkhead behind her faced the window. The bed smelled of aged leather and linens that needed to be aired.

After laying her in the bed, Marcus straightened. His gaze went around the cabin before it finally came back to her. His nearness filled the room like a storm cloud. It bespoke of pain and something else she could not name.

A lump formed in her throat. Her heart cried at seeing him so vulnerable. She'd wanted to protect him. All she'd done was hurt him.

And now she'd lost his baby.

She buried her face into the pillows rallying the strength

not to shed tears in his presence. She couldn't bear to further burden him with her pain.

"How are you feeling?" he asked.

Brass lanthorns attached to rings on the walls, banged with the ship's rocking movement. She was too nauseous and weak from the effects of the opium to form any long, cohesive thought. "Alive," she murmured. "Where . . . are we . . . going?"

He lifted a strand of her hair as if it was the most fragile lace. "After we take on supplies in Old Providence and drop off Carlos"—his silver eyes held hers—"we're going to Martinique."

Dios, he knew about his brother. Faintness fell over her. Somehow, she found the strength to hold his gaze. The deck no longer trembled as the men at the capstan pulled in the anchor.

A knock sounded.

At first, she did not think Marcus heard. Then he let his hand fall away. She caught his wrist, and felt the carefully contained violence inside him. His darkness frightened her. Yet, he was in control of his emotions when she was not. "Marcus—"

A finger against her mouth silenced her words. "Sleep, Liandra."

The knock sounded again. Harder this time. "Dutch said that he can't sail the ship alone, Captain. It's time," a voice called.

Time. Her breath hitched. There had been so little of that precious gift between them. And what there had been, she'd stolen.

She felt his eyes linger on her a moment longer. Then the door closed. Biting back the wrenching tears, Liandra shut her eyes. If Marcus had been harsh with her this day, he was also all that stood between her and Carlos. He could have decided to leave her. And hadn't.

Chapter Twenty

Liandra slept through the night and most of the next few days, waking as Marcus fed her bread and made her drink water. His gentleness surrounded her, even if nothing else about him was soft. His eyes remained shuttered.

She was grateful for the strength that kept her from shedding tears in front of him. She didn't try to talk to him. She needed to focus on healing, now.

But after he left the cabin, she buried her face into the pillows so no one would hear, and sobbed for the loss of her child. This was punishment for her deceit. She'd allowed the need to protect him to become something more. Something terribly selfish. Hadn't Marcus made it clear from the beginning that he never wanted to take her with him? All he'd wanted was to see his brother again. To resume life with his own family.

When Liandra finally closed her eyes again, she drifted into a deep, undisturbed slumber unplagued by nightmares.

Near sunset the following evening, the opiates Carlos had fed her finally wore off. She awoke to find herself in a clean, white nightdress. She fingered the cloth. The sleeves encompassed her arms in petal-like softness. Sitting up, she shoved the hair out of her face and glanced around. Someone had cleaned her and changed the rags between her legs.

A flush heated her face and she cast her gaze about the room. A lone lamp cast dancing shadows on the walls. Outside, it was dark.

Marcus sat at the desk, his head resting on his arm, asleep. He still wore the blue and white uniform of Carlos's guard. A half-eaten tray of food sat atop navigational charts. A quill had fallen off the desk and rolled with the ship's movement. The window was open and a breeze rustled the charts. Female laughter drifted across the water.

Liandra tossed back the covers. Most of the debris had been moved aside as someone cleared a path across the carpet to walk. She padded to the window and pressed her face to the glass. Campfires dotted the beach.

They'd arrived at Old Providence. Turning, she looked down at Marcus. In sleep, he didn't look nearly so threatening or angry. Only exhausted.

Drawing in a deep, salt-scented breath, Liandra stretched her shoulders. Her stomach growled. She was no longer dizzy. But she was starved. She sat in the chair across from the desk and made quick use of Marcus's leftover cheese, then ate the uneaten mango and bread. She was about to indulge in the wine when a knock sounded on the cabin door.

Fingers closed around her wrist. Her heart slammed. Marcus lifted his head. His eyes touched hers but offered no comfort as he seemed to assess her lucidity.

The knock sounded again. Harder this time.

Slowly, he drew back. Standing, he walked to the bed and, stripping off the sheet, tossed it to her. "Come," he called.

Dutch entered. Carrying a tray of hot food, he saw Liandra at the desk and his face broke into a huge grin. He looked no thinner than when she'd seen him over six months before. "*Ja*, I tell the captain that you are strong. But he does not believe me."

She smiled. "It is good to see you still healthy, Dutch."

"Der captain, he took too long to find me, I think."

Marcus stood near the door. "Put the food on the desk, Dutch."

Setting down the tray, Dutch aimed his one good eye at Liandra and winked. "He is testy. Maybe now that you are awake, he will get some sleep and make us all smile."

Liandra touched the Dutchman's arm. "I am sorry for what happened to all of you."

"It would take more than whip and Spaniards to get rid of Dutch," he boasted. Making a rude noise, Marcus folded his arms and leaned against the wall watching them. Ignoring his *capitán*, Dutch indulged her. "Is there anything more I may get you, mistress?"

"*Sí*. Some water for a bath, *por favor*." She touched her tangled mass of hair and wiggled her toes. "I would appreciate a comb, a pair of shoes, and some decent clothes."

"And maybe we can go shopping on the moon," Marcus snapped. "Or hasn't it crossed your mind exactly where we are?"

Turning away from the offending comment, Liandra braved a smile at Dutch. "A needle and a lot of thread will do. Perhaps you can purchase a dress from one of the ladies in town, maybe. Or cloth—"

"Let me clue you in on something, Liandra," Marcus snapped, "It's not clothes the ladies in town are selling."

"*Ja*." Dutch frowned. "Der captain would know."

Opening the door, Marcus pointed—"Out!"

Dutch ambled past. Eyeing Marcus, he rubbed his chin. "*Ja*, it is goodt thing I was already fondt of you. Otherwise, I break your teeth for being son of bitch."

The door slammed.

Marcus stepped back into the room.

Liandra folded her hands in her lap and attempted to look composed. Grandmama always counseled her on the virtue of patience.

Marcus took one look at her and whatever temperamental tirade he was about to let loose vanished in a disgusted snort.

Spinning on his heel, he quit the room.

With a shaky sigh, Liandra wondered if he would seek succor on shore now, since he obviously could not find it with her. The thought brought a sting of tears to her eyes.

Marcus crashed over debris in the gangway and took the stairs to the deck. There was no breeze tonight. Only an inland stillness that reeked of offal and the pungent scent of green-wood fires built to keep the cloud of insects at bay. He slapped at a sting on his arm. Murdering mosquitoes gave vent to his anger at Liandra. Both were proving to be a pestilence to his mood, already diminished by hunger and lack of sleep.

She had no bloody right looking like a glass Madonna. Making him the villain. Hell, when was she even going to tell him about their child? Or apologize for deceiving him about his brother.

Snatching up the perspective glass, Marcus climbed to the quarterdeck. Not that he would accept an apology from her even if she got down on her knees and prostrated herself before him. She'd lied to him. Her very silence condemned her.

And he hadn't even seen it in her. Not even a hint; he'd believed in her virtue that much. Needed to believe . . .

Marcus scanned the shore. Half of his men were on the beach. The crews of two other ships riding at anchor joined in the ruckus. Marcus kept *Dark Fury* farther off shore, with men on watch.

Raising the glass, he stared at the distant mountains carved by moonlight and the memories he'd left behind.

Aye, he'd believed in her goodness. Yet, for months, she'd looked him straight in the eyes and lied through her beautiful white teeth about something or another. And now that she was safe, his anger came full circle like a bloody fist in his face.

Noise on the deck saved Marcus from his temper. Dutch carried a wooden tub braced on his massive shoulders down to Liandra.

Where the hell had the Dutchman located that contraption here in this pestilence-ridden pirate lair? It annoyed him that Dutch had found the tub when he'd looked all day for one.

He braced his feet against the ebb of the sea. Leaning against the taffrail, his eyes caught a trail of green seaweed in the oily water before he found the launch tied against the ship. Dutch had personally rowed in a barrel of fresh water to go with the tub.

A soft rustling sound below him drew his gaze. The main cabin was directly beneath his feet. A shadow moved against the stern galley glass. He could see Liandra looking out the window. Chin propped on one hand, she watched the activity on the beach.

For a moment, he yielded to the desire that rose within him.

A frustrated groan crushed his onerous ardor. For better or for worse, she seemed too content with her plight. He didn't understand her peace. And felt more the fool for his own tumult.

He threw his gaze aloft, tempted to join his watch as far away from his wife as he could go without abandoning ship. Instead, his gaze stopped on the tattered sails and worn rigging.

"Jesu." With a deep gut-wrenching ache, he knew he had another serious problem to consider. Marcus turned to the man on watch. "Has all the canvas been brought out of the hold?"

"Aye, Cap'n."

He swallowed an impatient oath. "Maybe we can paddle to Martinique."

"Bugger me, Cap'n. I don't think we have enough oars."

Marcus opened his mouth to reply. Shaking his head,

he walked away. A voice stopped him just before he descended to the lower deck.

"How does it feel to know you will not make it out of here?"

Slowly, Marcus turned. His uncovered head caught the dying heat of the day, and contributed to the slow burn inside when his eyes found the one who'd spoken.

Carlos was chained to the mast. His reptilian eyes smiled. "Those other two ships make this one look like a piece of driftwood."

Marcus turned his gaze to the other two ships and let his eyes adjust to the darkness. A slow stir of excitement hummed. A brigantine and sloop rocked in the swell. Neither ship possessed a bell watch. If any man remained behind, he was sleeping or drunk.

Marcus took a step closer to the rail. The brigantine looked newly refitted. A little thievery will make a man smarter in this clime. Teach him how to live longer. Aye, there could be no pillows in this profession, not if a man wanted to win. And winning meant securing enough canvas to get to Martinique.

A slow grin formed. "Carlos, you may have the brain of a cockroach, but tonight you're a genius."

Marcus rounded up what remained of his crew.

Aye, he would have his sails tonight.

Liandra stepped onto the deck, and stopped when the sunlight hit her. The ship was alive with activity. Men perched along the ratlines like happy baboons, controlling the winches and pulleys that hauled supplies on board. Crates of chickens and geese were piled beside barrels of limes and casks of gunpowder waiting to be lowered into the hold.

Liandra found Marcus easily on the quarterdeck. His voice alone carried over the bustling chaos, and her pulse measured the uneven leap of her heart. He stood against the crystalline brilliance of the Caribbean dressed in the silver-gray knee breeches of Carlos's guard, boots, and a pristine, white, ruffled shirt, minus the blue and white frock. He'd wrapped a black sash around his waist that carried the sling for his cutlass.

How handsome he was, she thought, feeling like a silly young girl in the flush of new love. The deck was slick beneath her feet, and she slipped, barely catching herself on the rail.

Abruptly, Liandra pulled her attention back to her purpose on deck. She glanced over her shoulder. A pattern of bearded faces watched her with casual interest. Her hand brushed down the length of her white nightdress. Nervously smoothing out the letter in her hand, she squeezed past the press of bodies and made her way to the quarterdeck. Intent on talking to the helmsman, Marcus did not notice her approach until she stood directly beside him.

Conversation ground to an abrupt halt. Dropping his gaze down the length of her, he stared in disbelief. The smile she bestowed seemed to have had the opposite affect she wanted.

He took her by the arm and led her to the rail. "What the hell are you doing up here dressed like that?"

Sensing other men staring at her, she let her gaze go around the crowded deck in exaggerated concern. She was not to blame for her attire, and would not be shamed because he'd failed to secure a dress for her. Besides, her gown covered more than what she'd seen the woman wearing last night on the beach.

"I wish Ramón to take a letter to my brother when he leaves here with Carlos."

A lift of his brow conveyed his displeasure. "Indeed." He reached out to take the letter.

She stepped out of his reach. "It's personal."

"Not when it concerns El Condor." He plucked the missive from her hands and, shaking the letter open with one hand, scanned its contents. Swallowing hard, she knew what he would find. Scrawls and scribbles better suited to a five-year-old than a woman of supposed education. His eyes lifted to hers.

"Is this some kind of joke?"

Despite her vow of patience, she snatched back the paper. "I am not interested in meeting your standards for good penmanship, *capitán*. Nor do I care for your opinion on the matter."

He remained silent, assessing her as if trying to decipher a puzzle that was quickly shaping into something he didn't like.

"I want Isabella to have my house and part of the cane fields. She will need the income. Gabriel does not need anything I have. He is rich as Midas and, in addition, I want him to know where my feelings lie . . . with you."

"And where exactly do your feelings lie, *gata*?"

She was beginning to really despise that name. "You are my husband. I willingly go wherever you go."

The invisible mask went up as efficiently as the reckless grin, but failed to hide the fatalistic shadow hovering behind his silver gaze. "Ah, the noble sacrifice. Am I your next benevolent undertaking? No more bloody orphans to save?"

"I don't wish to save you from anything," she whispered.

He leaned a boot on the teak rail at her back trapping her between the sea and his body. "Good. Because it will be a pleasure to introduce you to my way of life since you are so intent to throw away yours."

A tremor inside took the shape of anger. He was an expert at playing the chameleon; she would not be baited. "Will you see this delivered to my brother?"

"Maybe you would prefer to give it to him personally. We can shoot it out of a cannon. A formal greeting between enemies when we meet again."

Heart pounding, she stared at him in disbelief. "I understand that you are angry—"

"Jesu," he shoved away from the rail in disgust. "You don't know anything about me, Liandra. You never have."

She hated that her discomposure was obvious to all.

A man approached wearing island breeches, no shirt, and a big strawhat. Liandra glimpsed the flicker of annoyance in her husband's eyes a second before he dismissed her. The man said something to Marcus that made him look toward the shore, where an irate, red-faced man stood brandishing a fist.

Taking the letter, Liandra left the quarterdeck with as much poise as she could muster. She'd wanted so much to say good-bye to her family, but that was hardly important now. Perhaps it was better that she didn't share her sentiments in a letter anyway. She had never mastered the strokes of penmanship. The skill forever escaped her. No doubt, her efforts would be lost as they had with Marcus when he'd looked at her writing with disbelief. This was something else for him to find disappointment in with her.

The deck seemed to have taken on an unnatural hush as she worked her way through the chaos. Despite the blatant gawking, the men respectfully stepped aside and allowed her to pass. A glance at the quarterdeck told her she was closely watched. While the man wearing the strawhat gesticulated in a furious repertoire of Spanish and English behind him, Marcus had moved to the rail. Her heart hammered wildly. The wood was slick beneath her bare feet as she hurried to escape the sudden scrutiny of all the eyes on board. Once back inside the cabin, she heaved a huge sigh and leaned against the door.

Her gaze ran around the cabin, taking in the melange of neglect and confusion, feeling a horrendous sense of loss inside for the lives that had been shattered here.

Marcus was so wrong when he said she didn't know him.

She knew him like he was part of her soul.

She knew that she'd hurt him, and burdened him now with her presence when he'd only wanted to protect her. She knew that he ached with the need to set to rights the sins of his past. He possessed honor and courage. He loved his brother and the country that had forsaken him.

No pardon from Spain would ever make up for what he'd lost at the hands of her family and those he'd trusted.

But Liandra also knew something about herself.

She was not one to quit. Grandmama had taught her how to fight. Marcus had no idea of her tenacity. In the end, he would see that she had done the right thing in protecting his life. He would see that she loved him.

With one final glance at the letter, Liandra shoved it away into the desk. Last night's bath still sat in the room. Tearing off the linens from the bed, she grabbed her soap and went to work on cleaning the room.

"You have been at this desk all morning, mistress."

Dutch set down the lunch tray as Liandra lifted her head and smiled. The tray rattled with the rise and fall of the deck.

"Are you now taking on the duties of a servant, Dutch?"

His deep-throated chuckle told her he did exactly what he felt like doing. "I am der only one der captain will allow in here. I take it as a privilege."

Liandra pulled at a loose thread on her sleeve. She wanted to ask about Marcus—she'd not seen him since they'd sailed from Old Providence.

Overhead, someone dropped a crate, making her flinch. Pigs squealed. Shouts and the slapping of bare feet followed as a mad chase ensued to capture the doomed animals. They would be having pork tonight for dinner.

"Der captain has his hands full," Dutch offered, reading her turmoil. "He signed on fifty-two men before leaving last week."

Liandra was surprised. "From the other ships that were there?"

"*Ja?* One of der captains had der swamp fever and der other was drunkard in no hurry to leave. Especially since der captain relieved him of all but his main topsail."

"Marcus did that?"

"He is goodt thief, *ja*?"

Liandra was stunned that Marcus had risked himself so, and she had not known. He was wont to keep her completely from his life.

"Is Marcus so famous a buccaneer that any man would sail away with him?"

"Many are just tired, mistress," he said thoughtfully. "What der captain offers is better than der lot had there."

"And what does Marcus offer?"

"He is good man. Like his brother. He goes to Martinique. For many, that is freedom from English or Spanish capture."

"*Sí.* If you swear fealty to the French."

Liandra fidgeted with the quill. For her, the French port might be a prison. It seemed so cowardly to admit that she was frightened sailing into the unknown. Perhaps because she felt alone.

Dutch's gaze dropped to the desk and the large family Bible that lay opened beside her hand. The book belonged to Marcus's family. She'd found it this morning while in the final throes of her cleaning frenzy.

Liandra resisted the urge to hide her work. I am writing my name. Or trying to. In English," she eagerly explained, hoping he might return some feedback on her efforts. "I believe this is the place where marriages are recorded." She angled the book so he could better see. "It could be where deaths are recorded for all I know about such things."

A wide-tooth grin broke his expression. "My dear muther was but a camp whore for the soldiers who fought the prince's wars in *de Nederlanden*. Do I look like a man who read der Bible?"

"You never knew your father?"

He shrugged his massive shoulders. "Maybe I did and maybe I didn't. Who is to say, *ja*? But I am here, so it does not matter. He did his part."

"You have an odd way of looking at things, Dutch."

"*Ja*, perhaps. But why fight what you cannot change."

Her glance fell back to the pages spread out before her. "I wanted to record our marriage. Perhaps Marcus will not appreciate the effort."

"Who is to say what is bothering him. He is not himself."

Liandra felt a small catch in her chest. Marcus had not spoken ill of her then. He had told no one what she had done.

Easing her scratch paper away, she replaced the Bible with the tray of food Dutch had brought. "Would you like to sit?" she invited the Dutchman.

He glanced around the room looking for the second chair. "You have built a castle out of stones, mistress." He straddled the chair and faced her from across the desk. "Der captain doesn't know what he is missing."

She peeled an orange and offered him half. "Thank you for taking the carpet out yesterday and airing it." Chewing the orange slice, she swallowed as she looked from the huge bed to the captain's wardrobe. "What will he be like, do you think? His brother, I mean?"

"Who can say, mistress?" Plying a knife, he stabbed at a hunk of cheese. "Englishmen are not logical. And I have learned that they hold very nasty grudges."

"Because I am Spanish?"

"You are El Condor's sister."

And therein lay a major crux of her problem with Marcus. Her presence clearly pitched him against his family. Maybe that's why he was so intent on leaving her behind. He knew what she would face outside the sanctuary of her sheltered life.

The Bible drew her gaze. Her hands brushed at the pages. She didn't wish him to defend her against anyone, much less his own family. Yet, at the same time, a part of her wanted him to stand up and fight for her.

Turning, she gazed out the huge stern, galley window. Lying over in the wind, *Dark Fury* ate up the sea. A shadow to starboard rippled in a graceful reflection of towering masts and crosstrees. From the look of her billowing canvas, *Dark Fury* was flying.

"Marcus is anxious to get to Martinique."

"*Ja,*" Dutch agreed. "We will be there in less than a month."

"Damn."

Marcus slammed the last desk drawer. A lanthorn spilled a furious circle of light around him. Bracing both palms on the desk, he tossed his attention over the cabin in complete disbelief and a little awe.

She'd cleaned it. Not a corner or crevice had escaped her eagle eye. Every square inch smelled of her touch. She'd even polished the walls and cabinets.

Hell, he'd been sleeping in the wrong place the past two weeks.

Her white nightdress hung from the captain's wardrobe like a saintly ghost, having gone through a thorough washing as well.

He looked over at the bed. Liandra was sitting up watching him. She'd wrapped the sheet beneath her arms, but it didn't hide the white curves of her breasts or the fact that she was naked beneath. Her sleepy hair framed her face. And a startling rush of lust chased through him.

He hadn't seen her in weeks except as a shadow against the stern, galley window when she'd stare out at the sea. Behind him, the curtains billowed, and he breathed in the salt air to cool the sudden tempest inside. He could not help the loneliness she stirred.

"Where are my charts, Liandra?"

Wrapping the sheet around her, she padded to the shelves built beneath the bed. "There aren't that many places to look, Marcus." Her impish eyes sparkled. "Unless you thought I threw them overboard."

His eyes narrowed as she flicked past. Her cheery spirit made him suspicious. She bent to retrieve the charts, and his gaze slid from her busy hands to her nicely rounded bottom.

Grinding his teeth, he swore. She stood, and he realized she was waiting for him to say something.

"I found this in a chest." She held out a Bible.

"What chest?"

She bent to reach beneath the bed. Marcus knelt and helped her pull out a black leather chest.

"The panels on the bed come off," she explained as if he didn't already know that. Only he hadn't expected anything of value to be left after Espinosa, and then Carlos, had razed the ship. He wasn't surprised that Liandra had discovered the compartments, especially with her penchant for cleanliness and order.

Marcus opened the leather lid and ruffled through the breeches and various shirts. They didn't belong to Talon. He closed the lid. Neither did the chest. His glance fell on the Bible. Setting it atop the chest, he opened the cover.

And knew at once what Liandra had found.

A chill swept over him as he flipped open the cracked pages. The leather cover was thick. Golden scrolls rimmed the worn page. His gaze fell on his mother's handwriting:

John Brendan Drake wed to Mary Francis Diego
October Fourteenth,
Sixteen hundred and fifty six in the year of our Lord
Puerto Bello

The names of his family blurred. Someone had written in the date of his death beside his two other siblings who had lived and died in infancy. Sarah's name was the last addition on the page. No date followed that of her birth.

"I thought it might be important to you?" she offered.

It was only a record of his whole past.

He flipped the pages and found where Talon's name

shared the same line with his wife's, and the date of their marriage.

What the hell had happened since Tortuga?

"Perhaps you should sleep, Marcus."

He leaned an elbow on the trunk. "Is that an invitation?"

She brushed the hair off his forehead. "If it is . . . would you accept?"

He clasped her hands and stood, bringing her to her feet in front of him. Her mouth opened slightly; so close he could feel the whisper of her breath against his lips, like he felt the wind in the sails and the force beneath his feet as the ship skimmed the surface of the glassy water. Her touch was no less powerful.

"Do women not have the same desires as men?" she softly queried.

"I wouldn't know, I never had to ask."

"You've slept with a lot of women?"

He could have told her that they were naught but faceless memories compared to her, but he wasn't inclined to ease her plight. "I did have a betrothed. Once." He smiled leisurely in reply. "We shared the room across the hall . . . on occasion."

Color filled her cheeks. "You were engaged to another?"

He turned away. His hands went to the laces on his shirt and hesitated. Moonlight trembled like fractured diamonds over the sea. "I suppose she had married by now."

"You . . . loved her?"

He said absently, "She was very beautiful."

Suddenly very weary, he let go of a sigh. He was returning to a life that he didn't know if he wanted with a wife who didn't belong.

A wife who plagued his every other waking moment and his dreams at night.

A wife who'd lied when he'd so desperately believed in her. She'd betrayed him, like too many others had, as if it made no difference to the worldly order of his existence.

Or their bloody relationship.

How could he ever trust her again?

Gripping his sleeves, Marcus yanked off his shirt. His muscles flexed with the movement. Turning slowly, he pinned Liandra with his gaze. All the light in the room centered in her blue eyes.

Without releasing her gaze, he stripped away the sash from his waist. Leaving a hip against the desk, he removed first one boot, then the other. Straightening to his full height, he approached her. "I want to throttle you; I want to make love to you." He cupped her face with his palm, feeling the silky smoothness of her cheek, aching to press his mouth to hers and drink in her essence. "I want to feel nothing," he said through his teeth. "My existence would be easier for the sentiment."

"Will time never heal your anger?"

"Anger?" He crowded her, made her take a step backward until he'd trapped her against the wall. "Anger does not even come close to what I feel. I will never forgive you, Liandra. I detest liars. I trusted you."

Clutching the sheet, she set her face at just the slightest tilt away from him. "You judge me too harshly, Marcus."

He grasped her chin and forced her to look at him. "Just when *were* you going to tell me about the baby, Liandra?" he whispered. Her face paled even more. "Or about my brother. Or anything for that matter? Hell, you can't even read and write. That was all a lie, too. My sweet paragon of a wife. You didn't even know what you were signing when you married me. Did you?"

"I would have married you anyway," she choked out.

Crossing his arms, he leaned a shoulder against the wall. "Lucky me, to be chosen from all the males in the world?"

Finally, her regal poise cracked and, for an awful moment, she looked so fragile he thought she might break. He hated himself for hurting her. But he could not reckon his guilt with the pain of her lies. Or his uncertain future with her.

"*Sí*, I cannot read so well. No matter how I try to decipher my letters they do not make sense to me." She paced furiously, dragging the sheet along behind her like a royal bridal train. "I write even with less skill than I read. But I know about medicine. And . . . other things." She wheeled on him. "I know how to love, Marcus Drake. Even with all your aristocratic education and two parents who loved you very much, you cannot let go of your fears enough to feel more than a mocking lust for life. You are so afraid of letting people down it is better not to be needed than to face the possibility of failing them."

For a long time he didn't reply, so incensed was he, his tongue would not work. "You've figured all this out on your own?" He concealed the tremble in his voice with derision, and pleasantly applauded her affect. "Bravo, Liandra."

"I think . . . I do not like you anymore, Englishman."

Marcus captured a teardrop and held it to the light. "Aye, I'm a heartless bastard, Liandra. It's whom you married. Get used to it." He walked past her to go to bed.

"Am I your prisoner?"

He stretched his long body out and laced his fingers behind his head. Her scent crawled all over him, filling his thoughts to their very core. "You're whatever you want to be," he turned his head and raked her scanty attire with a half-grin, "as long as you don't go on the deck looking like that. Or you will force me to kill my crew."

She tossed her head flippantly. "Why bother, Marcus Drake?"

"Because you belong to me, Liandra. And despite our many differences, I am still loath to share."

"*¡Ai de mi!*" she sputtered. Wheeling on her heel, she plopped down on the window bench beneath the stern, galley window and presented him with her back as she stretched out.

With narrowed eyes, Marcus traced the slim curve of spine illumined by the lanthorn above the desk. "You and I are well-suited, *gata*. A liar and a thief. Both masters of deception. You will make an excellent pirate, sweet."

"*Sí*, my wondrous husband, and yours will be the first tongue I clip with my sword."

Marcus laughed, but he was hardly amused. Her aplomb annoyed him. But not as much as he annoyed himself for wanting her still.

Chapter Twenty-one

Liandra heard the soft sound of his voice and thought he'd whispered her name. His hands were upon her, gently caressing, soothing, wanting. A rain-scented breeze snuggled against her senses and mingled with the pillow softness of his lips.

Nay, devoured.

For all the fury behind his touch, there was gentleness too, a need that Liandra recognized. She stirred as Marcus scooped her up still wrapped in the sheet, and carried her to the bed. His smoldering perusal plucked away the blanket of sweet languor.

Everything came rushing back with a groan. She'd fallen asleep.

Struggling, she shoved against him. "Put me down, Marcus Drake."

He tossed her onto the bed. She was too slow to escape. Her muscles ached from lying on the hardwood bench all night. Marcus pinned her to the bed with his thigh. Braced on an elbow beside her, his silver gaze unfathomable, he lowered his mouth to her temple.

"Are you still bleeding?"

The intimate question brought a hot flush up her neck.

Perhaps because she didn't think men knew about such things. The query intimated privileged knowledge shared between husband and wife.

Vaguely, she felt herself shake her head, nay, warmed that he even cared enough to ask her first. His mouth moved down her throat. Closing her eyes, she inhaled the salty scent of him. A barely audible moan escaped before she caught herself and stiffened.

"You have nerve, Marcus Drake."

He pulled back. Shadows bathed his face but did not dim the intensity in his silver eyes. "And you have the only sheet." A rakish grin lifted his mouth. With a yank, he dislodged the cover and slid beside her. He was naked!

"Get off me!"

"I was thinking—"

"Pah!" She shoved against the muscled wall of his chest trying to spread some distance between them. "When a man thinks, it is not his brain that worries me."

"We can share the cover."

"*Sí*, and after you have finished playing the roué, what happens then, O Intelligent One? You owe me an apology."

He drew back. "How do I end up owing *you* the apology, *gata*?"

"And quit calling me that." She rolled to her knees, hair whipping around her, and took her corner of the sheet with her. " 'Tis insulting. Would you like it if I called you a dog?"

He smiled. "From your own sweet lips, 'twould be a compliment."

Gritting her teeth, Liandra yanked the sheet and rolled off the bed. She came up short. Marcus held a fistful of the wretched cloth, abruptly halting her escape.

"Don't you dare touch me, pirate."

"I have never forced a woman. Even if that one standing before me now is my wife."

"Pah! You flaunt your love for your betrothed. Tell me you . . . bedded her right there." She shook her finger at the offending door that led out to the gangway. "Now, I am your wife?"

"By your own vow, sweet."

Her grip on the sheet tightened. This was war, far more grave than the matter of stealing the only sheet between them or settling the obvious logistics of their vows. But she would not surrender. He was naught but a thief. He had insulted her earlier with his attitude and mockery. He'd frightened her to death with his anger. Which, in her opinion, nullified anything she'd done to him out of love. He was too blind to see proper reasoning. If she didn't make a stand now, he would be the victor, and she would grow to hate him.

"One of us will have to yield," he whispered.

She held tight. "Apologize."

"Aye, I am sorry that I find myself wanting you above all else."

"You insult me, Englishman."

Hand over hand, with slow deliberate movements, he pulled her closer. "Tell me which part of what I said was a lie . . . and I will apologize, Liandra."

She let go of the sheet. But he was out of the bed blocking her escape before she took two steps. Warmth harassed her, filled her veins. He raised his arms and rested his palms on the ceiling timbers. She could not contain the urge to look at him. All of him.

His hair caressed his shoulders. Fire danced in his eyes. Then his mouth covered hers.

He didn't touch her anywhere else. He didn't have to. Her senses hummed, molding tightly to his, licking along every vertebra in her spine to settle relentlessly in her chest.

She would not be caged by her lust. Not with the matter of trust still unsettled between them.

She would not!

Her outraged protestations went the way of her reason, scattered by the chaotic pounding of her heart, and she was stunned to discover her arms around his neck, her hands threaded in his hair, her mouth clinging to his.

She felt him pull away. Felt his gaze on her face as he watched her curiously as if disbelieving. His mouth was damp. And she seemed unable to focus on anything else.

He would mock her lack of self-control, toss it back in her face with a cocksure comment.

She was not prepared for anything else.

"Ah, Christ. . . ." A tremor went through him.

With a ponderous groan that bespoke his own surrender more than any victory, Marcus wrapped her within the fierce band of his embrace and took her down to the bed. Braced on his elbows, he pressed full length against her, his muscles trembling beneath her palms as she met his gaze and wondered at the torment she saw in those silver depths. Curling his fingers in her hair, he lowered himself between her thighs and thrust deeply into her.

A cry broke from her lips, and he moved slowly at first, then harder as he drove against her, his breath ragged against her ear. She held fast as he rode her beyond the shadows and the darkness, away from the past and the future. Someplace safe. Someplace totally theirs alone. And for a moment, as they soared, Liandra gave him her soul.

Afterward, she lay silent in his arms as he drifted to sleep. All her body's aches didn't equal the one in her heart.

He had taken her.

He did not love her.

He had not apologized for anything.

A knock sounded. Liandra stirred and turned deeper into the pillow to block the sound. Sunlight penetrated the haze and pricked her skin with beads of sweat. She didn't wish to awaken. The days ahead no longer held any fascination for her.

Conscious of the soft mattress beneath her back and the

memory of last night's foray into her heart, she opened her eyes and sat up abruptly. She was alone.

Dutch called from the other side of the door announcing breakfast. Throwing her nightdress on, Liandra met him at the door. He was so tall he had to duck beneath the heavy wooden beams in the ceiling. "Goot morning, mistress."

Quickly averting her face, she went to make the bed. "Dutch?" He set the tray down and turned. "Is there such a thing as a woman pirate?"

Dutch laughed. "If there is, I would like to be the first . . ." Clearing his throat, he actually blushed. "Why do you ask?"

"Marcus said I would make a good pirate. I think I wish to prove him correct. It is time that he remembers that I am on board."

"In my fair opinion, mistress, der captain already knows you are on board."

He turned, and Liandra saw Marcus standing in the doorway. His hair was wet and off his face in a queue. He had washed and shaved. Darkly tanned against the white cravat of his shirt, as usual, he exuded masculine good looks and confidence.

"There is a squall to the south of us," he told Dutch. "I want you at the helm."

After Dutch left, Marcus walked to the desk and began rummaging the shelves. She awaited him to talk, react—anything that gave hint to his mood.

"Will the storm be bad?" Liandra asked.

"Rainstorms are part of these waters," he said, pulling out three charts and spreading them over the desk. "I made a mistake two days ago by putting someone else at the helm. When I took the altitude the next day, we were two points off course."

"Two points. Surely that cannot be so bad."

He gave her an impatient look. "Only if you preferred to go to Jamaica. We lost over a day."

Intentionally or not, he made her feel stupid.

"Is Martinique any different than Jamaica?"

He lifted his eyes from the charts and found her standing near the bed. Absently, she smoothed a hand over her hair. Clearly, he suffered some internal struggle and must have wondered at the weakness inside that betrayed him last night.

"I don't know," he said.

"Are you frightened?"

A brow lifted mockingly.

His arrogance miffed her. "Does nothing frighten you?"

If it did, he wasn't saying. Instead, he bent his attention back to the charts.

Plucking the tray from the desk, Liandra took her breakfast to the bed, as far as she could away from him. Despite his overpowering presence, she ate. He sat at the desk pouring over the charts, seemingly oblivious to her presence. Though, at times she puttered about straightening the room, she could feel his eyes on her.

But she could never catch him outright staring. It was as if he could read her thoughts and knew the instant she would look his way.

After straightening the room, Liandra kneeled beneath the bed where she'd found the Bible yesterday. Prying off the slats of polished wood, she reached beneath and pulled out the leather trunk.

Her gaze fell on the Bible. With reverent hands, she lifted it to her lap and opened it. Except for the one name, the page reserved for marriages remained unmistakably blank. A quill dropped near her leg. Black ink spattered her nightdress. She lifted her gaze to find Marcus leaning against the window, watching her.

"You're welcome to sign it."

Closing the Bible, she set it aside. "Is your brother anything like you?"

He gave a scornful laugh. "God, I think not."

"He is worse?" Liandra added her own mockery as she fluttered her hand about her breast. "*¡Cielos!* We are all doomed."

"Aye." Marcus's smile was bland. "It will be interesting to see what he thinks about my beautiful Spanish bride."

He struck a nerve, and Liandra clasped her hands. "Will it matter?" she hastened to ask as he turned to leave her. "What he thinks, I mean?"

The question didn't please him, as if she'd insulted him by even asking. Without a word, he quit the room.

In a temper, Liandra tossed the quill at the door, where it missed completely and hit the bookcase.

"*Sí,* 'tis my lot in life to be forever aiming at something I cannot seem to hit."

Already, she longed for Friar Montero and her mother. What she wouldn't have given even to talk to Isabella, and she missed little Christina terribly. They'd never been separated for so long. Liandra wondered if she'd ever see her niece again.

Wiping a treacherous tear off her cheek, Liandra flung open the lid to the chest and focused on finding something to wear. She withdrew breeches, shirts, and sashes. The clothes were of the finest velvets and satins. With needle and thread, she proceeded to spend the next week creating a new wardrobe. A nip here, and lots of tucks everywhere else, she'd have outfits worthy of any female rogue.

Marcus was on deck the first evening that she appeared topside in her new attire. He'd just taken a drink of grog when he saw her and spewed a mouthful, barely missing her as he choked.

Dutch clapped him vigorously on the back. "*Ja,*" he said, eyeing her up and down with masculine approval that made Marcus glower, "you should have gotten der dress like she wanted."

Liandra narrowed her eyes. "You said I wasn't your prisoner."

"Dutch, take her off this deck."

"And maybe you have der wrong rooster guarding der hen, *ja*?" With a wink at Liandra, he walked away, leaving her alone with her reluctant husband.

Liandra almost hugged the big Dutchman.

After that, Marcus grudgingly took his meals with her in the cabin. At night, he walked her on the deck and they shared the bed. He didn't touch her again. Not physically, but his presence always seemed nearby whether he was in the same room with her or somewhere else on the ship attending to some duty.

"We're in this predicament now because you wore pants once before." He said days later as she sat down to start mending the breeches that were suddenly appearing daily at her cabin door.

"You and your fishing lessons." She tossed her head. "How dare you blame that night on me. I think you don't even know how to fish."

Instead of anger, he perused her with eyes that burned like silver fire. And her heart skittered. Then he bent back to work on the charts. She continued sewing, prepared to ignore him. But she could not forget the way he'd looked at her or ignore the scent of bay rum coming from his presence. He'd washed that afternoon and his face was smooth. Someone had even trimmed his hair to the nape of his neck. Fingering her own boyish attire, she finally stood and summoned the courage to approach.

"Marcus?" Her voice sounded small.

He'd been twirling the quill between his thumb and forefinger and was slow to lift his gaze. She stood in front of the desk surrounded by the sound of creaking timbers and the look in his eyes. The room shrank around her, vanishing until they were the only two people left on the sea.

"I was frightened," she said after he waited patiently for her to speak. "I wanted to tell you about your brother. But you would have walked away forever. You were building the mill. Creating." Her fingers fidgeted with the loose folds on her breeches. "I wanted you to know that you were something more than what you thought you could ever be."

His face expressionless, he didn't blink.

She licked her dry lips. "I wanted you to believe in yourself."

Later that night, Marcus didn't come to bed. For a long time she lay staring at the timbers in the ceiling. Tomorrow they would be in Martinique.

Someone paced the deck above her.

And just before she drifted to sleep, a long ago memory snagged her attention. She'd listened to that same restless rhythm, the same heel-toe, heel-toe steps once before on the galleon.

Martinique loomed in the same way as the dormant volcano that dominated the island. On the hill overlooking the harbor entrance, a huge French fort stood guard over the bustling seaside town of Fort Royale. Brigantines, ketches, and sloops shared the bay with smaller fishing craft, which lined the golden beaches. A sizable crowd gathered on shore as Marcus disembarked from the launch.

A colorful bazaar dominated the square. His arm went around Liandra and he edged her through the bustle of humanity that overflowed from the narrow streets into the square. She felt smaller, more vulnerable walking barefoot beside him. She'd been right when she'd sensed that he was nervous about this moment. He'd wanted to find his brother safe and alive. But his first duty was to the welfare of his wife and crew. To that end, in case the French were not in a friendly mood, he'd ordered his crew on the ship to standby at quarters, and left Dutch in charge. The men who rowed the launch to shore nervously watched him now, as if he were God's own paladin. Today, he didn't care. He'd accepted a responsibility in bringing them here.

Before he could grant shore leave, he would have to clear the ship with the port authorities and contribute a tax to the governing coffers. Having been stripped of all Spanish signature, *Dark Fury* flew no flag or banner. He was surprised that the port authorities hadn't already met him.

"Marcus. Look!" Liandra pulled his hand and lead him to a nearby stall. She was smiling. "Combs. And real clothes."

She held a vivid red skirt next to her and whirled. They were hardly clothes of value. More like peasant garments: loose sleeve blouses and various bright colored skirts. She had nothing. She'd left Puerto Bello with only a firm conviction in him.

"Buy them," he quietly said.

"*Sí?*" She beamed like a child. "What shall you pay with?"

He tossed down Spanish silver. He'd done so little to earn that breathtaking smile. That he could have the power to engender that kind of happiness filled him with a keen sense of shame.

She'd never asked anything from him. Ever.

Except an apology for his atrocious behavior.

Holding her gaze, he reached out to touch her smile. It beckoned like warm sunlight on the sand.

"Marcus?" A feminine voice shrilled.

As one, the crowd seemed to grow quiet. Marcus turned. The people fell away, opening a path. "Marcus? Oh, my God. It *is* you. You're alive!" A warm feminine body launched into his arms. Her arms wrapped around him, her lips rained wet kisses on his face. "Can it really be you? Tell me I'm not dreaming."

He eased her out of his arms. He had no want to see her hurt. Her pink satin skirts caught in the breeze and wrapped around his legs. Blond curls framed her heart-shaped face, now colored with excitement. "We thought you had died in Tortuga." She kissed him on the mouth, and he tasted her tears.

"Arabella . . ."

"Regan saw you shot. She saw you drown."

His memory of his betrothed had not changed. She was still beautiful and kind, and he was a bastard for hurting her. But he was no longer the man she once knew. The only one his heart pined for stood beside him.

Mindful of the growing crowd and what this must feel like to Liandra, he disengaged Arabella's grip. Marcus reached behind him to draw Liandra forward. Clutching the forgotten treasures in her arms, she looked at him, anguish in her eyes. "Liandra?"

Her gaze dropped to his outstretched palm. She placed her hand in his and let him pull her in front of him. Arabella's eyes fell on Liandra. Out of respect for what he'd once shared with his betrothed and his wife's feelings, he'd wanted to spare the public announcement of his nuptials, but there was no help for it now. He made the introductions. Neither woman moved, and Marcus could not evade the burning question in Arabella's eyes. But his loyalty was to his wife. And in truth, what he'd ever shared with Arabella was not love. They both knew that.

"This is not the greeting I expected to find." Marcus passed his gaze across the peaceful setting. "Is Talon safe?" he asked.

She crossed her arms. "What are you doing on his ship, Marcus? We have been waiting months for *Dark Fury*'s return from England."

"It's a long story. One I'll tell later if you don't mind. I need to get my wife out of the heat."

Chin high, she opened her arm directing them toward the carriage sitting at the other end of the crowded bazaar. "I sent word back to the plantation the moment *Dark Fury* was spotted. Perhaps . . ." Her voice wobbled. "We will meet Talon on the road."

Marcus left orders with his men to return to the ship until he knew it would be safe for them to come to shore.

With Liandra walking ahead of him, he crossed the hot plaza, grateful to reach the shade where the carriage awaited. Nobody said anything. Two fine black steeds greeted the newcomers. Marcus recognized the driver as one of Talon's old crew.

"Bugger me, Cap'n Marcus." He hopped down from the seat to open the carriage door. His grin was missing two more teeth since Marcus had last seen the grizzled tar. "If you ain't a sight fer these sore eyes."

"Harry, it's good to see you're still kicking."

"The cap'n is goin' to be mighty pleased to see you."

Marcus handed Liandra into the carriage, then Arabella. Perched primly on their leather seats, both turned to stare out the opposite windows. Adjusting his cutlass, Marcus sat next to Liandra. He placed his arm around her shoulders and felt her stiffen.

Betwixt hell and high water. He considered riding atop with Harry. The carriage snapped forward and, in the icy stillness, his gaze alighted on his ship in the harbor.

"Why was *Dark Fury* going to England?" he suddenly asked.

"Talon finally had the proof that would clear your family name of treason." Arabella clasped her fingers in her lap. "He surrendered the ship to one of His Majesty's men, who was going to England to present your case before the king for a full pardon."

Marcus let his head fall back against the worn leather seat. He turned and locked eyes with Liandra. They both knew why *Dark Fury* never made it to England. And that those who had sailed the ship probably died as pirates on the gallows in New Spain.

Downstairs a door slammed.

Dressed in a simple white blouse and red skirt, belted at the waist, Liandra attempted in frustration to work her damp hair into a braid. But her hands trembled. With fury or pain she didn't know.

She stood at the window staring down into the gardens. Plumeria and hibiscus blossoms flavored the air. A breeze gentled the heat in the bedroom and mixed with the song of the young girl kneeling among the flowers.

The voices downstairs had gone from dark to black in tone. Closing her eyes, she leaned her forehead against the cooler glass.

His brother had not been at the plantation when they'd arrived. Working in the cane fields, he had never received word of *Dark Fury*'s arrival. The girl, Arabella, took Marcus into the fields to meet him.

Liandra shivered in frustration. By dint of incredible willpower, she hadn't clobbered her husband and his fairest true love after he'd allowed the woman to drool all over him like he was tonight's beef brisket. Then he'd reluctantly introduced *her*, his wife, like she was something to be ashamed of. Perhaps she was an embarrassment, dressed no better than a street urchin next to the blond queen of Sheba. But it was hardly her fault that she had no clothes.

Now, Marcus had to defend her to his own brother!

Maybe her reluctant husband would remind the tyrant overlord of the manor that she was merely El Condor's *half-sister*. That her Spanish blood did not make her an evil clawed creature of the night. That she wouldn't suck the blood from Talon's newborn babe.

"Hello."

Liandra shifted her gaze over her shoulder. Through a blur of tears, she saw a young woman enter the room. She wore a bright yellow gown. Her dark hair was wrapped in a thick coronet around her head. Brown eyes dominated her flawless oval face. She walked with a limp.

"I'm sorry I wasn't here to greet you when you arrived. But I see you have been able to bathe."

"Your servants gave me one of your shifts and a pair of slippers."

"You may have anything that you need."

Wiping at her face with the heel of her hand, Liandra let her gaze go over the woman in more detail, and at once discovered an inkling of kinship with this person. "I thought I was the only person on God's earth who wore bright yellow."

The woman laughed. "Yellow is my favorite color." Her skirts whispered on the sea-blue carpet as she came to stand beside the window. Her down-to-earth warmth was at odds with the regal elegance of this bedroom. And the rest of the house for that matter: all probably obtained with ill-gotten gains and Spanish treasure.

"You're as beautiful as Marcus said you were."

"He said that?"

"Aye," she smiled. "And a lot more besides. My name is Regan. I'm Talon's wife."

They spoke of trivial things, the weather, the stately beauty of Regan's new house. She and Talon had only just moved in when the baby had come. "It was a wonderful surprise to find Marcus alive. You don't know what that means to us."

"*Sí*, I do," Liandra whispered. The silence grew awkward and finally Liandra's gaze returned to the girl in the garden. "I heard her singing earlier. She has a beautiful voice."

"Like an angel," Regan quietly said. "All the Drakes sing like that. Though, you might not know it. I cannot get Talon into a church. That's Marcus's sister, Sarah."

"His sister?" Liandra pressed into the glass. She could do naught but stare. "I don't . . . understand. Marcus has always blamed himself for her death."

"Sarah didn't die with her mother. But her injuries left her blind."

Liandra faced Regan. "Has Marcus seen her?"

"He reacted the same way Talon did the first time he learned that she was alive. She has very little memory of either brother. It's been hard on Talon to accept. We thought perhaps with the new baby it would help to bring her here. But she will be returning to St. Mary's soon. This is the first time she has ever ventured out."

"St. Mary's is a fine hospital. I have heard of the place."

"It is also a convent. When it's time, Sarah will take her vows."

It was ironic that Marcus had gained a whole family when she had lost hers. Her throat tightened and she looked away.

Wrapping an arm around Liandra's elbow, Regan smiled. "We are sisters."

Liandra tried to smile. But it was no use pretending they were suddenly one big happy family. "Will Marcus be all right downstairs?"

"Marcus can take care of himself." Regan walked Liandra out of the room. "Though I fear my husband is rather set in his opinion about some things. And it will take time for him to adjust." Her voice was not apologetic, but neither was it cruel.

Unfortunately, Liandra was through proving herself to the Drake men. She was not ashamed of who she was.

Down the hall, Regan led her to the nursery. Yellow papered walls brightened the room. Tiny gurgling sounds emanated from the white cradle. A servant wearing a red and white checkered scarf, a white peasant's blouse, and red skirt similar to Liandra's stood when Regan entered.

Regan lifted her baby and gently kissed the child's forehead. Little hands and legs wiggled in delight. "You may hold her."

Her heart hammered against her ribs. Liandra's panicked response was to refuse, but Regan laid the baby in her arms. The little blanket of life was warm against her palms. Snuggling her nose against the little girl's neck, she inhaled the baby smells of sunshine and innocence. She stared in awe at the fine black hair and silver-blue eyes. The child looked so much like Marcus that Liandra could barely breathe for want of staring.

"Your husband must look like his brother."

"Enough that you can't mistake the relationship." The voice came from the doorway.

Liandra's head snapped up. The man in the doorway leaned against the jam with the air of an angry cat. Even without noting his mercurial gaze, she knew him at once as Talon Drake. He was as tall as Marcus and wore his shoulder length dark hair queued with a leather thong. Laces tied at the front of his white shirt. Buff breeches encased his thighs and ended where the tops of his dusty, black boots began.

Liandra handed the baby to Regan. Talon approached and took his daughter, holding her gently, as if checking her for broken parts. The baby cooed like a happy dove. And the brute cracked a strong white grin in response. The contrast between his harsh demeanor and the tender love for his child stirred Liandra with wonderment.

Talon lifted his gaze and caught her staring.

She gave him a nervous smile. "We haven't been introduced."

"I know who you are, Miss Espinosa."

Liandra flinched at the use of her brother's name. "Perhaps you English can learn a little from the Spanish about hospitality."

"I'm very acquainted with Spanish hospitality. Would you care to see the scars left from your brethren's generosity?"

"Are you always such a bully, *capitán*?"

Talon's mouth lifted just enough that one might mistake the gesture for a grin. "I'm usually much worse."

"Talon," Regan admonished.

The dragon suddenly turned sheepish. "But I've never been able to tell my brother what to do. He's been stubborn in that way."

Regan took the babe and laid her back in the cradle. "What's done is done." She told them both but her next words were meant for Talon. "Marcus is alive and has come home to us. He obviously loves Liandra very much or he wouldn't have brought her here."

But Liandra knew Marcus hadn't wanted to bring her at all.

Chapter Twenty-two

Fingering the missive in his hands, Marcus stared out across the fields of shimmering cane. The sun had set an hour ago but the sky still burned an exotic crimson. Nothing stirred his blood more than a Caribbean sunset, except maybe waking up next to Liandra and feeling her eyes on him. He clenched his hand around the missive. The message had arrived from Dutch.

"Bad news?" Talon's boots crunched the gravel behind him.

When Marcus didn't answer, Talon moved down the hill to stand beside him. "Arabella is packing her bags. She's moving into town."

"She's Regan's family. It's not my business where she goes. You damn well know it."

Talon's mouth kicked up slightly. "She married shortly after you disappeared. It seems she is unlucky in love. Her husband died some weeks later leaving her a wealthy widow."

"I'm not going to apologize for marrying Liandra. The two don't even compare."

Marcus kicked a stone loose and sent it rolling into the creek. A tiny waterfall bobbled over the miniature boulders, answering the breeze with a soft trickle. Dinner had ended abruptly on a note of disaster. Not that anyone spoke words in anger, but the discomfiture was there all the same, making him ache for wont of tearing into his brother. Marcus had carefully set down his fork, left the table, then the house. Only to meet his boatswain at the door.

And now this. He crushed the letter in his hand and tossed it into the creek, where it meandered into oblivion. Marcus didn't have to meet Talon's eyes to feel them peering inside him.

"El Condor has found a way on Martinique. He has demanded an audience with Liandra. Jesu," he said in disgust. "How did the bastard know where to find her so quickly? He must have returned to Puerto Bello right after I left. His ship must be well-hidden for the French authorities not to know he's here."

"Did you think he wouldn't follow? She's his sister for Chrissake. Where is he?"

"Leave him alone, Talon. I'll deal with him. And not in the way you think."

Something flashed in his brother's silver gaze and Marcus knew he was remembering things best left forgotten. The scars Talon carried ran far deeper than the physical ones on his body. Marcus made no excuses, nor did he condemn the Spaniards.

"We all have reasons for the thing we do, Talon. What makes another man's hatred more wrong than yours?"

"A year ago, I would have knocked your teeth out for being a bloody traitor."

Marcus laughed. "You've always possessed an over inflated confidence, Talon. I still don't know how it was I and not you who got shot in Tortuga." His eyes narrowed. "You left me there. I could have hated you for that. But I didn't."

"We were running for our lives. I went back . . ." His gaze dropped to the ground, something that never happened when Marcus faced off with his older sibling. "You had no idea what it did to me to lose you. The months I spent blaming myself for what happened. Regan saved my life. And then I learned that Sarah was alive."

Marcus closed his eyes. He was still reeling from his meeting with her earlier and torn because she didn't know him. "Will she ever regain her sight or her memory?"

"No one knows what happened. Maybe it's better that way. She's happy at St. Mary's. Harrison Kendrick is dead. He will never be able to hurt her again."

"Jesu . . ."

"It wasn't your fault what happened to us, Marcus."

Silence fell over him. "You knew?"

"About the map? That you blamed yourself for someone else's actions? For another man's greed? Aye, I suspected well enough. I also know that we can never get back what they stole from us. I've already lost too many good people trying. I won't be sending anyone else to England to plead our case. It's over for me. I've found the only thing that matters."

Marcus couldn't pull his gaze from his brother's face. "And there never was any treasure, was there?" he asked.

"*Nada.*"

Talon crossed his arms and for the first time that night, his expression grew warm. "Now, that all depends on where a man looks for his gold, brother." He shifted his attention to the fields. "This is all half yours. You can make a home here if you choose."

Marcus fingered the golden cross at his throat. The sound of the wind and the sky surrounded him. He had everything now he'd ever wanted. His brother and a sister he didn't know lived. He could be a planter. He had a home. The gold felt warm against his palm. Yet, he felt . . . cold.

"What about my wife?" he asked. "And there are many among my crew who are Spanish. Can you promise that they will not be harmed, and will be accorded the same privileges as all of my men?"

Marcus knew he could not.

Talon's mouth tightened. "Are you willing to leave and live among the Spaniards, then? What of your own life?"

His eyes picked up and followed the slim silhouette of a woman as she walked through the tangled gardens.

Liandra.

His heart skipped to see her outside in the moonlight. She stared across the fields, much as he had been doing all night. But her shoulders slumped and he felt an inherent depth to her defeat. She continued away from the house following an invisible trail. Then she stooped to smell a flower, cupping the silken petals in her hands as if she gleaned some strength from its life force. She didn't tear it out of the earth to hold it for her own pleasure. She merely possessed its fragrant beauty with an unselfish affection. Her love of life kept him in awe of her gentle power.

Marcus knew now that he drew strength from that bright force inside her. She'd fought her brother for him. She'd lost her home, and her child. Yet, through it all her belief in him never wavered. It had taken coming here to his family . . . it had taken him to hurt her.

She saw him then and straightened, almost nervously, as if she hadn't expected to see him standing there. Her hand tangled in her skirts. Pivoting on her heel, she quickly walked away. Something was odd about her behavior.

"Think hard, little brother," Talon quietly warned. "For what you give up, you may never get back."

"Maybe that's been my whole problem. I've been thinking too hard. I only hope I'm not too late." Liandra disappeared around the side of the house. "Where does that path go?"

"To the stables," Talon said. "My groom won't saddle a horse for her. Unless she can ride bareback, she won't be going anywhere."

Marcus's heart lurched. "Shit!"

She was leaving him.

He took off after her. When he reached the garden, she was no longer in sight. Nor were the stables. Moonlight shadowed the copse of trees and he guessed at her direction. He tore through the brush just as Liandra rode out of the stables of one of Talon's fine English horses. Marcus leaped aside, barely grabbing the gelding's red mane before Liandra could sweep past.

"Let go!" She raised a riding quirt and he stared, incredulous that she might actually strike him. "Go away."

The horse pranced in an impatient circle. It was all Marcus could do to maintain his grip on the halter. "What do you think you're doing, Liandra?"

"You *should* have left me in Puerto Bello. It would have been kinder than this." She was encased by moonlight, her luminous eyes wet with unshed tears. "Tell me you didn't want to leave me, Marcus."

"I thought about it," he answered honestly.

"Our baby is gone . . . there's nothing holding us together."

Marcus felt a stir of agitation at her cavalier dismissal of their vows.

"Gabriel forced you into this marriage," she said.

"Is that what you want? An annulment?"

"I wouldn't contest it, Marcus."

Christ. His grip on the horse tightened. It took all his strength to keep her from pulling the horse away. If he attempted to yank her off, he could lose his grip completely. "Liandra . . ."

"I will not stay," she whispered. "Please, Marcus. Let me go. For your own good. For both our sakes."

The pain in her voice made him ache. "Where do you think to go on an island? I will only find you."

Her gaze lifted helplessly to a point over his shoulder and at once his heart stopped. He sensed movement behind him before he felt the tip of a cutlass against his ribs.

"No sudden movements, Drake. I would hate for you to impale yourself on my sword."

"Gabriel . . ." Liandra hesitated. "You promised not to hu—"

"Did you think to keep me from my own sister, Drake?"

Liandra swung her gaze back to his. He pressed a rueful grin to his lips. But his eyes were hard. "That thought crossed my mind."

"You knew he was here! *¡Aiyi* Marcus! You are such a hypocrite as I have never seen!"

"Slide off the horse, Liandra. You're not going anywhere with him."

"Get away from her, Drake." Espinosa's tone remained cool. "She does not wish to stay with you. And I don't have the luxury to argue the matter."

Marcus didn't let loose of Liandra's liquid gaze or his grip on the horse. If he were going to be murdered, she could bloody well look him in the eyes and watch him die.

"Would you kill an unarmed man, Espinosa?"

"I have men all around this place. I would not like to think what would happen if you were armed."

A cold chill slithered down his spine. His blood screamed in his ears. Christ, he couldn't think. He'd just allowed his wife to take him into a trap.

And he'd led Espinosa to his brother. To Talon's family. Would she be a party to slaughter?

Jesu, she could not!

"Run me through now, Espinosa. Or on my word, I swear I will find you."

"And kill my sister's faithless husband? I did not come here to start a war in French territory. I came only for my sister."

"No, Gabriel! Don't—"

Someone hit him in the head from behind, knocking him to the dirt. Liandra's cry died in the darkness.

"Jesu, that hurts!"

"Really, Marcus," Regan said prettily. "You needn't be such a baby."

"You're lucky he didn't bash your skull in," Talon added. "Espinosa must be growing soft."

Talon's voice drilled into his head and, with an impatient wave of his hand, Marcus shooed the lot of bedside gapers away. Sunlight bore into his brain. It was nearly noon. "Finish the damn stitches, Regan. And get out of here so I can die in peace."

Regan wrapped a bandage around his head. Marcus flinched at her less than gentle bedside manner. "The only thing that's going to kill you is your temper, Marcus."

"Good riddance to her," he muttered.

"So, you've told us a thousand times," Regan commiserated, her less than compassionate voice making him nervous. She tied a knot on the bandage and with skillful flourish whacked off the loose cloth. "Truly, I can see that you're better off with her gone."

"Aye." Marcus peered up at her.

His sister-in-law waggled the knife before his eyes. "It's hard to love someone who thinks only of her own happiness. Especially since we treated her with such"—she aimed her glare at Talon—"English hospitality and graciousness."

Marcus met Talon's gaze, then set his own out the window. Framed by yellow, wispy curtains, the sky was a perfect blue. "She'll get an annulment," he finally said. "And I'll be free."

"She won't get an annulment. And you'll never be free, little brother. Because you love her." Talon dropped the family Bible on his chest and nearly broke his ribs. "And she loves you. Open it."

With trembling hands he did. He thumbed through the pages, stopping abruptly at the place where their family marriages were recorded. No fancy penmanship connected his name to hers. But with each crooked letter, he knew the painstaking effort it took for her to write their names. The vision blurred.

Below the date of their marriage, written in three different languages, were the perfect words: *I love you*. And the date they'd taken their vows. A date he hadn't even known.

Time froze in the pair of heartbeats that followed. In

that moment, he understood that logic is not found in the heart. That riches are not found in gold.

And that Liandra was the only true treasure in Puerto Bello worth dying for.

Surely, this was what his father felt for his Spanish wife.

"Your crew is waiting," Talon said.

Marcus lifted his gaze to embrace his brother's.

"Go," Talon encouraged. "Take the ship. A belated wedding present from me. My life is here, now."

Marcus swung his legs out of bed. He'd never cried in his life and it took all his strength not to do so now. "I may not be back."

Talon held his gaze.

"Tell Sarah," he choked. "Tell her that I love her."

"I will," Talon whispered.

Marcus looked between his brother and his brother's beautiful wife. He could utter nothing more powerful than a simple thank-you.

Liandra rolled the parchment and carefully retied the thin red ribbon. Her fingers refused to work the simple knot. Finally, Don Pedro reached across the supper table and took the roll from her fumbling grasp. The ship's sounds mixed with the clatter of silverware against porcelain.

"You have read and reread this many times, Doña Maria. The words do not change."

"Only because you told me what it says." Her brisket had chilled and she shoved the plate aside. "Why could we not find a way to give this to him."

Gabriel plunked his fork on the table. A dark forelock of hair raked one raised brow. "It will make a difference if you have a child. At least his father would not be a traitor to Spain."

"Marcus was never a traitor to anyone," she snapped.

Her brother's dark eyes lashed out. "You speak like a woman," he scoffed. "You cry for three days, weep over the man's pardon, and argue with everything I say. Why did you come with me?"

Liandra burst into tears. Both men suddenly looked helpless. She hated feminine hysterics and blamed Marcus completely for ruining her. Wiping her face, she stiffened her spine. "Because you came for me, Gabriel. Because you love me. He does not. But you should have made the effort to tell him everything before you hit him over the head. He could have been severely injured."

Gabriel rolled his eyes. "If you had stayed to coddle him any longer than you did, my men would have been caught."

"He had a right to know about the pardon." She looked beseechingly at Don Pedro. "Tell him I am right. Did you not go to all this effort so that he would be safe."

"*Sí.* He is an honorable man."

"A pirate!" Gabriel scoffed. "The only reason I am here at all is because I did not go to Spain, Liandra. I was delayed because of that man and his silly letter. First, I go to Havana. Then Cartagena, where I must sit and await an audience with the viceroy while my fleet sails without me. Pardoning a pirate. The idea is ludicrous."

"We have already argued this."

"*Sí,* for three days we have argued this and you still do not see past your prim little nose. I have much to answer for to the king."

She knelt before her grumpy brother. "Will you be all right?"

"I am in a lot of trouble," he grumbled sheepishly. "But what can they do to me? If I am relieved of command, then I will stay home with my daughter, which is where I belong."

She leaned into his arms until he was forced to surrender most of his anger. "Thank you for returning to Puerto Bello and bringing Don Pedro with you. Thank you for finding me."

"Carlos has been imprisoned," Don Pedro said. "You may return to the mission valley if you wish."

"I will never return."

Gabriel's arms tightened around her. "Christina is in Havana waiting for you to take her home."

"And I do love her, Gabriel. But I cannot go there, either."

"To Spain?"

She shook her head, nay.

Gabriel flung his arms out in frustration. "There. We are back where we started."

"Gabriel—"

The sudden slap of feet on the deck above silenced her.

"Something is happening." Snatching up his feathered hat, Gabriel went to the stern galley window. His demeanor darkened. "We have company, *querida*." Pivoting on his booted heel, he turned to Liandra. "Stay below."

"Will this ship be safe?"

"No lone ship is safe in these waters."

A knock sounded on the stateroom door. But Gabriel was already on his way out, snapping orders to the uniformed man at the door.

Liandra ran to the stern, galley window and stared out. The sun had not yet set. In the distance, silhouetted against the great ball of fire that dominated the horizon, a lone ship sailed. Every inch of canvas spread to the wind, she was lying over steeply, her whole profile presented to Gabriel's ship.

"She has a bold captain, I think," Don Pedro said coming to stand beside her. "She's weathering on us. Perhaps two knots faster."

"How could that be?" She leaned closer against the glass. Above her, she could hear Gabriel ordering his men to the braces. "I cannot see her flying any colors."

"She is a well-rigged black frigate."

Liandra's fingers knotted against the thick crystalline pane glass. Her heart began pounding against her ribs. There *was* something beautifully familiar about that magnificent vessel and the bold captain who dared sail her straight down El Condor's throat.

Liandra spun on her heel and ran from the room, slamming the door in her wake. Gabriel stood on the quarterdeck, feet braced wide, his hands clasped behind him. Over the white and cobalt blue waistcoat of his high rank, a golden braid attached a short cloak now battered by the wind. He saw her at once. His expression did not change when she ran to the rail.

He knew. He knew who was on that ship.

Wind whipping hair into her face, she swung her gaze to the masts of Gabriel's ship. With one hand braced for balance on the rail, she controlled the wild flapping of her skirts with the other. Both ships had the wind abeam as if they raced the moon and the stars.

But Marcus would still catch them.

She laughed. A tap on the shoulder, and a young seaman presented her with a perspective glass. She looked up at Gabriel on the quarterdeck just as he nodded the man's dismissal. Her heart burst and never had she loved him more than at that moment.

Raising the glass to her eye, she sought the ship.

"*Dark Fury* is truly glorious." The wind tore the words from her lips. And Marcus was coming.

He was coming for her!

"I think he will not let me get away this time," Gabriel yelled back. He turned his attention abeam to the slim formation taking shape on the horizon. They were approaching an island. Probably one of the hundreds of small islands that pocked these waters. "Are you sure you want this, *querida*?"

"Oh, Gabriel, *sí!*" she cried in the wind.

A tense minute answered her joyous response, and she thought Gabriel might still try to outrun Marcus. Then he snapped an order to the helm and her happiness took the shape of tears, for she knew what the order had cost him. What he was doing for her.

The men on the ship began taking in canvas. An hour later both ships lay anchored nearly two hundred yards apart off the shoals of the island. The yawning gunports were open on both ships.

Already she could see Marcus in the other launch, barely recognizable except for the white shirt that framed the breadth of his familiar shoulders. A bandage was wrapped around his head.

She and Gabriel did not speak on the way into shore. The fading sunset provided what scant light remained. Only one man handled the oars. The waves tossed the boat, and her brother barely leapt out fast enough to catch her as she jumped over the side. Already Marcus was running toward them in the waves.

Gabriel kept hold of her wrist. In his other hand, he held the naked cutlass. "Where will you live, *querida*?"

"I do not know, except that wherever it is, it will be with him."

Heartbeat racing, she could hear Marcus's boots slapping the water. Gabriel lifted his gaze as Marcus stopped a pair of steps away. Liandra turned. Her world tilted. He looked terrible and beautiful all at once with his clothes plastered to his body by the surf, his unshaven countenance grim with purpose as he held Gabriel's stare. Silver flashed from the heavy length of steel he gripped.

Gabriel's grip on her hand tightened. The striking white and cobalt blue jacket of his high rank in disharmony to the warrior expression in his eyes. Marcus raised the cutlass. And for a terrified instant, she thought they would go to war over her.

Marcus's voice lifted above the crash of the surf. "I love her." He looked at her and there was such affection in his face that she could not stop the rush of tears. A half-sob and half-laugh left her lips. "I have since the moment she stood in front of a cannon and taught a shipload of pirates about courage."

"You did that?" Gabriel's voice dropped in disbelief.

Marcus's eyes smiled. "You should see her wield a fishing pole."

"You truly wish to go with this madman?"

"*Sí*, Gabriel," Liandra whispered, placing a hand on her brother's heart. "Let me go."

Gabriel pinned Marcus with a glare. "I will know if she's ill treated, Englishman."

"Aye," he answered her brother. "You can end my miserable life if I so much as harm a hair on her head."

Gabriel let her go, and she flew into Marcus's embrace. He lowered his sword just enough to take her into his arms, kissing her deeply, dragging his mouth from hers only when Gabriel cleared his throat. Sea foam swirled around their calves.

"Drake." Her brother's voice seemed to push past something in his throat. He pulled from his jacket a thick scroll of vellum.

The pardon!

Marcus carefully took it. Unrolling the parchment, he lifted his eyes in disbelief.

"Don Pedro worked hard to get that for you."

Marcus's gaze moved to Gabriel's ship, to the lone figure on the quarterdeck. "You're free, Marcus," Liandra said, fingering the cross at his neck that he'd worn so close to his heart. His hand covered hers and his eyes told her again, how much he loved her.

"Find a nice island," Gabriel said darkly. "Settle down. The pirate life will only see you killed. Already, I will have to answer for letting your ship go."

For a moment longer, Marcus held Gabriel's gaze. "Good-bye then." He tapped the hilt of his cutlass to his forehead in mock surrender. They all knew Gabriel couldn't have taken *Dark Fury* even if he'd tried. Even El Condor wasn't invincible.

With her in his arms, Marcus walked back up the beach. When Liandra turned again to wave good-bye to her brother, he was but a dark speck on the sand swallowed by the shadows.

"You will see him again, Liandra."

"And what about your brother?" she quietly asked.

"Right now, we will find our own way. Our own life. This is a big place. I am through chasing windmills."

"You have chased windmills?"

He swept her up and whirled her in his arms. "I will have to read you *Don Quixote*, sweet."

"*Sí.*" Her feet dangled happily in the air as he wrapped her in his strength and kissed her, a melding of mouths that promised more to come. Then he took her hand and led her to the launch.

In the distance, the huge red sun finally settled into the sea. It was the end of the day, and the beginning of the rest of their lives.

Laura Renken is a Golden Heart finalist, a Maggie finalist, and a winner of the prestigious HOLT MEDALLION. A product of thirteen schools and twenty-two moves stretching across the United States and Europe, she is a self-proclaimed gypsy, whose passion for writing developed at an early age while living overseas where she acquired an appreciation for historical intrigue. She is a wordsmith, a creator of dreams, and a passionate believer in happy endings. Even after graduating from the University of Oklahoma with a degree in criminal justice, she soon learned that her passion did not lend itself to a career in anything other than writing romance. You can visit her Web site at: http://www.laurarenken.com or you can write to the her at: P.O. Box 144, Channahon, Illinois 60410-0144.